VIRTUOSO

DRAZOEN HERALDS

BOOK ONE

JULES PEACOCK

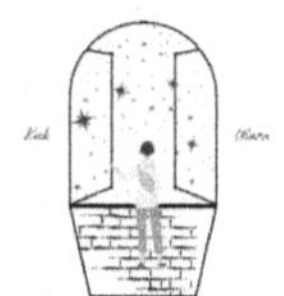

Virtuoso

Copyright © 2025 by Jules Peacock

This is a work of fiction. Names, characters, businesses, places, events, locales, and incidents are either the products of the author's imagination or used in a fictitious manner. No identification with actual persons (living or deceased), places, buildings, and products is intended or should be inferred.

LCCN: 2025900454
ISBN-13: 979-8-9923803-0-9 Paperback
ISBN-13: 979-8-9923803-1-6 Hardcover
ISBN-13: 979-8-9923803-2-3 eBook

First Edition: January 2025

10 9 8 7 6 5 4 3 2 1

❀ Formatted with Vellum

For Uncle Erich who introduced me to my first dragons and flies with them now

Fair winds and following seas until we meet again.

WELCOME TO THE AONI
THE TIME OF THE HERALDS HAS COME

Imagine

Before there were planets and stars, the Nine Drazoen flew the cosmos. You can call them dragons if you prefer.

No one knows why, but the Nine faded from our Universe, the Aoni, long ago. They haven't been seen since, though they did leave nice, vague instructions on how to find them. When the time was right.

That time is now.

In a Universe where ancient prophecies can come true... Anything is possible.

PRESENT

Humans learned they were anything but alone in the Universe on a Tuesday morning. Millennia of thinking themselves rulers of their solar system, shining examples of sublime evolution near perfected, gone in an instant. Not only were humans not the best species on offer, they barely cracked the top fifteen. Out of a possible sixteen.

Given time, much later, to contemplate Earth's interstellar wake-up call, Katy Phelan decided it was best discovered on a Tuesday rather than a Monday. Mondays were stormy, per the old song. Bleak and scary. Tuesday at least meant most humans had gotten a day of back-to-work normalcy before this sudden and forced confrontation of their cosmic inadequacies.

Unfortunately, per the same song, Tuesdays were just as bad. As it happened on this Tuesday in May, a massive shape had appeared in dawn's light over the Puget Sound, almost directly on top of a secret island in the San Juan archipelago. The shape eclipsing sunlight and spreading a shadow over the nearby ocean and ground below her feet was moon-like. Yet nothing like a moon honestly, or a planet, or any other celestial body Katy had studied in school. This new occupant of near-Earth space looked very like a Pac-Man about to gobble, or an open fan spread nearly three hundred sixty degrees? She blinked, trying to comprehend what she was seeing.

Djilbay jo Bikajo shifted beside her. He was polite, strong, a Mikanjo seeker capable of flight, and decidedly non-human. His species for sure made the top ten. Bay, wings fully spread in a massive thirty-foot span, said, "Now our journey can truly begin." As he spoke, something small that must have detached from the larger craft shrouding land and sea breached Earth's atmosphere and headed their way. Fast.

Katy glanced at him, captivated as always by Bay's presence. Half-bare frame, covered in tattoos, caramel skin stretched over bone and musculature capable of keeping those ridiculously majestic white wings aloft. She was glad he didn't have them pulled back in the compact hold. Her breath hitched in awe as she watched them lift slightly in the gentle morning breeze off the strait. She pointed at the ship then back to Bay. "That's the *Eternidad,* right? Your ship? We don't have to worry it's a surprise visit from someone else?"

Her gaze lasered in on the literal killer twenty feet behind Bay. That mofo was smirking, and Katy wondered how he would manipulate events to keep his current murder attempt in play. He'd made it clear he wasn't giving up just because they'd caught a ride off planet. That he'd never cease trying to get them. That man she'd never met, from another world, wanted to kill her, had promised he would with his dying breath if necessary. She shivered.

Bay eased closer, raising his wings to circle her and block the view of the killer. Her seeker was so much taller it was like a curtain of white feathers cut off the outside world.

"Yes, it's them. My people, not his. I can't wait to show you everything on our way to Centris. My sister will be so eager to meet you. Everyone will. You're what we've been seeking for so long." Katy shied from his gaze, still unsure of her hero's journey (alleged) about to begin, despite his conviction. He stepped closer and nudged her chin up with a gentle finger. "You are the one," he promised her. "The herald, the person who will return Sundancer Orange." He gave her his nothing-but-trouble smirk and took her hand. "Let's go wake a dragon, Katy Phelan."

Back when creation was young, when the Drazoen flew through spacetime, and sentient species numbered only in single digits, They created Centris. The Nine Drazoen, called dragons by many and gods by some, first beings in existence, foresaw how the rapidly increasing numbers of people from varied places and cultures in the Aoni would need a common gathering place. As each of the species conquered space travel, they would require a neutral setting, one where all were safe to meet. Where councils could form to provide guidance, and social interaction might encourage understanding and fellowship. The Nine flew to the center of the Aoni, pooled Their powers, and gave birth to the Wheel of Centris.

Three circular levels joined by nine spokes, one for each Drazoen. Each dragon's spirit and traits imbued Their region, lending the whole Wheel its color, vibrancy and disposition. Waterbringer Blue an exuberant cerulean filled with celebratory life, Earthcaller Gold a gilded wonder in combat and strength. Hu Ularu Black cloaked in the inky mysteries of faith, existence and the Aoni itself. Everything bound by the Drazoen to the Wheel as it spun and measured a time standard all species counted. One full rotation comprised a work day and relaxing night: a sal. Eighteen sals a buwan, and fifteen buwans made a tuig.

Here the greatest political force of the Aoni had been built: the Calling at Centris. Beside it lay the Chorus, sacred to Songmaster Silver. He had crafted it, laid out a blueprint for nine schools of specialized disciplines so that each Drazoen was honored. He then ensured the heads of the Chorus – the voices – formed a Cadre that advised the Calling on all matters. Their first and primary duty, though, was keeping the schools vibrant and filled with talented people from around the Aoni.

Dindal Orangevoice, current head of Sundancer's school, was performing that duty now, enjoying a fine meal at Lányok, one of the larger restaurants on Sundancer Orange's subspoke. On this occasion she'd gathered thirty robes for a celebration of their accomplishments – these students had graduated from tyros to robes by completing testing in their first school. Now they decided if they would continue to another school, or leave the Chorus with a single beaded necklace.

Each robe before her wore only Sundancer Orange's beads, and Dindal urged them to seek additional training. Dindal tried to stifle her dismay that, similar to the last several tuigs, distressingly few of these students would progress. Fearing the loss of oral history and talent this disinterest could mean, she resolved to be firmer, harder, call upon the intellectual curiosity and drive Sundancer Orange's school cultivated. Looking over the expansive table, filled with diverse species, Dindal raised a glass to begin her toast. She would chide, goad and demand their buy-in.

Without warning every light in Lányok went out, the room plunged into darkness. All candles, chandeliers, every light source had been eliminated, their table surrounded by staff and other customers they could no longer see. A nervous murmur arose, though no one seemed panicked yet, merely confused. Long minutes passed without a change in the darkness surrounding them, voices got louder demanding explanations.

Dindal readied to lead her robes to an exit when the lights burst on. They pulsed and flared momentarily before settling back to normal. Around her, other diners repeated messages they'd received that the entire orange spoke had briefly gone dark. Nowhere else on the Wheel, only Sundancer's spoke. Everyone in the restaurant shrugged it off, but Dindal was less sanguine. She'd been on Centris for hundreds of tuigs and nothing like this had ever happened. Raising her glass once more, acting normally for the student's benefit, she resolved to call a meeting of the Cadre and discuss what kind of portent this could had been.

1

(THREE DAYS EARLIER)

TEA WAS THE PROPER START TO ANY SUNDAY, IF YOU asked Katy. Workdays called for coffee's caffeine jolt, mayhap on Saturday as well to recover from Friday night carousing. Slow weekend waking could be embraced with a gentler approach on a Sunday, though. Catherine McEvoy playing in the background, light morning fog giving way to crisp May sunshine, a slice of lemon breakfast cake, and life was grand.

Katy considered if toasted oats coated in a glaze then dripped over the top of the cake truly earned the "breakfast" moniker, or if she might be stretching things. Another bite. Definitely breakfast cake. Katy's doctor could keep her thoughts otherwise to herself, ta.

Pouring another cuppa before returning to her spot on the couch, Katy resumed gazing out the windows of her Fremont sublet. She didn't always love the hike to the third floor, but couldn't argue it made the view nice. Housesitting for a cousin and living here rent-free wasn't bad either. Three years. Had it really been so long since she'd come home from Limerick? What was happening with her life that so much time could go by without much action, or even notice?

As a girl she'd thought the world was filled with adventure and magic she would uncover someday. A universe in a dew drop, werewolves, deceiving sprites who traded souls for stories, a sorceress who would set her a task of some terrible danger and importance.

Her mother had set the scene by naming her so theatrically, in Katy's opinion. Brianna Phelan grew up on a dairy farm in Antigo, Wisconsin. She said the most precious sight back then was a rare pink katydid. It was beloved by Gamgam Leona, who had passed her affection for the vividly tinted insect down to her daughters. Every spring they tramped through woods and fields, listening, trying to find those pink ones. Ma said they'd had dreams of catching a pair, and making baby pink katydids, but never could. Years later, when Brianna learned she was having a girl at last, she wanted to honor the cherished memory without "saddling you with Gamgam's name."

Her brothers turned Katy-for-katydid into Bug, because obnoxious nicknames are the raison d'être of older brothers, and Katy had four of the bastards to contend with. Despite their teasing, she'd loved being named after a pretty insect, especially because her ma said they were special bugs that made music. Made perfect sense to young Katy, given that as long as she'd had memory she'd been hearing a tune in her brain. One that rejected description and capture of any kind. It was simple and not; it wrapped around her and wove through her, and she knew other people didn't hear it. Didn't take more than a couple of strange looks on other people's faces before Katy figured out not to talk about it anymore.

Once she'd gotten old enough to use a computer, Katy researched katydids, the *cruicéad beag* her father nicknamed her (which was kinda just Gaelic for Bug but sounded way better). The katydids she found on the internet were…gross and cool, pretty much in equal measure. She'd found a database of katydid songs and played those short files over and over, cranking the speakers. Oran (twin brother and *such* a mank) had stormed into the room at one point to threaten her favorite blanket's impending demise if she didn't stop making those annoying sounds. Ma had interceded on her behalf and for once her evil twin got a time out. Result!

Her favorite of all the short chirps, cheeps and whirs was from the common virtuoso katydid. It was named for its complexity of song, and was a word that rolled around Katy's tongue over and over: virtuoso. It meant being a gifted expert, a creative genius, and that little katydid earned it, singing for all it was worth.

Then came a fateful day, snuggled in Da's lap waiting for story time, when she'd heard Irish flute for the first time. It didn't take long for budding ideas to bloom as her young mind interwove these foundational things: katydid songs; folktales and fairy stories that Da told; the secret music of her soul; a wooden flute playing what sounded like someone taking flight.

As only a child's mind could, Katy laid fantasy worlds, adventures and myths onto the backs of rare pink insects, imagining she could be transported to other realms and play her Air (she'd named it that and capitalized it, which is how you knew it was important). Once she realized her dream of becoming a world-famous flautist, Katy knew she would be a virtuoso like that katydid, a wee bug that gave its all with the instruments it had. She, too, was a wee Bug and someday she'd save the world with her music.

Of course, now she was twenty-eight with an arts degree fourteen shades past liberal that not only didn't attract employers, but actively repelled them. Katy knew she was good (certainly good enough to get her master's degree with honors), though one professor had suggested she lacked innovation. Not much call out there for flautists, though. There are only so many traditional Irish flute players the market can handle, a fact she'd realized long after setting her sights on a wooden instrument that to her childhood heart was the best of all worlds: it played music and looked like a magic wand.

Katy was determined nevertheless. Something called to her, prodded at a deep-seated need to perfect an ability that her large and (one might say) invasive family viewed as a strange quirk. Okay, it was her. Katy was the one who'd say invasive. Chaotic and wild, too. Jesus God above, how the bloomin' pranks and ransoming of her belongings had defined her childhood. Oran had been a terrorist from the day they left Ma's womb, and rallied her three other brothers to pile on.

When they weren't busy convincing her a poltergeist lived in her room, they were always giving their opinions, shouting her down when she tried to explain her dreams, loving her by attending every recital and concert, behaviors they undermined with backhanded compliments on her proficiency in a "useless pastime". Katy felt overlooked in a family that loved physical, tactile things. Sports, sculpture, fixing cars, building models, gardening, those were their likes; not some nebulous secret earworm that lived only in her mind.

They had jokes and things to talk about, athletes and artists, but no one had music like her. Not even Da, whose love of Irish music was deep but didn't reach far past the well-known groups. It made her feel like the Girl Who Doesn't Fit, and had driven her to try and be special, heard through the anarchy of their large clan. A feat she never believed she'd accomplished.

Her phone ringing jolted her from her musing. One glance told her it was her father, and she groaned internally, sure she could recite the conversation to come. "Da. Still gloating over the Kilkenny Cats winning yesterday?"

"Ah, *mo chroí*, more the treat they bested your Limerick lads!" Martin Phelan's voice was giddy. His Irish accent remained as strong as the day he'd come to Seattle.

"Da," she smiled as she said, "I don't care about hurling, much less my team from uni. You're the one who cares."

A dramatic sigh. "Sweet girl, where did we go wrong wit ya?" He chuckled. "Your ma, loves sport. Ian and his Deb, Patrick and his Vasuda. Paul. Oran. Everyone else does, but not my Katy. I've failed as an Irishman and parent."

Since he couldn't see her, Katy didn't bother hiding the wince. She knew he didn't mean anything. But always, always, she was the odd one out. Different from the rest. Forcing a light tone, she replied "I know, Da. I am your 'sore trial' in life."

"Never you mind that, now, you're my heart, the light of my life."

"Has Ma forgiven you for the fireworks?"

"Sparklers, love. Mere sparklers! Why she got so upset is not clear to me at all."

When Da had broken out gold sparklers at halftime the day before ("Like the amber our boys wear, bless them!") he and her brothers amped themselves up jousting with the fireworks-on-a-stick. Katy and Ma stood back and marveled that the five Y-chromos hadn't set the house on fire. "When did he even get those damn things?" her mother had murmured.

Katy waited, knowing what was coming next. "Speaking of being my light, I don't want you driving to session alone tonight, so I'll come over."

"And you're sure this is about my safety and not having a pint at Conall's?"

Da laughed. "Perish the thought, dove. I'll leave the island 'round about five, be ready when I text."

ANOTHER WEEK, another new city. Seattle in North America's Washington State. Djilbay jo Bikajo – gemstone artisan, generally pleasant guy, non-native to Earth – had been losing heart. Genuinely losing it this time. Not almost losing it, like the regrettable years that followed his unintentional aid of Kublai Khan conquering China's Song Dynasty. That had been a rough period, no doubt – turned out Great Khans were not forgiving men, and Divine Emperors even less so.

Today, however, Djilbay wandered through Pike Place Market feeling rejuvenated. He'd be spending the next few weeks here, thanks to a friend loaning him a table. His fellow jeweler, Scott, had spoken to Djilbay many times about this market, how it overflowed with food and flowers and flying fish and cheap baubles; leather goods and hemp clothing and tourist claptrap alongside wooden carvings so beautiful a man could weep. Just within eyeshot of the space Scott had loaned him, Djilbay saw such bounty: almonds in tempting flavors both sweet and savory; clogs made of recycled materials; massive bouquets in white buckets waiting to be wrapped in paper and carried away. A healthy inhalation brought traces of brewing coffee and frying foods, and the fainter aroma of briny water running off freshly caught ocean creatures.

Across the cobblestone street produce stands opened and lovely fruits were arranged in displays that kings of old would have envied. Ovens opened and closed, humid heat fogging glass panes as fresh baked breads were set on window racks to cool and entice early morning passersby. Two tables down a tinkling sound drew his eyes back to his immediate thoroughfare: stained glass window medallions being unpacked and hung, light catching tinted glass and fracturing, momentarily covering surrounding tables in soothingly muted colors. Everything combined to incite a feeling of overwhelmed awe and exultation in Djilbay's soul. He was exactly where he was meant to be, awaiting the person the Aoni created him to find and anoint.

A milenyo, roughly a Human millennium, had passed without Djilbay finding his Kawakona. He'd despaired, yes, but something told him this Seattle was going to close his search, give him what he'd sought so long. The Drazoen were coming back. All of them. Sundancer was just the first and She would lead the way. It was as Windweaver White, Hunanjanno jo Bikajo, had told his ancestor, Swailu. *When your descendants have uncovered the heralds the Aoni shall ring with your success, and The Nine shall soar again.*

AFTER A LONG SATURDAY watching hurling with family, Katy looked forward to seeing her session boys. Sundays at Conall's Pub was her refresh button. Kevin's bodhrán, Danny and James on fiddles, her flute, the rare treat of Sean's uilleann pipes, and the craic was grand tonight, as Da would say. *Had* said so, several times, during the drive down to Pioneer Square.

Tonight, as ever, they were early to session because her father would neither let her drive downtown herself, nor trust her about how long the drive took from Fremont to Pioneer Square. They'd had a rousing discussion about mapping apps and how they couldn't be trusted when he'd arrived from Mercer Island, annoyed she wasn't waiting at the curb.

Katy argued her father was an engineer, for feck's sake, and should have faith in the science and tools designed to be accurate and helpful. Da raised an eyebrow and said being an engineer was how he knew coding was inferior pseudo-science and they'd be leaving now. In the face of logic like that Katy threw up her hands and caved... and they arrived thirty minutes early, just as she'd predicted. Amazing how they had the same argument every week.

At least she got to nurse a pint, admire the warm and gleaming oak hardwood floors, booths upholstered in County Clare tartan, and the brass accents that gleamed from years of cleaning. Come to think on it, Da probably just wanted time for an extra pint as well. He was over at the bar, talking with the owner who was his supplier for kegs of Kilkenny ale. Katy could start swearing about wasting time, or love him and get over it, "because it's half a bloody hour, Lady Drama."

Her internal music was strong tonight, for no reason she could pinpoint, and it was raising goosepimples along the back of her neck. It generally came as it pleased: while she was awake or slept, when she met someone who became important to her, or when she saw something sacred. Beautiful places, sad events, moments filled with the kind of laughter that strained her abdominal muscles, everything added richness to the Air. For all that it was intertwined with every moment of her life, she wasn't able to make it whole in her mind, attach the right words to explain it. Which made times like this, when it inexplicably surged inside her, more frustrating.

"Katy dearest!" Tony called to her from behind the bar. "Planning to dazzle us tonight?"

She shrugged, sending a sly smile back his way. "Only if you promise to keep the ale flowing."

Tony laughed and waved her off, returning to conversation with her father. More people were gathering in the pub, and Katy felt the rising restless hum that built inside her each Sunday night. The desire to entertain and set toes tapping, to raise spirits or break hearts, whatever the song called for. That was her passion, and it was all in pursuit of giving voice to her sneaky personal song, without ever telling anyone that's what she was doing. Part of her had always been irrationally afraid that talking about her Air would make it go away. Like that science thing with the cat in the box, but her cat would be DOA for sure if she shone a light on it. The challenge of it, she'd believed as a girl, meant she was destined for a quest like no other. Lord of the Rings? Step aside suckah, the Lady of the Air was taking over!

Except no sorceress came, no Stone of Power was uncovered. Blades of Greatness and Destiny never planted themselves in her path. Years passed and she'd realized she didn't have a Quest teased out from prophetic riddles on a miraculously exhumed vellum scroll. She had a life. A single Human life, much like any other on a planet of billions of people who also didn't have Quests or Divine Journeys. Years of dedication to the flute, lessons, recitals, and travel had only built false hopes.

At twenty-eight, Katy wasn't in a "my life is over" phase per se. She was a normal, mundane adult woman who just… wasn't where she'd thought she'd be. She worked as a page at the Seattle Public Library (Aunt Mildred had gotten her in the door), and she played trad Irish music in Sunday night sessions. Not much else of note; no lovers, pets, or significant vacation, and that left her a little melancholy. Sipping the last of her pint, watching tables fill more quickly, she asked the Universe when her life was going to do something more than pass by uneventfully. Predictably, the Universe declined to respond.

2

Djilbay sauntered slowly from the market down to the waterfront. A fresh feeling of hope infused his steps. As a young boy he'd dreamt of finding Sundancer's herald each night for years. Post-fledging dreams had teased with scents of briny water utterly unlike the lake waters of Bankiri mimicked on the *Eternidad.* The closer his people had come to this part of the Aoni, the more his dreams intensified and seemed so real he'd felt condensation dripping from rainforest canopies onto his skin; boiling heat of sinuous lava building new lands or reshaping old ones; screams of prey and triumphant roars of predators on vast open plains; calls and songs of brilliantly colored winged animals dancing in air or in underbrush. He'd even heard trumpeting horns of great beasts that echoed strangely over salty waters.

He blushed now to think of decades spent regaling all seekers with his heroism to be: he, Djilbay jo Bikajo, was the One Who Would Return the Nine! His mamas would just embrace him, smelling of spicy raschai and maluwa flowers, chuckling at his fervor.

At least, in the earlier times they would. Before laughter

ceased, before Djilbay and his sister, Vailillia, stood at an observation screen, watching their family pod detach from the ship, course set for Bankiri. Their mothers inside, faith lost, so eager to escape they hadn't waited until the *Eternidad* returned to the home planet, but tearfully fled once Vailillia had taken her seeking mantle.

He'd had his visions and knew them to be a certainty, though, and he would not give in to despair. For a milenyo he'd camped on this water-heavy planet, knowing in every plumy filament of his hidden wings this was the right world. When he'd uncovered carnelian – a stone only found on this planet – and felt it sing through him, he knew he'd found Her essence, just as prophecy foretold: *We shall endow sacred materials with Our essence, the spark to cry out and wake Us when We are needed.*

Her primal spirit flashed through him when his fingertips brushed the deposit of a mineral that hadn't even been named when he unearthed it. Finding the Kawakona to wield the trigger and wake Sundancer? It was a mere matter of timing, no doubt. But so much time passed without a hint of the herald.

About three hundred years after his first arrival on Earth – post-Song Dynasty disaster – he'd weakened enough to use his beacon to signal his sister back on the ship. Non-contact was protocol, but Djilbay was desperate for her voice and the comfort of his own species. The AI beacon must have transmitted some of his misery because Vailillia hadn't just replied, she'd convinced the seekers to return to Earth. Their arrival was fairly easy to hide from Humans of the time, who hadn't yet invented telescopes. Someone probably noticed, but any records were lost to time.

Vailillia got him back on track in a few short revolutions of Earth, reinvigorating his sense of duty. His sister reminded him why he was doing this, praised how he'd handled Sundancer's trigger, and showed how much she'd progressed with her chemistry research when she gave him several drugs she'd concocted for his mission. Healing and harming draughts in equal measure, critical given what was at stake. If anyone tried to slow or stop his assignment, he had the tools to handle it. There were those who didn't want the Drazoen to return; it might signal an end to their power and darker ambitions.

This modern age, though… It had begun feeling nearly insurmountable. Humans now reached epic population levels – few in the Aoni were so fruitful, none with such short life-spans – and he'd begun to fear it was impossible to find Sundancer's herald, when so many of this species were born and died in each of their planet's minutes.

But Scott had given him somewhere new to explore, a city possessed of a subaudible hum, one that made his pinions ache with the need to stretch and be free of the suppression suit. Seattle was a splendid opportunity to travel somewhere he'd never been, with the added bonus of a nearby refuge for non-Humans. There was something about this Pacific Northwest that sang out, gave him hope, and Djilbay looked forward to using Sundancer's carnelian pendant to call Her Kawakona.

He'd come so far, afraid many times he was lost or wrong about Earth, age upon age culminating in this moment. He needed to focus on the now, open to the possibility he was finally where he should be: standing outside a cheerful Irish bar in a place called Pioneer Square. Live music spilling onto the street while a misting rain tickled his skin. Celtic pipes inside and ferry horns sounding behind him on the bay – *trumpeting horns of great beasts that echoed strangely over salty waters.* All of it daring Djilbay jo Bikajo to keep his faith, to pray wholeheartedly this was his moment to manifest his dream.

ONCE THE BOYS arrived and got situated, the group set to and played with gusto, filling the pub with warmth and joy. Regulars called out favorites, the players gave each other good natured ribbing, and one elderly woman sang along to any ballad she knew. Katy let the merry night wash away her stress. Playing her flute Sunday nights muted the anxiety that she'd wasted so much of her parents' money getting degrees that hadn't secured a viable future. Other than giving her a good in with the session groupies in Seattle, that is. When she'd first told her parents about getting a degree in Irish Music they'd been less receptive than anticipated.

"Waste of time and money" was shouted out, as well as "how much of a career can that be", capped off with "utter boondoggle!" Might not be marketable, but she'd gotten those damn degrees, and the least she could do was play the thing she'd spent her life trying to perfect.

For Katy life meant music, always had. There was both peace in that, and the goad of her ever-present restless internal hum. The atavistic thing Katy knew she'd been born with. Even now, in the twilight of her second decade and feeling decidedly less than a virtuoso, a fiery mote of belief remained in her. Her time would come, damn it, and she would play the crap out of that Air. Bend it to her will and let the stars themselves reflect the notes back to her.

Sean nudged her, and her mind returned to the session she'd almost completely zoned out on. Hopefully she hadn't dropped any notes. "What's up?"

"Your turn to call a reel, duck." Sean was the sweetest guy, a little older than her dad, quintessential Irish American, and Katy loved when he could join their Sunday sessions.

They went another twenty minutes before taking a break. Danny, James and Sean headed to the bar saying they'd grab pints for Kevin and Katy. The two of them, left in the corner, continued to play softly. Katy followed the other three with her eyes, thankful they'd opened their group to her two years ago. Her eyes tracked left, immediately snared by the sight of a striking man in a plain t-shirt and jeans. Conall's wasn't over-crowded, but they had a decent audience filling most tables and a few barstools. This guy stood out from the crowd.

Literally, because he was tall as a basketball player, one of the ones who could nearly reach the basket without jumping. Size-able enough to puff the feathers of insecure men, his soft black hair fell over his forehead as he slipped change into his front pocket. Well-worn denim, faded but no visible holes, comfy rather than trendy ripped-up skinny jeans. Her nape tingled yet again, and she had the strangest thought he was watching her despite not looking at her.

Someone this sexy wouldn't be looking at her awkward self, anyway. Frankly Katy was often suspicious of people this gorgeous. In her experience they were the most likely to cause shenanigans and instigate fuckery that would get *her* in trouble, never themselves. Case in point, all her brothers, their friends on every team ever (and in one sort-lived band), and quite a few guys at college. Katy was applying that healthy and hard-earned caution to this guy, because seriously. Who was this flawless and just casually hanging out at an Irish bar in Seattle?

He twisted to pick up his pint and Katy took advantage to blatantly check him out. Scanning down first to the cracked and scuffed tan hiking boots, then back up past a side-view of his very nice behind, wrapped like a gift in those soft jeans. Up to the simple white t-shirt that showed off his broad, borderline Mr. Universe-level muscled chest. A tee that had been clean if wrinkled, right up until James man-punched Danny's arm, thereby knocking Danny's arm into tall guy's hand, splashing the pint the poor git had just been sipping.

For the record, the shirt improved when wet if anyone asked Katy.

Her trio of session gents apologized profusely and she nearly lost her rhythm when tall guy waved them off with a broad smile and rich laugh. Holy Mary, mother of God. Straight gleaming teeth in a mouth designed to drop panties at twenty paces, plump lips surrounded by a short, boxed beard in the same warm black as his hair, the perfect foil against skin that looked as luscious and silky as crème caramel. For a moment Katy's brain flashed to an image of her own pale Irish skin with his draped over it, just like that sweet dessert. She floated away on a lust cloud briefly.

Came back to herself right quick when she dropped her flute, something that hadn't happened since she was a teen, and which drew tall guy's focused attention. Katy doubled down on her skepticism because he was a smoke show and that sort never looked twice at her. Was there a modeling agency actively hunting him? If not yet, there would be soon. His eyes were what happened when jade and turquoise had a baby, then that baby had a torrid romance with emeralds. A green-blue like exotic oceans, piercing without being electric or creepy. These eyes mesmerized, caught and held you. They had depth. Cobras could use those things to hypnotize prey.

Tall guy had way too much going for him to be anything but sus – big and tall without being an ass or the agro macho-type (he hadn't tried to punch James or Danny when they spilled his beer, after all). A striking smile, laughter a deep rumble like rolling thunder, eyes blessed by Beelzebub as a tool of seduction, and what appeared to be an easy-going temperament. And he liked Irish music? Perfection like that couldn't be trusted, much less when he applauded her clumsiness with the rest of the pub, saluted her with the remains of his beer, and grinned.

She ignored the Air stirring, raising its head and purring in interest. He was trouble, nothing but trouble.

3

Dꜱɪʟʙᴀʏ ᴇʏᴇᴅ ᴛʜᴇ ᴡᴏᴍᴀɴ ᴘʟᴀʏɪɴɢ ꜰʟᴜᴛᴇ ᴀɴᴅ ꜰᴇʟᴛ everything in him light up. She was the Kawakona! Sundancer's herald. The one he'd desperately yearned so, so long to find. Prayed for and cursed in equal measure. Praise to Hunanjanno jo Bikajo, Windweaver White, Mother of his people and She who gave them the prophecy. His search had come to fruition, and he wasn't letting this woman out of his sight until he could give her the pendant and confirm the trigger bonded with her. Let a Drazoen rise!

Was he looking lunatic-y? He knew his smile kept getting bigger, his relief and joy a challenge to hold inside. His wings ached to burst free, but they would fill this pub front to back and spill more drinks than the half of one he wore... Perfect. Nothing like meeting the single being you've waited a milenyo to behold, reeking of the ale staining your shirt. Not a shining moment.

No matter. She would be magnetically attracted to the pendant, just as he was drawn to her. He could signal the *Eternidad,* and regale her with his stories while they waited to be

"

picked up. So many stories. Tale after tale of adventure, some misadventures, her part in the prophecy. How happy she would surely be when they left this planet and travelled to Centris.

Djilbay wasn't terribly clear how they would get from "Hello Drazoen herald!" to "Arise Sundancer Orange!" But he believed someone had to know at Centris. The Cadre of Chorus voices, Calling ambassadors, or the Toledral speakers of his own people. He'd met the most recent one as a child and she seemed the wisest person he'd ever known. She had to be to serve the role, given they mediated for political peace regularly. He would provide them the Kawakona and they would figure out how to combine elements properly to wake Sundancer. If that didn't work he would just dream a damned answer, since that had been the way since his childhood.

He gazed at the culmination of his mission, enraptured. She wasn't quite what he'd imagined. Then again, he'd never known if the herald would be male, female or non-binary, young or aged. This one was adult by Human standards, and average height for her gender in this time. A wealth of deep red hair in corkscrew curls tumbled down her back, a braided coronet around the top to keep it out of her face. Her skin was fresh cream, freckled on her face and the shoulders she'd bared earlier. He'd been more interested than he should have been when she shrugged off her sky-blue sweater as the group played. The skin she'd revealed was dotted as if playful constellations had been sprinkled across her skin. This seemed even more proof to Djilbay that she was the one he sought. He'd voyaged galaxies to meet her, after all, and her skin mapped them in homage.

Her lips had been thinner before she'd played thirty minutes of enthusiastic flute, now they were puffed and reddened. She didn't favor heavy face paint, had eyes the color of lovingly burnished rosewood, polished and lit from within. When she walked to the restroom, he noted her figure was one more appreciated on this planet centuries in the past. Her arms were sleek, her waist small, hips and behind curved like a cello.

Was she in any way "expected"? Not at all, she surpassed expectation. She was in all respects a pleasant surprise and fascinating to him.

Djilbay headed to the back of the pub, convinced he could win over his Kawakona and begin their journey. Sundancer would rise, the other Drazoen would follow, the Aoni would rebalance, reach for unity and peace. He felt the prophecy egging him on, and his heart filled with determination.

KATY CAME out of the loo to see tall guy hovering in her path back to the main room. She knew it was deliberate because those gemstone eyes were focused on her, a half-smile rounding into a smirk. Lah! That soft black hair she wanted to stroke. One step, then two in his direction. A closer view certainly didn't disappoint, and from here she saw the hint of a tattoo on his upper arms. Not a tribal armband, but hard to discern what it was in the low light. Besides there was so much else to peruse. His chest was epic, the kind of thing she'd expect to see on a Halloween costume for He-Man.

Moving in his direction seemed a wise choice, not least because she'd just seen Da look up. He was checking out her stranger now, a practiced fatherly eye measuring him for a smack down. Martin, the Sainted Father of Katy Phelan, Bless Him and All His Travails, had been swatting boys out of her orbit for fifteen years. Was he going to let one sneak by him tonight? Not a chance.

As Da pushed to his feet, Katy race-walked the last few steps to the handsome stranger. She tilted her head back, gazed goofily up at him, and said "Hi."

To her shock he didn't laugh in her face at her lame opening. He extended his hand and said, "I'm Djilbay. You play flute like you were born to it."

No clue how to pronounce that name, he'd said it so fast and soft in an accent unfamiliar to her. Zhilba? Jill Bay? That couldn't be right... She'd stick with "tall guy" until she could get him to repeat his name a little slower. Maybe right into her ear. She shivered at that thought.

Letting him enfold her hand in his, she said, "Katy, and thank you." She used her free hand to grasp a pretend skirt and curtsey, acknowledging his compliment. The hand he held was warming up and her heart was going from moderato to allegro: zero to sixty, his touch and smell combining to give her a full-body shiver now.

His smile was full, no-holds-barred, and disclosed what she hadn't seen at a distance: an adorable snaggle-tooth in the front, ever so slightly turned at an angle while the rest of his smile was straight and white enough to glow. There was a high risk of imminent swooning. Even with the faint whiff of ale coming off his still-damp shirt.

"And I'm her father, boyo. What on our Lord's green Earth makes ya think skulking about near the toilets and pouncing on a young woman is acceptable?"

Mental face-palm emoji. Uncertain if her smile had turned manic or if she was maintaining any kind of poise and grace, Katy tried to calmly face her father rather than whirl on him like a furious harpy. Her tall guy's face had frozen at "skulking", he'd dropped her hand, and was now focused on the wall behind her head.

She heard him clear his throat and rushed to stop him from potentially digging a bigger hole. Stern but calm voice, channeling her Aunt Mildred and Ma, she said. "What did we tell you about this last time, Da?"

Her father's face froze, then flushed slightly. "Here now, love, a father must always care for his-"

Katy made a zipping motion over her mouth and he stopped talking, looking down in mulish shame. "And when Ma and I talked to you about it last time, what did she say you needed to do?"

Face even redder, her father came far enough around mystery man to look him in the eye. Sighing heavily, he raised his hand to shake and said, "I'm Martin, Katy's father and it's a great pleasure ta make your acquaintance."

"Djilbay," hot tall guy replied, cautious smile instead of the glory from before.

Da tried to stop there, but she raised her index finger and circled it once to tell him to finish it. Another sigh. "I apologize for my poor behavior and realize my daughter is an adult. She will make her own decisions, and I will support her."

Katy could see this dude wasn't sure if he should laugh or run from the insane Irishman still holding his hand. Hell, he was so confused he'd only turned partway to face her father, his feet still pointed back down the hallway behind her. She slipped around him, put her own hand on Da's arm and gently broke the handshake.

"Thank you. In a few minutes I'm sure Bay and I will join you at the bar and you can buy him a beer." She took a shot at his name, pretty sure that had been the back half of it.

Her father sucked in his objection, nodded once, gave her suspiciously handsome man the hairy eyeball, and walked away. Katy grimaced apologetically. "Sorry. I'm so sorry. He's sweet and overprotective and stubborn. I promise I'm a viable adult capable of speaking for myself, no matter how that looked."

His grin came back and he raised an eyebrow. "All is well. I envy you still having a parent love you that much." He absently scratched his beard and straightened again. "Bay? I've never had anyone call me that."

"Never? I'd think it was an easy nickname to get." Katy flushed a little. "I'll be honest, I wasn't sure what the first part of your name was, but I felt pretty solid about Bay."

The smile wattage increased a little more. "I guess you'd say we're more formal where I'm from. Djilbay jo Bikajo is my entire name, but Bay... I like it."

Katy laughed. "I'm glad you like it because saying your whole name will take some practice."

Bay put his hands in his pockets and shuffled a bit. Katy did too, but *way to be a copycat doorknob*, so she clasped her hands behind her back. Realized that choice was pushing her breasts out like they wanted selling, so she crossed her arms in front. But maybe that looked hostile? Then she dropped them to her sides and felt stupid, but it beat the other options. Their conversation had completely stopped while she figured out body language complexity, and she scrambled for a topic or a witty comment. Why was she so bloody hopeless at this stuff?

He beat her to it. "Do you happen to like jewelry, Katy?"

Random subject change ahoy! Please, please, don't let this be the lead-in to a weirdo pyramid scheme of direct-to-consumer sales crap. "I've only worn these. Family heirlooms," she said as she pointed to her lobes, touching her small gold Celtic knots. "Otherwise, I've never found anything that I couldn't live without."

Bay looked a bit stricken and she felt her bedamned pale skin flush to red. If he had a flirty fun reason for asking, Katy was sinking her chances with dumb statements like that. She hurried to follow up with, "But I don't dislike it or anything. Just thought it should mean something if I were going to wear it around all the time, you know?"

James Dean had nothing on this guy when he assumed a sexy, leaning-on-the-wall pose. He fished a business card from his back pocket. "I specialize in meaningful jewelry," he said as he handed her the card, an eyebrow going up again.

Katy decided his eyebrows were what swung him from sexy to smexy – those things were acting outright smutty, like darkly seductive wings over his incredible turqjadine eyes. Aquadeoise? She had to find a word to express that color, because it was unique and enthralling.

She glanced down at his card, gently curved from his perfect behind, and saw "Djilbay ~ Artisan Jewelry, Custom Design, Antique Repurposing and Rebirth". Not a marketing scam, then, but an independent artist like her brother, Patrick. Suitably impressed, she tried to hand it back, but he folded her fingers over the card and left his hand on top of hers.

"I'll be at Pike Place Market this week. I thought perhaps you could come by." Bay's eyes seemed to increase in brightness and his voice dropped. "We might find something meant for you. I specialize in making pieces that call to people." He paused, bit his lower lip, and continued in a deep tone, "I'd also simply like to see you again." Boyish smile now. Damn him and his cute wonky tooth peeking from behind succulent lips,

She stood no chance honestly. Forget being nearly thirty, her inner child shouted "A BOY! A BOY LIKES US!" Keeping it cool, Katy took a full second, possibly two before saying "That would be great! I work downtown, so I could try to swing by at lunch tomorrow, or should I come after work? I'm not sure how long you'll keep your spot open for the day." Excellent, totally played that cool. *Saints preserve me.* This was worse than trying to ask Jack Blanchard to the Sadie Hawkins dance when she was in high school.

Bay's eyes crinkled. "At the risk of angering your good father, I'll say the sooner the better. You're the only customer I'm interested in seeing. Tomorrow midday, then?"

She nodded, then jerked her head in the direction of the bar and Da. "Speaking of himself, we'd best get over there. There's only so long the threat of my mother will work against him." They both chuckled. Katy tucked Bay's card in her own back pocket, patting it for safety. Pretty things to look at and lunch with a smexy man were definitely worth the irritation of her father.

4

Unlike her usual Monday blahs, Katy felt excited. Enthusiastic even. Last night had been an unexpected delight and she hoped for more today. Bay and Da had been cracking on by the end of the night. So much so she hadn't been bothered leaving them alone together, when she went back to playing with the boys. As soon as Martin Phelan found out how much time Bay had spent in Ireland, they were off and talking through hikes in the West Country or north to the Giants Causeway, and debating the best casual dining in the Southern Region.

She wasn't a hundred percent sure she'd walk down to see Bay today (morning rationality made her more insecure than last night Katy) but she was pretty drawn to him… it scored in the ninety percent vicinity. Her hair, often a terrifying basket of frizzy un-wrangled snakes, was behaving. The day was shaping up to be a pleasantly warm one, so the walk from the Central Library branch on Fourth to Pike Place might be welcome and invigorating. A late lunch break would avoid any tourist crush, plus she could stop by the market's private library and try to schmooze her way into an interview.

Being a page at the Seattle Public Library started as a stop-gap, something to do when she got back from Ireland with a musical degree that qualified her for pretty much nothing useful in life. Art has its place, her ma had said repeatedly, but it doesn't pay the mortgage.

Katy had been at SPL long enough, while honestly enjoying it, to contemplate a future in libraries. She genuinely cared for the work, and could see herself following in Aunt Mildred's footsteps. The very Aunt Mildred who'd gotten her into SPL had recently been talking up the Folio at Pike Place – more formally known as Folio: The Seattle Athenaeum. It was funded by membership and considered a little slice of heaven for librarians. Auntie M had heard a rumor there'd be an entry-level opening soon and thought Katy should apply. She was considering it, but a voice inside Katy whimpered that would be the final death knell of her virtuoso dreams.

Katy finished her early morning tasks and treated herself to a wander through the Maritz Map Room. Rare maps, exotic maps, regular plain old NOAA charts from 2 years ago, all of it intrigued Katy. It fed into the part of her that had loved her da's stories; anywhere she hadn't already been was capable of being fantastical. You might not think a central Canada hiking trail was filled with potential magic…. But you couldn't prove it wasn't.

Today's detour to the map room brought her face-to-face with her co-worker, Raisa, rapidly dropping her level of enthusiasm. Raisa Leon was Katy's age, about five foot nine to Katy's five-six, and bombshell gorgeous. Chestnut hair and shining brown eyes that reminded Katy of a mirror glaze you'd see on competition baking shows. Persian ancestry, gifted with blemish-free skin that had a subtle bronzed glow.

"Katy, so good to see you. What are you up to?" Raisa asked.

Could she escape without being roped into coffee, lunch, or a twenty minute "chat"? The true danger with Raisa was her niceness. It made you agree to things you didn't want to do, since it was unthinkable to make her frown. Katy didn't know how to refuse without seeming grumpy or anti-social. But every time they were together she later felt like she'd heard a lot about Raisa without learning much. Either her co-worker didn't have a lot of substance, or she hid what mattered.

"Hey, Raisa, how are you?" Katy edged toward the door. "I'm meeting my aunt for lunch in a bit so I best move along." She gave a half-wave and tried to turn away.

"Are you sure your plans are for today?" Raisa followed Katy, soft voice mild but curious. "I saw Mildred prepping a meeting room for a lecture she's giving today. Maybe your wires got crossed?"

Damn it. "Shoot. I probably have a text from her and didn't see it." Katy tried to walk faster, but Raisa kept pace.

"Maybe we could go for lunch? I was interested what you thought about the rumors the First Folio might come back to Seattle." Raisa's long, obedient and not at all a bird's nest hair was slickly braided and slipped over her shoulder as she shrugged. "Sometimes I think we don't need to worship at the altar of dead white men anymore. But then I think, 'Shakespeare!' and get excited all over again."

Katy fell on the "can't be arsed to care" side of that debate, but Raisa was a literary woman to her core. In the simplest terms, Katy loved that people wanted to learn things, and Raisa loved the things people wanted to learn. In her years at SPL Katy had figured out it was a fine distinction, and meant they played in different parts of the scholarly orchestra.

"You know… I think I'm skipping an actual lunch, now I'm free," Katy said as they got in the elevator to ride to the employee break room. "Might dash down to Pike Place and look for some jewelry or a new purse."

"Oh, how lovely. Do you mind if I tag along? I would love to pick up a bouquet for my mom, and it looks like such a great day for a walk." Raisa beamed at her, opening the door to the small staff room.

Katy gave up. Saying no felt like kicking a puppy, and maybe she could lose her shadow by the time she got to Bay's table. Letting him see how amazing someone *else* looked wouldn't help Katy get a date. And Raisa looked gorgeous today; a blush cashmere cardigan over a marzipan blouse. Slacks in a color matching the blouse that fell loosely yet highlighted the curves under the fabric. She looked tall, elegant and warmly approachable.

Katy, meanwhile, had dark-wash jeans and a lightweight cable-knit sweater in moss green. Not because it highlighted her figure or flattered her eye color, but because it was the clean option. Laundry was Katy's least favorite chore, the one she left to the last possible minute, and over this morning's coffee she'd confirmed today was that minute. Wearing clean clothes to work tomorrow meant laundry tonight, because this sweater was the bottom of the barrel.

She sighed softly. "Sure, ready to head out now? Maybe I'll find a fun spring top, too."

Raisa clapped, bouncing a little in her ballet flats. "I love clothes shopping. Love. It." She reached into her locker and pulled out her purse. "I just need to use the bathroom first. Meet you out front?"

Katy, resigned, grabbed her own purse and closed her locker. "See you in a minute."

When she got outside she debated just taking off, then had a stern word with herself. She needed to wipe away the churlish attitude and reset. Raisa was kind, thoughtful, maybe a little pushy but overall a genuinely sweet woman. There were far worse things than an unobjectionable person trying to be friendly. Now she had a companion on a sunny walk to the market, not competition for the interest of a man she'd spoken to for thirty minutes all told.

If his eye was going to wander, it was best known early, and also entirely his right because she had no claim. One more deep breath and Katy had the surprising kernel of jealousy and cattiness under control. Good lord, where had that come from?

Raisa exited the building and linked arms with Katy. "This will be so fun!" She stepped forward. "Maybe if there's time we can snag some take away from Café Favahar?"

Katy matched her stride and replied, "What if you get kabab, I get Piroshky Piroshky, and we split them on the way home?"

"Perfect."

Katy felt her earlier excitement return and smiled at Raisa. No matter what happened at the Folio or with Bay (if he was even there), she was going to have a great break with her co-worker. Her positive attitude even held up as they wound their way past Benaroya Hall. As always, Katy slowed, stopped, and sent a prayer to the Universe that someone in the symphony decided to open up room for her.

"What is it?" Raisa asked.

"I play music, and have dreamed of playing here," Katy said, then let out a gusty sigh. "What I play, the Irish flute, isn't typically part of the orchestra here, but I still dream it."

They'd unlinked arms on their walk, but Raisa took hers again and squeezed. "I think I remember you telling me you got an MFA, right? In Ireland? If you believe, if you do the work, it will happen. I've seen your drive and competence at the library," she paused to wave at Benaroya, "so I can only assume it would be even greater for something you deeply loved."

Katy looked at Raisa and realized that, despite all the work events and casual chit chat, she'd never known her co-worker. She couldn't tell you if Raisa had family in Seattle or pets or a partner. Had she gone to college? Did she live in an apartment or a house? Did she have dreams like Katy? The most she knew was that Raisa drove a sensible four-door sedan in sensible blue, and only because Raisa had once driven them to an off-site conference.

This woman recalled things about Katy that Katy didn't remember telling her. Once again she was shamed to realize how easy it was to not ask questions of people who shared themselves less effortlessly. She could say they had nothing in common, but had no real proof of that because she'd never checked. Da had always told her people could surprise you; to be "ever open" and heaven knew her da had never met a stranger. That didn't come naturally to Katy, but she was determined to do better.

"I'll make sure you have front row seats when I debut."

Djilbay was apoplectic. No, wrong word. Euphoric? Yes, better. After a thousand tuig, years, Human languages ran together and the words jumbled. But euphoric was good. Blissful, eager, grounded in his purpose and certain of success. Katy was going to resonate with the pendant, use it to wake Sundancer Orange, and the Aoni would reverberate with the Mikanjo seekers crying in joy. Irojaku jo Faluji would rise from wherever She'd hidden at Katy's call, return to Her throne in the Calling, and reign supreme once more.

Dreams of an Aoni renaissance washed over Djilbay like warm air currents ruffling his downy interior feathers. Sundancer would outlaw Chitan slavery, stop the Krylar's blood-soaked march through the Aoni. When She heard what they'd done to Her brother's people, destroying their planet and forcing the Lunari to become wanderers, She would… Well, She certainly knew what She'd do even if *he* couldn't imagine it. She was about justice and truth and enforcing both. Maybe She'd be the one to awaken Songmaster Silver Herself, and He would take vengeance on the Krylar for the attempted genocide of His people.

Djilbay was getting ahead of himself. He rubbed his hands, the very ones that had touched Katy's skin. She was delightfully cool compared to his higher body heat, and her soft, fair skin showed delicate blue veins here and there, under the blushes of pink and red. If he were honest with himself, his excitement over her might have as much to do with her loveliness as with her being Sundancer's herald. Potential herald. He had to stop getting ahead of himself.

That's why he hadn't sprung the pendant on her in the bar; he could tell he'd pushed her away a little by bringing up jewelry. Did she worry he was only out to sell her something? He wasn't sure, but he couldn't afford any missteps so he'd eased off, praying he could coax her back to comfort.

She'd radiated energy that called out to his seeker side, and she'd smiled and talked. To him! She'd forced her father to back down just to keep talking to him. She'd awarded him a sweet-name; Bay. He'd never thought to have one since he'd spent most of his early adult years on this planet instead of with other Mikanjo. Normally he would have met someone to love, and he or she would have given him his sweet-name, but that time had come and gone while he was watching the fall of Constantinople to the Ottomans.

Which wasn't to say he was assuming she understood what she'd done. Humans were very fond of nicknames, a familiarity Mikanjo didn't share for the most part. For now, though, he could be Katy's Bay, even if only in his own mind.

He had spent all night going over his plan, which went perfectly in his mind, right up to the point he gave her Sundancer's pendant. Hopefully she immediately realized her destiny hung around her neck and they needed to call the *Eternidad* to come get them. But he couldn't be sure, so he intended to ask her to lunch if she didn't instantly understand.

He had to give it time to bond and a chance do whatever it would do to activate.

Would it be a sign only she recognized? Or would it be noticeable to everyone around them, an audible note resounding throughout the Aoni? He looked around at other craftspeople setting up tables and wares. How shocked they would all be, witnesses at ground zero as his quest was fulfilled. Would they run, cry out? Or was the sign going to be subtle, hidden, obvious only to Katy and him?

Brought out of his musing by aggressive honking on Western behind the market proper, he ducked out to Le Panier for coffee and pastry. The vendor beside him gave a thumbs-up and waved him off when he asked her to watch his table.

Ten minutes later he returned with a perfect café au lait, a slice of brioche to thank his neighbor, and a gorgeous, gooey croissant à la framboise for himself. Should have gotten two, he thought. Just then, a blob of raspberry preserve dove off his lip to stain his shirt in the most blatant way possible. No hiding it, and it wasn't coming out with a spritz of water and a prayer.

Of course. His best shirt, worn specifically to impress the Kawakona, ruined. And this after he'd sported a beer stain their first meeting. DAMN. IT. Djilbay eyed nearby possibilities, weighed the options, and sighed reluctant acceptance as he walked to the stall of handmade tie-dye batik clothing.

Hopefully he'd made a good impression last night, because he wasn't sure what the startlingly bright red t-shirt with rainbow-Om symbol he now wore said... or shouted about him. He loved it, but Katy had worn understated clothing the night before. The off-white sleeveless blouse under her sweater had been alluring, but as far from his flashy shirt now as could be.

No more time for panicking as late morning stretched into early afternoon and people began filling the market in earnest. A milenyo on Earth and Djilbay still hadn't lost the joy connecting with this species, even though he didn't need to make money from his craftmanship. The concept of investment had eventually sunk in and kept him from "couch surfing", a delightful phrase he'd learned a generation past. Being well-off by this time's standards hadn't lessened the driving urge to mingle with people drawn to his kind of art.

He'd always believed Sundancer's herald would be found amongst the artistically inclined, and this conviction had carried him through ages of bazaars, street markets, souks and fairs. Even a few high-end stores for short-term runs. It was always humbling – and a thrill – to see one person flush with delight beholding a piece that four others had rejected or ignored.

By the time Katy found him it was shortly past midday. He'd sold several smaller pieces already, and sent them off with silent wishes they would be long-loved. But as soon as he caught sight of her whiskey eyes, her curly hair trying to imitate flame and escape from a loose bun, all other business was forgotten. This was it. The pendant in his pocket seemed to pull toward her as she walked up to the table.

"Hi, Bay," she said with a shy wave. Her tentative eagerness was luminous and contagious. He grinned helplessly. She was perfect, regardless of whether the pendant awoke anything.

KATY HAD WATCHED him from a distance before approaching, seeing if he was different or the same as the night before. Her ovary-exploding, casually cool tall guy from last night had transformed into Bay, the gemstone artist chatting with his customers while wearing a siren-bright red tee. Less relaxed boating dude and more PNW enlightened spiritual explorer. Still a threat to her ovaries.

"Whew, so glad we found you," she said with a smile. Did she look as goofy as she felt? Within seconds of approaching him, the Air had exploded in her head, clearer than any time before in her life. It made her feel a little drunk, swelling like a wave. She despaired at having nothing on her to transcribe notes; for once she might be able to capture something if only she had paper. Maybe she could text herself. The need to compose left as fast as it arrived when his grin captured her attention again. She looked into those stunning eyes (*jaquatur?*) and felt blissfully caught.

Lord of mercy, those white teeth against warm tan skin. Irises more enthralling than any jewel on his table. Large physical presence that wasn't frightening, more comforting. What was it about this guy that had her so discombobulated?

"Hi," she heard to her right. "I'm Raisa, Katy's co-worker."

This was enough for Bay's gaze to release hers, and she took the first full breath since arriving. "Sorry! My bad," she blurted. Waving between them she continued, "Bay, this is Raisa, Raisa meet Bay." As they shook hands she said, "Raisa and I work together at the library. We snuck out for a lunch break and I wanted to stop by since you'd invited me."

Never let it be said Katy Phelan couldn't over explain something simple. Ugh.

DJILBAY SHOOK the co-worker's hand, strategizing how to get the pendant on Katy. His perfect plan scattered to the wind with this unexpected addition. Should he try to get rid of Raisa? Maybe in order to work he and Katy would need privacy when she donned the necklace? Why were none of these details covered in his dreams!

"Delighted to meet you," he said, reaching out to shake her hand. "Djilbay jo Bikajo. Do you like jewelry? I could show you some pieces-" He cut off, seeing a shadow cross Katy's face. Did she worry he was just trying to make sales to anyone and every-one? Was that why she'd shut down a little when he'd first brought it up at the bar? He had to ensure she understood the pendant was special, something to show only her.

Katy's companion seemed to understand the visit was about something more than a necklace. Her half-smile was rueful and kind. "I think my father would be much happier if I didn't look too closely," she chuckled. "But I do need a bouquet to take home to my mother, please excuse me." Raisa pointed toward the flower sellers. "I'll be over there when you're ready to grab food, Katy. Nice to meet you, Djilbay."

Did he hear that correctly? Dining with Katy was denied him as well? Despite his frustration, Raisa's gracious departure gave him an opening. He prayed to the Nine his Kawakona and Sundancer's trigger would bond instantaneously.

"I have something I've been saving, hoping you would come," he said softly. She had no idea just how true that was. "A pendant I would love to see on you. When I saw you last night, I knew it was meant to be yours."

Pulling it from his pocket, he cradled his most precious item in his left palm, holding the chain in his right. Every aspect of this piece was hand-crafted by Bay, the carnelian essence of Sundancer pulled from the ancient deposit in Africa himself. He'd carried it in raw form for many centuries before the design came to him: a thick baton of the gemstone, grasped vertically in the foreclaws of a dragon, the Drazoen who'd called to him his entire life. Djilbay had first thought it would be a faceted cylinder, but came to see it should be rounded and polished. A resilient pillar of this gorgeous mineral that She had birthed Herself.

Sundancer's wings arched down in a pose that simultane-ously protected the essence and showed it off, the impression of movement palpable. Her head was raised, hindlegs down, as though the wings were mid-beat and about to thrust Her into the air. She was taking flight with Her prize firmly and gently clutched.

He had waited long years for Human metal use to progress where he could get a material worthy of a Drazoen trigger. Each small platinum circle of the chain links had been forged painstakingly and individually; it had to be delicate, but strong enough to support a bigger piece. This pendant wasn't a lightweight filagree, it was bold, powerful. Heavy. One of the only pieces of this size he'd ever designed.

The mold of Sundancer had taken a Human generation to perfect. Carving the fine details was his fevered passion for decades. Casting test after test in inferior materials to ensure it was exactly as it should be, before completing the final version in platinum. Seating the carnelian and securing it, threading the chain. Polishing the final piece rarely, but enough to keep it ready.

All for this, here and now. This was it. The moment of truth: would it resonate with her?

KATY'S FINGER rose to trace the intricate and unique dragon necklace Bay held. She was unexpectedly overwhelmed, damn near choked up. It wasn't the kind of thing she went for, she tended toward minimalism, but how she wanted this!

Jewelry wasn't her jam at all, frankly. Earrings, rings, and necklaces all got lost so easily. To say she was surprised at how much she craved donning this pendant was an understatement. Hell, it was big enough it almost qualified as a medallion. This was what fashion blogs called a statement piece.

Shiny silver that would blaze in sunlight. An orange stone held by a dragon taking off and shooting straight up. Her fingers didn't encounter any sharp edges, despite the claws, wings, and swoopy crown-looking deal on the dragon's head. Even the stone was smooth and curved, giving Katy the impression of well-contained power. This was a dragon with places to go and the strength to get there. Katy wanted to ride this dragon. Or be it.

"This is fantastic. I've never seen anything like it, and," she trailed off sadly, "I'm confident I can't afford something so fine."

Bay looked happy at her compliment, then anxious about her trying to refuse. "Don't worry about a price. My favorite pieces are meant for the person they are meant for, I have little say in it." He huffed. "You could say this one isn't likely to be on any wavelength other than yours."

Katy tried to protest again, "But-"

"Please," he gestured for her to turn around. "Let me just see it on you." His voice nearly pleaded.

She decided not to argue and gave him her back as she said, "Okay, but I'm going to be very sad when you realize a library page doesn't have enough coin, even if it's *meant* for me."

His warm breath gusted over her neck as he sighed. "Trust me, it will work out."

Katy had subconsciously noticed the growing crowd of people moving around her and Bay, noise picking up as more cars drove past on Western or Pike Place. Raisa a few feet away getting her monster bouquet wrapped. Three women perusing the nearby tables, and a baby cooing from a stroller going by. Then the necklace, held in Bay's hands, circled her throat. The solid weight of the pendant came to rest on her breastbone, the chain closed and the Air swamped her. Time stopped.

Even though her eyes were open, she saw only orange. Spinning, writhing, transcendent, ascendent. Pike Place Market disappeared and she saw music in every shade of orange that could have ever existed. It was "Kyrie Eleison" in pumpkin and the "1812 Overture" in coral. A "Gloria" in tangerine, "Flight of the Bumblebee" in rust, a gamboling reel in carrot. Polyphonic, layered, shattering. Katy had never experienced anything in her life to compare, and fell back against Bay, legs shaky.

"I knew it!" she heard him declaim as he caught her against his chest. His arms were strong, his hands warm even through the sleeves of her sweater.

"Katy!" Raisa called out. She felt her co-worker touch her. Raisa must have dashed back toward her when she stumbled.

Her vision cleared slowly, and she pushed away from Bay, only to turn and face him in awe. She looked next to Raisa, saw the worried frown marring her normally relaxed countenance.

"I'm okay, just had a weird moment." She faced Bay and locked eyes with him. Her hand raised to the pendant, covering it, knowing she'd be hard-pressed to take it off again. This was hers now, by the saints! "I don't know what happened, sorry about that."

His face was excited, eager, nearly beatific. "It's you," he said. "You at last! I thought, I hoped... but it's really you." He beamed and threw his arms wide. "Yes!"

Bay's arm whacked Raisa's flowers out of her hand. Their triad bent down simultaneously to pick them up, knocking heads in the process. As all three laughed at the awkwardness and their lack of coordination, Katy, motivated by a force she could no more fight than name, slipped the pendant under her sweater. It was *hers* now. She might fight to keep it if pushed on the matter.

Rising, Katy stared at Bay again, caught in his vibrant gaze, excited in a way she couldn't fully grasp. Slightly nervous, too. Big shite was happening, change was coming, and it had something to do with Bay, this necklace, how it made the Air howl ecstatically and color the entire bloody Universe orange for a hot second.

His smile faded into a more serious expression. "We need to find somewhere to talk. I have to explain." He paused, running a hand through his hair in frustration. "How do I explain?" he whispered.

"Try the beginning. It's where my da always started all the good stories," she encouraged softly. "*Once upon a time*, or *In a certain land*. Or a personal favorite, *There was and there was not*. They all work."

"How about," Bay replied just as softly, "*long ago and far away?*"

Katy smiled, staring up at him, knowing incredible things were to come.

Raisa nudged Katy, mumbling "Don't feel great all of sudden."

5

Raisa's hand rubbed her lips as though they'd gone numb, her eyes appearing unfocused.

Bay and Katy, yanked out of their mutual admiration moment, turned to face her. Katy spotted a tall man in aged sorrel-tone leather lurking too close, right in their personal bubble. He had a strangely blank face under a drawn-tight hoodie, and loomed at Raisa's right side, leaning forward menacingly. Her co-worker's normally perfect skin was simultaneously flushing red and going blue around her lips and nose.

Wait, that man wasn't in a hoodie, it was a straight-up hood, like an over-committed renaissance faire attendee. And his face wasn't blank, it was missing, as in it looked like pictures online where someone's visage has been blurred for anonymity. Unable to process what she was seeing (and not seeing), Katy froze, confused, an icy sense of primal fear trickling down the back of her neck.

Bay reacted immediately, no hesitation. His left hand shot out, knocking the stranger's hood askew and clawing at the blank face. The blurring slipped on that side, a verdant green color peeking out around the edges. WTF? Was this a Hulk reenactment where they just used random bystanders as extras? The guy wasn't big enough for that, but maybe he was a modern, trimmed down version. Svelte Hulk.

"They *did* send one of you this far!" Bay hissed, swiping at the discomfiting, blank face once more.

What the hell was Bay talking about? He knew who this rude and maybe dangerous guy was? Bay struck out at the other side of the creeper's face for the third time, snatching at nothing Katy could see. He glided around the women to get a better angle at the stranger. More green peeked out, this time with puce whorls tracing to the edge of the face. This was serious makeup not-Hulk was rocking.

Still unsure, feeling more and more like this was a Very Bad Situation, Katy grabbed Raisa's hand to tug her closer. There was resistance; blank face had his hand wrapped around Raisa's upper arm, pulling her hard, back into his body.

"Let her go, freak!" Katy shouted as she yanked Raisa into her shoulder.

The hand bruising Raisa sported a fingerless half-glove with slim ridges lining the top of it. The fingers peeking out from the glove were so pale they appeared bleached, but with darker lines striped down the sides, like cracked and weathered tree bark. When the bastard let go to deal with Bay's assault, light flashed off something tiny and metallic that slid back into one of the ridges.

A retractable needle? Jaysus this was out of control, and happening so fast. Katy's self-preservation instincts started shrieking at her to run far and fast from whatever the hell was happening. But Raisa needed her, she had to stay and help her.

Blank face guy ignored his slipping mask and squared off against Bay, raising the same, partially-gloved hand toward Bay's neck. Bay anticipated the move and blocked, kicking out at the guy's right knee. The stranger took the kick without making a sound, punching Bay in the chest, which dropped her man to his knees, breath whooshing out of him.

At the same moment Raisa's knees seemed to give out, her near-dead weight taking both Katy and Raisa to the ground. Katy was eye level with Bay, who'd been gasping for air while she did her best to keep Raisa from hitting her head on pavement. *Help me, dear gods, help me. I'm so scared and confused!*

Bay, undaunted by the creeper's assault, punched the same knee he'd kicked before, which finally got a pained noise out of blank face. His leg collapsed under the hit, and he fell back into a neighboring table filled with fresh-made bouquets. Water and sweet peas blasted all over the tables and ground.

Passersby became spectators instead, stopping to stare. Startled shoppers exclaimed as the fight got more aggressive. Jostling got more chaotic, and when their attacker was pushed away from someone trying to pass by, his mask slipped further. More green face paint was revealed, along with extended swirling curves of rose.

"Look at my dude's makeup! Is there a movie being filmed or what?" Katy overheard.

Bay, still on his knees, spun and lunged toward Raisa and Katy. Raisa was leaning into Katy more deeply, nearly laying atop her now, mumbling "Why are things so wavy? My head…heavy…."

Katy's deep unease turned the corner into heart-racing panic. Bay pushed them and growled, "Go!"

Katy got to her knees, wiggling a shoulder under Raisa's, and turned as Bay lurched to his feet. "Pull," she begged, lifting her hand toward him. He clasped her forearm and yanked, managing to leverage both women to their feet.

"Which way?" Katy asked. Raisa was nearly unconscious.

Bay swiped something off his display table – a brooch of some kind – then swiveled the other way to see if blank face was up yet. Their attacker had gotten to one knee, but Bay had done real damage because he couldn't use the right leg. It was held off the cement and to the side, like it couldn't take weight.

Bay pushed Katy toward the nearest opening onto Pike Place. "Go, go, now!"

She glanced back as she angled herself to help Raisa keep walking with them, and she couldn't believe it. Mean greenie pushed up, almost fell when the table he was using as an anchor slid sideways. Then he resolutely put the injured leg down and brutally stomped his foot against the ground. It held, though she heard a distinct grunt of pain. His head came up, eyes still hidden under whatever was blurring half his face, and took a step. He was adjusting to the pain and overcoming it. How was he was still coming? Why hadn't anything put this son of a bitch down for the count?!

The man limped toward them, most people backing away from him. Less Hulk now, more Terminator. Two older teen boys tried to ask him who he was cosplaying, pushing in front of him, demanding selfies. Blank face brushed them harshly to the side, picking up speed. They responded to his aggression by shoving him from behind and he fell, barking an unintelligible word at them.

"Fuck you, bro!" one of them shouted before they took off running.

Bay got Katy's attention refocused when he took Raisa's other arm and growled, "We have to be fast or she isn't going to make it. My car, I have what we need in there. Go left!"

Questions later, Katy decided. "Isn't going to make it" sounded terrifying and time sensitive. The overriding fear she'd felt the first time she looked at scary guy had only increased in the three minutes since everything kicked off.

"Make sure you call my mom, not my dad," Raisa slurred. "Baba will be angry I was out with you."

"No, it will be fine. Don't worry," Katy reassured her.

Between the two of them, Katy and Bay essentially lifted

Raisa off her feet and ran as best they could. She followed his lead to an SUV. It was thankfully parked in the vendor-reserved spots just outside the market stalls. Bay threw open the closest back door, and Katy ran around to the other side so she could pull Raisa through. Bay angled Raisa's face up, protected her head, and together they safely slid her onto the back seat.

Sweet baby Jesus, it was a scene from a zombie movie now. The stranger was up and slowly limping in their direction when Katy peeked over the car's roof. "Hurry, hurry, he's coming!" she cried.

Bay leaned over Raisa's body. He pressed the brooch he'd grabbed earlier into the side of her neck, pin side penetrating skin. Katy cried out as her terror ramped up to a level she hadn't known it could reach. Why would he stab Raisa like that? Oh my god, who was this man? What if Bay couldn't be trusted? She'd put them both in the sights of scary men and she didn't know what to do. She couldn't run and leave Raisa, she was trapped with someone she had to admit she didn't know at all.

Bay slammed the door on a nearly unconscious Raisa, forestalling Katy's demand for answers with a raised hand. "Get in!" he growled. "I promise, I'm not hurting her, and I'll explain but we need to go. Now!"

She heard people cry out as the creepy attacker shoved through pedestrians to get to them. Katy yanked open the front door and nearly dove into the seat.

Bay raised the back hatch and grabbed at a bag. "It's in here, damn it! Why didn't I have it ready?" He continued to curse extensively, throwing things onto the cargo mat as he yanked them from the bag.

Katy saw their attacker mere feet from the car. Without thinking she locked the doors, setting off a high tone since the hatch was still open. Blank face recoiled from the sound, slowing him just enough for her to whimper "He's here!"

Bay whirled on the other man, an old-fashioned stickpin in

his hand. This time he thrust toward the guy's throat with his empty hand, making the creeper lean back. Then Bay jammed the pin right into the chest of his opponent. Somehow it penetrated the leather, and in one second flat not-Hulk dropped to the ground. Bay kicked at the man, ensuring he was completely out, before dragging him against the curb.

Asleep? Dead? Please not dead. Murder seemed like such a bad lunch time outing.

Bay laid their enemy down next to the wall of the market, facing away from the street. He also pulled off whatever mask the man had been wearing, clenching it in his hand. She couldn't see the revealed face since it was hidden at this angle. Slowly straightening, Bay turned and gazed at Katy through the window, his expression one of raging adrenaline high.

But it was fading to sorrow, twinned with resolve. She knew that last look well. Her mother wore it often. Her artisan jeweler had made a decision, one she might not like, but it was happening nonetheless.

6

He'd gotten them off Pike Place, onto Western, headed for Inter-bay. Not a peep. Katy was clenching her hands on her knees, bracing for his explanation, but he wasn't sure where or how to begin. At last he'd found Sundancer's herald, Her Kawakona, his dream come true, and a Pu'ulqaari assassin nearly took her. Raisa's rattling breaths from the backseat reinforced that horrifying fact. If he'd been slower, if he hadn't had antidotes prepared and to hand because his sister insisted... Vailillia would happily lord her prescience over him, and given Raisa was still alive because of it, he would honor his sister's greatness.

He needed to dig out his beacon and signal the *Eternidad* right away. If he could also set it to analyze the assassin's facial kuh he'd swiped in the fight, that would be ideal. Pu'ulqaari kuh were treasured by that species, capable of camouflage and mimicry better than anything Humans had dreamt of in Mission: Impossible or Face/Off. Why this one's mask came off as easily as it had was confusing, because Bay had heard stories of assassins who committed suicide rather than surrender them. An item of that technological magnitude, if it could be merged with his suppression suit tech, could conceal their flight to the refuge. Every minute they weren't away from here was an opportunity for the killer to wake up and come after them. Flight was the fastest and best way out of Seattle, but that brought its own dangers, if he couldn't hide them from Human eyes on the way to the safehouse.

Earth's sanctuary for off-worlders, a refuge in the San Juan Islands, had helped tempt him to visit Seattle. His chance at a momentary escape from reality. He hadn't thought he'd be in such a desperate race to get to it: if they were onsite, Katy would be safe from the assassin due to the non-violence mandate there. They could recuperate as they waited for his ship. Make plans, figure out how to use the trigger.

Myrtle Edwards Park was on their left when she finally spoke up. "I'm trying to be patient, I'm trying to understand what the hell just happened, but I can't stop my brain spinning out. You need to explain!" Her breathing was accelerating, panic crimping her features.

His suppressed wings tried to flutter. That killer had nearly ended his destiny just as it came in range. Bay reached for calm, hoping to settle Katy, too. "I need to get us to a safe place, so I can arrange transport to somewhere that assassin can't-"

"Assassin!" Katy cried. "I can't even-", her breath was shallow and shaky. "This is too much. What are you talking about?!"

Djilbay inhaled. "I'll try to answer, but a lot of this will be overwhelming. I am deeply sorry all of this was brought into your life suddenly. I thought we would have… I expected more time to explain. Gently." He adjusted in his seat, straightening his shoulders. "But we didn't get it, and have to roll with it. I've looked for you for such a long time. I've searched all these years, and just when I found you someone tried to take you."

"Roll with it! You've looked for me? How?! You don't even know me!" Her agitation ramped again. "Completely freaking over here! Why did you stab Raisa with a pin? And green makeup guy with the freaky missing face – is he still alive? You stabbed him too! You say he's an assassin, but maybe you're a killer! Oh god. Are you going to murder us and dump our bodies?" She moved a hand toward the door handle and he prayed she didn't try to jump from the moving car.

"Wait. Give me a second. He's alive, just sedated for a while." Bay glanced at her before back to the traffic on Elliot Ave. "This will seem outlandish to you, but when we get somewhere more secluded I can prove everything I'm about to say." Bay mentally girded himself, then went on. "Yes, he's an assassin, from a species called the Pu'ulqaari. I am from a species called the Mikanjo, I'm what we call a seeker. We aren't in a great place to give a lot more detail, though I promise I will. My people have been seeking beings like you for nearly a full kōmilen." He paused for Katy to ask a question or several dozen, given he'd just told her Humans shared Earth with multiple other species.

"What is a coo-mee-len?" She stared down at her lap, voice low and small.

Surprised that was her only ask, he clarified, "A kōmilen is roughly equal to a hundred thousand Earth years." Closer to ninety thousand, but this didn't feel like a moment to be literal.

Katy's head whipped toward him, jaw dropped. "You never looked for me for a hundred thousand years! Humans have only been legit civilized a few... a handful... maybe several thousand years..." Her pauses and ascending tone made the end of her statement a question.

"True. My people have been seeking a long time, but didn't know what species the herald would come from."

"You keep saying species, but I think you mean race." Katy's tone was still uneven, shocked at what she was hearing. "I've never heard of either ethnicity you said. Where are poo-ool-car-ee from? Where are your people from, for that matter? Mee-con-jo?"

A short whimper echoed from the backseat. Katy checked her friend, turned back, then threw up her hands. "Jesus wept, where you're from doesn't matter, why am I getting distracted! The important thing is whether Raisa will be okay and what was that fecking mess back there!"

How did he tell her that where he was from mattered very much? He'd have to cover that when they got to the park, it seemed. Reassurance was what she needed right now, not a steamroller over her preconceptions of life as she knew it. "Your friend will be fine. The assassin seems to have mistaken her for you, or he thought it was better to take out both of you to be sure."

Katy gasped and he pushed on, hoping she'd handle the shock better if he went quickly. "I had an antidote, the brooch you saw, which is why I pricked her with the pin. It needed to get into her blood immediately or she would have died."

"Raisa's my coworker." She trailed off, voice wobblier than ever, looking out the window, away from him and the unpleasant reality he was unveiling. "All Raisa wanted was a walk on a sunny day. A lot of the time she annoys me, but I didn't know how to get out of her coming along."

Katy's fingers pressed against her lips, hard enough to leave bloodless marks as her hand dropped to her lap. "She might have died because she's pushy and I'm a pushover? I don't understand any of this, yet I feel like it's my fault."

His heart broke a little for her. "I swear to you, this isn't your fault. I know it's confusing, I'll try to help you make sense of things."

"You promise she'll be fine? She'll recover?"

"Yes." He was firm, his conviction audible. Bay kept his sorrow hidden, knowing none of their lives would be the same, especially these two women. He'd been a naïve fool not to see what kind of impact revealing her role as the Kawakona would have. "We're going to Discovery Park, where I can signal my ship and make plans for us to get to a safehouse."

Katy was back to incredulous with a helping of pissed off. "Whoa. I never said I'm going with you. Unless you're kidnapping me, this ends as soon as the car stops and I can get out without breaking my neck."

"You'll feel differently when you have the whole picture. And, again, I am so sorry that this is world-altering news you're getting in a short period, no working our way up to it." He jerked and slammed the brakes as a driver cut in front of him. He heard Raisa's limp body slide on the backseat, and he threw an arm in front of Katy. She shrieked, grabbing his arm for a second before pushing it away angrily.

"No more, dude. No. More. Give me the CliffsNotes version or so help me God I will jump out of this car!"

A cartoon version of Katy would have steam coming out of her ears now. He also wondered what CliffsNotes meant, but in context he gathered she wanted concise and abbreviated. So be it.

"When I said species, I meant it. Mikanjo and Pu'ulqaari aren't from your planet. We come from distant places in the Aoni, the Universe. My people are from the planet Bankiri, Pu'ulqaari are from Ishar, both in the Grulat galaxy. Which isn't this galaxy you call Milky Way.

"Long ago, right before that kōmilen I mentioned earlier, the Mikanjo were given a quest by a goddess, one that is crucial to saving the Aoni. A mission that generations of Mikanjo seekers have followed, which is how I eventually ended up on your planet. I have wandered here for a milenyo, a millennium, believing I would find what I sought, and today I have found you."

Here he paused, but Katy remained silent, mouth agape.

"When we get to the park, I'm going to stop the car somewhere discreet. I will check Raisa to ensure the antidote is working as expected, since it wasn't calibrated specifically for Humans. I have a tool I will use to signal my ship. I will also have it try to jailbreak the assassin's mask tech for our use. As it works on those things, I will give you undeniable proof that what I say is true."

He took advantage of the red light stopping them to look at Katy for several seconds, peering into those wide amber eyes. She was fair by nature, but her face had gone distinctly pallid. He hoped his bullet-point explanation shortcut some of the fear she must be feeling.

"I swear you can trust me, but I am aware that takes time. The best I can do is keep my word to you, protect you, and that means getting us to the safehouse."

"Fine." She turned her face forward. "Light's green."

KATY WAS MOSTLY at sea over what Bay said, because it was nonsensical and awesome. In the Old Testament sense of that word. The *an archangel burned you to a crisp by revealing the glory of themselves* sense of awesome. Which made her a little angry, a lot scared, but she couldn't waste her energy on fears and panic right now. Bay was driving well over the speed limit when she'd last checked, and unless she wanted to risk a broken neck bolting from the speeding vehicle, she was stuck.

The hell was he talking about, not from Earth, blah blah? This whole day had gotten out of control. It was a flat-out dog's dinner, a chaotic "minus craic" as Da would say. She'd thought she was flirting with a handsome guy who made pretty things. She'd thought he was into her, too, that they'd had a moment at Pike Place and it would lead to something exciting. A meaningful instant where they'd connected…. Right before the freaky dude in makeup tried to kill Raisa. And would have gone after Katy, too, sounded like. Because of some prophecy? That was straight-up cult shite.

The longer she stewed on this, the more Katy got a sick feeling that it was all a prank. Oran could absolutely dream up something this crazy and get a friend or two to help him pull it off. Her twin started his windups unnaturally young, gluing her toys into the toybox when they were four. As he got older and more devious, he would make her belongings disappear then reappear in embarrassing places. Like her first bra hoisted in the school cafeteria. Once for Halloween he'd coordinated all the brothers and they'd convinced her the ghost of J.P. Patches, beloved Seattle clown, was coming to take her to hell. The logic was convoluted and relied heavily on Katy not being a Patches Pal (she was twenty years too late for that club and didn't even know what it meant). All four brothers frightened her for weeks leading into Halloween, culminating in her faking sick for trick-or-treating so the clown couldn't snatch her off the sidewalk. When her father finally got the story out of her, the boys were in so much trouble, but Da was openly impressed with his sons' commitment to theatrics.

Ipso facto it wasn't completely impossible for this to be another prank. It was next level, for sure. Yes, it strained credulity that he also recruited Raisa to pretend to be poisoned, but Katy put nothing out of bounds for Oran's fuckery. Oh damn, and if he got Patrick to help? That glove gauntlet thing the "assassin" wore would be right up Vasuda's artistic alley.

There was no way her almost-sister would help them do this to Katy, but Patrick could have taken it from her workshop!

"Tell the truth – did my brothers put you up to this? Pay you? Because the jig is up, Bay! This has gone too far." She twisted to look in the backseat. "Are you faking it back there? Hey, Raisa! You hear me? Get up and explain how Oran got to you!" Looking at Bay again she asked, "How much did those jerks pay you to do this? The fighting looked so real!"

Bay peered at her like she'd grown a second nose, then started laughing. It was a good sound on him, as rolling and deep as the lower register of a bass fiddle.

"This isn't a prank; your brothers didn't hire me." He sobered, pulling into the north lot of Discovery Park and stopping the SUV far away from other cars. "I promise you in fifteen minutes you will see with your own eyes it's all true." His hand dropped to her knee, squeezing gently.

She contemplated a few choices: smacking his hand, grabbing it and never letting go, or just leaving it alone. Each choice would be a message of some kind. Angry and reactive, clingy dingbat asking the big strong man to take charge and keep her safe, or the passive girl swept into events beyond her control. Katy decided, in the end, to be who she knew herself to be, never mind who he thought she was.

Calmly and firmly, she picked up his hand, returned it to his own leg, crossed hers in the passenger seat and said, "You've got your fifteen minutes, then no more BS. I'll have the truth then." Turning to look out her side window, Katy dismissed Bay, assassins and safe houses from her mind.

It was more difficult to set aside how intensely the pendant continued to resonate with the Air inside her. From the moment he'd dropped it around her neck, Katy had felt a surge as her always present soundtrack had responded to the incredible, heavy piece. Her lifelong, just out of reach, frustratingly semi-audible companion was finally clearer, though still playing peek-a-boo in her brain. Throughout the entire fight-and-flight, a resonant whirr ebbed and flowed in her bloodstream like a coastal tide. It had settled somewhat, but was more forward than ever before.

Back to Bay's bewildering explanation of being E.T.... His assertion that Katy was rather an important person (you didn't search a hundred thousand years for unimportant people, right?), and how that left her feeling unmoored had to be examined. A prank, while obnoxious, didn't hold the same peril this seeker quest crap did. A mission from a goddess sounded dangerous. And involved. Journeys like that led to rings thrown in mountains of doom, yellow brick roads with mean witches and false wizards, or very dark evil sorcerers who killed your friends and family. Fairy hills that snatched you up and spit you back out three hundred years later. Black holes full of stars.

No matter how much she'd fantasized as a kid, being slapped with the possibility this was real was shocking. There was a spreading numbness in her limbs. Physical jeopardy might be imminent, hell, it had already happened. An ancient, epic quest was on the line, and Katy might have to be a chosen one. She wasn't even like that, was she? Did a chosen one get a choice? Buffy didn't, and she'd died twice.

Katy was nothing more than an Irish-American chick who'd gotten a degree in an esoteric subject and super-specialized instrument, trying to find a way to express something she couldn't define or put into words. Now she filled her time at a library, dreaming of the day the Seattle Philharmonic decided they couldn't survive another year without a full-time Irish flute. Not a bloody thing about her screamed *woman most likely to save the Universe.*

As she ruminated, Bay opened the back door and checked Raisa's vitals. He lifted eyelids, measured pulse, things that seemed logical if he were telling the truth about trying to save her. Katy opened her door, ready to jump out and run in any direction. If she bailed, she wouldn't have to deal with the repercussions of Bay being for real. That an alien, a for-real-from-another-planet alien, had tried to kill her, had very nearly killed Raisa, and would eventually wake up from whatever Bay gave him and keep coming.

Bay didn't even lift his head as he said "At least wait for the rest of the story before you run."

She deflated, sagging back into the seat. And this alien before her, he was problematic because she wanted to let him save her, keep her protected. Explain this rapidly changing and expanding Universe to her. But how could she trust him when she barely knew him? The Air liked him, that was true, and he'd made the lovely pendant she currently clutched through her sweater, a gift she'd be loath to return. Katy's mind was slowing, tired from the adrenaline and shocks of the afternoon. She followed Bay in the rearview mirror as he circled to the back of his car, reaching for his bag once the hatch lifted. That triggered a memory of their escape.

"Hey, did you see how the alarm on your car made that bastard SOB slow down a sec? It was like he couldn't handle the pitch or note." She dug out her phone. "We should record the sound, just in case he catches up again. When you're done with whatever you're doing let's set it off again."

His head came up and she met his eyes in the mirror. "I hadn't noticed that, great idea." His lips curved. "Of course, someone musical like you would put that together."

"What are you doing back there? Getting irrefutable proof of your alienhood ready to dazzle me?"

Bay laughed. "I'm hoping my beacon can splice the kuh into my suppression suit. These things-"

Katy cut him off. "Coo? What's that?"

"Sorry. I forget you don't have aoiti ... another thing we have to take care of, getting some into you. First off, my beacon is a personal AI device, although it's more AGI in the Human definitions of artificial learning, and able to function creatively on a sub-nano-scale-"

"Dude. Getting in the weeds. I understood AI device and that's it." Katy was frustrated. Also nervous. She'd seen plenty o' sci-fi and had new worries he was about to whip out a needle to inject her with freaking ow-wee-tea something or others. Ow was in the godsdamned name! She didn't like needles, another reason the assassin had made her freeze like a deer in headlights back at the market. His had come out of his glove, or hand, like an even scarier Freddy Krueger. She shuddered.

Bay looked chastened. "Sorry. Again. Just think beacon equals very advanced AI, linked at a quantum level to the parent AI on the *Eternidad*."

"What is the *Eternidad*? Sounds like eternity."

Bay smiled. "You'll learn there are similarities to many words because of how the Aoni, the Universe, was created. I'll explain more later, but the *Eternidad* is my people's ship." He waved a hand covered with the killer's face mask, no longer blurry but a neutral, shimmery grey. "The kuh is this mask with stealth properties. You saw how it blurred his features to the point of near-invisibility? They are quite rare, protected by the Pu'ulqaari, often violently. If I can just get my beacon to crack the coding and reconfigure my suppression suit, broaden the display field, it would help keep alarm down when we leave."

Leaving didn't sound promising. Nor did the substantial detail Bay was casually throwing out about alien cultures and weird technology. All of that sounded authentic, real, and like Katy was destined for a long walk through a dark wood, in quest-speak.

"I'm lost again. Why will leaving cause alarm? Is this car a spaceship?" Despite anxiety over the unknown, excitement flourished. "Is that why it's so quiet?!"

Deep rumbly laughter again. "No, it's just electric."

Embarrassed and feeling her cheeks flame, she pretended to check her phone. "Ah, right. Are you almost ready? Your fifteen minutes are nearly up."

"I've started trying to jailbreak the mask, anyway. Come on, we need to walk a bit on a trail so we're away from people."

This was Katy's Rubicon. Either she listened to the logical

side telling her that going somewhere remote and isolated with a guy she barely knew was throwing herself at death's door, or she trusted and walked with him. She had no illusions she could outrun or overpower Bay; she'd seen how fast and fluidly he'd moved back at the market. He was strong; he'd mostly carried Raisa himself when they ran, and his punches had taken out the attacker's leg. He was good looking and charming, like all the best serial killers. Perfectly good reasons to climb out and scream for help from the couple she spied fifty feet away.

Something told her to trust, though. Instinct, a lifetime of reading fantasy and science fiction priming her for acceptance of the bizarre. The Air that felt so very strong at the moment, reaching toward him, raising the hair on her arms. She slipped out of the car and met him as he came around. "What about Raisa? We can't leave her."

"I'm coming back for her once I show you the truth and you agree to leave for the refuge." His gaze searched her face for something she couldn't pinpoint. Fear, pushback, disbelief? "I can't kidnap you, or force you to go. But he will find us again, and at least if we're there he can't attack you."

Sure, a refuge. Why not? Katy had no fight right then, just more questions she knew he wouldn't answer until he'd done whatever he thought he needed to prove his story. She shrugged. "Okay, let's see this evidence, Bay the Seeker.

7

Katy followed Bay north, into the Wolf Tree area. He'd locked his car after one final check on Raisa. The black bag with beacon and mask and who knows what else held firmly in one hand. Out of the corner of her eye she noticed him reach for her hand with the other, then stop himself. She wasn't sure if she wanted the comfort of his touch, or if it would be sensory overload on top of the earlier violent melee, headlong getaway, and out-of-this-world revelations.

A weekday this time of year meant the sometimes earthen-sometimes wood plank path was theirs alone. Sunlight filtered through newly grown deciduous leaves, a damp smell lingering as the wooded area continued to mulch gifts of the wet winter they'd had. A woodpecker was going to town on a nearby tree, angering a squirrel who chittered scornfully.

If they kept going this way they'd come to the Cultural Center, which might be booked for an event. That would mean an audience. They were five minutes in when she said, "Let's stop here. Show me what you've got, so we can figure out how we're going to proceed." She was proud of herself for being calm, nay, cool as a cucumber, facing down what she'd accepted was going to freak her out.

Bay slowed, turning in a circle, eyeing nearby trees. "I need a little more space," he said. "There, that will work," he added, pointing slightly northeast at an opening inside a ring of trees. One had recently fallen, leaving extra room on that side.

They set off beyond the path, stepping over ferns, moss-covered semi-buried trunks, and around pink-flowered salal and huckleberry shrubs. Their trek scared a jumping mouse who whacked the ground with its tail a few times before leaping away. Distracted by the rodent, Katy managed to face-plant through a spider-web strung between two low-hanging pine boughs. As Bay set down his bag, she flipped her hair maniacally.

"Do you see a spider? There's no spider on my shoulder, right?" Katy shivered. That damn arachnid could get into her curls and hide forever. "Or in my hair? RIGHT?"

Bay looked her over, his own dark hair falling forward when he leaned down to brush hers with a few fingers. How had she forgotten how incredible his hands were? Masterpieces of genetics... regardless of how alien that DNA might be.

Would they have DNA, she wondered. Or would that be a Human thing and they had something entirely new and weird and wonderful. Maybe DNA but a triple helix? His hands smoothing down her cheek to her chin redirected her attention, away from genetics and back to those beautiful mitts capable of making fine art and provoking lady shivers.

"No spiders." Bay's face smoothed, his Mediterranean eyes piercing. He withdrew his hand from her face, stepping back. "Are you ready? This might be overwhelming. Please don't be scared."

"Why would I be..." Katy trailed off, eyes glued to Bay removing his neon red Zen tee. The Universe had apparently decided such divine hands needed the support of empyrean arms. Ones anchored by a chest Katy felt sure could double as a blacksmith bellows. "Not afraid," she mumbled.

Bay stripped the t-shirt off, revealing smooth toffee skin covered, front and back, in exquisite tattoos that swept from shoulder to shoulder, down about a quarter of the biceps. Were they Polynesian, or Thai? She thought they had that vibe at first. Swoops and swirls, bold black without a hint of color. These told stories she couldn't read, but she knew they were there, and were probably pretty thorough.

This stunning expanse was framed by a leather harness wrapped around his shoulders and under his arms. That was jarring enough to stop her mental drooling and bring her back to reality. If he'd had a gun the whole time... but there wasn't a gun. Just the straps, which weren't leather now she looked closer. Futuristic something, she bet he'd say.

"I told you our goddess gave us our mission, to find the heralds of the Drazoen." His raised hand forestalled her question. "The Drazoen are supreme beings, as old as the Aoni itself. On Earth you would call Them dragons. Just over a kōmilen ago They left the Aoni, we don't know why, nor where they went. But our Drazoen, the one who chose the Mikanjo as Her people, told us to seek these heralds that would return the Drazoen to the Aoni. You are Sundancer Orange's herald. You are what my people call the Kawakona. I know it to core of my soul, and I need you to come with me, to finish our quest and wake Sundancer from her slumber.

"To get you to agree to this, I realize I have to make you believe. This is the only way I can think of to do it quickly, and we are pressed for time. Those of us who seek as She bade us often have to suppress Her original gift to our people. There are reasons in many places we are best served hiding our gift; for me it was absolute necessity because Humans are unaware of anything beyond their species. But I'm going to take off the suit that suppresses my true nature. Now you'll see that what I've been telling you is true."

Before Katy could ask more questions about these druhzhoon, or get too worked up about Bay removing a suit (hot), or keep him talking about his true nature (was he about to be unmasked as a vampire or demon?), he reached behind his back. A faint snapping sound, followed by a heartfelt breath of relief gusting from his lips. The straps slid from his shoulders and gargantuan white wings snapped out and up from his body.

Katy shouted, stumbled back, tripped on a rock and landed hard on her ass. Birds cried out and fled the nearby copse of trees. From this angle he towered over her, downy feathered wings expanding to fill the clearing. Had to be twenty or thirty feet across, wingtips reaching between the circle of trees and pushing tree branches aside. There were three distinct layers of wing, sliding together then apart, that joined in the same place. At least that's how it looked from her angle on the ground.

"Oh. My. God." Katy was breathless, in complete awe. Her eyes tried to track individual feathers, follow how they flowed into one another making a flawless whole. Three tiers, arching over his shoulder blades and back, distinct but harmonized in their movements.

Bay reached down, bending forward while his wings flexed behind him. "Apologies, there isn't really a way to ease into that." She took his hand, marveling at his shoulder muscles contracting as he rolled the triple wings a bit to stabilize them and pull her up. "Whenever I take the suppression suit off after long tuigs those muscles spasm."

Katy held up a hand, flabbergasted. "Let's start there. What is a suppression suit and why are you wearing it?" She badly wanted to circle him for a better view, but his wings were so large she couldn't easily step around him. "And too-igs?"

"Tuig means year, tuigs plural. Long ago, we Mikanjo knew we'd travel the Aoni and go everywhere, to seek as we'd been commanded. Travel was also necessary for diplomats, wander-ers, any Mikanjo who left our home. We knew not all of those places would be able to handle, or even welcome, winged people. So my ancestors created these." He pointed behind himself and down, at a pouch on the ground, still attached to the straps she'd seen earlier. "Suppression suits have been mission critical for many jo Bikajo, me in particular here on your planet."

Katy wanted so badly to touch his wings, but figured that was likely inappropriate, if not outright sexual harassment. Still wanted to, though. She settled for grabbing the pouch, which, while large, could not in any way have actually been hiding those massive freaking wings. "Jo Bikajo? Isn't that your name? How did you get those," she gestured over his shoulders, "into this? Magic?"

"Everyone who seeks is a jo Bikajo whether by bonding or birth. Descended of the original pair chosen by Hunanjanno jo Bikajo, Windweaver White, we alone carry Her name as our line." Clouds momentarily blotted out the sunlight. Bay shrugged each shoulder, rolling them over and over.

"I can tell you more. Everything, if you want. But we need to go, quickly. I'm not sure how long the drug will keep the assassin knocked out. With luck many hours, but if he's been trained to withstand drugs his system may flush it soon."

Katy's heart had slowed from the buzz of Bay's wing reveal, but stuttered at his reminder of their danger. "Okay, what do we do?"

BAY thrilled at the building trust he saw on Katy's face, her eyes wide, hands a little shaky, but determined. Small bursts of wind teased his wings on the underside, flowing over the leading free edges and slipping gently down the outside. After taking a "break" from seeking in the Dark Ages – he thought he might have inspired Beowulf's dragon – he hadn't allowed himself more than one or two minutes a century out of the suit. This was a glorious moment: his wings freed and his Kawakona willing to follow him.

Determined to project competence, he told her "If you're ready, I'll test if my beacon was able to get through the mask protections. If it was, I'll get it to merge that tech with my suit. Then I'll fly us to the refuge."

"What refuge? You keep mentioning it like I know what it is."

"Planets with advanced or soon-to-advance species will often get a safehouse or refuge assigned. When I first arrived here there wasn't one, but the *Eternidad*-"

"Your ship?"

"Right," he said. "It came back once, before I found you, and there were non-Mikanjo travelers aboard who took an interest in Earth. They petitioned to have one built here, and I understand it's been in use ever since. Located in the San Juan islands somewhere."

A dark ginger eyebrow quirked. "You'll fly us. As in, you will lift me up like some kind of Human-sized bird, carrying me? While you fly to the San Juans? Well sure." She smirked.

"Our musculature is vastly different from yours," Bay said. "Developed under different gravity and enhanced by a goddess. Carrying you won't be a problem," he stated, pulling the device and mask from his bag. She didn't believe him, but when he flew with her she'd realize he didn't lie.

Katy stepped closer to examine what Bay held. He flipped the kuh over and put it in her hands. It wasn't fabric, rather a hard but flexible piece of plastic or matte metal, small and bent to fit over a nose or facial ridge. These disguise units were relatively new to the Pu'ulqaari arsenal and little was known about them the last time he'd spoken with Vailillia. If his beacon could crack it and jump link it to his suit, he would have opened the door to new ways of Mikanjo wing illusion.

Bay slid his beacon, a white rectangle as long as his forearm and twice as thick, out of the bag and whooped, startling the surrounding wildlife, Katy included.

She gasped, nearly dropping the mask she still held, then slapped gently at his arm. "What the holy hell?"

"It worked, we're in!" He pointed to the blinking yellow light that indicated pairing. "Now for the next phase. With luck it won't take long."

Bay laid both his suit and the mask on the AI interface – intuitive cellulose nanofibrils that protruded from each surface of the beacon – and whooped again. "There, the lights show the beacon is successfully analyzing the properties of both items."

Katy peered down. "What lights?"

He was confused until he remembered Human eyes were less color perceptive than Mikanjo, something he'd noticed early in his residence on Earth. Vailillia thought it had to do with the blue sun of their planet – and therefore the sim-sun on the *Eternidad* – influencing how their eyes perceived color and light. Bay thought it came from Hunanjanno just like their other gift, but knew better than to argue with his older sister.

"Never mind. Just trust me, it's working." Bay slid his thumb over the security interface, verifying his identity and releasing the virtual console.

"Will I regret asking how the hell that works?" Katy said.

"That depends on how much you understand about neural wavelength alignment with non-biological systems, progressive inference programming, and artificial neural networks," Bay replied.

Hands on hips, eyes raised to the sky, she sighed. "Moving right along."

He hummed in sympathy, instructing the beacon to begin

merging the Mikanjo and Pu'ulqaari technologies. If it worked as he hoped, it would give him an effective means of cloaking. The device estimated a fairly short window for completion, so he was increasingly confident. Maybe the Pu'ulqaari protected these things so ferociously because, while they were exceptional, they were easier to hack than Human computers.

"It says it will take twenty minutes, but it might be longer."

"Can we afford to wait? There's almost no one here today, anyway. I bet we could just shoot out there, none the wiser," Katy said.

Bay was unreasonably delighted at both her impatience and practicality. "I thought as much a while back, let myself fly when I believed I was safely distanced from Humans. My antics over Human history have given rise to myths of angels, drakes, that kind of thing." He snorted. "I had a bit of fun more recently, and now there's kongamatos and the Mothman."

Katy's jaw dropped. "You mentioned a lot of time before, but this is... whoa. Drakes sounds medieval. How long have you been here?"

"About one thousand Earth years." He traced the soft shape of her face with his eyes, already sure he could draw it from memory. "I wandered far, but in the end I found you."

"I'm still not sure you're right about this..." She trailed off, looking away. "Listen, if we have a bit until it's done, I want to run back and check Raisa. I assume you're stuck here until you can put the suit back on?"

Bay was terrified at first. She wanted to leave; she wouldn't come back. He'd finally found the one he knew was Sundancer's herald, he couldn't let her leave! After the blast of panic, reason crept back in. Katy was a good friend, a caring person, looking after her companion. She would return to him, not leave him in these woods. His gaze zeroed in on the pendant under her sweater, the one she'd covered protectively with her palm repeatedly since it first closed around her nape.

"Of course. Take the key," he said as he fished it out of his pants pocket and handed it over."

She nodded, pensive, looked at his wings, and shook her head. As though she couldn't believe they were real. "Back in a flash."

KATY TORE back through the woods twice as fast as they'd come. She felt a strong urge to check on Raisa, to verify she was still breathing and maybe getting better. It was the only way she could convince herself it would be okay to fly somewhere with a bewinged alien who had futuristic rectangles that could re-engineer space doodads. An alien who'd seen Humanity from the fall of Rome to whatever the hell they were calling this time. Anthropocene with a side of hubris? How the holy hell could she live up to being a herald of one of his gods when she'd not even rounded out three decades? She didn't have the experience, the wisdom. But she yearned nonetheless.

If Raisa was improving and not dead as a doornail in the backseat, that meant Katy could trust Bay. Thirty-foot wings went a long way toward convincing her there were more things in the Universe than she'd been told. But they didn't guarantee the character of the one wearing them. Raisa being alive would mean Bay had protected both of them at risk to himself. He'd used some wonder drug to save Raisa, not left her behind to advance his dragon-assigned quest. He'd doggedly sought Katy for a good chunk of written history, and was positive she was this herald he kept talking about. He hadn't forced her at any time, even when things started getting dicey. That's what would guarantee his character in her eyes.

She was going to trust him, as long as Raisa was improving.

Conditionally, at first, but trust nonetheless. He'd earned that much.

When she got back to his car, she opened the back door and saw Raisa had rolled off her side and onto her back. Her long braid, partially unraveled now, trailed down to the floor. Her skin was still waxy, but color had returned to her lips and her eyelashes were twitching, eyeballs in REM behind them. Katy smoothed her hand over Raisa's forehead. She was both surprised and not to see it tremble when she reached out.

"I promise to make this up to you somehow, Raisa," Katy whispered. "I don't know what's going to happen, but we'll get you safe and sorted. I'm so sorry."

"'s okay," a tiny voice whispered back.

Katy examined Raisa's face, but her eyes were still closed. "Hey, you awake?" No response. But she must be on the mend if she could speak at all. Relieved, and letting herself get a little excited, Katy thought about flying to the San Juans with Bay. Would she ride on his back like she would a horse? Or Superman-style? Basket carry? This was going to be interesting.

A GENTLE CHIME sounded and the beacon was done. The mask and his suit were hybridized. Bay grabbed the enmeshed cloaking item that had been created, and tried to sort how to get it on. Experimental tugs showed it was vastly more expandable than before; compression traded for concealment, lending it substantial elasticity. It also seemed permeable; air would get under his wings in flight. He arranged his feet behind one edge, and the fabric fitted itself around his shoes. Pulling, he got it around his legs and waist. Every time he thought the garment would stop, it seemed to adjust and stretch more. He'd gotten it over his lower wings when Katy returned.

"Fecking hell, how is that even possible?" she shouted.

He shushed her. "Someone finding us before we can fly away, safely invisible, would be unfortunate."

"Sorry, sorry. It's just, well, wow. It was one thing to cover them up when you'd had them pulled against your back. Now they're open under there?" She came closer, peeking under his arm. "It's not truly invisible, you know. More like blurry blending into the background."

He reached for her, turning her back to his front. This close, her scent was like anabolu, the beloved fruit he hadn't had since before coming to Earth. The closest matches here were starfruit and lime, but with an added underlying note of pandan or vanilla. No one food here compared, but Katy's scent took him back to special moments with family, laughter and happiness.

"Hey. It's polite to ask before invading personal space," Katy grumbled.

"Time to see if this thing will work," he said in lieu of apology.

The edges of the new suit – with Katy's help and a lot of swearing on her part – were at last tugged over all three sets of his wings. The last step was to slide them around the outsides of her arms. After he got it spread out over the edges of her upper body, he felt straps fall forward.

"Hold on, I think you'll need to turn and face me, then I can secure you to me, both of us snugged up in here."

Katy started laughing. "Any other time in my life this would be the worst come on in the world!" As she shifted around, she asked, "How the hell is Raisa going to fit in here, too?"

"She's not," he said.

Katy's arms had been sliding around his waist but stopped. Impatient to get moving he tried pulling them but she resisted. "You said you'd be going back for her. You promised."

Bay stopped and looked into Katy's eyes. "I will be back for her after I take you to the refuge. This I swear. But only we can fit in the upgraded suit. The faster I get us up there, the sooner I'm back to take her."

He didn't add how fervently he prayed to Hunanjanno jo Bikajo that Raisa was still unconscious. Otherwise, the tattooed, winged man trying to tie her up in an invisible suit might be cause for alarm.

Katy turned fully into him, cuddling against his body, huffing her reluctant acceptance of his plan. He fastened the straps in place behind her back and shoulders, which pulled her even more tightly into him. A test flex of his wings told him he had freedom to fly as normal inside the boundaries of this hybrid suit, which seemed to coat his feathers without impeding their spread. The kuh was marvelous technology indeed! Wrapping his arms tightly around his Kawakona, he took to the air.

8

It was a bumpy start. Bay's arms and the suit straps secured her top half, but a little too well. He was so much taller that when they ascended at a gradual angle, his hold hitched her body higher to his chest, and that made her feet pop out of the bottom of the sack. Her legs had immediately fallen toward Earth. This had the effect of arching her back sharply and making her feel like she'd drop any second. Score one to gravity for always winning.

Thankfully they sorted the problem quickly. Bay rolled to his back and had her lock her legs between his, slipping her feet back into the lower pouch of the suit. Watching the Puget Sound race below them was exhilarating, his strength allaying all fears of falling. Flying only seemed to require two or three lazy swipes of those considerable wings followed by a tranquil glide. It was smooth, gentle, thrilling. She felt her hair tangling (the lazy bun of earlier long since fallen apart) and prayed there would be a jar of mayo where they landed to help get the knots out. Regular conditioner wasn't fixing this, but oh how it was worth the coming pain. Light blue sky above, darker denim

Pacific Ocean below, spring sunlight that didn't blind her to the view of Earth usually reserved for birds.

Speaking of landing, though. "How long will this take? To get to this refuge-slash-sanctuary, I mean."

Bay's grip tightened as he flipped them back over so he flew upright, and dropped his head closer to her ear. "We'll be there in another twenty minutes. Lanu's island is camouflaged, so we won't be able to see it because of the shield. But the beacon provided spatial coordinates; I know where to go."

"Who is Lanu?"

"The host. A sort of gatekeeper who protects the refuge from discovery."

"And you'll signal your ship from there?" She missed the panorama of water and coastline she'd had, but his bared upper body wasn't a bad view either.

Another couple of wingbeats, then he answered. "Already sent the signal, while you were checking your friend. Hopefully by the time I've retrieved her, and we're all back together, they'll have responded with their arrival time."

Hoo boy. Could this honest to God be real? Her life? An alien spaceship coming to get her? Too big, too hard to grasp, she needed to focus on the immediate to stave off anxiety about the future.

Katy rested her chin on his shoulder, wanting a closer look at Bay's wings. How did triple wings work together in flight? Very well, from what she could see. The two large sets of wings overlapped and anchored in the same area of his back. A fine stripe of aqua feathers, matching his eye color, lined the ridge of the third set. The accented wings were higher up and smaller, attached to his shoulder blades she thought. These had none of the fuzzy baby chick feathers she could see on the inside of the bigger two; the bone or cartilage also appeared thicker on them.

Her brain wouldn't let her relax. "I'm trying to roll with this, like you said. But it's a lot, not gonna lie. A lotta lot. We left

Seattle five minutes ago, because a whacko tried to kill Raisa, and probably me, and we are fleeing the scene. You're saving me and taking me somewhere safe because maybe I'm a herald. Except not the one of your goddess, but one of an orange dragon?"

Bay nodded against her cheek. "Sundancer Orange, Irojaku jo Faluji to the Mikanjo."

Katy took a brief mental detour to acknowledge that the pretty pretty man, strong enough to carry her in flight, smelled very good. Jasmine and a dark rich spice, like clove. She took a deep breath, soothed by the scent. Back to information gathering.

"Excellent. Still working on being absolutely grand about all of this, but..." She let loose in a rush. "You're saying we'll be in the San Juans in twenty minutes. Are we flying at Mach speed? Doesn't feel like sound barriers are breaking, but what do I know. Never understood that concept well. Maybe I wouldn't hear it if we're the ones breaking the barrier, or maybe it's a magic thing for Mikanjo?"

She continued before Bay could respond. "And I'm going to meet Lanu, another alien, I take it, since I'm guessing they don't put Humans in charge of intergalactic safehouses?" She leaned her head back to see his face.

Bay smiled, fingers rubbing her hip where he secured her. "No, it's not magic. Magic doesn't exist as far as I know. We're simply flying very quickly. Yes. Lanu will be our host at the safe house. They're Uilig, a species that acts much like your Switzerland here on Earth. Neutrality in a host's nature is a plus for havens where no guest may attack another. Seeing an Uilig reminds visitors of all species to keep themselves controlled."

Katy felt him banking right, dipping slightly, before taking a few strong wingbeats to regain height and speed. "Uilig come from Asinjo, a planet not well known outside their own. No other species may visit without invitation, which is rarely extended. They are all what Earth calls androgynous or non-binary, generally slow to act, and will always consider all sides of an issue before making decisions."

"Wee-lig?" Bay affirmed her pronunciation. "I'm going to need a manual." Katy paused, struck by a thought. "Ohhhh. Tell me there's actually a *Hitchhiker's Guide to the Galaxy*! Please, there has to be! Did Douglas Adams base that on knowing an alien for real?" She laughed at the absurdity of it.

Bay gave a rumbled chuckle, which rolled down the back of her neck, giving her yet another internal flutter. Hanging with this guy was a non-stop shiver-fest.

"Not to my knowledge," he said, referring to her question about famous books. "But if I find a primer on the Aoni in English I will share it. At least, until we get you some aoiti."

Her momentary amusement drained as she considered the reality of her life. An alien with big-ass wings had signaled his ship, which was supposed to be on its way to Earth. Another alien, homicidal in nature, was probably going to be hunting them soon, if not already. A third alien ran Earth's sanctuary, shielded from Human eyes and knowledge. Raisa was, hopefully, still passed out in the backseat recovering, but when she woke up what would Katy say? That Katy was now a cosmic big deal, despite having zero knowledge of what to do or how to proceed? What did a woman do to wake up a fecking dragon? How would she explain just how overwhelming the future gets when you throw prophecies in a blender with regular people's lives.

Nor was she touching Bay's second reference to owie whatchas, and what might be an impending injection nightmare. If you don't say it out loud, it isn't real. Choosing to stop that panic attack in its tracks, Katy returned her gaze to Bay's shoulders, eyes tracing over his tattoos. The intense black lines with traces of orange were bold. Arresting. This close up they were detailed masterworks of shading and varying patterns.

"Do these mean anything? Your markings?"

Bay shrugged a little, and given how tightly they were bound the movement shrugged her, too. "It's called our seeking mantle. When a jo Bikajo reaches maturity they get the first lines embedded. We add as we feel necessary. The designs speak of my path, the choices I've made, even mistakes are transcribed. My life leading to this, us in this moment." He squeezed her.

Would she become part of his inked tale, preserved on his skin? If so, she thought she'd like a space where the lines of "her" touched the place his wings attached on his back. No matter how critically or closely she examined them, they remained truly glorious. Unexpected and fantastic, they scrambled her brain's pleasure centers. She wanted to stroke them, pluck a feather from them and keep it forever. Be wrapped in them and sheltered from danger. Or steal them and attach them to her own back so she could fly free. Snuggle into them and feel the softness and warmth rubbing against her own skin. What it must have cost him to wear that old suppression suit, his wings so tightly bound.

Katy raised her head slightly and pressed her forehead against his neck, inhaling, letting her emotions and senses be overwhelmed by the incredible beauty of the moment. "Thank you. Thank you for sharing this with me, even if you're crazy for thinking I'm your special sparkle princess. Even if I spent half of today terrified a manky prick was trying to kill me, and I don't fully understand where we'll end up or how it will go. I'll keep this memory forever."

Bay hugged her tighter in wordless response, nuzzled her hair, and she thought he was maybe sniffing her too. "Time to land. I'm going to turn you around to face forward," he said. She tensed but he reassured her, "I think it will be less scary if you're seeing it happen than being blind to it. I'll turn you quickly, and it will be easier if you don't help or struggle. Just trust me."

There it was again. Trust. So far he hadn't played a bad note, despite copious opportunities. He'd done nothing but prove in many small ways that he was there for her, would support her on this ridiculous mission he believed in. That he was a man she could count upon. It was like her sessions with the boys at Conall's: the joy was in the safety of exploration and riffing with companions who knew what they were about. Ones who could deliver on promises because they had the skill and desire. The Air stirred like a sleepy kitten, agreeing with her thoughts on Bay, then resettled itself.

"I trust you," she said, meaning it wholeheartedly.

His maneuvered her face-front, her back warmed by his skin even in the chill of the wind moving past them. Her feet remained tucked into the cuff of the suit despite the rearranging, keeping her legs from falling out again. They were flying fast enough that when he started to descend she joked, "Brake hard, pull up, don't crash!"

"I wouldn't crash with my special sparkle princess." They leveled out, slowing gradually, everything ready to come back to Earth. Katy barely had time to lament the imminent loss of flight before she felt a distinct and unpleasant sensation. Like a full body wetsuit had snapped over her skin. Then it disappeared.

"We're through the shield now. Lanu will meet us once we touch down, I would expect. They'll have sensed the breach in their cloaking," Bay flexed his fingers against her stomach, securing her for touchdown, which was so even and light she barely noticed they were mundane pedestrians once again.

Caught up as she'd been in the excitement of flying and landing, Katy hadn't paid much attention to her surroundings. Earth's refuge was something well worth seeing. She turned from the view of the San Juan Channel to see an elegant chalet crowning a small clearing. Out of the forested land half an acre or so had been developed. Several stone and wooden buildings formed a semi-circle that was inviting. If she didn't know better, she'd think she'd arrived at an exclusive spa or pricey corporate retreat.

Dead center was the three-story main house, a modern upscale log cabin built in a gentle C-curve. It gave the impression the house beckoned you with open arms. On the left was a pool, to the right a large, outdoor fireplace circled by chairs and loungers.

"There's our host," Bay said.

Katy, busy gawking at the gorgeous architecture and décor, startled. Where Bay pointed, a figure crossed the veranda and moved toward them. Her third alien of the day was less scary than the assassin had been, slower paced than Bay, but far more colorful. Bright, splashy colors from head-to-toe.

They came closer and an abundance of blurred colors resolved into an attention-grabbing figure. Tall, not quite Bay tall, but closer to seven foot than six. They wore a purple caftan shot through with threads of silver, had straw-straight white hair cropped close to their scalp, skin color like toasted hazelnut, and makeup or paints coating their eyelids, orbital bones and just below their eyes. A profusion of blues, greens, purples and bright pinks, not blended in an ombre but dotted in overlapping patches. An eye mask designed by a drunken Georges Seurat.

Katy was enchanted. Lanu was her new favorite alien.

"Welcome seeker," they said, facing Bay first. They extended both hands, but made no attempt to touch Bay or Katy. "I am Lanu Ojala, keeper of this sanctuary. And you," they said as they focused on Katy, "are the herald, I think?"

Bay stiffened when Lanu's soft voice said the h-word. His arm, still around her back, pulled her tighter to his body.

"I mean no harm, seeker," their host continued, reading Bay's tension. "But it seemed a safe assumption after the message received five minutes ago from the *Eternidad.* They advise you should expect them in this orbit fourteen sal-angs CM from now."

"Thank the Nine!" Bay cried. "I prayed they'd received my message, that it wasn't intercepted."

Lanu's forehead crinkled, and Katy was sure an eyebrow would have been raised if they'd had any. "Indeed, message received and returned. Which is why I felt confident this Human with you must be your herald. Mikanjo would never violate the Law of First Approach for anything less. Your journey to find them has been long, I think."

Katy wondered if she was burning out on the ability to be surprised. Nothing Lanu said shocked her. Law of First Approach? Sure. Seemed like something that would exist in this new Universe she was learning about. She'd deal with Bay's people showing up when they did, but when exactly would that be? Fourteen of something. "What's sawl-aah-ngs sea-em mean?"

"A sal-ang is a time segment like an hour on Earth. Not directly equivalent, naturally, as all locations measure time using different suns." Lanu's sweet, high tenor was a charming way to have her understanding of time's integrity blown up.

"What the feck does that mean? Time changes in different places?" She immediately cringed. *Way to be an impressive representative of the species, ya dozy cow.*

Bay said, "Humans measure time by your own sun and its relationship to your planet. The rotations, orbits, time spent in light and dark. But that applies only here, only now. In the future as your sun changes or your planet's rotations speed or slow, so will time. Leave this planet, just for another in the same system, and time will be measured differently. A 'day' on Neptune is shorter than on Earth, on Mercury fifty-eight times longer.

"Imagine that happening for every advanced species, every galaxy and solar system they inhabit. To combat these myriad differences the Calling at Centris set up a primary standard clock. CM, which is Centris Measured, and safe to use as a base because that time will never degrade or alter. Fourteen sal-angs CM will be about twenty Earth hours."

Katy felt weak in the knees. In less than a day she'd gone from plain Jane to a dragon herald flying away in a spaceship. Now there was this Centris crap to try and assimilate. Where (and-or what) the hell was it, and why was it calling? "Stick a fork in me, I'm done," she muttered.

Bay, not hearing her, stepped away. "I should return for your friend. We have beaten the Pu'ulqaari here," he glanced at Lanu and got a confirming nod in return. "But I can't leave her there safely for long. Will you be okay?"

Katy grimaced, knowing Raisa was the priority now, not her encroaching freak out. She felt selfish for wanting him to stay. "Yes, go. I'm sure I can manage for an hour." He would totally come back. He wouldn't leave her stranded on an island no one could see with someone she'd just met. Things were good. Very fine and just grand.

Lanu extended their hands, asking, "May I touch you? I can escort you to a chair, be at your service for questions while your seeker is gone. Then you can answer my own questions about the situation we find ourselves in."

They peered into Katy's eyes and smiled. She saw their irises were almost as pale as their white hair, a calm if eerie center to the colorful powders coating their skin. Lanu had been gracious and thoughtful so far, maybe even a bit empathic, so Katy reached out to take their hand.

"We'll trade, question for question, then?" She laughed. "Fair warning, I have *so* many of them."

Bay recaptured her attention when he touched her arm and stroked down to her free hand, entwined their fingers, and squeezed once. He leaned forward slightly, like maybe he'd kiss her goodbye, but stopped short and moved back. That might be wishful thinking. No, it definitely had to be wishful thinking; she was just this Kawakona thing to him. The herald, not a chance for romance. What on Earth (or elsewhere for that matter) would interest him in someone so much younger and unsophisticated? That thought firmly in the front of her mind, she let go of his hand, keeping Lanu's for reassurance. One massive, near-invisible swipe of his wings and Bay was airborne.

Katy followed Lanu's lead to the fireside seats, past the house's portico. It was too early to light the huge stone fireplace, but that would be her first request when sundown faded to twilight. The area was decorated with Chinese lanterns and Turkish hanging lamps, a mix of vibrant colors. Comfy oversized chairs, benches and semi-reclined loungers; eclectic and original, a lush hygge-core vibe with a PNW twist. Thick wooden posts holding up the gazebo overhead were carved with totemic imagery.

Once they settled, Katy looked over at Lanu and said, "You first?"

They nodded. "You had a Pu'ulqaari confrontation?"

"I'm calling them PKs, I've decided. It sounds less dramatic and I refuse to rent them that space in my head," Katy replied.

"In English it would be PQ, I believe."

"Oh. Huh. Fine, they're PQs to me from now on. And yes, one attacked us today, nearly killed my coworker, Raisa, and was coming for me next. Bay saved us. Then had to explain everything faster than he was planning, I guess."

"Everything? Meaning what?"

"*Everything.* The Universe being more crowded than I'd thought, dragons who went to sleep a hundred thousand years ago, and that I'm supposed to wake one up. Supposedly. Wings! Prophecies and goddesses. All *that* whackado. Everything." She laughed ruefully.

Lanu crossed their legs. "This 'PQ' is still coming, you believe? Not gone?"

Katy liked how Lanu started using her term, it made her feel like they took her seriously. "I think so," she replied. "Bay knocked him out, but said it wouldn't last forever. He also assumes the guy will know we're coming here and try to follow."

"Your seeker is smart. This would be the most logical place to take sanctuary, and the PQ will most definitely come. But we have some time, even so. He will probably have to use regular transport, a ferry then a kayak or rented motor boat most likely. Getting this far out isn't easy, unless you have wings." They tapped a finger against lips a shade peachier than their nut-brown skin. "Given their history in the Aoni, this PQ should be very careful to observe the non-violence rules here."

"What's their history?"

They sighed. "Subjugation and rigid class hierarchy, sadly." Lanu paused, then elaborated, "They enslave their own people, as well as anyone foolish enough to fall into their debt. While they don't war and fight like the Krylar or Chitans, they have codified their caste system more deeply than the versions I've seen on your planet."

"Every time I think I'm getting my brain around this shit," Katy whined, "you throw new stuff at me!" She threw up her hands. "Here we go: who are kree-lar and kite-anne-s? Hey, do you have an encyclopedia for the Aoni??"

9

By the time Bay returned with Raisa, Lanu and Katy had run through A Short History of the Aoni (abbreviated) and she now knew the Chitans (brawlers) and Krylar (genocidal warmongers) tended to align with the PQs. An interstellar axis of black hats. She also learned Centris was some place designed and created by the dragons where every advanced species gathered. The Calling was the U.N. of the Universe. Aoni. Whatever it was called.

In return, she'd told them about meeting Bay at the bar, the attack at Pike Place, and her heartache that she'd dragged Raisa into the mess. "I know this isn't technically my fault, but it still feels like it is. If I'm supposed to be this herald person, that puts it all squarely on me."

"You know this is false," Lanu chided. "Your fate or destiny, if that is what is happening, didn't force that person to attack you. The violence is carried on their shoulders alone."

She tried hard to remember that when she saw Raisa's disheveled braid trailing over Bay's arm, her head lolling as he carried her from the landing zone to the main building. Katy was happy to see much more color in Raisa's face. Thankfully

80

her coworker was still passed out, presumably making Bay's retrieval and flight much easier. She ran over to them, checking Raisa's pulse even though she wouldn't have known what was acceptable. Steady state seemed good; if it had been rabbit fast or tortoise slow she would have gotten worried.

"Come with me, we'll put her in a room while she recovers." They followed Lanu into the refuge.

Bay wasn't even winded carrying Raisa the whole time, and that after flying with her for half an hour already. Katy had to assume the muscles needed to support those epic wings could handle one smallish Human. She turned her attention to where they walked, but left her hand on Bay's arm, near Raisa's head.

They zipped through a soaring entryway and great room with high, exposed beams. A staircase at the back of the room took them to the second floor, where ten or more doors lined the hallway. Luxurious carpet dampened their footsteps. Lanu opened the first door they reached, waving them inside. "She should be comfortable here, safely removed if your assailant makes an appearance."

Katy hesitated as Bay settled Raisa onto the large bed. "I should probably stay here with her. It will be so confusing for her when she wakes up." She choked up, trying to remember what Lanu told her. That it wasn't her fault. "I don't want her to be scared."

What Katy wanted most was to stop being scared herself. This day had been a nightmare roller coaster of exhilaration, terror, confusion, and anticipation. Her hand crept up to press the pendant against her breastbone, something she'd been doing ever since Bay had put it on her. As though she could meld it to her skin. This was the thing that started all of it, and she almost resented it. But she couldn't imagine not having it now, constantly touching to reaffirm it was there. Every time she made contact her Air thrummed gently.

"I want to call home," she whispered. "Can I call my family?

Aunt Mildred might have realized we're missing, which means she's called Ma, which means Da will try to marshal the National Guard."

Bay and Lanu held some kind of silent conference over her head, then Bay shook his own. "If the Pu'ulqaari pins the signal and traces it back to them... too risky."

Katy went ice cold at the idea. That horrible person couldn't get anywhere near her family. They'd be unprepared and he could mow them down. Even Oran didn't deserve that.

"All right, I'll stay with Raisa, try to keep her calm when she wakes up," she said.

"Her healing is progressing well, but she's going to be out a while longer," Bay said. Reaching out, he pulled her close. "We should try to eat and rest up."

"A sound plan," Lanu added. "I have plenty of food options for all species' tastes. Wine or spirits? I bring in excellent bottles from Vancouver Island and Washington State vineyards."

Katy was loath to relinquish her hold on Bay. She only moved her head far enough to see Lanu and asked plaintively, "Tea?"

Lanu smiled gently. "I have several Murchie's options." They waved at the door and hallway beyond. "Come with me to the kitchen and pick what suits you."

The lure of good tea was enough to get her moving, letting go of Bay and trailing behind Lanu. One last glance at a peacefully sleeping Raisa eased the tightness in her chest, and Katy resolved to be braver. Stolid and steadfast in the face of her fears. If this was her destiny, she was going to face it head-on, no more whinging.

Lanu led them to a nicely appointed kitchen, opened an industrial sized refrigerator and asked, "How do you feel about fish?"

Hours later, after drinks, a filling dinner of salmon and risotto, more education on the Aoni, and a tour of the refuge grounds, the sun was finally setting. This time of year in the PNW that meant it was nearly nine p.m. Their small group had adjourned to the outdoor fireplace. It was a temperate evening, and once Lanu had started the fire, Katy was comfortable with a light lap blanket, staring into the flames contemplatively.

Lanu and Bay were preparing beverages and stoking the fire, respectively. She'd learned so much and was reflecting on the latest bomb the two had dropped on her: most sentient, evolved species of the Aoni were symmetrical in features, bipedal, carbon-based and shared analogous core mythologies. This was because the Drazoen had seeded life throughout the Aoni, leaving genetically coded sense memories in their wake. Folklore and fairytales had similar themes throughout the Aoni as a result. Creation rising out of chaos? Dragons? Great floods? Fire as a gift from the gods? Check.

In some ways it made things simpler. All species shared some language fundamentals because one of the Drazoen, Tonguemaker Green, had created language. Each species had made their own contributions and developed distinctive varia-tions, but plenty of words were close or the same across worlds. Genetics allowed most species to intermix, though there were blood purists out there, just like the bigots on Earth. When they got to this Centris place, she would see all of these different people in person.

"I thought for sure you'd say there were hundreds!" had been Katy's response when she learned only fifteen advanced species were recognized. Another three were under watch for possible inclusion. Well, two now, because Humans were about to be thrown into the mix and make sixteen species on Centris. Her excitement built as she thought about it. What would the other fifteen look like? Sound like?

"Do all Uilig look like you, Lanu? Or will I see some in busi-ness togs instead of casual chic?"

They shook their head. "You won't see many Uilig on the

Wheel, if any at all. We declared ourselves officially neutral. No ambassadors to the Calling, non-intervention in conflicts. Most Uilig stay on our home planet, and those of us who travel tend to run these refuges."

That made her sad, because Bay had said no one could go to their planet, either. Lanu might be the only one she ever met, and they were so cool. But other species would be equally exciting!

It was nearly enough to overcome her worries of getting translator bugs injected. Her fear of that had started morphing into worry it might be a surgical splicing, so she shoved the thoughts out of her head and focused on good things. Like the fact she already knew three of the fifteen! Or was it four of sixteen…. Did you count your own species as one you "knew"?

Lanu's species seemed very cool, the Uilig with the bright colors and peaceful nature and whatnot. But not only were the Mikanjo real go-getters with their prophecy seeking gig, they had those wings! Which, it turned out, could be retracted into a very compact form. Like some kind of Transformer thing, feathers sliding over each other and snapping into a smaller configuration. Katy wanted a set for herself, so very badly.

When Lanu brought her another cuppa (Golden Jubilee blend in perfect harmony to the quiet night) she nearly dropped it when they handed it to her. Rays of moonlight revealed even more paint on their skin, nearly neon and glowing. "That is so cool!" she burst out. "Did you just do that? Is it blacklight or glow-in-the-dark?"

Katy reached out, stopping short of touching their face. But she wanted to trace the patterns, same as she'd wanted to do with Bay's tattoos. It was a subconscious compulsion: would the lines and dots be raised or smooth?

Lanu pulled back, although they didn't seem angered at her aborted movement. Just unwilling to be touched like that. "Some of my people celebrate adulthood with this decorative procedure. On this planet your people only notice the color in darkness."

"I had no idea you couldn't see it earlier," Bay said. "They're very bright."

"Hold up, you see that all the time, even in the day?" She pointed at Lanu's face, covered in color that illuminated their skin more warmly than the spots dotted around their eyes. Reds, oranges and yellows speckled and swept over their cheekbones, forehead and jaw.

"Mikanjo eyes are some of the most perceptive in the Aoni," Lanu said. "Where you and I see wings of a fairly uniform white, Mikanjo see a range of shades, isn't that right?"

Bay nodded. "I've had to hide how acute my eyes are over the tuigs, but it helped me source the finest gemstones, that's for sure."

"But," Katy asked Lanu, "do your own people not see it in daylight, then? If Uilig are getting these tattoos you must see it, right?"

"We do, and we have a yellow star like yours," Lanu replied. "It seems Human eyes haven't developed as far. Yet."

Katy fell back in her chair, miffed. Why'd her species have to get stiffed in the eye department? Thus far, in comparison with aliens, citizens of Earth weren't looking too special. No wings, poorer eyes, technologically backward. Short. Drinking her tea in silence felt like her best move.

After a few sips she gathered her courage to ask, "Why does this PQ want to kill me?"

Her companions looked at each other, then Bay waved for Lanu to start.

"It's complicated. Remember I told you that they enslave others?" They continued when Katy nodded. "Sundancer Orange is known as the Drazoen of justice. Righteousness and morality, I suppose one would say. The Calling at Centris still allows the Pu'ulqaari to participate and vote. But objections to their inclusion have been increasing over the last several aiwaks. Centuries. Many feel they should be ejected as the Krylar were."

"On the *Eternidad*, we theorized they might fear a Drazoen return ending their profiteering ways. They would object to Sundancer's return most of all, as She is highly likely to declare them ûpiøra." Bay leaned back in his chair, wings draped over the sides, stretching his legs before him.

"Oop-yore-ah translation, please," Katy said, fighting a yawn.

"One of the oldest words in the Aoni. It conveys being unclean, working against the flow of the Aoni, unworthy. Ûpiøra," Lanu said.

Katy curled tighter into herself, the implications making today's assassination attempt scarier than ever. "Let me guess. If they're declared ûpiøra there are sanctions or something? They'd lose money? Cutting into the bottom line makes killers out of Humans, lord knows."

Bay nodded. "Shunned, barred from Centris, sanctioned as you say."

Lanu continued, "It would be far better for the PQ if no one brought the Drazoen back to the present." They coiled their feet under them, mirroring Katy's posture, their purple caftan trailing below their chair. "So much to lose."

"And the Krylar?" Katy pressed. "You said they were proper baddies, but didn't mention they'd been booted from Centris."

"It was...perhaps fifty thousand Earth years ago?" Lanu looked at Bay who waffled his hand to signal *close enough*. "They destroyed the home planet of another people, the Lunari."

Katy actually gasped. "They went full Grand Moff Tarkin?!"

"I'm not sure what that means," said Bay, looking confused as Lanu laughed. "But they waged a sustained campaign for bisous. Decades. Poisoned land and air, while trapping the Lunari on the surface. Ultimately, they drilled explosives well below the planet's crust and disintegrated it, rendering it unin-habitable. Lunari, like Mikanjo, were one of the species who kept to a single home planet. The few thousands who weren't on Vonar when the war started are the only ones who survived."

"Why?" Katy cried, saddened for people she'd never met. "Are Krylar just evil through and through?"

"Krylar motivations were never spelled out clearly. They provided no justification or reasoning when summoned to the Calling to answer for their atrocities," Bay answered. "Regardless, they were declared ûpiøra. First and only people to be so judged. Most assume their purpose was to test if an act so terrible would bring back the Drazoen, either in fury or judgment. Or both. When there was no Drazoen awakening in response to the decimation of Vonar and annihilation of the Lunari...." He trailed off.

"But they've been cut off from the rest of the Aoni? They're being punished?"

"Well," Bay hedged. "There are embargoes, and penalties are assessed for any that do business with them. Pu'ulqaari and Chitans, however, find loopholes and declare exigent circumstances for keeping lines of trade and communication open."

"Where are the Lunari now?"

Lanu smiled sadly. "They have become the wanderers of the Aoni, though you will see their unofficial home when you get to Centris. The Chorus, while not exclusive to the Lunari, is heavily favored by them."

"And this Chorus is like a choir or something?"

"The finest performance and philosophical arts school that has ever existed," Bay clarified. "People who are accepted there train for a very long time. More than a Human lifetime, especially if they pursue learning over multiple schools. Concerts from there are broadcast widely and showcase the most supreme musical talents to exist."

More than a Human lifetime. Katy was abruptly reminded how old Bay was. "Lanu, do your people live as long as Bay's?"

They shrugged, such an oddly Human gesture on the Uilig.

"Close to it. Humans have the shortest lifespan of the developed species."

"Damn, another area we got the short end of the stick! Drazoen needed to seed longer life over in these parts, I guess." She laughed. "But I'm excited to see this school. I went to music college, too. Not one quite that intense, but still."

Katy wondered, could she possibly get into this school? Get a tour, stop by admissions and put in an application? She'd be the only Human student in Space School, learning music no one on Earth had ever heard. Damn it! More than her cell phone, in this moment, she wanted her flute. Then she remembered her real job: miraculously figuring out how to bring a dragon out of a coma. Somehow. While angry slavers tried to kill her.

Lanu's head lifted, and they started to say, "I need to tell you-"

"Nope, nope. I'm still processing. Can't take anymore." Katy waved a hand to forestall whatever the next revelation would be.

"I believe our host was trying to tell you I've arrived."

10

Katy's exhaustion vanished. She twisted in her chair, coming face to face with the PQ who'd tried to kill them earlier. He stalked to a chair in their circle, and she watched him like she'd watch a cobra who'd suddenly appeared by the fire. He was careful to keep clear of Bay, slouching stride, like a predatory big cat, hips rolling to keep his upper body relaxed, straight, and ready for action. Any limping from the damage Bay had done was completely gone. How had he healed so quickly?

His hair was a masterpiece, she had to admit. Peroxide blonde, shaved on each side, long mohawk platted down the center and gathered into a bun at the base of his neck. Beads and trinkets woven into the braid. This was Viking going raiding hair. Dude who might snowboard his way down a mountain after being dropped out of a helicopter hair. Pure bad boy you will regret in the morning but thoroughly enjoy tonight hair.

That face, though… Her first glimpse of his unmasked face reinforced the jaguar or leopard impression she'd first had. Most of his skin was the green she'd glimpsed at Pike Place, but smoother than a Human's would be. It seemed hard, like it was a carapace or mask rather than his actual face. Maybe this guy wore multiple masks to hide his identity? The vibrant lily pad facial color was broken up by finely drawn dusty pink lines. They were scattered over his entire face in feline rosette patterns. Kind of pinkish cheetah markings. His entire face was covered to the hairline. The flesh under his hair was a sun-bleached ivory.

His overall look was deeply, deeply unsettling. Despite a color palette that should have been ridiculous and off-putting, he was scary. You looked at him and thought of running away because your primeval hindbrain screamed DANGER.

Katy decided to shortcut her way through the wiggins he set off. "Is the hair high maintenance? It seems like it would be, but I guess you could leave it braided all the time and keep shaving the sides? Or does that turn into dreadlocks?" She tilted her head like she truly contemplated the questions.

His eyes widened microscopically, and she was sure he'd have raised eyebrows if he had any. That made two aliens without brows, Lanu and this baddie. Katy was going to make a scorecard for this stuff.

Their attacker looked at Bay, sat down, and remarked, "This is the savior of the Aoni? Your herald? Or was it the other one and I succeeded in ending the threat?"

"You fucking prick! Katy shouted, instantly nuclear. She pounded a fist on the armrest of her lounger. "Succeeded? You have shit luck for that, because she's alive. And when she knows you're here she'll come get even herself!" Katy was incensed, her "Irish up" as Aunt Susan used to say.

All three men said, "Violence is banned in refuge."

Katy grumbled and looked away from the PQ assassin. Bay took up the conversation. "Do you have a name?"

"Yfaun." His voice was mild and even, his gaze never leaving Katy's.

"Big bad Eeee-fawn," she drawled out to annoy him.

"Are you warrior class? How did you find us?" Bay was

outwardly calm, but her ability to read him was improving by the hour. His skin flushed around his ears, giving away his irritation.

"Artisan class. I've been assigned to your ship, then to you, for aiwaks. I'd lost you for a short period, but your undisciplined antics on this planet exposed you." Yfaun crossed his ankles. "It was clear from observation today you'd found Sundancer's herald. I merely needed to wait for my opportunity."

He faced Katy directly. "Destroying you is my life's appointed work, and I *will* complete the task. Your companion must go as well, since it isn't clear which of you…"

He trailed off as he caught sight of the dragon pendant, which had slipped out from underneath her sweater. His body tightened like he'd pounce. "That settles the matter, doesn't it?"

She recovered from her shock quickly. "You, sir, are such a charmer. Why is it the mission of an artist to kill someone they've never met?" Bay and Lanu had given their theories earlier, but she wanted to hear it direct from Yfaun. She also wanted to redirect talk away from the pendant's meaning.

"Artisan class, not artist. Pu'ulqaari are placed in their class at birth, but there are many paths open within each class. I am an assassin, artisan class, family Lu'upan."

At the name Lanu drew a sharp breath. Katy looked over and they murmured, "One of the ruling families, very powerful."

Bay opted for poking the slouching predator. "Artisan class, instead of warrior or spy. This explains how you were so easy to outmaneuver and overpower." He smiled and it wasn't a nice one. "A milenyo here gave me time to learn nearly every Human combat art. I take it you didn't sully yourself with the natives like that." He paused, then swiped his hand around his face. "How could you, your ruh is so incompatible with Humans. And the kuh, while hiding it, would be problematic in a different way."

Bay, Katy thought, had to quit throwing around words like

the whole class was following him. "What is a roo? The kuh was the blank mask thingy?" Her tone was exasperated, she knew. "I remember milenyo is a millennium because they sound the same."

Yfaun scoffed. "Your species is disgustingly ignorant. Of course there are similarities, the Drazoen scattered language through the Aoni, just as they did civilizations."

"Everyone's ignorant before they learn something," Katy sing-songed back. "Dickbag. Manky twat. Do those have the same meaning on your planet? Did it get seeded down your way, or are you the ignorant asshat now?"

Bay reached over to place his hand on hers. Cheering her on, or telling her to chill out? She picked cheerleading because she didn't need a man, no matter how impressive, telling her to calm down.

Or maybe he was just hoping she didn't reveal what he'd done with Yfaun's kuh because they still needed it. Bay said those PQs would fight to protect the stupid thing, and she didn't put faith in Yfaun obeying this non-violence deal.

Lanu finally answered her questions. "Ruh is what he bears on his face. The Pu'ulqaari are renowned in the Aoni for their crafting of nefeslo, which is a sacred and secret mixture from their world. In their species it's a symbol of prestige to bond the nefeslo to their body, usually the hands, neck or face. That is ruh."

Horrified and intrigued in equal measure, Katy leaned forward to peer even closer at Yfaun's animal-spirit mask. "That's attached? Permanently?"

"Yes," he replied quietly.

"Whoa. Hardcore. How does it move like it does? I mean, it looks rigid but you can move it more than someone who got Botox or glued a Halloween mask on."

He cocked his head, possibly confused why she kept asking questions instead of running in fear as anyone sane probably would. "It's bonded. At a quantum level. It was once separate but now is part of my whole."

Katy tried to come up with more ridiculous questions, thinking maybe it would encourage him to underestimate her. It also helped keep her from hyper-focusing on the fact she was sitting beside a firepit with a killer. One who'd baldly stated he would never stop until he succeeded in his mission to kill her. She thought her next questions should poke at the flowery designs on that ruh of his, and took a breath to speak. His head jerked up, nostrils flaring, mouth clenching, before she could utter a word.

Katy heard pounding footsteps echo from inside, Raisa's voice frantically calling her name. Crap. Would Raisa remember what happened at Pike Place, or would she have traumatic event amnesia? Was she about to meet the first aliens of her life without a clue of the danger they were in? This could be bad. Really bad.

Katy jumped up, hoping to stop Raisa before she came out. Giving her coworker a head's up in private about the things happening would go a long way to keeping this powder keg of a night from going off. Maybe even head her off and send her back upstairs. No such luck, though, and she watched anxiously as Raisa stepped out and shuffled toward the fireplace.

"I heard voices and came to find...." Her speech trailed off, clearly confused by what she was seeing. Raisa's disheveled state matched the fragile tone of her scared voice. Her clothes were heavily wrinkled, further enhancing her off-balance vibe. "What, I mean, who-"

She stopped abruptly, rubbing her forehead with the heel of her palm.

Katy began with basics. "Raisa, hi. Hey! So glad you're awake. Do you feel sick or queasy or anything?"

"I think I'm seeing things," she muttered, walking closer.

Katy was relieved to see her skin tone back to normal, lips pink not blue, no visible shaking.

"Alright, there are a few things we have to discuss because, well," she paused, trying to sort out how she'd explain this to Raisa. Katy took a deep breath, gaining a new appreciation for what Bay had tried to do for her. This shit was complicated. "Well. Yes. So, look, it turns out there's a lot more to the Universe than we previously knew. I'm trying very hard not to quote *Hamlet*, but you know how badly I want to."

Raisa stared, non-plussed, hands limp at her sides. Okay, the Shakespeare hint had failed. Just as Katy was about to start with dragons, confident easing into the assassin thing was for the best, Bay stood up.

"Voi khâdâh yeman!" Raisa shouted.

"Um, I don't understand that," Katy said, then caught a glimpse of Bay's wings silhouetted behind him. "Oh, right. That's part of the story."

Raisa started to tremble. Katy wrapped an arm around her shoulders, trying to lead her back to the house. Getting within easy reach of Yfaun felt like a very bad idea. Raisa, though, had her own thoughts; she twisted around and shuffled to the circle of chairs near the fireplace.

"Katy, he has wings. Why does your guy from the market have gigantic white wings? Why do the other two have crazy makeup?" She halted, jerking out of Katy's hold, looking wildly around them. "And you're all sitting around with drinks, chatting?! Where are we?! What happened today?" Raisa was shaking all over, eyes wild.

"I know you're confused," Katy started.

"I'm past confused. I'm scared and nauseous and completely pissed off!" She rounded on Katy. "And you're not answering anything, just trying to drag me back inside! What are you trying to hide?"

Whoa. This wasn't everyday Raisa. Today's events had

brought out a whole new, saltier side. Katy didn't think she'd ever heard Raisa's voice raised, much less borderline swearing.

"I'm sorry, I'm trying to think of the easiest way to do this, but screw it. Ripping off the bandage now." Katy stepped in front of Raisa, grabbed her hands, and said, "Turns out there are aliens. Loads of 'em. We're talking Star Trek, Star Wars numbers. They're way more advanced than we are. There used to be dragons, who went to sleep for some reason a long time ago, but we need to wake them up now."

Raisa's jaw dropped after Katy's first sentence. Her eyes slowly widened, until Katy worried they might pop out.

"Bay, the one I introduced to you at the market, has wings. His whole species does. They were hidden before in a compression bag thingy. Lanu is the one with glow-in-the-dark tattoos, they're the owner of this whole island – did I already say we're on a secret island in the San Juans? – and they're a totally different kind of alien than Bay.

"That last one," she dropped her voice, "is the piece of shit who attacked us at Pike Place."

"Attacked us?!" Raisa shrieked at the same time Yfaun called, "A piece of shit who has very good hearing."

Incensed, Katy shot back, "Is that why they look like freaking whelk shells? So you can funnel the sounds in like a creeper?" Yfaun didn't answer.

Katy's anxiety was mounting. This wasn't going well; she was scared how Raisa would react to Yfaun, more afraid of him going after one or both of them. Her coworker was yanking her hands away now, moving toward the killer, posture stiffening.

Bay walked toward them. "Raisa, it's best if you can stay calm while the poison is still working its way out of your system."

"Poison!" Raisa was getting a good head of steam worked up, turning all that fear to anger. Her voice had bypassed loud and headed for shrill. "Somebody better start answering questions right damn now!"

Yfaun watched them lazily, utterly unconcerned with the aggressive posture of the woman headed his way. Katy wondered if that bored look was part of his training.

Lanu's turn to stand up. "Raisa, I believe you are called?" When she nodded in confirmation, they gestured to a divan close to Katy's original seat. "Please join us. I appreciate much of this is shocking to you, and we'll be able to give you the answers you want, but not if you overtire yourself."

Looked like their voice was the one Raisa responded to, because she slowly sank down onto the offered seat, though she didn't recline against the puffy arms. Her back was unbending, her fingers clenched together so tightly they'd turned white. "Fine. I'm skipping everything Katy said because it's insane. Start with poison. With him," she pointed at Yfaun, "attacking us. Is that what happened? I remember dropping the flowers and not much else."

"He is an assassin, here to stop the events Katy mentioned," Bay baldly stated. "He injected you with a fatal poison, but we had an antidote. You've been unconscious, recovering, from then to now."

"But you're just sitting here with a killer, shooting the breeze?" Raisa's voice was sharp. "Why haven't you arrested him? Locked him up?!" She tried to stand, but shrank back from Yfaun, who bared yellowed teeth at her.

"They cannot do anything to me while we're here. Even though you're in my sights, *I* cannot do anything to *you* while we're here. The ban on violence at this refuge is the only reason you still live." His voice dropped lower and lower, as though imagining killing them excited him. "Ridiculous neutrality rules. But sometime you will leave here, and then I will finish what I started."

"Motherfucker, Shut. It." Katy ground out. "There is something deeply wrong with you, you know that? Is your entire species like that? Jesus."

Raisa looked helplessly at Katy. "My father told me not to be friends with American girls. Said they behave badly, would lead me into danger." Tears filled her eyes. "Still, I wanted to be your friend so badly. But Baba was right all along."

Katy's heart twinged, guilt at her past behavior pinging in her chest. Even just now she'd thought of Raisa as a coworker, not a friend. Given the news she was about to break to her, Katy thought it was time to dive into camaraderie, no more reluctance and distance. They'd be the only Humans on the way to Centris and would need each other.

"I'm so sorry, Raisa. I've been guarded, I know, and no good reason for it. But I swear, I'll do better. By the time we get where we're going, I hope we'll be the best of friends."

"Where we're going? *We* aren't going anywhere," Raisa ground out. "*I* am going home. You crazy people can go wherever you want."

Bay, Lanu and Katy looked at her sadly, unwilling to contradict her immediately. Yfaun had no such compunction.

"They think they're taking you with them, atachelys," Yfaun crooned. Lanu and Bay's sharp inhale made it clear awe-tah-kell-ees wasn't nice. "You shouldn't go. It will only get worse for you out there. Your species is stupid, you yourself know less than nothing. Navigating the Aoni will break you, drown you in politics, worlds and people your species can't imagine. Your precious friend tells you tall tales about Drazoen that have no meaning in this time." He sat back, a hand raised dismissively.

"If they're tales with no meaning," Bay drawled, "why would you try to kill these women today? If a herald isn't a threat to you there would be no need for terrorization. Your own actions make lies of your words to her." Bay knelt before Raisa, taking her hands gently. "He wants you to run so he can chase you down. Try to ignore him, Katy and I will keep you safe."

Her head shook side-to-side, trying to negate what she heard. "I'm going home."

Katy sat on the low couch next to Raisa. "We can't. I think you know that, and why," she replied with genuine sorrow. "We'll give you more details when the ship comes."

Bay's eyes closed and his head drooped. Katy realized she'd just shared something she shouldn't have. Raisa's next words forestalled her apology.

"If I've understood this nightmare: there's a prophecy about waking sleeping dragons. The daiva over there," pointing at Yfaun, "wants me to buy his claim it means nothing. But he's a creepy green-faced demon so I'm not listening to him.

"You," she tapped Bay on the shoulder, "are a species of alien with rather spectacular working wings?" Here she paused, he shrugged, and she smiled wanly. "Are your wings how we came to this magical island run by the other alien in a gorgeous caftan?" Katy, Bay and Lanu nodded.

"I can-"

Raisa cut Katy off. "Stop, please. I'm still working through what you've already said. Now, because of the dragon wake-up mission, he tried to kill us today, very nearly did kill me. None of us may reach out to loved ones without putting them in grave danger. We are, therefore, leaving for somewhere else on a ship? A safe harbor?"

More nods all around.

"Is it a big ship? I don't get seasickness as such, but if the boat is small, I get a little queasy. How do we keep him from following us?"

"Ohhh, no," Katy whispered. "Different kind of ship, Raisa. Think Battlestar Galactica."

Raisa's face blanched and she rolled her lips inward, probably biting them on the inside to keep from screaming. She blinked slowly, clearing her eyes of the liquid sheen that disappeared as fast as it had appeared.

"What did I tell you, atachelys? You're not prepared for this and will die quickly when I find you." Yfaun leaned forward, hands on his chair's arms as though he would rise to attack her then and there. Katy wondered why he was determined to separate them. Were they easier prey apart? Or did he just like to play with his quarry, like the predatory felines he resembled?

Raisa calmly asked, "There's a non-violence rule in effect here? He can't hurt me right now?" When Bay and Lanu said yes, she asked, "What's the penalty? What's bad enough to stop someone this evil?"

"Instant death. Drones and other defensive technology would trigger if he attempted anything," Lanu advised.

"Great," she said, reaching around Katy for the half-empty mug of tea. When she had it in hand she cocked her arm back. Katy grabbed her arm and the mug before it could fly free.

"The rule applies to us, too!"

Raisa sagged against Katy's side, rested her head on Katy's shoulder, and said, "I'm tired. Hopefully this is a bad dream and I will wake to sanity once more." Then she passed out.

11

There was no relaxing after the confrontation. Lanu and Katy had gotten Raisa back to her bed, then returned to the fire. Yfaun stayed seated, menacing and vile, making no move to follow Raisa inside. He knew Katy was his true target now, and would keep her in sight as much as possible.

Bay could have ignored him, perhaps even enjoyed taunting him with the failure of his assignment. Katy wasn't as calm, though, and the killer's presence made her nervous and angry. Her tension was visible in the clenched line of her jaw and hunched shoulders. He asked Lanu to show them somewhere they could rest, away from the Pu'ulqaari killer's unnerving pink eyes.

"This room should suit you both," Lanu said as they led the way to a large suite on the second floor. It faced away from the dining area and heated pool, presumably with an island view during the day. "I'm assuming you don't want to be separated?"

Bay agreed and looked around. Two rooms were visible from the suite living area they'd entered. He knew they likely wouldn't sleep before the *Eternidad* arrived, but perhaps relaxing on the large sofas would help settle Katy. She was wound tightly after the revelations and fight earlier.

"Can we bring Raisa in, too?" Katy asked. "I don't want any of us apart while that psycho is here, roaming free. Feels like we're rabbits trying to ignore the tiger circling."

Lanu's head tilted. "While Yfaun cannot harm her, I understand your caution. I will ask her if she feels strong enough to resettle in this room."

Katy opened the French patio doors. "I know he isn't supposed to breach the peace, but this all feels like it hinges on the rules of nice." She turned back and smiled grimly at their host. "If he decided not to play along anymore, I'd feel pretty dumb we just assumed he would. Ma always says 'hope for good, plan for bad.'"

Starlight from beyond the doors caused Lanu's markings to flare as they nodded and left the room. Bay agreed with Lanu that Yfaun was unlikely to make a violent choice, but appreciated Katy's pragmatism. He also very much wanted to meet her mother, remembering how the threat of her had made Katy's father back down from his posturing at the pub. Was that truly a mere day ago?

Katy stared outside, into a fully darkened night. Did she look at the stars and wonder what it would be like to travel to them? Bay wasn't sure how she felt about this day's developments, if she shared his excitement or feared the unknown. Her arms twitched then wrapped around herself, and Bay couldn't help but go to her. Everything about Katy Phelan called to him; all the dreams of his destiny, the aching pull to seek and remain on this planet for the centuries it took for her arrive, the resounding bell in his soul when she had Sundancer's pendant around her neck. It all coalesced into a need to comfort and support, to lend his strength without blocking the wind she would need to soar.

He came up behind her, and laid a hand on her shoulder,

letting his thumb brush against the base of her neck. The pendant's chain rolled as he stroked her skin softly. She made a noise he couldn't categorize, neither assent nor dissent. Before he could move away lest he'd offended, she leaned back into him.

"My brain is treacle, Bay," Katy murmured, settling more firmly against him. "I thought I was smashing this whole 'hey the Universe has a few surprises for you', but I think I'm not that cool."

Moving his hand over her shoulder and down her arm, he took her hand. "You are remarkable. Everything I could have imagined and more." He squeezed her palm. Her anabolu scent teased his nose, both comforting and arousing.

Katy shifted, rotating to face him. Their hands separated, both of his coming to rest against the small of her back. She was cradled in his arms and it felt natural, easy, fated. Her palms stroked up around his biceps, and she leaned back to make eye contact. A mischievous smile played at the corners of her mouth. "You imagined me?"

"Of course," he replied.

"Was I always a short, Irish chickadee with whack hair and a fear of spiders?" she laughed. "Or have there been variations on the theme, since you waited so very long for me to get here?"

Bay looked into her tawny eyes, taking the question more seriously than she'd perhaps intended. The dreams had, after all, been persistent and with him nearly his entire life. There'd been centuries of fodder for his imagination. "The heart of you always remained the same. In my dreams you had no form, but I *felt* you. The core that made you Sundancer's herald. It was how I knew to craft this," he said, bringing a hand up to the pendant. His fingers rubbed the carnelian, something he'd not allowed himself to do too often after making it. It was Katy's talisman, marking her as Sundancer Orange's herald, Kawakona, and never his pendant though he'd crafted it. But he allowed himself this small gesture in the intimate space they'd created together.

Katy looked down, reached for the pendant herself, clenching it tightly. He relinquished his hold as she asked, "Dreams told you to make this?"

"Dreams told me I was destined to find the herald of Sundancer Orange. Dreams pushed me to seek in parts of the Aoni none of my people believed held advanced sentient life." Bay's wings relaxed and wrapped around her in a cocoon of white. "Dreams kept me on this planet, long after I thought I'd lost hope."

She gazed at him, eyes shining a bit in the room's lamplight. "What did the dreams tell you? I mean," she chewed on her upper lip, "were they more like visions, or did they have that trippy dream logic that makes perfect sense while you're dreaming and seems surreal when you wake up?"

"Both, I suppose," he said. "When I was very young, before I'd fledged, I dreamt of flying through an ocean of orange. It coated my skin and the feathers I didn't yet have in my waking life, even my insides. I knew in my heart I flew with a Drazoen, over and over, night upon night. I never saw or heard Her, but felt Her in the marrow of my bones.

"As I grew, I begged for our ship to seek further and further into the Aoni. Into areas younger, less known, likely empty but potentially burgeoning with new lifeforms. The dreams I had then," he said, his voice dropping, "were even more formless, but pushed at me. As though I needed to be somewhere and trod the wrong path."

Katy made a sympathetic noise and put a hand against his chest. "But you were right. Eventually."

He huffed a laugh. "Eventually. Once we found this planet, the dreams shifted to longing and desire." Katy raised an eyebrow and he hurried to clarify, "Not that kind. This was more...covetous. There was something I needed to obtain." He reached up and tapped the carnelian. "It took many years for me to find this. Many sals, days, to separate it from its protective, rocky sheath."

They both looked down at the resplendent dragon clutching its blood orange-colored baton. "Where did you find it?"

"In what's called Botswana now, near the Tsodilo Hills," he replied. "This gem doesn't exist outside your world, and I had trouble understanding what the dream was showing me. I had the word from our prophecy, but no practical knowledge of the stone. Fortunately, a San healer was willing to commune with me and understood what I sought. She led me to the site where I found the carnelian.

"It took longer than I'd anticipated to dig it up – my tools were poor for the job – and many nights I stared up at the cosmos and doubted my power or right to handle something so sacred. My dream coming true in this way worried me. If I had found Sundancer's stone, would I understand what to do with it? Once I did have the gorgeous, rough stone in my hands, though, I knew instantly. The design, the intention, the meaning. A single rush of inspiration."

Katy smiled, taking the pendant in her fingers once more, rubbing it absently. "It's perfect. I wanted it so badly the second you showed it to me."

"It was destined for you," Bay murmured. "Sundancer's essence. Her spark, the prophecy calls it. My hands called to your spirit with every action. Shaping, carving, heating, buffing. I took decades to fashion it, scared to ruin what I had been gifted. And once I finished, the dreams eased." He sighed. "They were less frequent, less urgent. I feared I'd found Her trigger, but had lost the foresight I'd used as my compass to locate you." His wings rustled, reliving his aching memories.

"But you hadn't," Katy comforted. "Obviously, because here we are. I take it the dreams came back?"

"Yes, after some misspent years," Bay said, irony in his tone.

"Had I known little to no writing would survive the time, I would have called the *Eternidad* back more than once. Rejuvenated for a while."

"Oh!" Katy exclaimed. "I get it now. I kept wondering why you weren't just regularly touching base. But you couldn't because that would draw some pretty major attention, yeah? That Law of First Approach Lanu mentioned?"

"The one time the *Eternidad* returned they kept our ship well out of Human sight so as not to violate the law. This time, though," Bay chuffed. He tilted his head at her and grinned, his eyes impish. "Knowing I have you at last and that we were attacked already? We'll see in a few hours just how major the attention is."

Katy's excitement blossomed on her face. "I can't wait for this! My whole life I've had fantasies and wishes about other worlds and species and adventures." She paused. "Less of the stabby, 'kill the girl' mood from today happened in my imagination. But still!"

Drawn to her, wanting to connect on a basic and profound level, Bay hovered over her lips with his own, whispering, "Kawakonas won't be stabbed on my watch." He scanned her face for fear, nerves or rejection but saw only acceptance and eagerness. His lips descended.

Before they made contact, he heard Raisa call out, "No sex in common areas! That was the rule in college and it stands here."

Katy jerked away guiltily and rushed to her friend's side. She trailed her hand over his arm as she left. Bay sighed and turned, spotting Lanu who carried a tray of water glasses and a pot of tea into the room.

"Need any help?"

They looked at him, white hair floating in the gentle wind lofting through the open French doors. "You might retrieve mugs from the kitchenette. I made chamomile. Excellent for soothing Human nerves." They winked at Bay, a gesture so unlike a typical Uilig he was struck dumb.

"You might have been here too long, Lanu," he warned, grabbing the mugs. "That was disconcerting."

"Camouflage is all part of the job description. One must learn to fit in for those times shields may fail."

Bay considered Lanu's moonstone eyes, shock of pearly hair, nut brown skin covered in moon-reactive tattoos, and their pangender form clothed in luxurious silk. Bare feet peeked from beneath the purple hem.

"You aren't likely to fade into the background if there's a malfunction of the cloaking device. But these modern times mean you'll just be 'groovy', I believe they say."

Lanu chuckled. "Groovy, I'm sure." They set down the tray on the coffee table and poured some tea. "I regret to inform you Yfaun knows which room you're using and insisted on the room adjacent. As I am unsure just how acute his hearing is, I'll be discrete." They inclined their head, speaking low. "The *Eternidad* sent another message through. They're on schedule for the time mentioned previously."

"Many thanks." Bay was chagrinned he hadn't remembered the killer's taunt at the fireplace, and had shared so much with Katy when they could have easily been overheard. He looked at Katy helping Raisa settle into one of the couches, handing over a cup of tea. "Tell me, could I fly from here? Without being spotted, that is to say. I realize Humans are about to learn the truth, but I prefer no military investigation tonight."

Lanu asked, "Can you not wear the-"

Bay cut him off quickly, whispering, "I prefer not to utilize that while other parties can see it." The kuh merged with his suppression suit needed to be kept secret, hopefully until the Mikanjo back on the ship or Bankiri could replicate it.

"Yes, I believe you could safely fly in this area. We're far enough from other islands and the mainland that you'd be unseen unless someone is flying at night." Lanu said. "Or stargazing at just the wrong moment."

"Okay," Bay said. "I think I'll ask Katy to go with me, to help her relax. Getting away from Yfaun would help immensely."

"Indeed," Lanu replied. "I'll leave you to unwind, then."

Bay refused to admit to himself that his motives were anything other than altruistic. The fact he never once considered Raisa might need to get away from the refuge – even more than Katy, in all honesty – didn't trouble him. His herald needed an escape, and he would be the man to provide it.

LIGHT POLLUTION this far beyond the shores of Washington State dropped to nearly zero. The farther northwest they flew, Katy beheld the night sky unfold before her like a blanket leisurely shaken to cover a bed. Stars ripened from distant cold pinpricks on a hazy charcoal background to brilliant gems piercing a velvety onyx ceiling, one she felt she could nearly touch. This was how the Universe painted its own Sistine Chapel. One equally sacred and grander in scale than the one in Rome. She saw an inky vault above Earth dotted with white, pink– and blue-tinted winking starlight. Closer stars were brighter, she knew, but between them stretched swaths of smaller jewels that looked like groundcover planted by cosmic titans in a time before Earth was fully formed.

She loosened one of her arms and pointed down at a large island, tapping Bay's arm with her other hand. It was far bigger than the one hiding the safehouse, or the San Juan islands they'd flown over earlier to get to Lanu's. "Vancouver Island?"

"Yes, I think so." His lips were close enough to her ear that she heard him over the wind of their flight. "Better to stay away, even this late."

Katy nodded and continued to marvel at what she could see of the water and land below her, colored in sable, violet and blues so dark they bordered black. She was flying. Flying! Ignore the attempted assassination, or understanding next to nothing about this magic herald crap. Or the odd ache from how Bay had to hold her bridal style, or her hair trying to escape a hastily rewrapped sloppy bun and fly up her nostril, because this was the best night of her ever-blessèd life! Katy's Quest of Great Importance had begun! Katy's Voyage of Significance might work as a title, too. All those years of waiting for it, giving up on it, and here it was complete with winged space people, and hooded killers, and shielded safe houses hiding in the Strait of Juan de Fuca run by glow-in-the-dark space people.

"I think you might like the view best if we turn you around," Bay rumbled in her ear. She pulled back, baffled, unclear what he meant. Her head at his feet? He sensed her confusion. "Your back to the water, hold again around my neck. Like earlier today, feet tucked between mine. I promise to hold fast, you'll not fall. Trust me."

"Absolutely." Katy wondered if this was a ploy for Bay to feel her breasts as he moved her, or to sneak a kiss (and who would complain if he did, not her, no way no how). She knew the tiny risk of slipping was worth it to be held a little closer. She could take another breath of his heady scent, clove and jasmine with a bit of lemon. Earthy with a wee twist of brightness. Definitely worth possibly falling to her death over the water. Bay adjusted his hands carefully, however, and helped her move around until she could circle his neck and feel anchored again. His gaze dipped to hers and he grinned.

"Now, let your head drop back and look up."

Trusting him, Katy did as he said, and what she saw was enough to steal the air from her lungs. A gorgeous midnight sky made up the boundaries and background of all she could see. A whirling astral tide pool simultaneously arching over them and pressing in on them, as though her fingers would trail through the Milky Way if she but reached for it. Her hair, completely freed when her hairband was lost to the coursing wind, streamed below her, pulling her head gently back. Her eyes watered from the current rushing over her face.

Yet it was the closest sight that most stunned her. Bay's wings, all thirty-plus feet of them, stretched wide, gliding while she adjusted to her new position. They were a white that glowed ethereally in the moonlight.

"We're almost back to the refuge," he murmured.

Katy made a small noise of protest. She voted to stay up here for hours if he'd keep them gliding through the night, marveling at the cosmos she wouldn't see from this view again for who knew how long.

"Do you want me to land with you like this, or turn back around? Backward landings might be scary even though it isn't your first time."

"If I turn around my hair is going to be in your face making it a blind landing on your end. That seems scarier," she replied drolly. "Let's give it a go this way."

Bay laughed. "As you command." With that, his wings did a tilting kind of thing, shifted against each other, flapped once, and they dropped like meteors. Yet their touchdown back onto the room's balcony was soft and controlled.

Her arms were reluctant to let go. Looking up at him, she was struck by how momentous her life felt that very second. Soon, a very scary soon, they were going to the center of the Universe: somewhere important to meet with important people who would have answers, which meant she was leaving her home planet. Hell, she'd be leaving her home solar system! Going on a bloody spaceship that could travel the Universe in ways Humans still debated were possible.

Because you had to figure all these cultures and planets and places were far enough away scientists hadn't found them using all the telescopes and radios listening for messages from distant lifeforms. If it took Humans three days to get to the moon but their group was heading halfway across the galaxy...or was it another galaxy entirely? Either way it meant aliens weren't just among us, they'd scripted a show Humans didn't even realize was on air. SETI and that lot were going to lose their minds in the morning.

All these thoughts floated through her brain as they kept sharing a smile, standing in place, still holding one another. Katy decided to forego waiting and leaned in to steal a kiss; just one, because the day and night had been so incredible and he was glorious in ways her mind still couldn't quite process. She felt confident Bay was going to kiss her back. Until she heard a throat clear pointedly, off to their right.

12

They managed to calm Raisa when they returned from their night flight, but it took some doing. She had, understandably, been scared and confused when she roused from a light doze to find Bay and Katy gone. Katy had thought they'd get back before she woke, but that was a miscalculation. One that disappointed Katy in herself; how could she have just taken off when she knew Raisa was still feeling unsettled? After interrupting them on the balcony, Raisa laid into them for disappearing, leaving her in the dark in general, and kept repeating how her baba had been right all along about Westerners.

Katy felt that was unfair because Bay wasn't Western, Eastern or anything bound by the terms of Earth.

"This whole day has been a nightmare!" Raisa slapped the coffee table for emphasis. They'd settled on separate couches, and Raisa leaned forward as they talked, swathed in a heavy blanket, hair loose and falling around her shoulders. Tears pooled but stubbornly didn't fall. "And you two," she shook her head. "I deserve better from you. You've evaded questions and hidden information from me!"

"Raisa," Katy tried to soothe. "The only information we

didn't share was about-" She stopped quickly, glancing at Bay, recalling the need for secrecy. "There are one or two things we haven't mentioned because we don't know if we can be overheard. Yfaun is a wildcard, and we can't risk exposing the few advantages we might have."

Like the hybridized kuh, when the *Eternidad* would arrive and where it would take them, or that they had a recording of a sound Katy was sure would give them a critical second of slowing that psycho killer when they'd most need it. Things like that could wait to be shared until they were safely away.

"I already blew it by mentioning Bay's people were coming for us, and by letting him see the pendant." Katy grimaced.

"At least he'll attack the right person next time," Raisa whispered. Immediately her face blanched, what color she'd managed to regain gone in half a second. "Oh no, I didn't... I would never want that." Her tears finally overran confinement and trailed down her cheeks. "I can't do this. I'm not brave, I'm not adventurous. I'm a library mouse who wanted a walk, maybe kebab for lunch."

Bay's wings rustled. He stood behind the couch Katy had taken, and now he leaned down to put his arms on either side of Katy's shoulders. Both supporting Katy and trying to catch Raisa's downturned gaze. "I respect your honesty. And your fear. To be unafraid now would be a fool's path. It's this very danger that means you will remain a mouse, only in a far bigger library. Yfaun will not stop, the Pu'ulqaari will not stop. They, too, are afraid. We represent a threat to their livelihood and, in some real ways, their very lifeblood."

Raisa shook her head. "What does that mean?"

"The PQ are into slave labor," Katy spat. "I'm sure there's a nice little word or phrase they try to use. 'Indentured servitude' or 'serfs who can't leave'. Some kind of shite like that. But it's fecking slave labor, and Lanu says they've built their entire society and economy around it."

Her friend physically recoiled.

"So you can see," Bay said, "why the Pu'ulqaari are deeply against the return of a Drazoen instrumental in creating the Calling of Centris. She is most likely to outlaw what they've been doing for so long, denying people rights and a voice."

Centris? Raisa mouthed to Katy, flapping her hands like wings. Katy nodded and gave a thumbs up, pointing between all three of them and copying the flapping hands.

"I don't know if I can do this," Raisa moaned.

"Would it help if you thought of it more like 'what other choice is there'?" Katy offered, reaching her hand toward Raisa's. She hadn't known Raisa's face could make that expression. Non-plussed mixed with irritated and sad. The hand she'd tried to touch jerked back.

"No, that does not help," Raisa ground out. She looked directly at Bay. "*We* do not represent a threat to anything. *You* do. You two. If I've got all this straight, Bay the Seeker and Katy the Herald are going to wake up a dragon. In space." She took a deep breath. "Raisa the Nothing has no role. Other than collateral damage, and I've already done that job."

Katy quailed. She wasn't wrong, but Raisa's stark assessment was bleak, and brought all the guilt from earlier surging back.

"I am not important anymore, nor am I mission critical for the future awakening of Sundancer. Ergo I should be able to go home." Raisa slouched back, drawing the blanket tightly around her.

"I don't think-"

"Wrong." Bay spoke at the same time as Katy, and his firm tone captured their attention fully. "You would continue to be at risk. You would put your friends and family in danger. We would leave, you would stay on Earth, as will Yfaun. He has seen that Katy protects you, cares for you, so he will exploit that bond by doing anything necessary to ensure she keeps you from being hurt or killed."

"But-" Raisa started.

Bay rolled over her objection, implacable. "There is no un-ringing this bell: the essence found its herald; we can't change that. If Katy is stopped from bringing Sundancer back to the Aoni now, all is lost. We cannot risk that, just as you cannot risk the ones you love most. I truly appreciate the pain of this path for you, but Katy was correct. There is no other viable option. The likely peril to anyone outside this refuge is vast, so until we have completed our task you have become an interstellar traveler."

He came around the couch, sat beside Katy as his wings contracted, and took Raisa's hand. She didn't jerk it away this time. "The very moment I can get you back to your family I will ensure it. You have my word as a seeker, and as a man who counts the atómi until he can see his mothers again. Return to family is second only to waking Sundancer."

Raisa clenched his fingers and Katy teared up, both women crying for what they were losing. "I promise to be the best friend you've ever had, Raisa. It will be exhilarating, terrifying and confusing. We'll do it together, I swear."

"Man nârâhatam," Raisa murmured. "I am sad, but I hear what you're saying. I'll find a way to get through this." She smiled tentatively. "With my new best friend apparently."

Katy beamed, relieved they'd gotten over this speedbump. "Can I hug you?"

"Yes, please," Raisa said, her eyes filling with happiness instead of tears.

Wiping her own wet cheeks, Katy moved next to Raisa and wrapped her arms around her. Da would be so proud of her, finally saying the right thing to someone. Bluster, silence and discomfort were Katy's usual methods of handling social inter-actions, be it with family or friends. All her emotion had gener-ally been reserved for (and sublimated into) her music. But in this moment the Air hummed gently in support of this new and still-forming harmony.

"We'll also learn together," she muttered into Raisa's hair. "What the hell is uh-tome-ee? Time, right? Has to be time."

"Seconds, in English," Bay chuckled.

Raisa raised her head. "Is there a dictionary they can give us?"

Great minds, Katy thought, beaming. "Right?! I asked for a Hitchhiker's Guide but they say it doesn't exist."

"Yet," Raisa said.

Truly, great minds did think alike. Between the two of them, Bay, and all these Centris geniuses he'd promised could help them, they'd knock this herald summoning gig out of the park. No worries.

KATY DREAMED of the last time her entire world had shifted and presented her with a challenge.

Four years old, she ran from her meanie twin brother straight to her father's lap. Da was her refuge when her brothers ganged up on her. Ma said that having four brothers would be wonderful as she got older, but Katy didn't agree. They smelled funny most days, they hogged food at meals and TV all the time, and they picked on her. So much!

Da protected her when her horrible brothers were their worst. Sometimes when he was in this room (where the model planes lived), he needed her to tug on his leg to remind him she was there. But then they would cuddle in his big chair while he told her stories from the fairy land where he grew up. He could spin tales for hours, which was her favorite way to spend rainy winter afternoons.

Ireland sounded very exiting – way more than Seattle,

because Irishes had leprechauns and toothy Dannons (it was a mystery to Katy why yogurt over there had teeth). She hoped to go there someday. If only Da would take their family back where he'd come from she could have adventures like in his fables. Rainbow bridges and secret hills and outsmarting Little Folk! She could sic dark elves onto her brothers…. But Da said the airplanes in Seattle had called to him forever ago, so here they were. Where Oran was a doody head.

"*Mo leanbh*, why're you fussing?" Da swung her into his arms and hugged her.

"I hate Oran." Her father shook his head at her, but she insisted. "No, Da, I do! He took all my blocks and hid them! He says I have to pay pirate ransom or I'll never see them again." Katy crossed her arms and pouted. "Can't you get them back for me? They were a present from you to me, not for Oran."

"You have to outwit him, *cruicéad beag*, not get him in trouble." Da's little cricket continued to pout, but started thinking.

"What will it solve in the long run if your mam and I always save the day?" he said. "Learn to think your way out of troubles and soon you'll have none."

"Fine, I'll do it myself." Katy sighed dramatically. "Can you tell me about the toothies again?" Maybe those sneaky folk would give her an idea how to be smarter than Oran the Evil.

Her father chuckled. "Tuatha Dé Danann, not toothies, my sweet." He rubbed her head gently. "I think we'll listen to some calming music first, so you can relax." Da always said music fed Irish souls.

"Okay, but stories later."

She always listened a bit to whatever her father played; it was usually Irish music, and it was soothing background noise. When the music came on this day, though, suddenly the world seemed different. Stories took a backseat for the first time. Today, in Da's lap, the room filled with a sound that brought her super-secret song closer. "What is that?"

"Matt Molloy playing the flute. Do you like it?" He pulled a blanket from the back of the chair and draped it over her.

Flute. Whatever that was, it was magic. Both high and low, breathy, fast then slow, then crazy fast. She wanted to leap up and dance then lay down and let the notes wash over her like ocean waves.

"Will the music feed my soul, even if I'm not Irish like you?" she whispered.

Da squeezed her tightly, gently rocking her. *"Is ceol mo chroí thú,* Katy. You're my heart's music, and you're more than Irish enough to appreciate a traditional air like this one."

"An air?"

He gently tapped his fingers along her spine, matching the unhurried rhythm of the song. "An air is what we call music like this. An older song, something slower, not meant for dancing, but still grand. Moving and tender, like as not to bring a tear to your eye."

At last Katy had a name for her beyond-reach music. An Air. She promised herself then and there that someday when she grew up (after she learned to outsmart Oran the Hideous) she would play the Air and bring a tear to Da's eye.

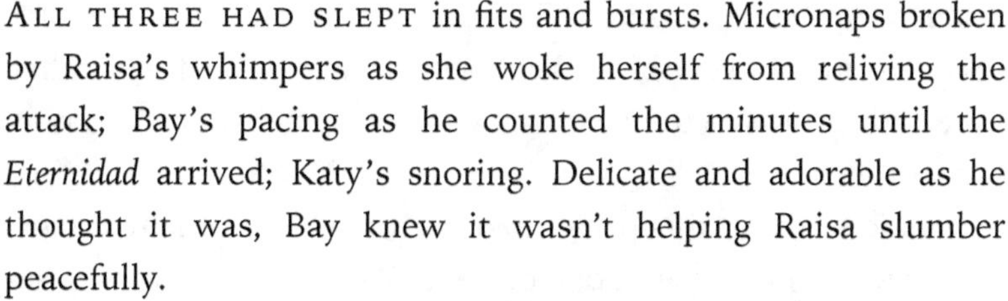

ALL THREE HAD SLEPT in fits and bursts. Micronaps broken by Raisa's whimpers as she woke herself from reliving the attack; Bay's pacing as he counted the minutes until the *Eternidad* arrived; Katy's snoring. Delicate and adorable as he thought it was, Bay knew it wasn't helping Raisa slumber peacefully.

They'd found a notepad after their heartfelt group talk the night before. Katy and Bay been able to write Raisa a note, explaining what they weren't willing to say aloud. They shared that the ship was expected around 10:30 a.m., and they also promised all information would be openly shared once they were aboard and off-planet. Safely away from Yfaun and on their way to fulfilling destiny.

Bay had nearly worn a trench into the lush carpet by the time the women roused completely. He watched Katy fondly as she stumbled toward one of the suite's bathrooms. She grumbled something about "feckin' sunny" and "hair will never recover". He took in the frizzy poof she sported and suppressed laughter. Djilbay might not know much about women and relationships, but he knew if he wanted to have one he shouldn't laugh at morning hair.

"You care for her. More than just the seeker/herald thing," Raisa said, passing him on the way to the second en suite. Her color was good, her walk strong, no lingering effects of the poison affecting her. "Looks good on you, and she deserves someone who can bring her this kind of wild escapade."

He dipped his head in both acknowledgment and shyness.

"It's like a story from the *Šāhnāme* of my people. Book of Kings, but with a heroine queen." Raisa's smile was soft, though inscrutable.

He didn't reply, letting her move on to her morning ablutions, and considered what she'd said. What if the feelings Katy seemed to share with him were actually about the thrill and adventure? What if she didn't want him, Djilbay jo Bikajo, rather what he represented? The danger, the pursuit, the storybook nature of everything they'd been through and what they expected to face in the coming days. Perhaps that was his only draw for her.

His journey on this planet had been filled with many things, but relationships weren't one of them. As a Mikanjo who would live far beyond many human lives, forming attachments led only to heartache. Bay had also always known he might have to leave in a hurry once his herald surfaced, which had further contributed to the lack of connections he was willing to make. Finally, there was the issue of biological differences that couldn't be ignored once clothing came off.

Katy was different to him, worth risking everything…despite the small kernel of doubt just planted. Yes, she was still Human with that short lifespan, but there were things the aoiti did beyond translating. Healing, boosting, enhancing. All of which she'd need to survive the near future; Bay wasn't even sure how well Humans would handle interstellar travel. They'd never done it. Raisa and Katy would be the first test.

Maybe he'd keep that to himself until they were safely aboard the *Eternidad*.

Freshly showered, both women rejoined him in the common area, wearing caftans Lanu had dropped off the night before. There was a knock on the suite door by a cart-pushing Lanu. They'd brought a large selection of breakfast items, and news that their Pu'ulqaari nemesis had retired to a room after midnight and hadn't been seen since.

Despite the nerves the quest mates felt, they sat together at the dining table and exchanged small talk over coffee, pastries and fruit. Lanu and Bay shared anecdotes and details about the Aoni and species the Humans might encounter. They'd met three, and twelve others could be on the Wheel. Raisa particularly appreciated learning things Katy had already been told while she'd been unconscious, recovering the day before.

Lanu spoke of amusing off-world visitors to the refuge: their observations and impressions of Earth. It seemed tourism had picked up substantially after the *Eternidad* visited hundreds of years past. Centris wasn't mentioned, but Bay had concluded during the night that Yfaun was likely to assume that was their destination, whether he overheard them or not. If they could afford not to go there, Bay would have suggested it to throw off their tracker. But the wisdom of the Toledrals and voices of the Chorus would be critical to resolving the task.

He'd gotten Sundancer's essence into the right hands, but they were stuck trying to figure out how to turn it into the trigger that would bring Her back to the Aoni. That wanted wise heads and information those people might have.

LANU PRESSED two boxes of teabags into their hands: Sadaf cardamom for Raisa and Murchie's Irish breakfast for Katy. "You'll want these, to teach the replicators how to make it."

Katy was humbled by their thoughtfulness, and how much Lanu had taught her. She wasn't fully prepared for what was to come... really, who could be? But thanks to Lanu's efforts she wouldn't be completely in the dark. That was worth its weight in gold. Or teabags.

Her first sight of an alien spaceship happened around 10:45 a.m. Pacific Daylight Time, near as Katy could tell. They'd all gathered outside, back where Bay and Katy had landed the day before. Everyone including Yfaun. He was probably waiting for someone to take a single step outside the boundary of the refuge, ready to strike. He wasn't an ounce less menacing in daylight, his threats from the night before nearly a tangible minefield between him and their group. It took all her strength to ignore him as Raisa urged.

Distraction was easy once a second moon appeared in the sky. Not quite as large as Earth's moon, but no one was mistaking that thing for a plane or satellite. Katy wasn't an astrophysicist and even she could see this thing had moved fast enough to be the ultimate Unidentified Flying Object. Or that other term they liked in those declassified government docs: Unidentified Anomalous Phenomenon. Katy was all for modernization, but would probably always think UFO over UAP.

This one wasn't unidentified anyway; had to be the *Eternidad* as expected, but it was an anomalous phenomenon. Literally not there one second, present the very next. Presumably they were slowing or stopped now they'd come into near Earth orbit, because it didn't get larger in the sky after that first sudden manifestation.

Skies were clear enough that Katy could see the shape plainly. It wasn't a full sphere, more like a set of Mikanjo wings flared and meeting at the tips. The distance and angle of the sun meant it looked black, but Katy wanted to believe it was white like Bay's feathers.

Raisa stepped forward as though she could get closer to something so vast outside the atmosphere. "Âlist. Incredible. I never in my life thought to witness anything like this." She shaded her eyes with a hand to see better.

Bay stepped up behind Katy, brushing her arm first with his wing edge, then a palm. She spoke quickly with him, confirming this was indeed the *Eternidad* and not the PQ or worse arriving. He reassured her, enfolding her in his wings as something descended to them, growing larger as it neared.

She turned her head just far enough to catch a glimpse of Yfaun, a single stride or two behind them, watching the inbound shuttle with a grim expression. Yfaun must know what their next steps were, headed to Centris. But he was still bound by refuge law, and couldn't do a damn thing until they'd left. If he already had a ship on Earth it could take him days to get to it. From what Lanu and Bay had described, she and Raisa would have extra protections once they got to this big floating wheel in space.

Screw him, she was wiping him from her mind right now. Katy looked back in time to see the shuttle come down thirty feet away. Jesus, Mary and Joseph that thing was quieter than a whisper! Something the length of a trolley carriage and the shape of a throat lozenge shouldn't be able to sneak up on a woman. Their group moved in concert as they walked toward the vehicle, Bay taking her hand. She didn't see any legs extend to rest on the ground, the shuttle just sort of hovered in place like a hummingbird, steady, and emitting a lower register thrum now she got closer.

She was a wee bit disappointed that her first ride to space would be in something that looked like any basic shuttle science fiction had ever depicted. Farscape, Star Trek, the spaceship from the game *Subnautica*, they'd all pretty much captured it. Katy had barely begun to lament imminent stellar travel being too ordinary, when a ramp lowered. The woman who emerged dialed things right back up to eleven.

At least, she presented female, and a powerhouse of one to be sure. This being owned the air around her. This one gave zero fucks, took no shit, and Katy aspired to (but could never actually) be like her. Height alone took Katy out of the running, because this woman was tall. Lanu or Yfaun size, not quite Bay tall, but definitely towered over Raisa and Katy. Had to be over six foot, especially in the knee-boots she wore. Dressed like a Scandi death metal fan, black bracelets halfway to her elbows, a pair of four-fingered ring-adorned hands, solid neon yellow choker around her throat, torn shirt and frayed shorts. Did they have denim everywhere in the Universe?

Green hair peeked from between the myriad of intertwined multicolored ribbons and yarn threaded throughout. Skin smooth as butter and the color of tahini. When she raised a hand to tap a finger against her lips, Katy saw claws painted grass green to match the hair, with vibrant orange dots as accents.

Like the Irish flag, she mused. That had to be a good sign.

Raisa took one look and stumbled back a little. "From what they told us this morning she's a Chitan, right?" she asked Katy under her breath. Only then did Katy notice the tail raised behind the new woman; it was a pale color matching her lips, covered in nearly translucent fur.

Her friend had not spoken as quietly as she thought, because the woman fastened her gaze of mottled hazel on Raisa instantaneously. "She's a Chitan, right?" she said back in a snide but perfect mimicry of Raisa's voice. She said something else in a language neither Human understood, and it didn't sound friendly. Her tail whipped against the ground in irritation as Bay stiffened at Katy's side.

"I, sorry-" Raisa started.

Making a noise of dismissal the pissed alien strode past them and stopped in front of Lanu. More words were uttered they couldn't translate.

Lanu looked at the Chitan, nodded, and waved her toward the safehouse. "Fumi Ly you are welcomed. In the wake of today's events we may have to lock down, but you will be safe."

Fumi tilted her head, shrugged and walked away. No look or last word back in their direction. She approached Yfaun, narrowed her gaze, and brushed against his shoulder. Not aggressive, but definitely testing. In sixty seconds, Fumi had ignored Bay and Katy, insulted Raisa, demanded a place at the refuge and poked at an assassin. Katy could only dream of being that badass.

"What was that she said?" Katy asked Bay.

"She said if you were examples of what your species represented, Centris would not be improved by your joining." He hastened to clarify, "Humans, she meant. Not you two specifically."

So much for first impressions, Katy thought.

THE CHITAN HADN'T USED such kind words; he'd politely paraphrased for Katy. She didn't need the added stress of Fumi's nasty comments. They all needed to head into the coming journey with clear heads and optimism.

Bay locked his eyes on the one person in the Aoni he'd longed to see as much as his herald. Vailillia, adored sister, friend and confidante. He wasn't prone to overwhelming emotion, but this moment was an exception. If they'd had time, that is. Her expression was serene on first glance, masking the thrill he knew she'd be feeling. For nearly a third of his life expectancy they'd been separated while he stubbornly pursued his belief his Kawakona was on Earth. They'd been apart longer than they'd lived together on ship, but how he adored her. To see her again was a joy he allowed to wash through him like a cleansing wind.

Her stride down the loading ramp was measured and brisk. Katy leaned back into his chest and said "She looks like you, is this your sister?"

"Yes," he said as Vailillia met them. "Vailillia jo Bikajo, please meet Katy, Sundancer's herald. Our Kawakona. And here is Raisa," he continued, gesturing to Katy's friend, "Katy's companion and another who needs our protection from active threats." A glance at Yfaun showed the killer looking intent, stance primed for action.

Vailillia smiled at Katy and Raisa. "Aw, she has a snaggle-tooth like you do!" Katy cooed.

"You cannot know how thrilled we are that Djilbay has at last found you," his sister said.

"Why," Raisa moaned, "can't we understand anyone except Djilbay, Lanu and the devil?" She didn't bother glaring at Yfaun, her tone scorned him enough.

Vailillia had received and processed Bay's transmission of some English, so she could understand their speech, but that didn't work both ways. She still spoke Mikanjo and neither Human woman had aoiti yet. Fumi Ly may have done something similar, or simply hadn't understood what Lanu had said to her.

"We'll take care of getting aoiti into you both when we reach the *Eternidad*," he said, surprised at the flash of fear on Katy's face. Why would she be scared of that? Raisa just looked confused and he realized they hadn't covered the process over breakfast. He'd explain on the short trip up to the main ship.

"Let us go," Vailillia said, stepping aside and gesturing to the shuttle.

"I demand ambassador accommodation on your ship," Yfaun's voice rang out, closer than Bay expected. The bastard must have inched forward while they were distracted with welcomes.

His words stopped everyone cold. Technically someone with true ambassador status could commandeer travel on Centris-bound vessels if they were stranded off their own world. Bay hadn't considered this, and looked to Lanu for some kind of confirmation. They inclined their head, which twisted his heart in despair. They couldn't get this far and have to endure a killer's presence – and evade his ongoing murder attempts – while they tried to safely reach the Wheel!

Vailillia put a stop to Yfaun's forward progress by stepping in front of him and looking directly into his face. "Denied."

"What is happening?" Raisa whispered. Bay realized Yfaun had stopped talking in English. No doubt he'd seen it made the Humans feel off-balance, which was the kind of thing this Pu'ulqaari would enjoy.

He sneered down at Vailillia. "You just delivered a Chitan here with lower status and will now take me. Unless you deny you are bound for Centris, which will be checked and dispute registered against your contingency if you lie." When she didn't speak, he hissed, "You have no right for denial, Mikanjo bekina'a."

"I am not your 'drudge', killer," she replied, shocking Bay with her implacability and directness. It seemed some things had changed since he'd last seen her. She was still clever and stubborn but no longer prone to stuttering during conflict.

"You will not board," she continued, "nor will you have grounds for complaint to the Calling. Your ambassador status doesn't overrule that of the first Humans to travel to Centris. They are Prima, the sacred class unseen at Centris for a kōmilen."

Yfaun locked his hands behind his head, growled, then sucked his teeth in genuine fury. "I will board!"

Vailillia looked back at Katy and Raisa, smiled to soothe their nerves. They still had no clue what was being said, but could read the tense atmosphere. The face she returned to Yfaun was blank and more intimidating for it. "Given your violent and unprovoked attack on these women only one Earth sal past, your right to safe passage is invalidated. There is provision for exclusion in such scenarios."

"Witnessed," Lanu called out in a clear, loud voice.

Bay was hard-pressed to keep his face composed. This moment was jaw-dropping, evidently prepared by his sister in advance, and the logic impermeable. Vailillia had become a formidable woman he thrilled to have on his side. The bag holding his beacon and the hybridized camouflage suit shifted against his back and interlocked wings. It put him in mind of an old practice he and Vailillia used long ago when scrapping with non-Mikanjo children who often thought them soft and easy targets.

Stepping to her side he extended his wings, careful not to hit Raisa or Katy, providing a safety curtain of feathers in front of them. Vailillia stretched hers just under his and now they formed a wall of white blocking Yfaun's view and progress toward the shuttle.

"Scurry back to the refuge," Bay said. "You've lost."

"Hold on to those wings of yours, Mikanjo freaks." Yfaun was so furious Bay thought he might start foaming at the mouth. "I know people who would happily carve them from your backs as you screamed. I should call them, encourage them to pay you a visit on the Wheel."

"Try us," Vailillia replied. "We have an entire room on the ship devoted to displaying Pu'ulqaari ruh of those who thought us easy targets."

They turned in perfect unison, keeping their wings between Yfaun and the confused Humans, precisely retracting them only enough to avoid brushing against the furious Pu'ulqaari. It wouldn't be a good time to accidentally break the non-violence rule.

Katy and Raisa might not have followed the conversation, but they understood very well it was time to go. They nearly race-walked to the shuttle and scampered up the ramp. Bay's last sight of the refuge was Yfaun's face hardened in a rictus of wrath.

13

"Questions, I have a million of them." Katy looked at Raisa. "You too?"

"Oh yes. Most critically how long until we reach a bathroom, followed by how many languages will we have to learn?"

Katy grimaced. She thought she knew the answer to the second question, and just hoped the injection or procedure wouldn't be painful.

Bay's sister said something to him, gesturing in their direction. He shook his head, eyebrows pinched. "Vailillia says the *Eternidad* has reported rapidly approaching aircraft, most likely military in origin. We have to leave quickly to avoid a confrontation. I'll show you how to buckle in, then we'll get to your questions."

Ah, yes. They were in the neighborhood (aerially speaking) of McChord Field for a USAF response. Presumably Canada had its own air force it would scramble to try and figure out what the hell was happening, though Katy had no idea how far away that base might be. Either way they were better off getting out of Dodge posthaste.

Her first real look around the inside of the shuttle revealed it aligned well with her subconscious expectations. Sides lined with webbing to hold loose items secure, like the bag Bay was stashing now. Twin rows of passenger bucket seats down the center, back-to-back, eighteen in total. Facing forward she saw panels that blinked with a lot of lights overlaying a 360° view of the surrounding land and ocean, the *Eternidad* visible far above, and the planes headed their way. Definitely military; this shuttle's resolution was so good Katy could see the missiles hanging under the wings.

Vailillia retracted her wings and sat at one of the two pilot seats, arms to her sides as the chair essentially buckled her in on its own. Bay waved at side-by-side seats and, once they sat down, their chairs auto-secured them, too. Katy considered making a bondage joke but rethought it when Bay kissed her head sweetly and dashed to the other pilot seat. She heard a new voice echo through the shuttle, Vailillia responding, the cadence of preparing for takeoff familiar even if the words weren't.

"Do you think a steering wheel or yoke will magically pop out of the console?" Raisa whispered.

Katy clutched Raisa's arm and laughed. "We think so much more alike than I ever knew. I wondered the same thing."

Beneath their feet and all around them the persistent low thrumming they'd felt when they entered the shuttle increased dramatically. Katy's eyes started bugging out. This was it. Her so-called quest kicked into high gear right here, right now.

She would have to do something vital and people would be counting on her. God only knew what was required. But she thanked heaven, as she looked around, she wasn't doing it alone.

The shuttle gained altitude with a speed belied by the lack of screaming engine noise. Whatever technology the Mikanjo (or maybe everyone in the Aoni) had… Humans were nowhere near this level. No joystick or other steering device had appeared so this was either controlled from the mothership, or worked on verbal commands. Katy barely felt any g-forces, less giddy roller coaster feeling than she would've experienced on a commercial takeoff. Those poor fighter jets didn't stand a chance of catching them.

Raisa put her hand on top of Katy's, which hadn't let go of Raisa's arm as they rose. "Why, when I am scared and bereft that I can't talk to my family, do I feel such a thrill? Look, look!" She patted Katy's hand and pointed to the screens. "That's the atmosphere and we're breaking through. I cannot believe this is real."

They watched the *Eternidad* fill the screen, absolutely massive and pewter gray against a backdrop of velvet black. As she'd seen from the ground, it wasn't a rounded sphere. Disc-shaped, vertical, and covered in a feather pattern. Her first impression of nearly touching wings had been accurate, and from their vantage it was breathtaking. Katy couldn't wait to board and see what the interior looked like. There were a jumble of comparisons running through her brain because she'd consumed so much science fiction and fantasy when young.

Bay's Seeking Ship could be anything from cramped International Space Station reality, to generation ships from The Expanse, to echoing chambers with their own weather systems like *Rendezvous with Rama*. Impatience to get in there and see with her own eyes surged, then receded as they got closer and the sheer size of the *Eternidad* sank in. *Bloody hell, I am going to get lost like a wee babe in there.*

The shuttle slipped over the face of the *Eternidad*, finding a slot amongst multiple other craft. This external parking lot formed the feather pattern she'd seen from afar. Once their shuttle locked into place, Bay and Vailillia came to them, Bay grabbing his bag out of the webbing as his sister talked. Vailillia faced them as she spoke, but knew they didn't understand so waited for Bay to translate.

"She wants you both to be prepared. A large greeting party gathered for us, so it might be overwhelming. Particularly as the language barrier will get in the way until we can get you aoiti." He pursed his lips, eyebrow raised at Katy. "Why do you keep making that face when I mention aoiti?"

Raisa piped up. "I, for one, would love to know what they even are."

Bay scrunched his face this time. "Apologies. I meant to use the shuttle trip to explain, but we needed to ensure no hostile contact and the fastest possible reconnection with the main ship." He shouldered his bag as he continued. "They'll help you, make you understand what's being said, let you connect-"

Vailillia cut him off, pointing at the shuttle door and sounding like an irritated big sister. With her long shining black hair, brilliant smile, crooked front tooth, and slightly greener but still incredible eyes, she was indisputably related to Bay.

"Looks like she wants us to go," Katy said to Bay. Her nerves flared at the prospect of meeting an entire ship of Mikanjo. If only this caftan had pockets she could hide her shaking hands inside them. Bay solved the problem by taking hers in his.

"If it's too much, for either of you," he included Raisa with a glance, "just lean on me, or Vailillia. Tap our shoulders or say something. We'll explain to the others. They're just very excited and want to welcome the first herald. After a kōmilen of seeking, we've succeeded with the first part of our task from Windweaver." He took a steadying breath, his face lifting. "Many stopped believing this day would come, so to those of us who remained and had faith, it's cause for much celebration."

Katy tried to lighten the mood. "Can I do the bougie queen wave? Or is that a Barbie wave?" She raised her eyebrows at Raisa, seeking clarity.

"Uh," her friend said, possibly for the first time since Katy had known her. "Both, I think?"

Linking elbows with Raisa, Katy turned to the doorway. "Let's do this."

They exited a short hallway to some kind of loading bay. The eruption of music, cheering and singing when they emerged was deafening. The space overflowed with Mikanjo. At least, Katy assumed they were, since Bay had said they were the only people with wings and she saw wings everywhere. And these wings were attached to people jumping into the air, performing quick loop-de-loops, and dropping back into a mosh pit of dancing and singing. Each one shouting "Kawakona!" over and over.

In the short time Katy had known Bay she'd gotten the impression Mikanjo were a formal society. He was often very precise how he spoke, eschewed contractions, took care with physical contact, all the hallmarks of more circumscribed people. And this despite a millennium on Earth. She'd assumed they were one hundred percent a Masterpiece Theater-style, quiet-of-manor people. But this was delightful pandemonium and triumphant excess. They had a hundred thousand years of destiny to celebrate, and the cork on a bottle that tightly sealed was as like to detonate as merely pop.

Raisa shrank back a bit, sliding behind Katy's right side. Katy opted for enthusiasm and threw up her arms while shouting "Hello!" She was embracing this and living in the moment. Never let it be said a good Irish girl couldn't party with the best. A great cry washed back over her in response and she laughed, giddy from the bedlam.

Her eye fell on one solitary figure in the back of the bay. A woman without wings, subdued, watching the festivities with aloof observation. Her hair was halfway down her back, loose, and a ghostly lavender color. This far away her eyes looked dark, her skin pale. Unlike the Mikanjo surrounding her in a subdued chorus of white, beige and tan loose clothing, this woman had a skin-tight body suit of gunmetal gray. Her boots and the high collar of the suit were red.

"Wonder who that is," she shouted at Raisa.

Her friend zeroed in on the woman across the bay. "No tail this time. No wings, no tentacles, no gills, no third eye. Not a levitating ball of interconnecting polyps. That leaves nine other possible species."

Trust Raisa to have already memorized major traits of the fifteen species registered in the Calling. She giggled. "You're going to be the ambassador for Humans, out of the two of us. That much is clear."

Raisa shrugged. "Knowledge is power, all librarians know that."

Bay and Vailillia had stopped behind them, waiting for the triumphant revelry to slow. It showed no signs of calming, though, and actually seemed to be feeding itself. Finally, Vailillia raised her arms, quieting the gathering somewhat. She spoke, they cheered. Bay spoke, more cheering. The crowd looked at the Humans and performed a lithe bow-curtsey-arm sweep move as one. After this they dispersed, except the woman across the room, who straightened up and moved toward their group.

She looks stern. Hopefully she's not in charge of administering aoiti shots.

BAY WATCHED the Jadoube pilot approach their group, slow and casual. She was new to him; by now their old pilot would have retired. A gruff but beloved crewmate, he'd been approaching elderly when Bay left the *Eternidad*. This new pilot emanated brash confidence and the typical belief she was immortal; the same foolish attitude every teen Human or newly fledged Mikanjo evinced. She was not a young Jadoube, but not very long into adulthood either. Given a lead position on the last Seeking Ship could mean she was stronger than he guessed, or that she was being punished by her people, forced to wander the distant black of the Aoni with an atrophied quest-following crew.

Regretting that Raisa and Katy would be left out of the conversation, he waited for Vailillia to greet the Jadoube woman with lilac hair and eyes of the Aoni itself. "Yuhwa Bon-Gil," his sister started. Her tone was friendly, which was good. That meant Yuhwa wasn't one of the diva Jadoube pilots. Too many times he'd heard of ships stranded by pilots who felt they hadn't been paid the proper respect, or Jadoube too high and mighty to speak with their own shipmates.

"Vailillia. I see your famed brother has returned, and apparently with the bounty he sought." She turned to him, took his measure with a glance, and said, "Greetings, Djilbay jo Bikajo. I am Yuhwa. I've been pilot for the last aiwak, happy to meet you at last."

Bay inclined his head in response, slightly surprised by the Jadoube's politeness to someone who was causing commotion on the ship. While pilots didn't run the ship, they still tended to feel possessive and more in charge than many captains liked. "These are my companions, Raisa Leon and Katy Phelan, Human ambassadors," he said, in English for their benefit.

Yuhwa laughed, a light but hearty sound. "No need for that story, I helped your sister concoct it in case there were any problems at the refuge." She looked at Vailillia. "I guess the good thing about picking up the desperate hail from that Chitan was having extra time to review the regs. I've had dealings with enough Pu'ulqaari to expect it might be needed!"

His sister laughed back, nodding her agreement. "Speed reading never meant so much!"

Bay looked down to see Katy and Raisa's confused and tired faces. Time to get back on task and help them start following the conversations. "We should go as quickly as we can. We need to get to Centris, to the Chorus and the Calling. Someone there will hopefully have a clue how we bring Sundancer back. In the meantime, we need to give them aoiti so they're ready to communicate easily by the time we arrive."

Yuhwa turned fully toward the Humans. In slow but clear English she said, "Hello. Me Yuhwa. You come. I fly."

Bay could have been knocked down with a raschai bloom. She'd taken the time to learn enough English to help ease the Humans' transition. That spoke to a character grounded in empathy and intelligence. The *Eternidad* had been lucky indeed when Yuhwa came on board, and he looked forward to hearing that tale.

Katy's eyes looked wet, and it was Raisa who bowed and whispered a hoarse "Thank you." They were weary and stressed to the very brink; he wanted nothing more than to get them settled and rested.

He reached for Katy's hand. "Ladies, this way." He tugged gently and they walked farther into the bay. This wide room felt welcoming even after so long away, still covered in sheer fabric panels of white as tribute to Hunanjanno jo Bikajo's wings.

Bay remembered days racing sleds through the ship with friends. This area was the key to getting between all ship sections, but speeding recklessly through here got pre-fledged kids in trouble. Nostalgia hit him unexpectedly hard, slowing his steps. He'd been gone so long, would anyone remember him fondly? Share recollections and laughs?

"It's huge!" Katy marveled, head swiveling between the four adjoining chambers and the sights revealed therein.

"The ships were built to be permanent traveling homes for up to five hundred Mikanjo seekers, originally," he said. "Each. Nine ships total were built. This is the last one operating. Over there it's designed for soaring," he pointed directly ahead where canyon-like walls swept up and out from the entrance bay portal.

"There," he pointed, "is the meditation and relaxation zone." A different opening, slightly offset from the first, revealed lush greenery and waterfalls, little more than dappled pinpoints of sim-sun breaking through the near-tropical canopy above.

In the third of the four openings, furthest to their right, snow-covered plateaus under twilight sim-skies surrounded a liquid amethyst reminder of home. "That one is a replica of Lake Mwanaburo. On our home planet our people live in homes surrounding the lake, farm land nourished by its waters."

"And fish those waters too," Vailillia interjected, wiggling her hand and arm like an eel when the Humans looked over.

"Feesh," Yuhwa clarified.

Bay lamented not carrying aoiti in his beacon pack. All those sals dreaming about finding his Kawakona and he completely failed to think through the basic logistics of post-revelation. He supposed in his head it all just magically worked out. As though Sundancer would have appeared instantly upon Her herald and spark being united, and then She would have handled the language issues.

Shaking his head at his lack of foresight, he steered their group left, toward the smallest of rooms, utilitarian and stereotypically spaceship in appearance. An amphitheater of circular traveling decks nested within graduating ledges, smaller cargo sleds parked below them on the floor. The decks required active drivers, rather than relying on the passive AI of the sleds, though they were still somewhat autonomous. Above all of this were more portals which led to housing chambers, dining areas, and all the rooms necessary for milenyo of lives lived on board.

Vailillia called a platform down as he explained to Raisa and Katy they'd go to medical to get them flight-ready. Nothing scary, just quick checks that Kweza, the ship's AI, gave good odds Humans could handle Jadoube-piloted travel. And to give them aoiti at last.

"But," she whispered, "do we need them? That woman who got off on Earth, she spoke perfect English when she made fun of Raisa."

"Chitans are expert imitators," Bay answered. "Fumi Ly probably didn't understand the words, just repeated them. You two will need aoiti to understand what's happening on the Wheel." There went Katy's face again, Raisa looking similarly unnerved.

Yuhwa noticed, her eyes narrowing. "Have you explained the process? That's it's nothing more than a liquid suspension of self-replicating nanobots?" Her tone was acerbic. "Or did you assume they would miraculously be familiar with advanced alien technology? Which they aren't. Meaning now they probably have imagination-fueled fears of something you've been telling them they can't survive without?"

Bay hung his head. By the Nine, he'd been scaring Katy every time he mentioned it because he'd forgotten she would have no idea what to expect. This whole "new species to the Aoni" thing was going to take more work on his part, he realized. Vailillia pinched his feathers, a retaliation method from their childhood.

Yuhwa had already assumed his negligence and spoke to Katy and Raisa in her basic English. "Aoiti mean small small," she said holding her fingers pinched together. The women hung on her words. "Aoiti not hurt. Trink." Here she mimed drinking out of a glass. "Rahh-eesa trink aoiti, Kay-tee trink, we talk."

The relief on their faces shamed Bay once more. He would do better, take their inexperience into account and be an improved seeker. Maybe he needed to stop thinking of himself as a seeker, in fact. He'd sought and found. Now he would become a … guide? Teacher? Partner? Much of him liked that idea exceedingly well. Katy's partner, in all senses. But that was assuming too much. He would 'chill', as he'd heard young Humans say. He would… Shepherd. Yes, that was it. No longer seeker, but shepherd to a precious flock.

14

Katy was in love. Yuhwa was the best alien they'd met so far.

Sure, Bay was hot, Lanu fascinating, Vailillia sweet. Yfaun and Fumi, well, dragging the bottom of the barrel there, were they not? But Yuhwa Bon-Gil was a dream come true. She'd learned enough English to help Katy and Raisa until they could help themselves through the power of these aoiti. Which turned out to be more than just trinkets that translated, they were everything in this wild west of a Universe. Aoni microtechnology that combined cell phone, computer, smart device of your choice, as well as your banking, educational and wi-fi needs all programmed via nanobots of something-something drastically impressive having to do with a biting brontosaurus.

Unclear on that part of it, really. She'd lost the plot a wee bit as Bay talked about the "Brontobyte quantum interface cloud" Bibbidi-bobbidi-boo, while she and Raisa waited for them to take effect. Her seeker had technonerd tendencies, and wasn't it grand to see something so adorable crossed species lines.

Yuhwa had handed them the aoiti cocktail and soothed them

in the medical wing when small whirring machines had begun circling the Humans like metal piranhas. Bay tried to explain what to expect, but kept getting distracted by Mikanjo swooping in to congratulate him. Lots of forearm-clasping and bowing, Mikanjo version of handshakes. Katy assumed these folks had known him before he left, and were proper gagged he was back with a potential herald in tow. Bay was able to break away long enough to say the ship AI, Kweza, pronounced them safe for travel, and that the language translation would slowly start to kick in over the next sal-angs.

Sal-angs *sawl-AAH-ngs; Human equivalent hours*, her aoiti helpfully supplied, right into her brain.

Fecking hell. That was going to take some adjustment.

Yuhwa had also been the one to bring them new clothes, a damn sight better than their refuge caftans. Sturdy bodysuits like she wore, since they didn't need Mikanjo clothing designed to accommodate wings. The Jadoube pilot's greatest asset, though, was not being so bloody tall. Finally, an alien sized for Katy!

Her anxiety, which had been on a low simmer ever since Pike Place Market (with occasional spikes during all the literally-fly-for-their-lives moments), was at its lowest around the Jadoube pilot. This woman was chill, calmly prepared for whatever situation they walked into, and that was bolstering. Raisa responded similarly, standing close to Yuhwa as they rode a deck to the pilot's platform, which Bay said was on the ship's bridge.

Katy asked, "Now we go somewhere to strap in for take-off?"

Two Mikanjo and one Jadoube glanced at her, trying to keep their faces impassive, but clearly she'd said something fairly dumb. "We've been in motion since we left the landing bay," he replied.

"No!" Katy cried.

"But," Raisa sputtered, "I thought Yuhwa was the pilot?"

Katy's earlier panic returned. "We can't have left without saying goodbye to Earth! Raisa, we didn't get a last look."

"We can't be that far out yet, we'll still say our farewell."

Yuhwa broke in. "I pilot, yes. Only important. Big."

Katy's face must have matched the confusion she saw on Raisa's. Vailillia, speaking to Bay but gesturing in frustration to herself, said something, still incomprehensible to the Humans.

Then, quite suddenly, the last part of her sentence became clear. Just a wee little lag between Vailillia's moving lips and the words turning to English in Katy's head. "...very frustrated I didn't learn the actual words, just let Kweza program my aoiti with what you'd transmitted so I could understand them."

Kweza *kway-zah; artificial intelligence bound to the Eternidad*

Katy gasped, as did Raisa, and Katy grabbed Bay's arm. "It's working! I understood her!"

Bay smiled wide, catawampus tooth on full display. "Very good! Faster than expected."

Yuhwa said, "Thank the Nine. This will make it much easier." As she spoke, their ride slowed, turned a corner, and stopped at the entrance to a short corridor. It was closed off by huge doors at the end.

Katy was continually reminded this ship had been built for a species with the wingspan to rival small aircraft. These doors were portal-style, the kind that would swirl open from the center, like a flower blooming in time lapse. Raisa managed to get off the platform herself, but Katy still needed a hand from Vailillia.

"Thank you, Lia," she said. At a nudge from Raisa she looked up to catch an odd look flash over Bay's sister's face. "I mean Vailillia. Sorry! Bad habit. My family uses nicknames as much as possible." Christ on a cracker, what if she'd just mortally offended the sibling of the guy she desperately wanted to kiss?

"This is," Vailillia paused and glanced at Bay. "This is acceptable. In Mikanjo culture what you call a nickname is termed a sweet-name. Usually a potential partner bestows it, but in this case," she smiled as blindingly as Bay did, "I will be able to brag to all that Sundancer's Kawakona awarded me mine!"

The whole group laughed, but once the portal activated and swooshed open, Raisa and Katy dropped their jaws. "Holy shite," Katy whispered. "Ensign Chekov would have given a lung to have this at his fingertips."

Raisa said, "I don't know what that means, but I know what you mean. This is surreal."

A walkway over what looked like thousands of computer servers with blinking lights led to a suspended platform in the middle of the room. Everything was covered in that same gunmetal silvery-grey she'd seen on the ship exterior. Stylistically it also matched the nearly-touching tri-wings motif Katy had noticed all over the *Eternidad*. From the design of door access buttons to the shape of the ship itself, that was a recurring image. Two other walkways branched out from the middle command center. All three paths were bounded by railings, though at a height meant for much taller creatures than Raisa and herself.

Futuristic terminals circled a raised dais in the center of the platform. Stools with no backs rose from the floor in front of the screens and panels, where several Mikanjo sat touching things with apparent expertise. Katy guessed that was how the ship was flying...sailing? Moving. And she knew for sure now that they were in motion, because overhead the entire roof was a domed window of unbroken clarity, showing space wheeling by.

It reminded her of summer evenings visiting Ma's family in Wisconsin. Katy and her cousins snuck out in the late-night hours to lay in a field, staring up at the stars. Vast inky infinity spread over their heads, the stars surely close enough to touch, as though they would alight on the ends of their noses like midnight butterflies.

This was like that. Except the stars slowly moved across the dome, the same way you look at a station platform when your train begins to move. That second where you wonder if the station is moving or you are. Holy Mary, Mother of God, this was the entire bloody solar system just flying by!

"I think we missed our chance to wave goodbye to Earth..." Her knees started to buckle a little. Bay steadied her from behind, a strong palm in the center of her back.

Raisa mumbled, "Oh pashmam! I can't look at that. Vertigo."

"You know," Katy said, taking her friend's hand, "these aoiti didn't help with that translation." She laughed weakly, hoping the absurdity of her comment would help distract Raisa from the overhead display. Raisa just moaned a little in return, face bowed to the floor, and squeezed her hand like a vise.

"Kweza focused on translating to English as the priority since you both speak it," Bay said, rubbing a gentle circle on Katy's back. "Eventually it will process all the languages I shared with it, Farsi being one. The upgrade will broadcast to everyone's aoiti on the *Eternidad* once done."

He turned eagerly to Raisa. "Someday I can tell you of the time I worked on the Sun Throne. I was blessed to see the Daria-i-Noor and Koh-i-Noor in that time, such incomparable gems. Just huge and the brilliance..." His tone was wistful, eyes unfocused, smile heavenly.

Raisa's face expressed *What the Fuck* flawlessly. "I don't understand who you are. In any way. Holy diamonds from centuries past? Wings of pure white like a Peri made large? Space dragons you want to awaken. My baba would either chase you from his home or adopt you." She shook her head.

"Your baba would have to fight my da over the adoption," Katy said. "Bay is the equivalent of walking folklore and he'll try to hoard him."

"Moving along," Yuhwa said loudly. The Jadoube pilot moved at a rapid clip down the walkway, and they followed as fast as they could. She led them to the central hub, passing through an opening between workstations. The Mikanjo officers, or whatever they called themselves, bowed to Yuhwa. "Majio attends," she heard them say in unison.

Majio flashed internally, but no explanation followed. That was the name for Yuhwa's job, Katy guessed. Pilot? Her newly supplemented brain told her it would sound like mahj-ee-oh.

Yuhwa, having reached the edge of the raised dais, turned and faced their group. "We're approaching the center," she said, "so I need to retreat and focus. I'd like you stay close, so we can continue discussions once we're through."

"Center of what?" Katy asked.

"Your galaxy," Lia said at the same moment Bay answered, "The Milky Way."

"Whaaaa-" she and Raisa spoke simultaneously.

Katy gawked. That hadn't been the solar system flashing by overhead, but the entire bloody galaxy? "How can we be there already? It's been less than 2 hours of travel. We take three *days* to get to the moon! And just what do you mean by 'through'?"

Raisa piled on, "The only thing in the center is a black hole. We aren't going to be spaghettified, are we? I've read about that."

Yuhwa held up a hand for silence. She also gave Bay a little side-eye, so this must be something she'd expected him to share before now. "I am a majio, which is a gift Songmaster Silver gave the Jadoube people long ago. It means we can navigate the Aoni through a sensitivity to, and harmony with, veṣu. What you're calling black holes."

Veṣu veh-shoe.

"Songmaster changed us genetically so that we could sense veṣu and travel quickly between galaxies. We navigate the fastest ways between planets as well, speeding journeys. Since the earliest days of Centris we've been the majio – able to link with ships and sail them on whatever journey we require."

"These Drazoen, they went around giving people wings and

changing species' DNA?" Raisa sounded curious and offended at the same time. "Did they ask, or just changed your ancestors on a whim?"

Every Mikanjo in the room sucked in their breath. Katy had put together that the Mikanjo were the True Believers of the Aoni; Raisa's words were borderline heresy to them. Yuhwa, though, just laughed. "That's a very great part of their mythology. You'll learn more when we get to Centris, but if I don't enter the river's communion we won't ever get there."

Katy's aoiti supplied **dao** when she thought "river". These aoiti were still working out the kinks of translation, but every little bit helped. She opened her mouth, ready to ask more questions. Like what dao was. Or how a river in space could require harmonic resonance with a species, because that felt more like magic than biology.

Bay slowed her roll. "She has to concentrate, a meditation of sorts. It's part of their genetic code, but still requires effort. Just as our wings emerge but we must be taught to hold ourselves aloft."

Yuhwa had ascended the dais, which had nothing on it but whatever passed for the advanced space version of a zero-g adjustable bed. She lay down, face lifted to the clear dome framing a part of space Katy had never thought to see. Just at the lowest horizon of the translucent window she could make out a brilliant circle of light surrounding the blackest pocket of nothing that could possibly exist.

Raisa edged closer to her. "I think that's a feeding black hole." Her voice was weak. "If I remember correctly, when you see an accretion disk that means the black hole is eating. Sucking matter down to disappear forever. Nothing gets out of black holes." She clenched her hands in a prayer position, raised in front of her chest.

Lia lightly touched Raisa's arm, a big deal from Katy's POV

since personal space and physical contact between alien species seemed minimal. *Unless they were trying to kill us.*

"Do not be afraid, we have been through this veṣu many times over the milenyo Djilbay waited on Earth. This is the way of intergalactic travel, Raisa. All trees look unforgiving as spears until your first safe landing amongst the branches. Once you have been through you will see how little you need fear."

Bay snorted. "Breaking out mama's old sayings? You *have* changed since I've been gone."

A Mikanjo at a nearby station barked a laugh, light and uplifting. Skin of milk chocolate, close-cut lemon-bright curls, and a rakish air. "Lealli jo Bikajo is a woman of rare sense and wisdom, fledgling. You'd do well to listen to her words issued from your sister's lips!"

Bay greeted him as she'd seen him do with most old friends: bow first, then clasp right forearms, left hand tucked into their own elbow. They started a low conversation she couldn't hear. Lia was still comforting Raisa, so Katy turned her focus to Yuhwa, laying on the Craftmatic of dao.

Dha-ow. All right, she'd take pronunciation if she couldn't get the whole meaning yet.

Yuhwa's wide open eyes were pinned to the black skies carpeted with stars and colorful nebulae. Her body vibrated, flexing rhythmically, like there was music only she heard, and she danced to it with her whole body.

The *Eternidad* very deliberately closed in on the black hole, the veṣu, and Katy's pulse accelerated. Her heart was aiming for two hundred BPM with a twelve-eight signature, felt like. Delightful Mikanjo clichés aside, everything Humans knew about physics and the Universe told her they were heading for guaranteed death. Acting insouciant was out of the question. She was just hoping she didn't collapse or gawk what little she'd eaten for breakfast over the railing.

"Katy," Bay called her over, happily distracting her. When she neared, he said, "I'd like to introduce you to Wiremu jo Bikajo, our captain, and a man who was old when I left the ship, which makes him ancient now."

Wiremu laughed heartily and clasped Bay's shoulder just as she chided, "Bay!"

She didn't miss the surprised-morphing-into-sly look the yellow-haired man gave Bay. She recalled what Lia had said about sweet-names and potential partners. If she'd done that to Bay and he hadn't objected… did that mean he liked it? Maybe liked her? Or was he just humanized to the point it hadn't meant anything to him at all?

"I'm very pleased to meet you," she said, offering her hand to shake before remembering that wasn't how they did it here.

Wiremu looked down at her hand first, then reached for it slowly. As he gently took hold she felt his tremble. "Kawakona, it is the greatest honor of my life to greet you." He smirked. "Apparently my very, very long life."

He'd used the word she'd heard Bay and Lia use, and the same one people were singing and shouting earlier when they boarded. **Kawakona** *ka-wah-KO-nah; Mikanjo term for herald of the Drazoen; the one foretold; precious; savior; hope for the future; duty fulfilled.* Looked like the aoiti would be giving her the flavor and nuance of words, too.

"Djilbay, you live a blessed life!" Wiremu was as happy as his hair was sunny. "The Nine will surely write your name in stars when they have all returned. Which begins with Irojaku jo Faluji as you always dreamed Her. She who will soon be among us once more if the Nine will it so!"

Bay put his arm around her shoulders, knowing the pressure of figuring out their next steps would give Katy some angst. "Indeed Wiremu, we have faith the great minds of the Calling and the Chorus can guide us. For now, however, we'll guide our Humans through their first veşu."

Raisa and Lia were a few paces away, Raisa looking paler by

the moment. Katy hoped Lia could keep her friend from completely freaking out.

Bay asked, "Ready, steady, go? Or would you prefer the ostrich approach?"

Katy straightened her spine. "I want to see it all. This is every dream I had my entire life coming true and I don't want to miss a microsecond of it."

15

Bay watched over Raisa, Katy and Yuhwa from the back of the room. All three had retreated to a private panorama chamber after Yuhwa transited the veṣu. Katy had wanted so badly to watch the entry and exit, but Raisa had collapsed almost instantly and Katy succumbed shortly after. She swore to him sympathetic fainting was "totally a thing". He'd never heard of it in his time on Earth, but he chose to give her the benefit of the doubt.

Yuhwa was having none of it once she came out of her trance. She demanded they confront their fears and brought them to this observation lounge: they could recline on couches, have drinks, and slowly acclimate to flying through space. Unlike the main flight deck, this room wasn't covered by a dome, but had widescreen windows letting them get more used to the view. She was trying to explain to the Humans what dao meant to the Jadoube, and how they accomplished the process. The discussion had been more successful before they'd consumed two cannisters of rusim, a drink beloved by the Jadoube and no one else. Except, improbably, Humans adored it.

"Mmm. A light fruity wine up front that knocks loose your molars later," from Katy.

"I have a cousin who makes aragh sagi, moonshine, a little like this," from Raisa.

Vailillia joined him watching over them. She leaned against his side and he slid his arm around her, reassured by an easy return to their old habits after so many years apart. Duty was a cold comfort when you'd been long separated from loved ones. He'd known she would forge her way without him, just as he'd done without her. But he couldn't deny a bit of longing to return to early days; when their mothers still spoiled them with love, laughter, and treats. Anabolu puddings if there'd been a recent visitor from Bankiri, or baijur crackle, nutty and sweet, melting on their tongues. Slow waking mornings filled with talk and silliness, all of them together as a family.

Bay knew part of him was also jealous of the ease and amity his sister had with people he barely remembered. That was part of the sacrifice he hadn't known he'd made until this very sal. Everyone on this ship was closely tied to him as seekers, his own sister most of all. Yet, he stood apart now, changed by his milenyo on Earth. The time he'd spent with Humans, she spent with Mikanjo struggling to keep their beliefs going.

"Do you begrudge me the time I spent on Earth, sister?" he murmured.

She didn't immediately respond, which caught him off guard. He'd asked it as a perfunctory thing, a way to establish he'd done what he must, and she would affirm she inherently accepted it. Duty was, after all, duty.

"I struggled with your absence, over the tuigs." Vailillia finally answered. "I knew what you dreamed. I knew you believed you had to wait on Earth, and I hoped with all my heart you would find your Kawakona there. I didn't lose faith in our obligation." Her arm tightened around him. "Still, I felt lost and alone sometimes. No mothers or other siblings to watch me learn and grow into my role. More seekers leaving each time we passed Bankiri. News of Mikanjo becoming targets of abuse and nasty bigotry… it seemed as though only cruel winds blew."

Bay was crushed. He'd completely failed to appreciate her perspective, and never considered how much it would feel like an abandonment on top of their mothers leaving, despite how she'd urged him to go. "I will never be able to apologize enough."

Her upper wing snapped out to whap his temple. "Stop it, Djilbay jo Bikajo. You were chosen by a deity to find Her herald. That leaves little room for niceties and comforts. I consoled myself over time with the knowledge we'd be reunited. That you would return and with something precious. Now, look. I was right."

Both of them refocused on the small group in the center of the room. The merriment and giggling were a balm to his spirit. Katy hadn't had much of that since he'd come into her life. Thank the Nine, Yuhwa was able to give her some ease and, the Nine willing, he would do a better job in the coming days.

"She's incredible, brother." Vailillia's voice dropped. "I think you have feelings for her, more than a seeker for their Kawakona."

Bay gave it a minute before saying, "I do. I never considered that as part of what could happen. How could I? I never knew who the Kawakona would be, much less what our relationship would be after the essence was transferred. But she is… She is everything I didn't realize I needed."

"I don't wish to hurt you, but there is a fundamental biological incompatibility. Kweza says Humans have lifespans of less than one aiwak. You have already lived thirteen times that, and will live another milenyo and more. I trust you are considering the realities of such a union." His sister rested her head on his shoulder, offering the kind of physical solace only family could.

By Mikanjo lifespans he was reaching middle age at nearly

thirteen hundred Human years. Bay was very aware of the numbers, the vast difference in life experience, and the current reality of Katy's aging prospects. Regardless of all the logic and sound reasoning he'd wrestled with since meeting her, he refused to believe he wouldn't get just as many tuigs with Katy as he'd already lived. The aoiti would do impressive things for her ability to regenerate and combat aging cells, fight off cancers and common disorders Humans suffered.

And… if not…. The pain of loss would be just as great when she left him than if he'd never reached for the joining. The thought of not being beside her was a spike of pain in his chest that shortened his breath. "The thrill of soaring great winds is worth the risk of fall," he said. More of their mama's wisdom.

"LIA!" Katy's voice carried from the center of the chamber, possibly out to the entire 75-23 quadrant. "C'mere, c'mere, c'mere! You hafta try this wicked brew! Say it again, Yuhwa?"

"Rusim" Yuhwa's voice was a little slow, but equally loud.

"Jesus, Mary and Jospeh this is grand bevvy! Riri might be a wee banjaxed in the mornin', but not I!"

Raisa, newly nicknamed Riri apparently, tugged Katy's leg and shouted, "Shush! The stars are trying to swim for me jus' like for Yuhwa. But I can't hear them over you."

"Ahhh, 's all jus' grand. The craic is GRAND!" Here Katy stumbled and sat back on a couch heavily, crashing into the side of Raisa, who just stared at the expanse of space in front of her face, entranced.

Vailillia looked at him and laughed. "I thought you transferred all their English, but only half her words make sense."

"Culturally specific slang. It will come in time." He nudged her. "Best join them before they get so drunk they pass out. Again."

Katy and Raisa were doing that a little too much around him, though at least this time it was their choice. A deep sense of peace and rightness filled him while he watched the group.

Cosmic prophecies and sacred duties could wait just a little more. They deserved some fun for once.

Alas, Bay feared Katy was having far less fun the next morning. She'd answered his hail slowly, and he could hear her swearing behind the closed door. When she remembered how to open it, he came face to face with a woman regretting just how much rusim their party had consumed.

"Hrngh." Katy turned away from him and slouched back to the bed.

The night before, Yuhwa declared she'd need to stockpile more cannisters of the drink if their team was to continue travel beyond Centris. The majio's voice was astonishingly slurred as she proclaimed it, something Bay had never heard from a Jadoube before. Even Vailillia had imbibed, though she'd reached for a Mikanjo preferred drink. Despite joining the group late, she'd done her best to make up for lost time. By the end of the night, Bay had to recruit help getting them all to their berths.

Now he looked down on Katy fondly, happy she was handling the transition from Earth-bound Terran to intergalactic wayfarer fairly well. In less than three of her planet's days she'd been confronted with a huge amount of information and change, but she'd adapted and pushed through her fears and anxiety. A rush of warmth flooded his chest as he beheld his Kawakona, a woman he wanted to make his own heart's companion.

"Good morning, *qania*." It felt right to call her his breath and light. Though their time together hadn't been long, she was already that important to him.

Katy moaned. "I profoundly reject this rise to consciousness. I'm in a hoop, go 'way." She rolled over.

Smiling to himself, Bay said, "Since we have time before getting to the Wheel, would you like to set up a call home? To your family?"

His beloved shot up, hair a Bacchanalian mess, eyes blood-shot amber. "I can do that?!"

He nodded. "Yfaun or other Pu'ulqaari aren't likely to intercept signals we encrypt on the *Eternidad*. Vailillia says we have no other travelers on board at this time, which means no one to try and grab the signals to sell, either."

"Riri?" she asked. "Can she call her family, too?"

"Yes," he said, helping her out of the bed gently and steadying her. "It will take a little time to set up, but we can do it for both of you."

"Yes!" Katy pumped her fist in the air, immediately grimacing and clutching her head. "I'm going to need time to recover first, though. That joy juice of Yuhwa's is a little too good. Have to be smarter next time." She looked around herself in mild confusion. "There's a loo in here somewhere? I can't remember what all you showed us yesterday."

Bay pointed her toward the door she needed. "I'll go get some food and drink ready while you wake up."

"Can I have a clean outfit?" He heard from the personal chamber, just as the door chimed. "Ohmygod, who is that?!"

Bay checked the viewscreen. "Vailillia and Raisa. They can explain the cleansing functions while I get Kweza going connecting to Earth's satellites.

He let them in, explained what he was off to do, and marveled at the comfort all three had with one another. Bay remembered an old Earth adage that crisis makes families of fellowships and thought it very true. The last thing he heard as he left her room was Katy, incredulous, sputtering, "What do you mean I shower *in* the suit?"

Bay greeted long-missed shipmates as he made his way to a dining compartment. Wiremu was already in the room, pouring a mug of nropita, the bitter, umami aroma instantly lifting Bay's heart. He recalled mornings with his family, watching moons and planets pass by as they talked and shared their plans for the days over breakfasts together. It was the first time a reverie like that didn't pain him as it had in the past. They had all done what needed to be done. His mothers couldn't stay on the Seeking Ship when they'd lost hope. He had to leave to seek as his dreams instructed. Vailillia had remained, growing into an accomplished chemist and his staunchest ally. The Aoni made all things possible; someday perhaps she herself would find a herald for a Drazoen. With his own Kawakona in tow, Bay could release some of his long-held anger and newly minted guilt. He accepted this was how the Aoni, or the Nine, had intended things to develop.

Bay walked in Wiremu's direction, debating if his Humans would prefer jurakeke or zoroia. He didn't know if a porridge-like dish would be better received than one of seafood. Or should he make a simple platter of fruits with a carafe of nropita to help them recover? As he greeted Wiremu he decided he'd get all of it. Let them decide what suited their tastebuds best.

"Ahh, good morning to you, Djilbay." Wiremu sipped from his mug. "Have you lost your Kawakona already?"

"They indulged last night. Substantially. Now I'm to fetch a morning meal and prep Kweza to let them call family back on Earth."

Wiremu volunteered to help him carry everything back to Katy's room. As the food was prepared Bay put his request in to the ship's AI. Once they'd made it back to Katy's chamber, laden with extra foods the chefs begged to have the Humans try, Kweza was ready for specific details on which Earth IP addresses to ping.

"Baba ignores his computer, sometimes for days," Raisa said. "Can it connect with his phone instead?"

A freshly bathed Katy, meanwhile, was strangely reluctant at the same time she appeared excited. "Can we give them a heads-up first? A little warning we'll be calling in an hour or two? That way we can eat first while preparing for the shouting?" She shrugged, looking to Raisa. "Let's be real, how mad are your parents going to be? Mine are like to be fuming."

"This is quite true," Raisa concurred ruefully. "How sound-proof are these rooms?"

Eventually Kweza used mobile numbers to text expected times for video calls, as well as the path to return message via chat app, if that was preferable to a call. All heavily encrypted as Yfaun probably had interceptor tech running back at the refuge. Bay knew rationally that Kweza had no feelings, but part of him sensed a new level of hum in the ship background noise. Something different from what he'd felt all his childhood on the ship. He thought maybe Kweza was excited by all the new tasks and experiences Humans were bringing to its databases. It was a fanciful idea, but fulfilling a prophecy seemed to bring thrills to both the living and to machines.

Katy loved the warm, oatmeal-sago hybrid dish best. **Jurakeke** popped up via her aoiti. *Joor-ah-keh-keh; a flower grown in the fissures of the Wairua Canyons.* She didn't get more info than that, but it wouldn't have made the food more delicious anyway. Covered in a gently heated sweet broth, just a little chewy, and pure comfort. There were also juicy and tart fruits, something fishy she couldn't handle but Riri devoured, and what looked for all the world like fiddlehead ferns. Here was more proof of synchronous universal stuff from all over the Aoni because of how the dragons had mucked about. Fiddlehead ferns grew on Bankiri just like Earth.

Didn't make her any more inclined to eat them, despite her mother swearing for years they were healthy and tasty treats, though. How could they taste good, they were bloody ferns. Unless... "Do these taste like chocolate?" Katy asked Bay. When he shook his head no, she passed over that bowl and went for more of the jurakeke. This was the thing to cure hangovers.

After they'd finished eating (and explaining chocolate to Lia and Wiremu), Raisa announced she wanted to take her call privately in her room. "I might put the caftan back on," she mused. "Maman and Baba will like that better than this bodysuit."

Wiremu, who'd stayed to have breakfast with them, volunteered to walk Raisa back to her room. Katy couldn't get over the fact that the captain of this huge ship had casually eaten breakfast with them. Hell, he'd carried half the dishes that they ate. He wasn't a man to stand on ceremony, and Katy liked him all the more for it.

Vailillia left at the same time, wanting to check on a couple of experiments she had cooking in her laboratory. Katy met Bay's eyes, hyperaware this was the first time they'd been alone since their night flight when they almost kissed.

Feelings were messy and awkward. This quest thing would be a damn sight easier if the man in front of her wasn't so bloody distracting. Katy could admit that, outside of a stray thought or two, her focus had been entirely on Bay and not on how the hell she was meant to resurrect a hibernating dragon demigod.

Would sacrifice be required? Blood, or life, or a precious belonging? She cupped the pedant, safely tucked under her suit, realizing it was the only belonging she had now, and it was certainly precious. It felt like part of her, it called to the Air and her very spirit, something she would fight to hang on to.

Katy wouldn't give it up. Nor would she give up the man sipping the most intense, high-octane version of coffee she'd ever drunk. **Nropita** *en-roh-pit-ah; made from the steeped hearts of galambah pods*. Nropita was the stuff of which caffeine addicts dreamt, and after one mug Katy felt confident she could scale Mt. Rainier. "Molly Bán" was playing in the back of her mind, merrily piping along with her allegro-bordering-on-presto rushing blood. Racing it was, both from the drink and contemplation of just leaning over and planting one on Bay.

Consent was key, she knew, particularly with a culture as circumscribed as the Mikanjo. Well. More than a culture, weren't they though. A whole species. Her mind spun out for a moment: in just a few days she'd learned so much, and that was only scratching the surface. Soon they'd get to Centris. Since she couldn't imagine a dragon-designed planet wheel that was the center of creation, Katy was using a Disneyworld/ComicCon hybrid as a placeholder image in her head.

A hazy memory surfaced from the night before; Yuhwa and Lia explaining how the Drazoen had sandboxed travel within the Kéntro system. That's the one they'd created at the same time they built Centris and the Wheel. They meant to ensure ships moved only at cruising speeds. It had been set up that way to give hotheaded species, or angry individuals, time to either calm the feck down, or to mount defenses at the Calling. Yuhwa's fancy dao didn't work here, which meant after transiting the supermassive black hole, or SMBH (Riri taught her that one) and jamming through multiple other systems in this galaxy, they flew at a stately sub-light speed toward Centris. There wasn't much to see, since no species was allowed to build satellites or waystations in Kéntro system. The Drazoen hadn't left other planetoids or moons floating about the place, either.

Such a slowdown meant they'd had yesterday to settle in and get pissed to the gills, today to recuperate and (soon) make calls home, with the afternoon earmarked to mend from Ma's expected tongue-lashing. Centris would happen the next day. Right now, though, this was for seeker and herald. Katy and Bay. She gathered all her courage.

"If I had my flute, I could play you a song that captured how you make me feel. But I don't and I'm utter crap with words," she rushed on, "so here's the deal. I want to kiss you. A lot. Do you want to kiss me?"

Bay froze with a piece of fruit on the way to his mouth. Was that a good sign, or had she just ruined everything? He coughed, setting the morsel back down uneaten. "I," he started, stopped, continued, "yes, I too would like to... share that with you."

They eyed each other over the small table for roughly two seconds before they lunged and met in the middle. Katy's heart thumped like a hummingbird, she knew her hair looked a whole lot like an active Tesla coil, but she smelled good from the bizarre ion-something-something shower. Her head had stopped hurting after the cup of nropita and second bowl of jurakeke. There was nothing going to stop her from enjoying Bay's kiss.

Because this kiss, St. Brigid and all the saints! It was a *show-stopper*. Urgent yet sweet, a little untutored as though he hadn't done it much, and yet it delicately expressed all his years of longing and the joy of succeeding. His admiration of her, his hope for their mission. Katy didn't know what her lips were telling him, though hopefully there was a hint of the safety, trust and thrill he'd brought into her life. Danger, yeah, that too. Her eagerness and trepidation, how much she wanted to be the answer he'd sought for so long, and just a dollop of her longing to stand out and matter in the Universe. Everything mixed up in a cocktail sure to spin her head, the Air going bonkers, surging and rolling, leaving her feeling like she was soaring.

Eventually Katy realized they'd stood, pressing together, knocking over food and drink between them. She didn't care, because finally she was able to trail her fingers down the insides of his triple wings, caress the edges closest to his shoulders. *Softsoftsoft*, just as she'd fantasized. Bay rumbled out a sound that clenched her stomach when she stroked tenderly, and then flared his wings. The room, built for Mikanjo habitation, only suffered slightly from the wind his sudden movement produced.

She traced the small line of aqua feathers, his only non-white ones, wishing she had eyes like he did so she'd see every shade and variation in his wings. Tilting her head to the side so he could kiss his way down her neck, all she could manage was to inhale his addictive scent. She let him take lead: Katy wasn't wildly experienced (college only yielded four brief relationships which all petered out rather than ending in fireworks), but her sense of the here-and-now was that she shouldn't push. Respecting boundaries was far sexier than unintentionally galloping over them.

Bay's hands went around her waist, just as they had when he'd first held her, flying them from Seattle's shores. This time was very different, and she trembled with want. His hands, large and inventive, capable of fashioning some of the most beautiful things, were gentler than the brush of his feathers against her fingertips. Their mouths met again, and again, intensity growing, at last peaking when they had to break for deep breaths.

Their eyes met again, Bay's had deepened to malachite and glowed from within. "*Qania,*" he whispered.

Qania *khan-yah; beloved, literal "dawn light's first wind lifting the heart"* floated through her mind. Katy couldn't contain her giddy, beaming smile, and threw her arms around his waist in an exuberant hug. "*Mo chroí,* you are for me too. In my heart."

Their urgency had subsided a little, and Katy savored the warmth of Bay's arms, how his wings draped around her so naturally. They'd had their opening movement, dolce and espressivo. She couldn't wait for the second and third movements. The full symphony of Bay and Katy would be amazing.

It would wait, though, because Kweza announced it was time for the call home.

16

Controlled chaos. That was the result any time the Phelans came together, whether in person or virtual. Throw in the Rollins side, and it was sure to get loud. Katy was relieved and chagrinned in equal parts now the time had come for the spaceship-to-Seattle call. Bay had met her father briefly, but this would be his first introduction to what she felt sure would be the entire clan. Knowing her family, the other side of the call would likely include extended relatives, neighbors, and possibly random Irish tourists Da had met in a store.

"I'm starting to regret giving them notice we'd call," Katy said as she watched Bay sort the room to look less wrecked-while-making-out. It seemed unkind to tell him nothing about the room would make her family happier than looking like they were sharing it. At least, she presumed her family would be all for it, given how much crap they'd given her about being single.

Bay looked up at her through those charming locks that always fell perfectly in front of his eyes. They'd evidently trained themselves in K-Pop-level cuteness. "What did you say?"

"I said, I think we should have just called, no warning, because there is going to be a carnival of my family on the other end." She laughed. "They can't help themselves." The crowded, not-one-ounce-of-privacy aspect to her family had been part of why she'd withdrawn from them as a confused teen and frustrated young woman. There was a level of reassurance to it, though. Her people could always be counted upon, despite the ribbing coming her way.

He crossed the room and encircled her in his wings. "I don't mind. You need them after the events of the last few days. The *Eternidad* arriving and their inability to reach you probably terrified them. And they don't yet know about Yfaun." Her arms came around his waist and squeezed.

"Ever. They don't know about Yfaun ever." Katy shuddered, her mind whirling with visions of what her family would do if they found out someone was trying to kill her. Oran might cheer them on, but the rest would be her very own brute squad.

"How will you explain what made you leave your planet then?" A warm turquoise gaze traced her face. "I should know what you're going to say so I don't make a mistake."

Katy shook her head, knowing this was going to be a goat rodeo no matter what she shared or hid from her family. Trying to manage their access to the truth was a fool's game, mainly because she was a terrible liar as she never could keep things straight in her own head. "Scratch that, I'll tell them the truth. Just.... Prepare for excitement. Raised voices or clapping. Definitely yelling, I'd say. We'll have to see how it plays out."

Bay did something that turned a wall of her room into a large screen. In short order they'd dialed her ma's laptop. Katy chose not to ponder what kind of physics had to be involved to video chat from outer space. One hundred percent the kind of physics Humans probably didn't know about, or at least know how to manipulate. Especially a part of outer space being traversed by an alien species who could "swim" the spacetime continuum. Yuhwa was going to have to explain that river idea again. Sober this time.

On the large screen in front of them, Bay and Katy suddenly faced a healthy chunk of the Phelan and Rollins families. Immediate and extended, live and in full chaotic glory. Ian and Deb on screen-left looked put-out, nothing out of the ordinary there. Patrick, Paul and Oran were to the right, Vasuda in front of Patrick. Katy's da sat down front, shouting over his shoulder at two teen cousins shoving one another. Her ma sat screen-center, eyes running frantically over Katy as though expecting wounds. Aunt Mildred stood behind Ma, next to Ma's other sister, Aunt Susan. Both had supportive hands on Ma's shoulders.

Paul shouted, "Everyone! Quiet, she's on!" Her da's head swiveled like an owl, eyes comically wide. Katy and Bay's screen filled with rare silence, dropped jaws and startled faces.

"Holy shite," Katy heard. "Boyo has bloody wings!" Ah, cousin Keane, visiting from Dublin. Her uncle's only son, twenty-five, and you couldn't tell Uncle Frank his boy wasn't perfect because he'd never hear ya.

"Hey," she said, waving lamely. Just how did one start a conversation about escaping the planet with an alien because a prophecy said so?

Oran cocked his head, raised an eyebrow, then asked, "Is there pie left?" With that he wandered out of frame. Paul smacked the back of Oran's head as he went, then the two were wrestling and Ma was yelling, "Knock it off!"

"*Cruicéad beag*, my girl. You're all right?" The sound of Da's concern choked Katy up. She could only nod in response. "Is this not our young man from Conall's Sunday night?"

"Yes, Da. It's complicated, I can try to explain-"

"I need you to come home." Her mother's wobbly voice threw Katy for a loop, her eyes instantly meeting Ma's on the screen. All her life, Ma had been steadfast, calm, mostly non-interfering in the hierarchical silliness of five children. Always proud of any accomplishment, but never effusive or overstated. Constant was the definition of Ma. Hearing her distress was appalling, and seeing her aunts bending closer to Ma in sympathy broke her heart.

"I can't, Ma. I wish I could, but..." Katy made a frustrated noise. "There are so many things I need to explain-"

"Gerrup outta that, is no one gonna address that our man HAS WINGS?!" Keane again. "For feck's sake! Do we even call you a man? Was that your spaceship what caused the entire planet to wreck the gaff?!" His face popped up sideways, in front of her parent's faces; freckled cheeks ruddy with outrage, brown irises nearly eclipsed by dilated pupils. "It's bloody feckin' chaos down here!"

"I'm trying-"

"This is all fake. No way any of this is real." Great, now it was Jake, teen cousin from Ma's side. "First of all, aliens? Puhleez. And even if there were aliens, why would they take someone like Katy?" He snorted. "Think, people!"

Katy took a deep breath, rubbing her forehead with shaky fingers. This was both exactly as expected, and worse. Oran wandered back into the frame, chewing something, just as Bay wrapped his arm around Katy's shoulders and kissed the side of her head.

"Jaysus! Katy's finally got a man and he's from outer space!" Patrick and Oran cracked up before Oran added, "So that's what it took, Bug? A guy has to be from waaaaay out of town to want you?"

Katy looked at Bay and murmured, "If I tell Yfaun this asshat is my twin and there's a chance he could be the herald, you think Yfaun'll try to kill him instead of me?" She realized she'd spoken too loudly when every voice on-screen erupted in various levels of outrage. Sighing, she tried again.

"Let me start from the beginning. Please! This is Bay, he's from a species called the Mikanjo. They're from a different galaxy." She paused, letting it sink in.

"You're taking the piss!" Keane and Da barked.

This was going well.

OVER TWO HOURS later Katy and Bay had answered questions to everyone's satisfaction, and escaped further inquisition. Mostly. Ma kept telling her to come home, which cracked Katy's heart a little more every time. She had always been more of a daddy's girl, but this visible show of her mother's pain and fear had wormed its way into Katy's already bruised spirit. By the time they'd wrapped up (with a promise to come fetch the family "in yer fancy spaceship" once it was safe), she was a little dejected and a lot tired.

What had Riri's call been like? There'd been more than one hint her friend's family was as close as hers, though her baba sounded far stricter than Da. Bay showed her how to call Raisa's cabin and the two women commiserated over the inability to fully share with their family members. They'd both tried, but aliens alone was a tough sell, much less cosmic prophecies and comatose dragons.

Katy hung up and turned to Bay, still in her room, wings retracted, looking slightly unsure. "You heard the dinner plans? I'm counting on you to get me from here to the cafeteria." She came closer as she spoke, reaching out to stroke his arm.

His tension dissipated and he smiled. "I can handle that, *qania*." His hands slid around her waist and pulled her closer.

She went willingly, loving the Mikanjo endearment, and eager to rekindle some of the rather excellent shiftin' they'd been doing before the call. Bay's lips were soft and warm, their tenderness easing any angst the call home had riled up. Katy allowed herself to relax, not pushing for more than the comfort Bay's affection offered. After several kisses she pulled back to rest her head against his chest. His steady heartbeat thumped against her cheek and reassured her, a sweet bolero rhythm.

At her request, Bay took her to another observation chamber so she could gaze at the stars and galaxies winking just outside the Kéntro system they flew through. Soon to get to Centris, and meet the voices of the Chorus. Yuhwa had said something about Jadoube Swords and Truth Arenas, but that was rather lost in the haze of the drunken night past.

"Is it okay to lay down on the couch and stare out like this?" Katy whispered to Bay. There were other Mikanjo in the room this time, and while most had smiled at their entrance, one or two had grim looks. "Am I doing something wrong?"

Bay reclined on the low settee, perpendicular to her, pulling her legs onto his own. "You're fine. This place is meant for relaxation and quiet observation. However you accomplish that is your choice."

It was peaceful at first. But after just a few moments Katy heard a sharp female voice snap "Kawakona? I think not!"

Katy scrambled to sit up and face the newcomer. It was a shock to hear the Mikanjo word for herald-plus spoken so negatively. Bronzed skin, eyes that resembled hazel but with brindled turquoise instead of green, and brown hair that hung down the woman's whole back. Her face was not welcoming. "I, I don't, I'm-"

"Djilbay," the woman plowed through Katy's stammering. "I am shamed on behalf of your mothers to see you have brought this pretender into our midst, making wild claims of her prowess!"

"Couri jo Bikajo, I would like to say well met," Bay growled. He rose to stand between Katy and the nasty woman staring down at her like she was rotting fruit. "But your rudeness is a shock. Perhaps that should be your shame. Leave my mothers' memory for Vailillia and I to carry."

The woman, Couri, didn't back down. "You were barely a

fledgling when you left, and time on an untested, infantile planet didn't mature you further. For you to think this," here she pointed derisively at Katy, "is Irojaku jo Faluji's Kawakona? Preposterous!"

Katy, realizing Couri was attacking her home as well as Bay, surged to her feet. He was flexing his wings a little, so she ducked under one and looked up at the harpy before them. "Are you saying there's something wrong with my planet and people? We might not have known about all these other species and places, but we're not backward. We'll learn quickly and be a major part of everything, trust that."

Couri's face soured further, if possible, raking Katy with her gaze. A man came to stand shoulder-to-shoulder with Couri, taking her hand. His cocoa brown gaze was anything but warm, making it evident he shared her feelings. The weight of their combined disapproval pushed at Katy's barely suppressed qualms. If she wondered whether she was an imposter, why wouldn't these people? They'd been seeking for thousands and thousands of years and here came Katy Phelan, no credits to her name other than a talent with an Irish flute and a narrow escape from an assassin. Even that last one wasn't completely hers to claim, since it wouldn't have happened without Bay's help. Okay, maybe she wouldn't have a lot of faith in her either, but they should have some in their own seeker for feck's sake.

"Abou, I hope you are here to escort your wife away." Bay looked at the man beside Couri, keeping his face blank, though she could feel his muscles had tensed. "I can only assume she is ill and in need of rest. The woman I remember would not have offered words of such disrespect to anyone, much less the Kawakona."

"Couri and I are of the same mind. We see nothing of a prophecy fulfilled in this one." His gaze on Katy was condescending. "If you are indeed the Kawakona, where is your Drazoen? What delays the awakening, Her return to the Aoni?"

Katy's heart sank as Abou voiced thoughts she'd had herself. The Air, which had been a lilting, quiet tune as they'd looked out the observation windows, turned lachrymose and sluggish. Sundancer Orange wasn't any closer to coming back than before Bay had met Katy.

"I dreamt of nothing other than finding the Kawakona, from my earliest days. You know this, everyone knows this. Before I even fledged, I knew it was my destiny, I felt it in every nerve, in the pulse of blood under my skin. And I tell you, Katy Phelan is the one. Sundancer's essence resonated with her, I could feel it. A Pu'ulqaari killer believed it well enough to try and destroy her. She will raise Irojaku jo Faluji, mark my words."

Couri's tone was pure venom as she spat, "Tell us then, what is Her truename, oh lauded Kawakona."

Katy looked at Bay in confusion. "Sundancer. Irojaku jo Faluji, right?"

Abou and Couri laughed; ugly, vicious chortles. "Prophecy says '*The herald of Orange shall bear Carnelian and know Sundancer's truename*', but this one shares only that which is already known. She is a false hope!"

Bay's hand smacked his own chest as he snapped back, "She carries the essence, a stone from her planet alone, one which I ensured was named to the prophecy! Do not presume to lecture me on those words, I have repeated them to myself for a milenyo." He dropped his voice even lower when he asked, "I wonder, do you dare think you would be worthy to hear Her truename? That any of us besides the Kawakona would be?"

Katy's hand went to where the pendant nestled beneath her bodysuit, protecting it from the disbelief and anger of the two seekers confronting them. She couldn't decide if the pair had lost faith, the way Bay had described his mothers, or if they just didn't like her. It was possible they had issues with more than her coming from an unrecognized species and planet. Perhaps they'd expected to find the herald themselves? Or believed a Mikanjo savior would fulfill the prophecy?

Whatever the problem, it wasn't one they were going to solve having a pisser in this public area, where multiple other seekers looked on in shock at the vitriolic confrontation. She didn't know how to put on the brakes, though. These two were proper furious and Katy didn't handle aggression well.

Thankfully Lia stormed into the chamber just then, a stunning woman at her heels. If Bay's eyes were luminous emerald, this woman's were neon sapphire and they flashed like warning lights. Her long legs carried her to their face-off in seconds. "Papu! Mama! Word of your umwana has spread all over the ship. How could you?"

Umwana *oom-wah-nah; to give offence, do violence and hurt with words, to harm the spirit.*

Katy could get quite comfortable with the aoiti talking right into her brain, especially when it told her this new woman was taking her side in the conflict.

Blazing blue eyes turned to her, apologetic. "Kawakona, please accept my regrets. My parents do not speak for all." Her frustration refocused on her mom and dad, who looked anything but cowed.

"You do not know everything in the Aoni, Orihei," Abou started. "We have asked and the Human doesn't know the true-name. She hails from a deficient species-"

"No more!" Orihei cut him off. Her gaze pinned them both. "What else does the prophecy say of the Kawakona? *'They will be precious and need guarding'*, something you have conveniently forgotten." A momentary flash of shame crossed their faces. "How can you declare Djilbay jo Bikajo lies simply because you have given way to the same disease of his mothers? Do not poison all with your weaknesses."

Whoo boy, Christmas at their house wasn't going to be a picnic, Katy thought.

"Djilbay," Orihei nodded at him. "Vailillia," another nod to the woman at her side, "thank you for telling me what happened here. I am so sorry-" Orihei broke off, rustling her compressed wings in agitation. "Kawakona," she looked at Katy now, not rushing her words. "Once more, I offer to you my deepest apologies."

"Oh," Katy hurried to reassure her, "please don't worry. I'm just happy to meet another friend of Bay and Lia, and I promise I'm okay." That was stretching the truth to be sure, but now was the time to move past this argument, not marinate in negativity.

Orihei tilted her head then gave a single, sharp bob. "Very well. I give thanks for your understanding and forgiveness, Katy Phelan. You must be as much the miracle as Vailillia has told me you are." Features going grim she opened a wing and swept it toward the doorway. "Papu, Mama, I will escort you out." Her words and tone left no room for objection.

Their faces mulish, Abou and Couri walked away, refusing to speak or make eye contact with anyone else in the room. Katy saw several bystanders take deep breaths and shake their heads. It hadn't been pretty, that was for sure. How naïve she'd been to think everyone would jump aboard the herald train. She'd taken her lead from Bay who was such a believer, and Lia and Yuhwa. Even Lanu had accepted it without question. Yfaun was scared of its truth, so much so he would kill her for it. She'd kind of assumed everyone on this ship would be like the boisterous group that met their arrival yesterday.

No one else knew what the pendant had done once it went round her neck, though. How it had stopped time and rewritten the color of the Aoni for an eternal second. One second that altered everything inside her. Bay had gotten the tiniest hint of it, he'd said, but for Katy it had been a shift in her blood and marrow, her very soul. The Air had chimed in to let her know this was important, fundamental and big in a way nothing before it had been.

This was what she had to remember when faced with skeptics. Faith only took you so far. Hell, these two weren't even the first of the day: Oran had made it very clear he didn't think there was a fart's chance in a hurricane that Katy was any version of a foretold savior. The whole herald thing was crazy, impossible, and yet she knew it was fated. Destined.

She turned to rest against Bay, hoping physical contact was acceptable in public. Katy needed his support and calming touch. He didn't flinch, nor did Lia drop her jaw or grimace, which seemed like a green light. Bay's arm slid around her shoulder, his hand gently massaging the back of her neck.

"When did they become doubters?" he asked Lia.

"It's a recent manifestation, Orihei says." Lia crossed her arms. "I think it's possible she's been ignoring signs for longer, though. Let's put that out of our minds now," she said in a bright voice. "Raisa says we are to dine together and has tasked me with 'picking her up' on our walk. Aoiti haven't helped me understand why I should lift her in the air, can you clarify?"

Katy laughed for the first time all day.

17

As he watched his sister explain various foods to Raisa and Katy, Bay fought to glide beyond the anger he felt. That Couri and Abou would confront them in public – air their loss of faith to everyone around them like it wasn't their problem but his – it seemed impossible. Yet it had just happened.

Katy laughed, amused by one of the cooks pressing her to try something freshly made. There would be no replicated food for the Humans tonight with all four on-duty chefs vying for their attention. This would be good for their little fellowship, a reset after the discord and hopefully restful before they arrived at Centris. Once they were on the Wheel Bay feared it would be a whirlwind; non-stop meetings, talks, studying manuscripts and getting the Humans used to interstellar governance and land-scapes, all the political nuances.

Should he send a message ahead? He and Vailillia had debated, both erring on the side of caution. It was unlikely a message could be intercepted, but there was no guarantee of the recipient keeping quiet. And as his shipmates had just proven, not all would believe or respect Katy's role just because he knew it to be true. On the other hand, any sal-angs remaining before arrival could be used to begin research, to locate ancient texts or anything that could help them determine how Katy fulfilled her role as Kawakona.

All the seekers had was the Prophecy of Hunanjanno jo Bikajo, something they were taught from birth. It was often part of scholastic call and response exercises, and only the jo Bikajo line knew all of it. Bay didn't think there was much in there that would be useful, though. They needed more than names of Drazoen essences and flowery words that invoked their divine mandate. If all he'd needed to do was get the herald linked to the spark, it would have happened already. Sundancer would be here. But She wasn't, so they must need more.

Wiremu entered the dining hall, disrupting Bay's increasingly negative thoughts. The captain led a contingent of entire families, Wiremu's own and many more. Quite rapidly a room that had felt spacious seemed close and jovial. All the newcomers stood arrayed behind Wiremu, looking over at Raisa and Katy with combinations of awe, excitement, and intrigue. Children yet to fledge peeked around adults, jostling for a better view of the Kawakona.

"The wind favors you tonight, Djilbay," Wiremu called. "It brought me rumors of recent unpleasant conversation, so that I might gather those who see things differently as an antidote. As all know, ugly words are no more than bad breath we dispel with revelry. Singing, storytelling, a drink or two – this cleans foul air." He gestured behind him to the forty or more seekers and laughed. "If your Kawakona and her friend don't object, we would like to share food and festivity. In honor of our long-held task as seekers coming to fruition!"

Another voice cried, "And jubilation at the future to come!"

Their words triggered hoots and shouts from the whole group, which startled Raisa and Katy into glancing over. Katy looked nervous walking to Bay's side. "This isn't a mob of angry villagers, right?"

There was a short, silent moment while each of the seekers' aoiti translated her words. Kweza had been updating the *Eternidad* database with English the whole time, refining it as Katy and Raisa's aoiti gave feedback. But for most it would be the first time they heard the Human language. A brave young boy darted forward, looking up at Katy in adoring wonder. "Do you live in villages on your planet? In these mobs?" His attempt at the unique English word came out like *mawps*.

Katy, charmed, bent down. "We live in all sorts of villages, towns, cities. Big and small. You name it, we live in it. But not in mobs, those are … temporary. Usually made of angry people, not cuties like you."

Rapt, the boy reached out, stopping short of touching her. Mikanjo always requested permission for physical contact, but Katy didn't know that when she took his hand in hers, smiling. "I'm Katy, what's your name?"

Assuming the handshake was permission, he launched himself at her for a hug. Thankfully he didn't have wings yet, otherwise Bay knew he'd have slapped Katy in the face with them. "I am Zazi jo Bikajo, Kawakona! I can call you Katy?" He pulled back to whisper, "I will be envied by all, and it will be *wonderful*." His eyes rounded, nearly bulging out of his cherubic face. "Can I tell everyone we are friends now, Katy?"

Her grin was equally enthusiastic. "I insist, Zazi. Having a smart and brave friend like you is what I need if I'm going to find my dragon."

She booped his nose with a finger, a Human gesture unfamiliar to Mikanjo, but Zazi was overjoyed. Bay was thrilled himself to hear Katy refer to Sundancer as her dragon. Surely that was a step toward whatever spiritual alchemy was necessary to fully become Kawakona.

"Son," Wiremu called out exaggeratedly. "Will you introduce us to your new friend? You know we are all eager to celebrate her." Katy smothered her laughter when Zazi gave his papu a dirty look. Wiremu's tone turned teasing. "Remember that Vashti has brought her ship-renowned baijur crackle for dessert?"

At those words Zazi's face transformed and he clutched Katy's hand, pulling her toward the group. "It is the best baijur you will ever have, friend Katy!" Delighting in his role as Katy's companion he bellowed, "Everyone! This is my friend, Katy. She is Kawakona and I love her. You must too, even if you can't be her friend as I am."

Raucous laughter erupted, and Bay felt every last measure of stress from earlier dissipate. Orihei's parents had clouded his mind with their vitriol, but this? These were the Mikanjo he knew, loved, and had missed every tuig on Earth. Compassionate, inclusive, honest and good. Katy had signaled Raisa to join them, and she, too, was enfolded into the melee of seekers trying to be simultaneously respectful and attention hogs, as Humans might say. Zazi never left Katy's side or dropped her hand. Wiremu looked Bay's way and nodded. How like the wise and honorable man, to hear what had transpired and organize the perfect counterbalance for it.

Vailillia called him over. "They're cooking a true feast for everyone. This will be like Pisha Bayo."

Bay agreed. Whether it was called Pisha Bayo, Thanksgiving, Ostara, or Ramadan, species Aoni-wide understood the value of shared food and celebration. He also knew once Katy and Raisa tasted the baijur crackle, let the nutty sweetness melt on their tongues, they'd be hooked. He couldn't wait for his own share of Vashti's treat.

Vailillia looked at the happy, hopeful faces of the seekers surrounding the Humans. "I think we all need this, a way to accept that the obligation our people were given has been met."

They gazed at the group, busy reconfiguring tables and getting seated. "You realize this means we can all go 'home'?"

Bay's mouth dropped open. He'd honestly not thought of it, focused as he was on Katy and the work still to be done. But Vailillia was right. Once Sundancer awoke the seekers were free, not bound to the ships any longer. It had never been the prophecy that Mikanjo would wake all the Drazoen or find each Kawakona, not the way he read it…. But that was his reading. He knew others interpreted it differently. There would be many thrilled to assume Katy's arrival meant an end to their wandering. Just as many might argue they couldn't return to Bankiri until all Nine Drazoen were back and they'd sought each herald.

This was an argument for philosophers and academics, he decided. His place was with Katy, and wherever she landed so would he. At the moment that meant he needed to sneak back to the group and secure his spot at her side before someone could steal his chair.

BAY HAD SHOWN Katy to the part of the ship that simulated other environments. She was happy and relaxed, lightly buzzed from the magnificent elixir Yuhwa had brought to the party when she arrived.

"Started without me, I see," Yuhwa had laughed as Zazi climbed back in Katy's lap, giving the pilot back off side-eye. The boy was very into claiming her. "There were a few final course adjustments the navigation team and I had to perform. But we are on schedule to arrive at Centris in eleven sal-angs. Time enough for a drink!"

Katy was smarter today than yesterday and stopped after two glasses of the wickedly good drink. **Rusim** *roo-sim; Jadoube wine brewed from fermented unripened vài.* The bevvy itself translated to a warm, soft buzz in her veins and tingling in the hand holding Bay's. Even more lovely sensations in the shoulder brushing his wing.

He'd said he wanted to sit on the shore of Lake Mwanaburo with her before they slept. She wasn't sure if he meant the kind of "slept" she'd like him to mean, and still didn't feel confident pushing for more physical intimacy. In lieu of nookie, Katy wanted to enjoy these last hours before docking. Her half-ass math had calculated their time remaining on the *Eternidad* was about fifteen Earth hours. Minutes aplenty to spend with her handsome man by a lake under midnight sim-skies.

Eventually the party ended and Bay escorted her to the huge section of the ship designed the replicate the lake of their home planet. Bay said it was effectively the center of their civilization on Bankiri. Everyone lived near its shores, which were surrounded by forests and canyons. This version just had the lake, but it was gorgeous. Royal purple and big as one of the Great Lakes. They held hands and meandered along a natural dirt path illuminated by white paper lanterns.

Would paper be something aliens would use? Or was this made of an advanced material? There were trees in this simulated landscape, but maybe advanced species didn't use their natural resources with the same abandon Humans did? Katy filed those as more questions for another time. Boy was that list getting long, between her and Riri having five or ten new items an hour it seemed.

As they circled the edge of the lake Katy asked, "Is this actual size? Compared to back home, I mean."

Bay's expression was stress-free and open. "The real lake is several times larger I'm told. There are cliffside dwellings, some cultivated plateaus, different styles of living depending on whether you fish or farm." His eyes seemed to dim a little. "That is, of course, only what I've been taught and seen in vids or photos. When our mothers call us, we catch glimpses of the lake far below them, so we think they have accommodations in the upper cliffs."

"You 'think'?"

He steered them to a bench built for Mikanjo; it had no back and her toes didn't touch ground. Katy took the opportunity to snuggle into Bay.

"I've been out of contact for a while," he said wryly. "But even before then, calls are restricted. Vailillia might know more, have had other calls with them after I left."

"I don't understand. Why would there be restriction?"

"When seekers falter and doubt, they can leave the ships and return to Bankiri, but must also resign themselves to only contacting those who remained once a bisous. A decade." When Katy lifted her head in shock he explained, "The hope is that their failure… their doubts don't carry through to others, infect those still on ship. You heard Couri and Abou. Imagine if they were back home, calling Orihei and demanding she leave as well. For those reasons there are limits on communication."

Katy hugged Bay tightly, reminded anew how lonely and difficult the path was for these seekers. She hardened her resolve to be the Kawakona they needed, so their people could reunite or, at least, ease up on the sacred duty thing. The Air, she noted with amusement, had composed a brief high and piped phrase whenever she thought of herself as Kawakona. And when did that change from herald, she wondered? Herald wasn't entirely right in her mind anymore, because Kawakona was what Bay and the others believed her to be, and she was determined to succeed. Her aoiti had layered shades and nuance every time one of the seekers used the word, and it had come to mean so much more than herald. It was harbinger and hero, it encompassed hope and potential, the fulmination of dreams, even a hint of cosmic mystery.

She thought of the night flight she and Bay had shared back on Earth. What she'd felt that night, staring up at a carpet of stars, reveling in the glory, wondering what was coming next. That was the feeling the word Kawakona gave her now. Katy pressed into Bay's warmth, turning her head to get a sniff of his scrumptious natural scent. She wanted more of it, of him, but they weren't completely alone out here. Mikanjo walked behind them on the path, some flew overhead. All very respectful, but watching them nonetheless. She decided to overrule some of her cautious thoughts and ask for what she wanted.

"Can we fly again? If that isn't presumptuous?"

Bay's smile was a hint roguish. "I would love to fly with you, *qania*. You had only to ask."

Soon they soared up toward the black sim-sky, making lazy loops all over the lake, cliffs and trees. Over and over, Katy thrilling and laughing like it was an amusement park ride. Best of all was having Bay's arms wrapped so tightly around her. He was heat, excitement and safety rolled into a dazzling package. Her thighs clenched with desire when he nuzzled the side of her neck, kissing below her ear.

"If you wrap your legs tightly around me, I can do a dive almost to the lake surface." He pulled back, gave her a wicked smirk. "But you have to hold on tight. Very tight." They'd climbed so high they were alone in the sim-skies.

Full steam ahead, Katy thought. Sexy innuendo meant she could get a little more of what she wanted from this man. Exhilaration, sensuality, and something starting to feel deeper. Not love yet, but in that neighborhood. He was fast becoming fundamental to her happiness.

She did worry this was all going too fast. That maybe she was filling a role he'd dreamt about for so long none of this was about her. What if someone else had pinged and zinged the necklace, would he want that person they way he seemed to want her tonight? Katy knew she was young to him, and still naïve about the Aoni she and Riri were scrambling to learn. Would that come to bother him?

Katy notched her thighs on his hipbones. Those were worries for another time. When she locked her ankles above his bubble butt, the bottom of his wings brushed her shins. She shivered at the sensation, her mind whirling when she thought she might get to feel that everywhere. If not tonight, soon.

Bay clamped his hands hard on her hips, not bruising but firm. One hand slid to the small of her back and she cursed the bodysuit denying her skin-to-skin contact in that sensitive area. She pressed up with her thighs so her lips were even with his collarbone, where first she kissed, then licked. He shuddered and squeezed her tighter in response. Katy went in for another taste, higher on his throat. Bay's spiced scent married with a hint of lemon on her tongue, very addictive.

His voice rumbled over her eardrum, so deep it was like a double bass bowed at the lowest register. "Steady now, hold tight."

They dropped straight down. Katy tried not to shriek, but they were stones falling from the sky and it was a tie between thrilling and terrifying. Trust, always about trust. She intertwined her fingers, hands already behind his neck, and looked into his eyes. He watched her with growing hunger, ducked in for a quick kiss, then threw his head back. Suddenly they were flipping, looping, twisting. She thought they'd score tens from the Olympic high dive judges, her stomach clenching from more than arousal, her heart pounding. They ended the tumbles, now rocketing head first to the water, closer, closer, until his wings spread, turning their freefall into a glide. Fast, shooting them across the surface of the lake, its plum-tinted water glassy until they passed, trailing a wake of navy caps.

Bay studied her eyes and face, checking how she'd handled the daredevil moves. Katy, giddy with adrenaline, lunged up to kiss him with no thought other than she would never get enough of her seeker. He flipped them as they kissed so she rested on his body. That freed his hands to wander, which they did with great liberty. Caresses to her sides, her butt, sliding up to her breasts. The suit stopped him from doing much more than stroking them, but it was incredible. Perfection. Their kisses heated, and she let her hands do a little exploration, too.

Bay's chest was hard and absolutely gigantic under his bodysuit. She supposed the muscles he needed to fly with those wings required substantial real estate. He was just so big. Tall, broad, thighs bigger than any hurling or rugby player she'd ever seen. Arms sure to rival Atlas holding up the Earth, steady and roped with muscle. Katy rubbed her hands over his biceps which bunched as he continued his exploration of her chest. She felt her empty core clench, looking for something to grab onto. She was more turned on than she'd ever been, but wanted one more trip before they (hopefully) went to bed and kept exploring thrills of a different nature.

Breaking off their kiss, gasping for breath, she managed to blurt, "Again?"

Flipping them back over, Bay roared with laughter and elation as he started their ascent. "Once more for my special sparkle princess!"

BAY FINALLY SHOWED her to his room, after they'd had their second grand swoop and another heavy petting session. Katy was trembling with want by the time his door shut behind them. Forced to behave themselves on the longest journey in history to get back to the living quarters, she hurtled into his arms now they had privacy. Which wasn't much of a hurtle, to be honest, because he'd not gotten more than three inches away from her the entire walk back to his place.

They picked up where they'd left off in the lake chamber, kissing and rubbing, stroking still-hidden body parts, licking available skin. Katy had never been this aroused, and had revised her opinion that Bay might be untouched. The man knew where to put those fine craftsman hands, deadly precise all right, and she was unravelling. She didn't know how far they'd go, but she knew she wanted to get her hands on as much of him as possible.

Bay obviously felt the same: he picked her up and carried her to the huge bed in the corner. Laying her down gently, he came down at her side and put a finger to the tab that would open the bodysuit. Breaking their kiss, he looked down and said, "May I?"

"Yesyesyes," she moaned, pulling him back down for another kiss. Before she could even register the cooler air against newly bared skin, the heat and light touch of Bay's palm shocked her. Goose pimples erupted in the wake of his gentle brush.

"Want to touch every inch of skin, *qania*, lick you head to toe and hear you cry out," he murmured. Bay suited word to deed. Katy couldn't be mad at the loss of his mouth on hers when he put it to better use against the hollow of her throat, her upper chest, the underside of her breasts and finally her nipples. "Have never desired anything, not even seeking, as much as this," he rasped hoarsely before reapplying himself to his good works.

Bay kissed Sundancer's pendant as well, each time he switched breasts. He treated it as though it were a sacred object or luck charm, which she supposed it was. Each time he bussed the carnelian, Katy would swear it warmed against her chest.

She was nearly coming out of her skin. He felt so good, perfect pressure, suction, giving each breast equal time and attention. She thought that deserved recognition and reward, so she pulled one hand out of his hair and reached for the fastener to his suit. "Please?" she whimpered.

Bay nodded but didn't break off from his suckling and licking. Her breasts felt so heavy and ripe in his hands, worshipped by his tongue. She struggled to open his suit and push it over his shoulders, where it caught against his wings. Damn the shite, this was beyond her skills at the moment. "Help," she whined.

He reluctantly let go of her to sit back, doing something twisty, and the top half of his suit fell to his waist. She took the opportunity to shrug out of the top half of hers, and then they came back together. More euphoric kisses, caresses, a shiftin' session to beat them all. If Bay applied this kind of time and attention to details on his jewelry designs, no wonder his pendant would raise a demigod. The longer they went on, the louder the Air got in her mind, surging and releasing, cresting and plunging, a mimicry of the act she desperately wanted to engage in with Bay.

Katy's hand slipped down to his crotch and he jolted before crushing her to him, trapping her palm. He pulled back, chest heaving, and put his hand over hers. What she felt was substantial and eye-widening, but she was eager to keep going. Bay's hand stopped hers, though.

"Wait. We're, I, you, I don't know if you're ready," he started.

"More than," she replied, changing from an open palm to a tender grip. "But we won't do anything you don't want." He wasn't pulling her hand away, so she left it there, hoping this wasn't the end.

He groaned and pressed into her hold. "We're different than human men," he said. "His gaze was earnest and slightly worried. "Not in basic form, fit, function, but appearance..." he trailed off.

Katy was nothing but more intrigued. Was it a different color? Did it have surprise tricks? Felt like the same shape. "Show me," she pleaded.

He took a deep breath and shoved the suit down to his thighs, dislodging her hand. She looked down and said, "Oh!" When she looked back at his face there was dismay and she hurried to reassure him. "You just have wee feathers instead of hair, not a big deal. Oh, look, they're the same color as the accent ones up here." She rubbed the top wing ridge of aqua feathers. "I love it."

Bay's expression eased. "Our reproductive center is internal, too. No Human scrotum. Those two differences meant being very careful about nudity on Earth." He shrugged, still uncomfortable, and Katy couldn't have that.

She put her hand back on him, thrilled when he responded instantaneously. The moment wasn't lost. "You had to hide so much of yourself for so long," she whispered as she started stroking him. "But not anymore. Not with me, *mo chroí*." Katy shifted closer to his body as her fingers squeezed and caressed him and his breathing shallowed.

He let her have her way for precious minutes, his muscles clenched as he shook from her ministrations. At last he broke, teeth gritted and a hoarse cry echoing in the room. They kissed intently as he finished, then languidly as he relaxed. Katy was so happy he'd trusted her enough to let her touch him intimately, she'd almost forgotten her own need.

Bay hadn't, though. His touch became purposeful once again, not stopping at her breasts this time, but slinking down inside the front of her bodysuit, still clinging to her hips. Those master craftsman digits slipped around then into her core. She was very wet, the excitement of touching Bay having provoked waves of damp arousal that slicked his way. Their kisses became frantic as he touched her all over, discovering all the spots that made her squeak and quiver. Katy might have been embarrassed about the noises she made, but each one made him grunt or groan and work her harder, faster.

In a mortifyingly short time she shattered, his long fingers bringing her over the edge with perfect touch and timing. Katy was panting, sweating, and grinning like a loon. Which beat the crying she'd been a smidge worried might happen. Emotions were tricky. She rolled into the crook of his arm, over part of his wing, boneless and sated.

"Is this okay?" she asked, stroking the feathers cradling the side of her body. "I'm not too heavy, or trapping your wing?"

Bay kissed her forehead, her nose, her lips. "Any bit of you is always welcome to lay on any part of me."

In a few more hours they would get to Centris and the crazy chase to solve the Sundancer mystery would kick into high gear. But for now, she was happy down to the bottom of her toes, wrapped in an alien's wings on a spaceship headed to the center of the Universe. Maybe it was the steady childhood diet of folk-lore and tall tales, maybe it was just her nature, but none of it seemed scary anymore. The Air, which had crescendoed right along with her, was quiescent now, a calando purr. Katy's eyes closed, body replete and enjoying the shelter of Bay's arms.

18

Arrival at Centris was perfectly choreographed, despite the unceasing traffic and overwhelming size of the docking port. Yuhwa said as far as she knew the *Eternidad* hadn't stopped here in several milenyo, longer than Bay or Lia had been alive. But she had lived here after an earlier pilot gig, before joining the *Eternidad*, and was familiar with recent protocols. A hundred years ago was recent in alien life, something Humans were probably going to struggle with.

Katy stood with her nose pressed to the windows, side-by-side with Riri, both of them gasping as the station and multiple port openings came clearly into view. Forced to go as slowly as they were, the sights had plenty of opportunity to boggle their minds. Smaller ships darted in and out of other portals to the right and left of the one they aimed toward. Compared to the station and the *Eternidad*, those smaller craft looked like flies zipping around a massive cylindrical tube. Basically this port was like a quarter of an inner tube plonked out here as the first stop on the way to Centris.

Most of the movies and TV shows she'd ever seen made the outsides of every spaceship, station, or galactic building look like some bored kid got hold of a two-thousand-piece model set and glue. Not this one: the sides of the curved port had a smooth surface, neutral matte finish. No random and unruly antennae or ladders here, just an expanse of tan panels broken only by huge swathes of windows facing incoming ships and the system beyond.

Before they'd gotten so close, Katy and Raisa had glimpsed Centris beyond the dock. Where they would land was attached by a corridor to the top circle of the Wheel. Lia said that was called the sky ring, and just beyond it they could see another wheel (mid ring) and finally a sphere in the center (core). All were attached by nine spokes, one for each of the Drazoen who'd created this place. Lia said the primary port would drop them into Giftgiver Red's spoke, and from there they'd take the tram to the Chorus.

"I was attacked and poisoned, have flown on a spacecraft that can go through black holes, met aliens with tails and wings and fluorescent tattoos, yet only now do I feel we have really left Earth." Riri's voice was coated with excitement. She grabbed Katy's arm. "We are in deep space, somewhere light years beyond 'outer' space. This is incredible!"

Katy shared her delight. "We'll be the first of our kind!" Her smile turned wry. "Nearly guaranteed I'm going to say or do something gormless. There's a risk Humans won't get accepted as an advanced species if I'm left to my own devices." She sighed. "Bay says we have to plan strategically before making announcements. I can't damage too much if we slow roll our reveal, right?"

"That's a problem for bureaucrats to handle, I say," her friend consoled her. "Our job is to figure out how to wake up your Sundancer and fulfill your great destiny. Ready?"

They clasped hands and turned from windows that had dimmed as they entered the landing pad. Lia and Bay were a short walk down the corridor, ready to lead them off the ship and into this bustling hub. The Wheel of Centris. Something that seemed a distant tale when she'd first heard it, like legends of fairy mounds or kingdoms hidden in magical mists. But now they were here, it was extremely real, and Katy was ready to see everything.

Only after a tense standoff with Centris customs and immigration, apparently. Over an hour after docking they were still on the ship, not allowed to disembark. Katy tried not to fidget at the delay, or worry that Yuhwa had now joined Bay and Lia in an effort to expedite the process. Their group had been stopped right away when they tried to leave, which Bay told them he'd expected and planned around.

One of the two port officials was a Jadoube that Yuhwa had greeted; unlike Katy's friend, this Jadoube had silvery tattoos lacing their forearms. The second station lackey was honest-to-God a piece of floating coral. As in, if you took part of the Great Barrier Reef, coated it in a rust-colored metal, and let it breathe in regular air, that was this.

Eng, *ancient species; multi-planetary, able to link consciousness.*

"Did you just get that?" she murmured to Riri, who confirmed with wide eyes. "We get tips on everything, not just word definitions. That's cracking!"

"We cannot process this pair, no matter you say their aoiti are malfunctioning." This from the floating coral, though Katy hadn't a clue where the voice came from. "No one without documentation enters Centris. Without aoiti, they have no documentation."

This was the standoff initiated sixty minutes ago: they were unable to pass the exit portal because while the Humans were being vouched for by the seekers, they didn't have anything close to a passport for Centris. Announcing they were the vanguard of a brand-new species to the Wheel (and the Calling) had to be handled carefully; Bay was relying on his Mikanjo contacts and the Chorus Cadre of voices to navigate that political morass. Until then no spoilers.

Katy heard various noises just outside, a bustle and energy that reminded her of Heathrow airport, or Frankfurt Central Station (where she'd gotten very lost once). But she couldn't see anything and it was frustrating. Her anxiety to get out, off, free of the *Eternidad* mounted. Raisa, beside her, must have felt similarly because she kept raising on her tiptoes trying to peek out the doors. Even before getting off this boat they'd seen another new species! Except for the Krylar who'd been banned and Uilig who opted out, they might get to see all the other species out there. Not to mention the food, clothing and architecture waiting to be admired! It was all so thrilling they could barely restrain themselves.

Bay was frustrated despite anticipating this hurdle to disembarking. Their morning had been perfect, slow and sweet with cuddles and kisses and a tad bit more shiftin' to be had. Katy thought she could spend all her time snuggled in bed with Bay, warmed by his feathers and touch. At this moment, though his ire didn't blatantly show, he wasn't his usual friendly self either. He didn't raise his voice when he demanded the officials contact someone called Swailu jo Faluji, but was short with them. He'd given this Swailu a title that came through as **Toledral speaker** *toe-leh-drawl; revered counselor roles held by only two Mikanjo at a time. Act as mediators and advisors to the Calling.* All right then, Bay was calling in the big guns.

After a brief wait where she tried not to gawk at the Eng (who defied her entire understanding of what sentience could look like), Katy saw a gorgeous woman in flowing fabrics join the officials in the passageway. Sable hair, styled away from her face, fell to her shoulders. Regal posture, yet soft and friendly. Sophia Lauren with a complexion of fresh nutmeg and snow-white wings. Bay's face lit up, almost childlike.

After a moment of blankness, Swailu beamed with recognition. "Djilbay jo Bikajo, I think? By the Nine, it has been long tuigs. And yet your smile is the same as that impish boy I met on my journey here." Her genuine happiness at seeing Bay immediately set Katy at ease.

"Yes, Speaker. You told me *"You must reach for the impossible to do the unimaginable. To raise dragons, one must swim through stars"* and I carried those words the entire time I traveled." He looked back to Katy, warmth in his smile.

Lia greeted Swailu, and the conversation with the officials continued anew. Swailu never lost her serene countenance as she suggested the word of a Toledral speaker should be accepted by these administrators. This woman wouldn't doubt Bay or be acrimonious, Katy sensed; she would smooth their way. They would be off the *Eternidad* in no time and out into the exciting beyond. Just as she thought that, the man who stepped into the entry beside Swailu made her take an involuntary step backward.

If he'd been Human and not Jadoube, Katy would say he looked like a character from a Wuxia drama. Long black hair pulled back into a top-knot with a slick waterfall of loose hair cascading to his shoulders. Silver tattoos like the Jadoube offi-cial, but his were all over his neck and possibly continued down his chest. He fairly bristled with competence, the end of a bō staff peeking over his shoulder, and had an attitude that said he expected to be obeyed.

"Pashmam!" Riri hissed. "They've called intergalactic police warriors and now we'll end up in jail. Baba was right again!"

Pashmam پشمام *posh-mom; Persian slang indicating shock, surprise.*

"Your dad thought we'd end up in *jail*? Of all the possible options, death still being one of them, he went with jail?"

Raisa shrugged. "I didn't tell him everything about Yfaun. That would have gotten," she paused, "very unpleasant. If he thought daiva, demons, were after us there would have been so much shouting. You would have heard it in your own room."

Swailu's voice interrupted their side conversation. The armed Jadoube now stood slightly behind her right side, out of the way of her wing if it were to extend. Katy had the impression they'd known each other a long time, and this was a subconscious habit.

"Presumably you know Tangun Ye-Na, Head of the Swords?" she said to the bureaucrats. "He, too, vouches for the pair with malfunctioning aoiti. Once we get them back online we will register them properly, as we have asserted. Repeatedly."

Maybe it was the intimidating presence of this Tangun dude, maybe it was Swailu's implacable resolve, maybe they were just fed up, but at last the officials relented. As they departed the ship, Bay and Lia beckoned to the Humans. This was it!

Time to begin Katy's Great Adventure Phase Two: Hopefully Less Deadly.

As they approached, Swailu turned her head and smiled kindly. Katy felt like she'd been hugged, the kind of warm and loving embrace her Grandmum Brigit would give. No matter Swailu looked younger than Katy herself, there was a powerful grandma vibe there.

When they reached a safe distance from people milling around the *Eternidad* she said, "Kawakona, how I am honored to meet you at last. Your seeker promised me long ago he would find you, and it seems he told no lies." She laughed. "I am Swailu jo Faluji. My Mikanjo line was named in alignment with your Drazoen, Irojaku jo Faluji."

"I thought that was a great portent when we met," Bay interjected. "You must have tired of my proclamations and antics back then!"

"You were a sign to me as well, Djilbay. My first work as a speaker was with you." She refocused on Katy. "And his dreams came true. It is a great privilege to meet you. May I ask your name?"

"Katy Phelan," she said, sticking out a hand to shake. She lowered it, embarrassed, when Swailu and Tangun just stared at her palm. She kept forgetting it wasn't the norm to casually touch amongst the Mikanjo. Even when they did, this was the wrong greeting anyway. Two seconds in and she was borking this Kawakona thing!

"The custom of their species is to clasp hands and move them. Like this," Bay said, shaking Katy's hand.

Tangun's left eyebrow came up and he tensed slightly when Swailu leaned forward to try the handshake. What was the story there? Had he needed to protect her in the past, or acted as her bodyguard even now? How safe was Centris if so-called beloved mediators needed protecting by the head of the Swords? Yuhwa said they were like the special forces of the Calling

Swailu's skin was soft and dry; she wasn't nervous about meeting the prophesied herald of a dragon. "A delight, *Kaytee Pheelan*. This is momentous, there hasn't been a Prima in nearly a kōmilen. Not since the Muškikal presented. Your species, they are called by what name?"

Katy waited for a translation of that mush-sounding word but nothing happened. The pause had gotten awkward, meantime, and she blurted, "Human! We're Humans, from Earth. This is my friend, Raisa Leon. Also Human. From Earth."

Riri stared at her like she'd thrown a gutter ball to lose the game. Tangun and Swailu had matching puzzled expressions.

"We haven't uploaded Human languages to the common frame," Lia said. "But they understand you." She translated what Katy had just said for their benefit.

"*Hewman*," Swailu repeated, exaggerating the middle ew sound. Then again, "Katy Phelan and Raisa Leon the Humans from Aarth. Meeting you is another honor, Raisa Leon," she added. Riri was smart enough to just bow her head respectfully and avoid the handshake awkwardness.

Katy was dumbfounded. This astonishing winged counselor had brought home just how out of their depth they were with a single sentence: *Katy Phelan and Raisa Leon the Humans from Earth.* How the hell were two librarians from Seattle supposed to represent their entire species in this huge assembly? The beings before and all around her weren't the aliens, she and Raisa were.

Swailu said to Lia and Bay, "I regret cutting short our introductions, but we shouldn't allow the clerks a chance to rethink their decision." She gestured over her shoulder at Tangun and smiled wryly. "My faithful compatriot can only induce fearful obedience for so long. Shall we go? I brought a Toledral sled, which will get us to the Chorus faster than the tram."

"Yuhwa, you will accompany us," Tangun spoke for the first time. His voice wasn't deep but had a roughness to it, a spent-all-night-at-a-concert hoarseness. Looking at him Katy was pretty sure a bender hadn't been the case, but there was no telling if he'd suffered trauma or if that was just his voice. The dude openly carried a weapon: previous injury seemed plausible.

"After we leave your fellows at the Chorus we'll speak at the Arena."

"I can't leave my friends," Yuhwa tried.

"They will be safe, and we need to discuss what you will do after the nawa calls you home." His face was fixed and cool, his voice measured, but his words made Yuhwa blanch.

"You've heard?"

"No, not yet. But I would expect soon."

Katy took her newest friend's hand and squeezed. "The aoiti are failing me right now, but we'll be here when you need us for whatever that nah-wa thing is."

Yuhwa's gaze shuttered, though she tightened her grip briefly before dropping Katy's hand. "If you can keep me busy waking your dragon and off that path a while longer, I will keep you in rusim for life."

"Deal," Katy murmured. To break the tension she chirped, "Time to get this show on the road!" forgetting Swailu and Tangun couldn't understand her. Bay translated, understanding blossomed on their faces, and finally Katy stepped away from the *Eternidad* and fully into the docking bay of Centris' primary port.

"It's so…organized," Raisa marveled.

Katy agreed. There was plenty of noise, given the number of spaceships docked in this wedge of the bay. Tubes and machines hooked into the Mikanjo Seeking Ship, fueling or cleaning or who knows what, and Katy saw rapt faces all around them. Mikanjo docking must be a pretty rare event. Clear dividers, floor to very high ceiling, revealed several other wedges that grouped craft together like theirs. It was a space port built like an octagonal Trivial Pursuit game piece. Most of the spots were filled with ships much smaller than the *Eternidad*, parked in an orderly and accessible way. Shockingly tall, thin aliens with three eyes and skin of solid color (chosen from the whole rainbow) walked quickly through the structured floor plan. They must be the mechanics, based on the uniforms they wore and their proximity to every spacecraft. Katy bet Raisa remembered their name, but was scared to ask and blow their cover if she were overheard.

She and Riri followed their party to a large travel sled. Fancier than most on the *Eternidad*, this one had solid half-walls going around it, and even a couple of couches. The paint job was neutral, a pair of spread wings wrapping the sides.

New species were everywhere, as far as Katy could see. They passed more Jadoube, a couple of the Eng, whoever the Gumby-style ones were, and Chitans with tails a-twitching. Even a few PQ, which made both her and Riri shrink back. Logically not every Pu'ulqaari would be evil like Yfaun, but that terrifying day at Pike Place was too recent for them not to flinch. The PQ didn't even give them second glances, far more interested in the sight of three Mikanjo. Looked like what Bay had told her about their wings being equally coveted and shunned was true. More worrying was Yfaun's threat back at the refuge. Katy prayed these weren't wing-hunting PQ.

Once aboard the sled, Katy and Raisa migrated to the front so they could watch everything go by. Those clear walls between the docking sections meant they'd seen the large portal leading out of the bay, but passing through it felt momentous. Particularly when they caught sight of multiple other portals exactly like theirs.

"How many?" Katy asked Bay. He moved over and put his arm around her. "How many of these docking thingies?"

"Six full landing pads, I believe, in the primary port," he said, glancing back at Swailu and Tangun to confirm.

Swailu, seated, her gorgeous floaty dress draped perfectly, confirmed. "Six here to accommodate all the tourism and business travelers. There is also a smaller port; only for members of the Calling, or citizens vital to Calling business. Just three docks there, heavily guarded."

Tangun remained standing, near Swailu as always. Yuhwa had picked the second couch to sit on, and looked down at her hands rather than their surroundings. Whatever Tangun had said to her put her in a major funk. Katy made a mental note to check on Yuhwa later, when they were away from the stern Sword.

Their sled continued at a sedate but intrepid pace. Things Katy desperately wanted to stop and see passed by too quickly: this wing, jutting off the main Wheel of Centris, was jam packed with people coming and going. Luggage, cargo, families and business people, it was all familiar and yet completely foreign. The style of a help/information desk was universal, even if she couldn't read the sign. PQ faces (with their funky face bonding thing) were less shocking now, even the Chitan tails and the third eyes of the mechanic people had stopped surprising her.

But here came new people, ones with eyes two- or three-times Human size, brightly dressed, carrying instruments and running for the tram. Were these the Lunari, the ones Bay and Lia said ran the Chorus? The ones Lanu said had lost their planet to the scary Krylar?

Their instruments closely matched Earth versions of them: violin, saxophone, a clarinet; each was just like what she'd see at home. She marveled how the Drazoen had entrenched these things into the base materials that ultimately evolved into sentient species. Music was part of every culture, and it made her long for her flute. This journey was the longest she'd ever gone without music, either playing or listening.

"Look there!" hissed Riri, pointing to the left side of the sled as subtly as she could. Being gawping rubes was one thing, being rude and disrespectful was another.

What Raisa had noticed was a group of male models at the mouth of the port. Would they have modeling in the Aoni? If they did, this crew had to be favorites for the industry. They were bipedal like most, but their skin or makeup highlighted scales and seaweed patterns all over their faces and exposed arms. All four of them had slicked back hair, body-hugging clothing, lips that looked tinted and sugared, and they slouched against a counter in a way James Dean would have envied. They were tall, naturally.

Good lord, did the Drazoen only like tall species, was that why there were nothing but giants everywhere she looked?

These weren't fish people or mermen… but they were very aquatic looking. Katy couldn't remember which species they were, but had a vague memory of hearing about one favored by the blue dragon. Waterbringer, that was it. Guess the aquatic thing made sense if that was the name of the Drazoen in their corner.

Rixat *rix-ought; young species, home planet is Shilmand, located in the Tilhar system of the Ankhen galaxy.* Aoiti were back, thank the Lord.

The tram came into view, a sleek street-level multi-carriage conveyance with swarms of people boarding and exiting at the stop. They had been told the trams ran throughout the Wheel. It reminded her of Dublin's LUAS, or the tramlines she'd ridden in Vienna. These ones had no overhead lines or rails underneath, rather they floated an inch or so above the ground like the sled she rode on.

The far side of the sky ring, beyond the tram, was filled with trees, flowers and parkland. Not a cold, metallic space station, Centris was verdant and alive. Bird-like creatures flitted amongst the leaves of abundant, fantastical flora. Pumpkin colored tree trunks with chartreuse leaves shaded ponds of chalky, baby blue water. Teal bushes lined the paths meandering through peach lawns.

The near side of the ring was dotted with cafés, tables, and hotels or the equivalent, spreading out from the port entrance down the concourse. It was early, maybe nine in the morning CM, and Katy could smell nropita being served to passersby. After just a few days she knew that scent, had come to love it more than coffee back home. She was delighted to see carts serving it exactly like Seattle did. Right now, though, it was a gentle but distinct slap in the face.

The dissonance between mundane Earthlike activities (grabbing coffee and commuting) happening with people that looked like coral polyps floating through the air, car lot waving inflatables, or underwater Calvin Klein fantasies, was turning Katy's brain to mush. She could be looking at Marymoor Park back home, but for the head-height ferns that resembled creamsicles of swirled white and orange. This was Wonka-level whacky.

"I think," she said quietly to Riri, leaning more heavily into

Bay's side, "I'm out of processing power. I'm just going to look at everything and stop trying to categorize it."

Raisa agreed, voice muted. "There's so much, it's too much. In the best way, but too much nonetheless. My cousin calls it 'being out of spoons' and that is me right now."

"Same cousin who makes moonshine?" Riri shook her head. "You've got as many cousins as me, I reckon." Katy sighed. "It's pretty here. Proper gorgeous. That's all I've got."

Bay patted Raisa's shoulder. "I share your feelings. This is the first time Vailillia or I have come to Centris. We've met all these species before, when they travelled on the *Eternidad* over the tuigs. Seeing so many of them in one place, in large numbers, is astonishing, though." His left wing stretched a little, then resettled.

Swailu spoke up. "This is the upper spoke area of the Wheel, primarily suited for tourists and traders." The sled rose into the air, lifting above the people and trams. "We want to avoid the Calling assembly, which is why we'll travel down Giftgiver's upper spoke to the mid ring and enter the Chorus from there."

Realizing her explanation didn't mean much to the travelers on the sled, she clarified. "The Wheel is composed of the sky ring, mid ring, and core. Sky ring is mainly for the Calling, the Truth Arena of Swords," she gestured at Tangun, then pointed at herself, continuing, "and the Toledral speaker chambers. Along with short-term lodging for visitors. Mid ring houses the Chorus as well as offices for the multitudes it takes to support Calling ambassadors. You will also find extended stay establishments mid ring, places for those who may stay months but not perpetually. The core is where long-term or permanent residents live."

As Swailu spoke, their sled gathered a bit of speed. They were still well above people and trams below, but nowhere near a ceiling. Rationally Katy knew she was in a fabricated environment, a closed system created by marvelous creatures in a time long past. The size of this place, enclosed though it was, made it impossible to feel claustrophobic or trapped.

"Each of the rings is transected by a spoke, one for each of the Nine. We are now in the upper spoke of Giftgiver Red. Her subspoke is between mid ring and the core. That is generally how you'll navigate here. Should you need me after today, come to Windweaver upper spoke. Tangun and the rest of his Swords are found at Earthcaller's upper spoke."

Tangun nodded, serene. The man said a lot with a look and no words; Katy sensed he'd handle anything thrown at him in a level-headed way that cut through the bullshit.

In no time the sled reached the mid ring and turned, moving along the ring rather than down the spoke. Rather quickly they came to a nearly walled-off section of the ring and coasted to a stop. A flagstone path ran from the tram station on their left up to a grandiose door-gate combo. Blue vines, so dark as to be nearly black, climbed the walls surrounding the door at the end of the path. Teardrop-shaped flowers bloomed from the vines, silvery white and delicate.

"We're here," Swailu said as she stood. There had been a crowd jostling their way to the entry, but one look at her and they all shuffled to the side. Guess it was good to be a counselor respected and revered on the Wheel.

Bay looked down at Katy, saw the signs of her nerves, and snapped his wings around her to form a cocoon of safety. "Don't be worried. These are the most learned people on Centris, they'll know the right direction for us."

"I don't want to make trouble, and I'm worried sneaking us in here will do just that."

He smiled, crooked tooth peeking through, lifting her heart. "All will be well, Katy Phelan, I promise."

19

They weren't eaten or held prisoner by the flowering blue vines covering the entire wall, not that she'd seriously worried. But one of those things could have sung out "Feed me, Seymour!" and shame on Katy for being unprepared if it did. She knew she couldn't assume nature here was safe just because it was pretty. That's how people disappeared in foreign locales, presuming they knew how it all worked and everything would be fine. This was uncharted territory and she'd need to be smart.

Their party, headed by Swailu, was politely ushered through a hand-carved double-door made for great halls or royalty: this was an entry for triumphant parades of explorers returning on elephant backs. It towered over all the people but swung open quietly and smoothly.

A vast arts complex spread beyond the gate, so gorgeous and filled with color it stole Katy's breath. It was greater in scale than any college or university campus she'd ever seen. A riot of hues and textures; a flat plane of flagstone lined walkways demarking the tall buildings and natural spots.

"Look, each building is one of the colors of the dragons, of the spokes. And the lawns of that peach-colored grass!" Raisa trailed off. "Maman would weep in joy to see this."

They were quiet after that as they followed behind Swailu. The Toledral moved with grace and the speed of a setter flushing prey. Katy cursed her shorter legs as she jogged to keep pace. They passed rapidly through several courtyards, between beautifully designed buildings, until they arrived at a palatial manor. It reminded Katy of a petite Schönbrunn in Vienna, if that palace were covered in a rainbow of ceramic tiles instead of Habsburg yellow. The colors were patterned to create an abstract mosaic, one that made her Air surge loudly in response. The facade embodied the essence of music in an indescribable, almost subliminal way.

The entire walk they'd been watched by hundreds of students, each one wearing bone-colored robes, some with colorful necklaces and some plain. Most carried an instrument: it was a parade of every instrument Katy had ever seen, and several she hadn't. Once their group started down the walk to the estate, though, there were no more students. Just a clear lane that shifted from the muted grey flagstone they'd been on, to mandalas made of white stone threaded with veins of silver. The overall effect was one of radiating light pulsing below their feet.

"This is the home of the Chorus voices," Swailu said. "The Cadre."

Bay asked, "They expect our arrival?"

Swailu shook her head. "There was no time, and I thought it best to come quickly without ceremony. Until we decide how we're declaring the Humans Prima, we don't need songscribes involved as well as the voices."

"Can we stop for one sec?" Katy pulled back on Bay's hand, trying to slow their pell-mell race to the doors of the imposing not-quite-a-castle. "I just need... help. Remind me, please. Prima, first of the species, yes? I remember voices, the top of the top, advisers and leaders blah blah. But who are songscribes?"

"Songscribes are the members of the Chorus who have completed all nine schools. The voices will give you better answers, but for now the closest equivalent on Earth would be the pope and the College of Cardinals." Bay paused. "If there were nine popes, and they were also illustrious performance artists."

Tangun spoke up, "I urge you to save your questions for inside. The less time we stand exposed here the better. Eventually some will realize these aren't Mikanjo in suppression suits, nor do they resemble Nyakisi enough to pass." His words carried more weight for the rarity of his speaking, and the group hustled to the building's entrance.

Katy tried to query her aoiti by thinking at them really hard. Maybe that would help her get deets on the new species Tangun had named. No such luck.

"Bougainvillea!" Riri burst out. She referred to the glorious creeping flowers surrounding the doors before them. "This is bougainvillea from home." Her hand reached out to stroke a few of the fuchsia blooms thriving on normal Earth foliage.

Lia spoke for the first time in a while. "This is common throughout the Aoni. I am not surprised to hear you have it on your Earth." She patted Raisa's shoulder. "Hopefully it brings comfort to see the familiar."

The cobalt blue double doors before them swung open to reveal a medium-height woman. She had a beaded necklace of all nine colors over her ivory robe. It was more like a collar, beads couched in silver. Bright and shiny. Lunari, she must be, because her eyes were double the size a Human's would be. Unblinking liquid jade with no discernable pupil. Her pink hair was cut short in a bob that swayed a little when she bowed to them.

"Greetings Toledral Swailu. When I was told of your arrival

at the gate I consulted our schedule." Her tone wasn't chiding, per se, but Katy definitely heard a wee bit of shade. "I didn't see you or Head Sword Tangun had appointments this sal."

Swailu's lips pursed wryly. "We have no set time for this particular meeting, Songscribe Voltan Asad. Many thanks for your courteous welcome, and your discretion which we will soon call upon." Tangun slid closer to Swailu, lending even more weight to her words. "Please go directly to Mara Silvervoice and with haste. Tell her that I have invoked the Kaltor Protocol."

Voltan didn't gasp, faint, or otherwise react beyond a head tilt in query. "She will understand what you mean by this, I take it? Shall I inform the other voices?"

Shaking her head Swailu said, "No, she will take care of the rest. Quickly, please."

Reluctant, but seemingly well-trained to act as a go-between to powerful people around these parts, Voltan bowed again as she took a step back. Before turning on her heel she said, "I will send someone to show your group to a meeting chamber."

Katy admired the smooth grace of Voltan; the Lunari climbed the large staircase at the back of the grand foyer fast as a chee-tah, but with poise. She wandered to the left side of the entry hall, admiring the array of musical instruments displayed on a series of podiums: violin, coronet, steel drum, a gorgeous mandolin. A chandelier made of colored crystals hung above their heads. The floor below her feet wasn't marble but more of that white stone shot through with silver.

Riri joined her, hands clasped behind her back. Katy whispered, "When these folks commit to a theme, they go for it, yeah? Drazoen colors everywhere."

"Very…lively," Raisa whispered back. "I have noticed that most of the Aoni we've seen likes color. Quite a lot. This is not a place for neutral minimalists."

They giggled, before quieting when another songscribe came down the vast staircase and bowed to Swailu.

"Speaker, Head Sword, companions, please follow me."

Three flights of stairs and two long hallways later they arrived at yet another set of double doors, which the songscribe opened and waved them through. The room wasn't what Katy would have thought of as a meeting room. But she was used to modern, corporate versions of that term. This hearkened back to medieval chambers where heads of state gathered, mingled, and made policy. Or maybe more like how the Habsburgs she'd thought of earlier would have handled important ambassadors. She walked across the room, bypassing a large square table, to the wall of windows looking out over a stunning vista: apricot lawns and teal shrubs trained into shapes of animals she couldn't possibly identify. More flowers, trees, ferns and bushes ringing a large pond filled with milky blue water. Was Katy in Oz and flying monkeys were en route?

A dark-haired woman burst through a side door on the right, one that Katy hadn't even clocked. Her silver-backed collar of rainbow beading was similar to those of the songscribes, but she wore a silver robe that glimmered under the room's lights. Two smaller ivory panels inlaid on the front of it; maybe a nod to the songscribe robes voices left behind?

"Is it true?!" she called in excitement, startling the entire group. "You've brought a herald?"

"Mara Silvervoice I greet you-"

"Enough of your formalities, Swailu! Speak plainly and fast. You can't invoke Kaltor Protocol and waste time on niceties." Mara stared at their group, trying to make sense of everyone. "One of these is the herald?" She turned in a circle, taking in Katy at the windows, pausing, eyes narrowed and assessing.

Tangun bristled at the near-insult from the voice, but Swailu was sanguine. "Yes, the Kawakona is with us." Her statement refocused Mara. "But there is more at play: she and her companion hail from a new species. We've managed to get them here without revealing it to the Calling and have avoided status checks. How we decide to have them defined and introduced remains a question. Their species' languages must be uploaded before we can communicate, but they have incomplete aoiti, and there is risk of premature exposure should we do so. Most pressing of all, we need to research how she will awaken Sundancer Orange. I believe the entire Cadre of voices is needed to find our way forward."

Mara, frozen while Swailu spoke, moved haltingly to a nearby chair and sank down. "I never expected to see this day. And we," she faltered, words thickened with emotion. "We are a fractured Cadre."

"In what way?" Swailu asked. "I saw you just sals ago at the Calling and all looked well."

Mara's grimace warped her lips. "We work hard to hide it. There is a good reason we will wait to bring in Zina and Trey. The recent tuigs have seen a lot of strife and those two are at the heart of it. Zina most. I think she..." She shook herself.

"Never mind that. First," she said to the room at large, "we should decide the best way to address the language conundrum. That will slow us the most and we have to be very careful how we share the information. Do they carry any aoiti mature enough to transmit person-to-person?"

Bay stepped up. "Their aoiti are still learning and translations would be incomplete. Additional issues may arise because their species is new to everything about the Aoni. But I am a seeker and gathered many languages seeking the Kawakona on their planet. My sister or Yuhwa" he pointed to them, "would have the next best patterning."

"How many need the update? You've already shared with the Toledral and Head Sword?" They shook their heads no. "Start with them, then, while I summon more Cadre members. Ones who will be most open to the herald's arrival." Mara left no room for argument.

By the time Bay had connected to Swailu and Tangun (presumably via wi-fi because no one touched physically), Mara had called for refreshments. She sat down, closed her eyes momentarily, then said, "I've sent a private link, use that to transmit, seeker."

Katy thought Mara would have done well as a drill sergeant or executive assistant. Who would argue with a force of nature like that? Voltan arrived, wheeling in a cart of pre-filled glasses. Whatever was in there was new to Katy, because she hadn't been given anything Kool-Aid red yet. Voltan left, closing the door. Before Katy could help herself to a glass, though, the doors swung back open and three new people arrived.

Two more Lunari and one of the aquatic Rixat people she'd seen at the port; he had a blue robe. The other two, both women, wore orange and green robes respectively. All three of them halted just inside the doorway, clearly thrown off balance. Katy assumed they weren't sure why a Toledral speaker and the Head Sword were there with total strangers.

"Kaltor Protocol has been invoked." Mara nearly barked the words.

Their gasps were audible. "You cannot possibly mean-" said the one in orange.

"I do," Mara cut her off. "Dindal Orangevoice, Golgun Greenvoice, Kalim Bluevoice: as your Silvervoice I hereby command absolute secrecy in accordance with the Kaltor Protocol. Do you comply?"

All three nodded, though the blue dude took his sweet time. His eyes traced over everyone in the room, lingering longest on Katy and Riri. She thought he could tell they were different, just as Tangun had said people would if they looked long enough.

"Who is the herald?" This from the woman in green.

"We will hear all once we update our aoiti." Mara stalled their questions with a sharp gesture. "We can make things clear once we have the updates. Time is critical here. Instruct your bots not to share to the parent servers, we aren't ready for that. Now, let us begin."

Between Bay and Lia, the process was done relatively quickly. Katy barely had time to get anxious. To combat her nerves, she examined the voices. Each wore a robe in the color of their school (presumably), with those same paler fabric panels in front like Mara had. The Orangevoice intrigued Katy most, probably because the orange robe meant she would align with Katy's Sundancer. Would this powerful woman be excited to meet Katy, or disappointed her Drazoen's herald was a mere Human?

This was the A-Team, best of the best. They'd completed every discipline of the Chorus and stood at the top of the pops. Mara in silver had actual wrinkles, and, from what Katy had seen, that meant she was probably a couple thousand years old. Katy was an utter infant in comparison, and she was supposed to be a chosen one? From a species no one had heard of here?

"Now," Mara called them back to attention. "We have a herald, or an aspirant to that role. Toledral Swailu vouches for her, says she is the Kawakona the Mikanjo have sought. Our Cadre will make our decision after examination. Which of you is it?"

Katy would later blame the academic feel of the Chorus for why she thought raising her hand was the right move. She felt ridiculous immediately, followed even faster by chagrin. She and Bay hadn't talked about this at all: was it safe to announce herself to this group? They were exalted according to Lanu, but plenty of those sort back home weren't deadly trustworthy. Why should these be different?

Citrine eyes flew to Katy and her stupid raised hand. "Your name?"

"Katy Phelan." Wow, she wished she weren't standing alone over here, like the odd one out. She waved vaguely in Riri's direction. "That's my friend Raisa, she's also from the new species. Humans."

Mara held up a palm. "Name only, please. Again."

Shite, this woman took her back to every music professor she'd ever had. *Stop. Change your fingering. Soften your breath. Again.*

They went over names of both Human women, their species and their planet, repeated a few times slowly. Was this group dimmer than she'd been led to believe? Bay had finally crossed the room to stand beside her, and his presence reassured her.

"Calibrated?" Mara looked to the other voices, as well as Swailu and Tangun. Each person nodded. "Katy Phelan, please speak freely now. Tell us of your journey and how you came to be revealed as herald of Sundancer Orange."

"Uh," she started. *Brilliant, ya numpty.* "I suppose it started when I met Bay at a bar where I play flute."

The woman in the orange robe spoke softly, but with excitement. "Ah, she plays the instrument of Sundancer's discipline. Promising, and surely a sign! How long have you performed?" She walked to the windows where Bay and Katy stood, sim-sun casting a honeyed glow on her dark skin. Her black hair was bound in dozens of braids, each end secured by orange ties. She was Katy's height and barefoot, which was when Katy saw Lunari apparently had seven fingers and toes.

Katy's gut told her this woman would be a friend, so she looked straight into peridot eyes and smiled. "Most of my life, more than twenty years."

That caused a mild uproar, and precious minutes were carved out to explain Humans in a bit more detail. Short-lived? Yep. Have barely left their planet and certainly not long-term off-worlders? Correct. Know about other species? Not a chance. Well. Now they did, since Bay, Katy and Raisa's Great Escape.

Katy went on to describe events of the past four days, Riri and Bay adding comments here and there. Tangun made a deep noise of disgust when they got to Yfaun and his attack. When she reached the end, she added, "And now we need help. Where do we go? Or do I need to do something? We're just... stalled, and looking for advice or expertise."

"First," said Kalim, "we need the entire Cadre. All must concur on whatever actions we take."

"I thought a staggered approach best," Mara hedged.

"Yes, we know Zina will be a challenge." Golgun Greenvoice looked so much like the actress who played Echo on Disney+ it threw Katy. "But at least bring in Olak, Pijo and Gudar."

"Sorry," Katy interjected, "why is this Zina a problem? Mara never finished saying."

All four voices regarded one another, Mara giving a tiny shake of her head.

"We'll cover that later if it becomes important," Kalim said. "For now, Mara, I urge you to include the others as Golgun suggests."

"Gudar may present a problem, too. He's a tough old bird, set in his ways." Dindal's tone was concerned.

Golgun was firm. "But he's a believer. If he can be convinced, he'll work harder than any of us."

Mara did whatever she was doing via her aoiti to call the next three voices, and Katy tried to sort the politics as they waited. No one could accuse Katy of being savvy when it came to undercurrents and machinations; she'd always been fairly straightforward, for all her head was forever in the clouds. She could see that Mara was in charge, but only barely. Whoever Zina was, she was the biggest threat to Mara's leadership. Katy thought Bay had said the Cadre was comprised of equal roles for the nine voices, but it looked more like eight reporting into the top Silvervoice. If there was a power struggle underway, Katy needed to sway every voice to her cause.

20

On her second time through the story, Katy got better at telling it. Riri got worse. Reliving Yfaun's violence wasn't good for her mental health, which gutted Katy anew. Trying to hang on to Lanu's reminder the blame was the PQ killer's and not hers, she pushed on.

She was intrigued, though, when the new woman in a purple robe, Olak, reached out to soothe Raisa. That seemed pretty bold for having just been introduced. Perhaps, though, Katy was hanging out with too many reserved Mikanjo and the Lunari were a lot more tactile. Case in point, the Orangevoice took Katy's hand once this second group had heard all the new information and started arguing.

This time the herald news was meeting more resistance because the three new voices weren't as on-board as the first three. These ones had argued more about the Kaltor Protocol requiring a cone of silence, and pushed back at the person-to-person aoiti updates.

"We have skipped all proper introductions in our shock at today's revelations," Dindal said. "Katy, please let me present Gudar Redvoice, my friend and fellow voice for several aiwaks.

Gudar, this is the herald of Sundancer, so you can imagine my delight at meeting her today."

Gudar seemed suspicious of everything going on. He kept frowning and looking between Raisa and Katy. Despite that, he gave them both a shallow bow. Katy appreciated the way Dindal threw in "herald" along with her name, trying to cement her place for the guy Golgun had said would be their champion, if he could be sold on the idea.

The newest woman, still touching Riri, spoke up to introduce herself. "I am Olak Purplevoice, this one here," she brushed the arm of the man beside her, "is Pijo Whitevoice."

"Great! Now we have seven voices of the Cadre to ask: what next?" Katy hoped someone had an answer. She was getting hangry and tired. All this show-and-tell was wearing on her.

"That is a complicated question," Gudar said.

Pijo asked, "Why are we not at full Cadre? The Kaltor Protocol is for the entire Cadre, not portions of it."

"We're trying-" Mara began.

"To avoid conflict," Olak laughed. "We all know Zina will be negative, and Trey will quietly support her as he always does." Katy was discomfited by Olak's frivolous tone.

"That can't be helped," Gudar insisted. "And she isn't a fool, despite her recent attitude. She'll know she has to attend the matter seriously."

Kalim scoffed. "Zina Blackvoice knows nothing but what she decides is true. If this doesn't suit her, she'll make it impossible to move forward." He eyed Mara. "But we need her and Trey, nonetheless."

"As the rest of you request, so I'll comply. We are not ready for this.... But we must play on, always play on." With that Mara Silvervoice rose and went to the side door from which she'd originally entered.

Mara's strong leadership had wilted over the several hours all of this had taken. Katy sensed the Silvervoice had hoped to get further before bringing in the last two. In all honestly, so had she. Right now there were seven voices, a Toledral, a Head Sword, two Mikanjo seekers and a Jadoube pilot present. None of them had offered a lick of insight on how Katy turned herself into a dragon apostle, or how to wake up Sundancer. Had they come all this way for nothing?

Irritation mounting, Katy sat at a tableside chair waiting for the last two voices to arrive. Yuhwa was murmuring something to Tangun close to the door, shaking her head. Katy didn't like seeing her new friend stressed and ran through options of separating the Sword from Yuhwa. Stage a dramatic exit from Centris so that the *Eternidad* would be forced to ferry Katy and Riri somewhere else? Anywhere else, where people were willing to shelter them from PQ assassins and tell them what to do?

Before she could fully flesh out her escape plan, Voltan opened the room doors. She was followed by the last two voices. Once they'd passed the threshold, Voltan closed the doors and everyone heard an electronic click.

"Mara, what is this?" the handsome woman in black demanded. "Why have you summoned us on a day we don't attend the Calling?"

Mara's nostrils flared in response to Zina's aggression. "Kaltor Protocol has been invoked. Voltan locked the room to siege setting when she left; we are unseen and unheard until I give the override."

Everyone was dumbfounded at this turn. Mara hadn't done the siege thing until Zina the Crabby arrived. Talk about not trusting her!

"Kaltor Protocol, you cannot be serious! That's mythology, not reality."

"I ask you to respect the Toledral who first declared it, Zina," Mara responded. "I have faith in her judgement, and find that I concur this is the herald. Therefore, I'm declaring that all discussion going forward is deepest confidence level."

"I have never heard anything so ridiculous in my life! You, Mara Silvervoice, wouldn't be able to sense a herald if your life depended on it." Zina's rancor was vicious.

"Zina," chided the man who'd entered the room with her. He must be Trey Goldvoice, Zina's enabler. "The Silvervoice has invoked the protocol, we must adhere to that until a decision is made."

"Fine, let us hear it then." Furious black eyes swept the room. "Bring forward the alleged herald."

Mara had stiffened ramrod straight at Zina's insults. "Zina Blackvoice, Trey Goldvoice: as your Silvervoice I hereby command absolute secrecy in accordance with the Kaltor Protocol. Do you comply?"

Zina actually hissed at Mara in response.

Jesus, Mary and Joseph this was going well.

THIRD TIME through wasn't a charm. Riri was a numb wreck after reliving it yet again, Katy's voice was wearing out. Probably because the third round had taken the longest. Zina had fought calibrating her aoiti, so she didn't grasp large chunks of the story. Others had to fill in using their language in the most annoying game of Telephone ever.

Now they'd been left to their own devices while the Cadre debated and argued. If Katy had to bet on the outcome of this Kaltor huddle they were having, she figured Mara, Dindal and Golgun were believers in her as the herald. Trey, Kalim and Gudar were possible doubters. Olak and Pijo, they were hard to read, especially because Olak kept her focus (and hands) on Riri.

Zina was a guaranteed naysayer. An imperious woman with yellow hair and dark eyes, she reminded Katy of those people who are never happy with whatever they get. Not even when it's exactly what they asked for.

"If only," Zina growled, "you had been given full Silvervoice passthrough from Hugo Ti." Her face held scorn. "Of course you did not, you were the first Silvervoice in Chorus history raised up only by the songscribes' vote. Which means we are in the middle of a crisis without all the pieces we need to solve this riddle!"

Katy saw more than one set of eyes rolling. So this was a hoary chestnut of an argument, then. Sounded like this was the problem Mara and the other voices hadn't been willing to share earlier, the source of their divisions. Was there incompetence on someone's part? Or lost mail? Did Mara become the Silvervoice by hostile takeover?

"'Scuse my ignorance, but why didn't he give you everything you needed when he left?" A sad silence clued her in that Hugo Ti might not have retired.

"He died," Trey said. His generous mouth pulled into a sad frown. Sable eyes met hers as he continued, "He was Silvervoice for over a milenyo, and suddenly passed one sal. Dropped in his chambers from a heart blockage that hadn't been caught in his physical, only one hinaharap before."

Hinaharap *hee-naw-har-AP; closest Human equivalent one week.*

Kalim pinned Katy with his gaze as he stepped closer. He was possibly the most attention-grabbing alien Katy had met so far. He had skin white as a polar bear, that shimmered faintly in the room's light. His face was angular, patches of flesh replaced with iridescent scales that glittered, sea glass green edged by a darker kelp shade. The scales traced over part of his jaw, left eyelid and right under-eye, streaked his cheekbones and marked a widow's peak. Instead of eyebrows and lashes he had fine, small fins in a shade complementary to the scales. His green lips were textured, like superfine crystals had been applied.

"Hugo," he mused in a slow, drawling tone, "died in a

surprising way. Some might say suspiciously. Right around the time you were first learning to play your flute on a world none have ever heard of." He bent closer to peer even more directly into her eyes. "Do you think that's coincidence, herald?"

Was this prat blaming her for the last head dude's death? What the ever-living hell!

"How dare you!" Riri shouted. "Katy has done nothing but tolerate all of this insane prophecy mess, answered your questions, and you accuse her of murdering someone? Someone we didn't know existed because we didn't know ANY OF THIS existed!"

Holy Shinola. If Katy thought Riri had gotten loud at the refuge, this was booming. Once again, Olak Purplevoice reached over to calm her, stroking her forearm softy.

Kalim's face creased with a smile, then he laughed. Turning to Raisa he said, "Your ferocity will serve you well here, Human." He stepped to the main table, his gait decadently nonchalant, then leaned. These Rixat were leaners.

"I merely put forth an idea: the possibility that the Supremacy Beyond recognized the coming of the first herald. I might also suggest that those who watch for portents and signs would want to ensure the knowledge was lost. They could have taken action."

Gudar grunted. "Krylar or Pu'ulqaari assassin? I would not have thought of that," he said. Katy knew Gudar didn't believe she was the Kawakona yet, but she was enchanted by the pudge around his waist and almost double-chin he had. She wanted him to be her Uncle Redvoice.

Swailu interjected. "Mara Silvervoice, what does this lack of 'passthrough' mean? You don't have something we may need?"

Mara paced. "Part of the Silvervoice duty is to carry our oral stories, the works of our greatest poets and philosophers. Kaltor was one of those. He was also one of our earliest Silvervoices, as well as a prophet. The Kaltor Protocol hearkens to that side of him, and it has always been said the Silvervoice keeps his 'Adugagio of the Returning Child'."

Adugagio *ah-doo-gaj-ee-oh; Lunari sacred animal, ran free on Vonar desert lands; the word has come to symbolize Lunari freedom through travel/wandering, and an opening of the mind/spirit through experience and learning (extinct when Vonar destroyed).*

"But," Zina said, "it isn't written, it's passed ear to ear, in Lunari tradition. Hugo dying as he did, long before he expected to pick a successor, means Mara doesn't have it and we are blind. We have no idea how to proceed, where to begin. If we even believe this foolishness, which I do not. Trusting Mikanjo seekers, so desperate to be believed. That is a fool's trek, and your most grievous mistake, Mara."

Lia and Yuhwa, both of whom had stepped away to sit in chairs against the wall, looked up at Zina's accusatory whining. Yuhwa, apparently offended on Mara's behalf, said, "Why do you lay this roadblock at her door?" Her eyes narrowed at Zina. "Do you think you should have been Silvervoice, is that it?"

Katy could see Zina puffing up, Mara looking unclear how to rein in the argument, and the others bored of this long-standing fight. "I'm hungry," she said, looking to Bay, her Gibraltar in this frustrating place. "I'm tired, still fairly scared, and have an elaborate fantasy involving waking up to discover this has been the most vivid dream I've ever had."

Seeing she now had everyone's attention, she pinched her arm. "Nope, not asleep. That means I need the people who are supposed to be smart and mighty to stop cat fights and power struggles and help. I'm suggesting a break, so everyone can take a moment to absorb what's happening, because we're supposed to wake up a dragon. One who could be anywhere. Where do newcomers stay while we sort this out?"

Absolute silence, a few shocked faces and even more smirks. Her parents would be so proud of her: Katy Phelan, being a ninny across the Aoni.

21

His *qania* knew how to handle herself. She spoke aloud what others would hesitate to air, demanded the group stop behaving like unfeathered babes, and asked for what she needed: a moment to stop and adjust to these monumental shifts in her world. Bay struggled at times to remember it had been just days for Katy to absorb the wider Aoni and all it contained. He knew how deeply some Humans believed they alone were the apex of creation. Even though this woman was not so shortsighted, she still had to confront actuality and that required a lot of mental dexterity. He adored Katy's ability to face uncertainty with a pragmatic approach. She believed the work needed doing, so she found a way to do it. He'd never loved anything or anyone so much. Particularly at this moment, when she stood in a small room with him, half-dressed.

After her plea for a break and refreshment, the voices had grudgingly concurred and the group split. Zina Blackvoice had been seething as she walked out. Katy called her "a hissing cat on a mad." Swailu, Tangun and Yuhwa had left the Chorus to attend other business. Katy had made Yuhwa "pinky-swear" to return as soon as possible. Vailillia and Raisa had been with Katy and Bay at first. Dindal Orangevoice escorted the whole group to this room down the hallway from the meeting chamber. But Olak Purplevoice knocked, asking if Raisa would like to see more of the house, and when Raisa accepted, Vailillia joined them.

Bay and Katy were left alone for the first time in long salangs. For precious moments they'd gazed at each other, not moving, existing in brief peaceful harmony. One of them moved first, he couldn't say which, and then they were embracing, kissing, reassuring themselves of their connection. Lamentably that respite had been interrupted by a knock; Golgun Greenvoice bringing a set of ivory robes and clean undergarments for Katy.

"I think the tyro robes will serve us best, right now," she said.

Katy thanked her, asking, "What are these? I mean, what do they represent... oh, wait,. Got it. Tyro are beginners, and you voices are the head honchos."

Golgun's kind face froze, before relaxing once more. "Goodness, I enjoy this Human word. Honcho." She smiled. "We'll get less attention from those outside the house if you and your friend appear to be members of the Chorus."

"Could I-" Katy broke off, taking a sharp breath. "Sorry, I didn't realize how much I wanted to ask this. Choked me up, there." She shook her head, taking the clothing from Golgun and stepping back into the shelter of Bay's body. "I don't have money to buy one, I know. I just miss playing so much. Is there any way I could borrow a flute?"

The voice laid a reassuring hand on Katy's. "The herald will have her pick of instruments. If I know my friend at all, Dindal will take you to pick one later, after we resume and set our agenda." Her soft brown eyes twinkled. "Sundancer Orange is her school, after all, and were I to offer she might think me poaching."

"Thank you, thank you so much," Katy breathed out. "I feel incomplete without one."

Bay cursed himself soundly for failing to see to her need, or even explaining she had plenty of money she could access with her aoiti. His goodbye to Golgun was perfunctory as he turned back to tell Katy he was sorry. But all thought stopped because she'd stripped the top half of her bodysuit off, was in the process of removing her bra, and the sweet wind of lust whipped through him.

How had he won this astonishing, gorgeous woman? Her mass of red curls had come loose and spread out over her shoulders and back like puffed feathers. Skin like unpainted porcelain, warm tawny eyes, those adorable freckles begging to be traced with his lips. Her creamy breasts topped by sweet shell pink nipples he'd spent a sal-ang this morning worshipping. He watched as she shook her hips to slide the bodysuit completely off, following its journey as it whispered down her generous hips and thighs. Bay spied more freckles on her shoulders when she turned to grab the fresh clothes. Taking two steps forward got him close enough to run fingers down her spine. She shivered, looked over her shoulder at him, eyes intent.

"You're making good on that later," she said, raising to her toes and lifting her face to kiss his chin. "Right now, I'm expecting them to call us back together any sec."

He acknowledged her words with a small groan, but left her to dress without his help. "Later I intend to make up for every atómi we aren't in a bed this day."

Katy's face brightened. "Every second, yes."

When their group reconvened in the main meeting chamber, Raisa wore tyro robes just like Katy. Bay noticed Olak and Pijo were quite attentive of Raisa. His memory was that Lunari were sexually adventurous, non-monogamous and rather fickle. Transient even before their planet had been destroyed. A sheltered woman like Raisa might struggle to understand their ways. Bay tried to get Vailillia's attention by rustling his wings. When she looked over, he tilted his head toward the two voices and the Human. How did his sister view the situation? Vailillia didn't react openly, just gave him a hand gesture they'd created as children to mean all was well. He accepted her appraisal and refocused as Mara closed the room doors and reactivated siege status.

"I apologize for the frustrations you heard earlier. It has been a struggle to keep the Cadre of voices stable, missing the oral histories. Much of how we govern ourselves was lost." Her tone was sorrowful.

Katy jumped back in. "My mother says there's nothing gained if folks keep moaning about what's been lost. Not that I mean to belittle what happened, but we're in a new situation. We can't linger in regret for the stories or prophecies we *don't* have." She looked around at the mulish faces circling her. "What *do* we have? Is there nothing we can go on? Nothing that tells us what Sundancer would do, where She would go?"

Dindal spoke up. "There is the 'Song of the Nine', with a verse for each Drazoen:

> *I am Sundancer's son, I wear Her orange*
> *She has given me to be powerful and sage*
> *Hardest of the Gods She is, Mother of Justice*
> *Truth She will reward, lies She will punish*
> *I am Sundancer's son, I wear Her orange*

"We learn this as children, all nine verses, and we teach it as part of the Chorus curriculum. The song encompasses our moral framework as Lunari, and reinforces the principles of each school's discipline. Not much in the way of prophecy, however."

Katy asked her to repeat it, then again, by which time half the voices said it along with her. "I get it better now," she said, reaching back to Bay. "What you and Lanu said about Yfaun and the PQ. How they fear her return, because any Mother of Justice isn't putting up with slavery and lying liars who lie."

"Djilbay," Raisa said, "what about the Mikanjo one?" She looked eager. "Can you share it here?"

"I defer to my sister, she's far better at remembering it word-for-word than I am." He looked at Vailillia. "It's up to you if you're open to share." Bay knew this broke a major taboo of their people, to hold secret and sacred Hunanjanno's words to their seeking ancestors alone. But if ever there were a time to end that convention, now was it.

"All nine are mentioned in our 'History of Hunanjanno jo Bikajo', Windweaver," Vailillia started, after taking a deep breath. "Most of the tale is about how She gives rise to the Mikanjo of today, giving us wings and leaving us when the Drazoen faded from the Aoni. The naming in that tale is a nursery song often repeated to children on ship:

Hunanjanno jo Bikajo, Windweaver White, Herself
Irojaku jo Faluji, Sundancer Orange, Her sister
Seraji jo Milabika, Songmaster Silver, Her brother
Jimandago jo Kalda, Giftgiver Red, Her sibling
Wanalika jo Pomareja, Tonguemaker Green, Her brother
Bankiraji jo Nanakal, Earthcaller Gold, Her brother
Kiashan jo Taljabo, Waterbringer Blue, Her sibling
Anamama jo Mwanakiri, Great Mother Purple, Her sister
Erokava jo Nbali, Hu Ularu Black, Her sibling

Nothing new for most of us, but I share for Katy and Raisa's sake."

"I could use a notepad," Raisa joked.

"The 'Prophecy of the Kawakonas', is a feather from a different wing. It has been heard by seeker ears only, our secret kept for a kōmilen. But there are parts that may mean something if we analyze... I believe we need to share now." Vailillia shifted slightly, her wings flexing nervously before returning to their tight, retracted state. "First there's talk of Windweaver White choosing the couple She means to engender the seeking line, Swailu and Kintabo. They became the first jo Bikajos. She tells them, *'After I have gone, many milenyo shall pass before any of The Nine are again seen. This has been decided, for reasons I cannot here explain. Just know that The Nine shall retreat from the People of the Aoni.'*"

"Has anyone ever known why the Drazoen left the Aoni?" Met with shaking heads or blank looks, Bay added, "I've long mulled over that part. That She doesn't want to leave, but must. What could make Them do anything They didn't wish to?"

"Only someone or something bigger, more powerful," Kalim offered.

Zina, who'd been broodingly silent until now, scoffed. "Ridiculous, absolutely ridiculous. There is *nothing* more powerful than beings who created an entire world and the system to put it in. Not even your 'Supremacy Beyond', a divinity in which I have never put any belief. The Drazoen gifted the people of the Aoni with language, music and arts, life and death itself! Then they left, never to be seen again. Dead? Bored? Unknown! All of this is pointless and I'm finished here." She stood, shaking her robes as though they'd committed an offense. She pointed at Katy. "You are not a magical herald, there isn't such a thing. These are folktales told to keep children in line."

"You deny the Nine exist?" Gudar asked in shock.

"I can't, we live on the proof They did. What I do not accept is this fantasy of Their return. How could They need the help of species' so far below Them? The Drazoen left the Aoni when They were done playing with Their toys. No more to it than that."

She tried to sweep out of the room, stopped short by the locked doors. "Let me out. Now."

Mara Silvervoice held her palm over the door lock, barely checked furiosity in her voice. "I remind you of your oaths sworn this day. This will be the only chance given to leave, to violate Kaltor Protocol. You will not be welcomed back for any reason, and you will keep your silence or face consequences. Is anyone else of Zina's mind?"

"I can't say I believe the Human is the herald," Trey Goldvoice spoke up. "But I do believe someday the Drazoen will return. If there is any chance They need help opening that door, I intend to do what I can to provide it."

Zina looked gutted at his refusal to follow her, and snarled as she pushed out of the room. Bay knew it was fanciful, but it felt like there was fresher air in the room with her departure.

"Can we proceed without her?" Pijo asked. "We are not a full Cadre. I thought that was a requirement for the protocol."

Kalim snorted. "She hasn't been part of this Cadre for ages. Let's not pretend any longer. We have work to do, we'll do it without her."

"Well then," Katy said. "Back to it, Lia. What comes next?"

His sister gathered herself, launching once more into the story. "Much weeping and wailing at the coming loss of Her presence, then She tells them:

Before the Nine retreat, We shall endow sacred materials with
Our essence, the spark to cry out and wake Us when We are
needed. These materials shall be scattered to the Aoni, perhaps
found over the ages, but inert until matched with Our herald

"Then we're told seekers will have the ability to sense the essence, and are given a list covering each of the Drazoen. The relevant one here is *'The herald of Orange shall bear Carnelian and know Sundancer's truename'*. Before Djilbay went to Earth," she said, smiling at him fondly, "no one knew what carnelian was."

Eleven pairs of eyes focused on him, and he felt slightly embarrassed. "It took single-mindedness, but I'd been feeling the pull of something for tuigs. When I finally found the right place it was... not easy, exactly. But correct. Smooth. I knew I'd found the essence from our prophecy."

Katy's hand moved to cup and cover the pendant hidden under her robe. He'd watched that become a new habit of hers. Multiple times a sal she would touch it, though she always kept it covered. He didn't know if that was out of a desire to protect it, to keep her potential role private, or if she was hoarding the piece to herself. Probably a combination of all three. Now, however, her gesture drew the attention of the whole room.

"You have this essence? You wear it even now?" Dindal Orangevoice asked eagerly. "May we see?"

"I don't-" Katy hedged.

"Yes," Olak cajoled. "You must show us. Then we'll know for sure this part of the prophecy is true." She leaned forward, an almost salacious energy radiating from her.

Pijo, seated beside Olak, put his hand on her thigh and squeezed. "Olak is pushy, you don't have to do anything you don't want. I admit, though, I'm also eager to see this."

"I guess it's a silly fear," Katy shrugged. "Part of me is so scared to lose it, and Yfaun knew straight off it was important. It's the thing that ensured I was his target, but it feels part of me now. I'm just being protective, I reckon." She reached into the collar of her robe and pulled Sundancer's pendant out. It rested against her chest, platinum gleaming, carnelian glowing with an inner fire.

Bay heard a collective gasp in the room and flushed with pride when he beheld the piece anew. For so long it had been with him, something he didn't consciously think of day-to-day, but always in the back of his mind. Irojaku jo Faluji had imbued this stone with Her essence; created a way for Her Kawakona to call to Her, bring Her back from wherever the Nine had been banished. And he, Djilbay jo Bikajo, had found it, honed it, made it into the thing Katy needed in order to succeed. It was beautiful, he knew, and complemented her spirit.

"*That* is hard to deny," Gudar said with no little reverence. "There is a power that emanates from it." He stroked his moustache.

"Agreed." Mara spoke decisively. "We clearly have the essence. Do we have the truename?"

Katy shook her head. "When I first put this on I heard a symphony, I saw and *felt* colors behind my eyelids, but I didn't get words. No name blazing into my brain, I'm afraid."

"We have a start, though," Raisa interjected. "We know the basic principles of Sundancer, that She wasn't fleeing but forced to leave. Maybe that means She isn't well hidden, that She left us an easier path to Her?" She crossed over to Katy, raising her hand to hover over the pendant without touching. "And this is like something from my childhood tales. A sacred object that chooses the bearer, knows who it needs to fulfill its purpose."

"Wish *I* knew," Katy muttered.

"You will," Raisa hugged her. "The object knows what it needs, and this one needs you. It will help you. You'll have to trust your instincts, but you can't have much of those until we find possibilities for you to review."

"What do you mean?" Golgun said, her voice frustrated. "Without the history from Hugo Ti we have little more than vague children's rhymes."

Raisa put her index finger in the air. "Truename. You were right, Mara, that's where we start. I understand from Olak the Lunari don't keep written records anymore because of what the Krylar did. But I assume other species do?" Trey assured her they did. "Katy and I are librarians on Earth. We know how to research. Point us to a well-stocked library and we'll find a way to dig up something that will help us."

Bay saw Katy's face light up, and though he'd never say it aloud, blessed the moment Yfaun forced Raisa's inclusion on this journey. She'd been a stalwart friend to Katy, he and his sister both liked her, and now she offered them a path forward. If they were lucky, her optimism would prove true and give them answers they desperately needed.

22

Voltan (sworn to secrecy and aoiti freshly upgraded) escorted Katy, Bay and Riri to the Chorus main library, along with Dindal. Lia had opted to return to the *Eternidad*, saying she would check with others about any hints of other tales. She hoped other seekers might have gleaned things from milenyos of travelers on the Seeking Ship. Gudar went with her, intending to memorize the rest of the Drazoen essences from the Mikanjo prophecy. Katy wasn't one hundred percent sure, but she thought he was coming around on the herald idea. Olak and Pijo had wanted to accompany their small group, but Mara vetoed that. As she correctly pointed out, too many voices walking around with them would raise suspicions beyond what they had been already. Their group had showed up at the Chorus with the Head Sword and one of the two Toledral speakers, for feck's sake. There were plenty of eyes on them, to be sure.

"Stunning," Katy murmured as they circled around a Husky Stadium-sized amphitheater. It combined natural and fabricated elements in a seamless way, a happy combination of an ancient Earth coliseum and London's O2 Arena.

Dindal smiled. "Concerts performed here are transmitted throughout the Aoni. One of the final tasks for robes to become songscribes is to play a concert perfectly."

"No pressure," Katy huffed. From what she'd gathered, no-necklace-tyro were undergrads, robes equaled a master's degree per necklace, and songscribes were PhDs with a full collar backed by shiny metal. If she'd had to play a "perfect" concert televised to the entire planet to get her one master's she might have blown it, much less if it aired to the entire galaxy.

Riri stopped them long enough to peer through a door, and Katy couldn't resist sneaking a look at the interior, too. "Imagine if you played your flute here," she said. "Benaroya would have to let you in, then, I bet!"

They giggled at the absurdity, but a cleared throat from Voltan had them back on the pathway to the library. Right, yes, destiny... and books or scrolls, and other things. That took precedence. But oh, how Katy wanted to explore. Her curiosity and xenophilia were barely on the manageable side of insatiable.

All of her attention refocused the moment Dindal ushered them through the library's front doors. Beside her Raisa uttered a low moan of wonder. Katy stopped in her tracks so abruptly that Bay, only a step behind, bumped into her.

She wasn't sure if wood here was like back home (if it even was wood) but this had a tone and gleam similar to the teak accents at Conall's pub. The ground floor stretched for a seventy-, maybe one hundred-foot diameter, bookcases both lining the walls and standing free, forming peaceful alcoves and nooks of couches and tables. Built like a castle turret, three balconied floors rose above them to a stained-glass dome. Each floor, covered in wall mounted bookcases, circled a central pole carved with stylized animals and painted in the by-now familiar Drazoen colors. They drew closer, and Katy couldn't help but compare the huge column to the totem poles of Pacific Northwest indigenous tribes.

"Do you see there?" Riri pointed to a couple areas. "That's a lotus flower. Must be another twin of Earth, like the bougainvillea."

Now that Raisa highlighted it, Katy realized she'd glimpsed the image in all parts of the Wheel they'd seen. From topiary shapes to light fixture design, that lotus had been consistent. "Ready to dive in?" she asked. "Where do we even start? Do you suppose they Dewey Decimal here?"

Several nearby robes gave their snorting merriment frowns. Okay, so that stayed the same no matter what world you were on. Dindal's look was slightly less severe but still didn't invite them to keep yukking it up.

"Being unnoticed was the goal," she reprimanded gently.

Riri sobered. "I'd say we start with the oldest. Histories, ancient stories that involve the Drazoen," she whispered.

Voltan, pink hair even brighter while surrounded by so much warm wood, spoke quietly. "I can take us to a few volumes of genesis stories. I used the Tschuele's "Origin" as inspiration for my red robe final."

Tschuele *shoo-leh; one of the oldest known species; all female; require dietary supplementation to live off home world of Quiltac.* This time the data stream came with a fleeting picture: a woman's face, the top third covered in lacy, dark-hued tattoos, like an elaborate eye mask. Unlike Lanu's, though, these were baroque style, precise in design, and a single color.

"Many thanks, Songscribe Voltan," Bay was saying. "Lead the way."

In short order they'd ascended two floors and circled halfway around the room from where they'd entered. Voltan led them to a shelf and pulled a few volumes, explaining they were different renditions of the same "Origin".

"On our world," Riri mused, tucking some loose hair behind her ears, "we have many myths and folktales of how the world was created. How gods and people and animals came to be.

Often they have core shared truths across disparate cultures, like a flood that wiped out creation or volcanoes that changed landscapes."

"Yes," Katy added. "Perfect. We need all the oldest stories because maybe they'll have hints we can use. How did Drazoen come into being? Maybe if we know that we can start thinking through where they'd go under duress. Humans are famous for returning home when we're in trouble, sad or just lost for purpose." Not that Katy had done that after uni. Not exactly. And not that Humans were in any way comparable to demigod dragons.

Voltan nodded. "Nothing exactly like that comes to mind, but I'll try to find a copy of Lonah Yuādo's work. Fragments only, but they're considered some of the oldest writings in the Aoni. I don't see the volume here, but I'll ask a cataloguer if they know where one is." With that she walked away, leaving them to carry the tomes she'd handed them to a table.

"This is a problem," Raisa said sadly. "Look, Katy."

Katy dropped her gaze to the page revealed when Riri opened the book. It was gibberish to her Human brain, barely even resembling words or a language as she knew it. "This is like the first time I saw Cyrillic or kanji characters." She looked up in despair, then turned pleading eyes to Dindal and Bay. "Are the aoiti going to teach us written languages, too?"

Their grim countenances didn't bode well. Shite. Riri's inspired plan to research the hell out of this mystery would take much longer if everything had to go through other people for translation. Just as she straightened, wracking her brain for another idea, Voltan returned with a large squid.

Not just any squid, but a six-foot-tall cetacean with dozens of arms. Katy prayed her mouth hadn't dropped open like a poleaxed cow. The coral polyp official from the landing bay had floated in the air, this person shuffled along the ground with tentacles rolling and rotating as they moved. Metallic armor, close to a chainmail pattern, covered most of the appendages and the head that poked out from the robe. A bulbous area up top she took for a head, anyway. She couldn't find eyes or a face and didn't know where to look in order to politely converse.

"This is Rácz, third discipline robe and library cataloguer," the songscribe said. "They will help us look for the Yuādo materials. They also had an idea where to look for something the Jadoube wrote of their founding."

Muškikal *mush-kih-call; newest species recognized by the Calling. Insular society, rarely leave their home world of Kan-Xibyui.*

Bay spoke over Katy's shoulder. "We're honored to meet you, Rácz, and thank you for your help."

What followed was a scene from a cheap horror movie. Rácz's head bulb split down the center, folding back to reveal a nest of very small tentacles. These shifted around until they formed the kind of face Katy had seen on most species so far; symmetrical, two eyes, one mouth. But these were all formed of wee fleshy fingers. She tried with all her might not to recoil in terror. On Earth this Rácz embodied an antediluvian fear: Cthylla and Cthulhu, Charybdis and Scylla, the bloody damn Sarlacc.

"I am pleased to be of aid," they trilled. The voice was in no way a match to the visual; high, sweet and light. *Feck, it's like a Demogorgon jack-in-the-box.* Didn't help that the little tentacles made the faux mouth move in time to the words. "Voltan tells me you seek stories of genesis and Drazoen?"

Riri recovered faster than Katy. "It's for our research into Sundancer Orange," she said. "We thought we might get some inspiration for Katy's flute solo."

Katy gawked at her friend fibbing so easily. She'd never have been able to dissemble that way, off the top of her head. Her worry it wasn't a good idea was borne out in the next moment, after Dindal repeated Raisa's English in a language the Muškikal's aoiti could process. Someone was bound to realize Katy and

Raisa's aoiti malfunctioning should have only stopped the women from understanding others. Being understood by everyone else with perfectly good nanobugs should have stayed normal.

"Flute? Then we are in Orange school together!" Rácz said, the dozens of arms conveying a happy and exuberant feeling. "But I have not seen…" Their words trailed off, and their twin eyes (the only facial features that weren't made entirely of tentacles) focused on Katy's chest. Or rather the pendant she'd left out of her robe. Then they took in the Mikanjo at her shoulder, the Orangevoice beside him, and their whole body flushed teal and purple. "And your words are unknown, meaning you are an undocumented people, I think. This is…. Stunning."

Katy's Air wove through her mind, gaining volume in syncopated time with the rippling colors racing over Rácz's skin. The pendant itself warmed against her body, feeling heavier than before, and the hairs on her neck and arms rose. Everything was reacting to this Muškikal, telling Katy the moment was critical.

"You are *not* a student, I think." Rácz's voice had dropped to a whisper. "I think you," tentacles undulating in Bay's direction, "are one of the fabled seekers. That talisman tells me this is your Chanticleer. Am I correct?"

Herald, Kawakona, now Chanticleer. Katy had a lot of titles these days, to go with not a whole lot of knowledge how to do the job.

No one spoke, unsure how to handle being unexpectedly outed like this. "I understand, please forgive my forceful questions. I, too, must be circumspect. Your silence tells me I am right." They dropped the simulated face, leaving just two eyestalks. "I believe I have knowledge to share, but must verify before I pass it on. My people, we have-" Rácz cut themself off. "May I come to you when night falls, if I have secured the proper permissions?"

"I don't, I mean, I'm not sure," Katy waffled and shrugged,

which seemed to translate even though her actual words wouldn't. She hadn't given any thought to how all of this would progress, where they'd eat or sleep, nothing beyond her singular plan of Find Sundancer, Wake Sundancer.

"I dislike waiting, but respect this is secret and most likely valued information," Dindal spoke at last. "Come to Voice House. We'll await your arrival. For now, please show us the volumes Voltan mentioned."

Bay, Dindal, Voltan and Rácz went back to the bookshelves and looked over quite a few books. Katy, who had started shaking in the aftermath of being called out like that, appreciated Riri taking her arm and quietly anchoring her in the moment. Then the Muškikal closed their head up, light armor falling back into place. They took one last look back at Katy before departing. It was bloody amazing how fast they moved on those splayed arms.

Voltan was walking away, too, while Dindal and Bay came back to the table with four or five tomes. Katy looked closer and realized these weren't cracked and ancient weathered volumes by any means. Other species must have invented better systems than paper or parchment. In fact, she wondered, why wasn't everything digital? On Earth print was facing an inexorable slide into disuse because online was how most people consumed their news, books, social media. Hell, when she'd left uni they were debating the merits of digital music stands instead of paper scores and sheet music.

"Dindal, do we need the physical books? Isn't everything here stored in a database somewhere?"

The Orangevoice's answering look was put-upon. "Of course. But you both asked for a library, so we are here."

"Physical isn't helping us as we'd hoped," Raisa said apologetically. "We'll have to rely on someone else to either read aloud or paraphrase." She looked at Katy. "If we go back, we can get everyone focused and sharing. Brainstorm session to beat all brainstorm sessions?"

"Works for me, Riri," Katy answered. "Are there people here who still prefer holding something physical? I assume you have very advanced versions of e-readers, so is paper a throwback?"

"Just so," Dindal replied. "Chitans are very tactile and prefer printed or written materials. While Lunari don't write our stories, we enjoy reading others' and sharing them widely in places like this."

Bay threw in, "Mikanjo also love physical texts. Books are printed on recycled materials, not natural resources like on Earth."

"So we leave these books here? I feel bad we pulled all of this for nothing." Katy frowned. "I also feel a little sad. We had such hope and verve, now it's back to the big house having wasted everyone's time."

"Not so!" Dindal exclaimed. "Without this trip we would not be expecting to hear from Rácz tonight. The Muškikal are rumored to be meticulous record keepers, the chosen people of Tonguemaker Green. This might be extremely advantageous." She looked around. "Mara was right, though; even a single voice is getting notice, three would have been impossible. Time we retreat, I think."

They returned to the mansion in short order, back to the room where they'd been all day. The books came with them, just in case. Yuhwa wasn't back yet, or Lia, but the rest of the voices (sans Zina) gathered once more. Their unanticipated hiccup with reading was lamented, but everyone accepted that's how it would be and dove in. One thing you could say about people who'd studied in a college like this for centuries, they knew how to cram. Refreshment arrived, more food and drink names Katy could barely keep straight. She dropped into an armchair, away from the larger group, to give her brain a chance to slow down.

Eyes closed and head resting against the chairback, hand covering the pendant, Air humming gently, she was startled when Riri lightly touched her arm.

"You okay?" her friend asked.

"Just," she sighed, rolling her head to look at Raisa who'd settled into a companion chair. "I wanted there to be an easy answer, which is daft because when have these kinds of stories ever been easy? After the fourth 'no, this one doesn't say anything helpful' it got to me."

"We've had a lot of mental gymnastics, I get it." They sat in companionable silence a while longer before Raisa spoke again. "You know what I keep going back to?"

"That one thing that was like hot pot?"

"It was delicious," she laughed. "But no, it's the lotus iconography. It's everywhere here. Olak told me on core, where most Wheel full-time citizens live, the symbolism is even more intense. Giant statues and fountains, housing architecture, that kind of thing. All in lotus shape."

"You think it's more than a decorative motif?" Katy wasn't sure. "Walk me through it, what you're thinking."

Riri's face scrunched. "I don't know if I have a cohesive theory. I have pieces that are nagging the back of my head. You noticed how what little we've gotten about origin stories have only been the beginning of species still around the Universe? Tschuele, Mikanjo, Rixat, all sort of the same: humble creatures visited by dragons who give them 'gifts'. Very special gifts that helped their people develop and eventually join the wider Aoni's respectable society."

Laughing, Katy said, "Respectable society? I'm flashing on Victorian ladies promenading through Hyde Park or Kew Gardens."

Joining her snickers, Raisa clarified, "Consortium? Congress? Is that better? The point is, none of this, so far, has included anything about how the Nine came to be. Where they came from, where they lived, things like that. They're complete mysteries. Think about all the Human mythology where gods are born, fight, get hurt, stories that are detailed and colorful."

"But they almost never die. Not permanently."

"Sure, because there's dying and then there's staying dead. Most gods don't go for that option."

"Why would they? Gods can be put back together, or slumber eternally, or never get hurt in the first place," Katy said.

"Yes, and behind all of *those* stories, even farther back, are the creation myths. Those are shorter, less detailed, because no matter how cataclysmic the idea is, making something out of nothing doesn't take a lot of words. Or," Riri mused, "it's that the words aren't there to explain the complete absence of existence very well. But no matter how you describe it, movies are made about the big stories – the ones filled with battles and love stories – and the beginnings get glossed over."

Katy thought of her da's fairy tales, always speaking of darkness as something that had its own presence. A weight to it that harkened back to days before humans harnessed light, when they knew scary things lived in the world after the sun went down. Maybe this carried over to other species, maybe not. But if it had, Riri was right: nothing they'd heard so far tonight had that fundamental storytelling root.

"We are a very young species compared to these others," Katy speculated. "You think, what? That their greater distance in time from their most basic mythology means we're not going to find what we need? That's it's been lost to them… the way we haven't got a clue what Cro Magnons would have believed?"

"That's where I keep coming back to the lotus. Back home, Lanu said that a lot of 'truth' of the Aoni repeated across worlds because they were things that came from the Drazoen themselves. Languages, tales of dragons, music, etc. Now, here we are, on the world the Nine built from scratch and designed down the last detail. Olak says very little on Centris is changed from the time of the Drazoen. Same buildings for the most part, because whatever those dragons built with, it lasts forever. If my math is correct, the Wheel is a quarter of a billion years old."

"Whoa," Katy sat up. "Did mammals even exist then?"

"Protomammals, maybe?" Raisa answered, then shook her head and put her palms in the air. "No getting off track! Back to the lotus, or I'll lose the idea. On Earth the lotus is heavily tied to the earliest, most basic, creation myths. Egypt, India, China, the Middle East. There's always a story where a lotus emerges from the primordial waters of chaos, it blooms, and a god or goddess is born from inside its unfolding petals."

"I think I feel bad that I've eaten fried lotus," Katy whispered.

"Don't, it's delicious and has fed people for thousands of years. But it's much more; sacred symbol of purity and moral conviction, the rights of pharaohs to lead, even embodying the dance between yin and yang. The Greeks associated it with narcotic stupor, the Lotus Eaters from the Odyssey, but most cultures have revered lotus as a divine thing." At Katy's inquiring eyebrow lift she tagged on, "I briefly considered getting one as a tattoo, so I did my research first."

"As one does," Katy acknowledged. "Okay, so where does this leave us?"

Riri relaxed against her chair's back. "Like I said, I'm not sure it's a valid thought, or a full one, despite all I just said on it. I just... I keep circling back to the relentless repetition of imagery the dragons built into this place. A world they essentially gave birth to. If the lotus meant to them what it means in a significant number of our myths, maybe it signals they were products of the beginning of time?"

Katy's breath whooshed out. "As in, Big Bang beginning of time?"

Raisa nodded. "And if they're products of the beginning of existence, I'd think they could be hiding anywhere. Unless there's a prophecy or poem that gives us more specific directions, we're going to struggle to get to wherever they are. The possibilities are literally as infinite as the expanding Universe. So, I was thinking, it might be a better bet to focus on your necklace. How you say it makes you feel."

"That seems very woo woo," Katy said, doubtful.

"So does every single part of this," Riri shot back. "Djilbay's dreams and instincts got him to Earth, to the carnelian – only found on Earth, I'll remind you. To Seattle and an Irish bar on a Monday night. Maybe it's quantum superstrings vibrating at a cosmic level communicating. Maybe it's magic! There's no logic here, Katy. Just subconscious and what was foretold a hundred thousand years ago. That's what a kōmilen is, you know. Well, ninety thousand-ish because they do everything here in nines." She shook her head. "That's how long your Bay's people have been seeking. I think it might be worth it to try meditating or playing music, or whatever will get you to a holy space, one that opens you up to more hints of what we need to do. Baba calls it spenta armaiti, and that's what you need to find."

Spenta Armaiti *spen-tah ar-mai-ee-tee; Zoroastrian reference to sacred focus, or holy meditation that can reveal the divine*

Katy gazed at her friend in wonder. "I'll never be able to thank you enough for being here, being my friend. Even when I couldn't appreciate you the way I should have, you were an absolute rock. Now I could never go a day without you."

Riri closed her eyes. "I am quite fantastic."

Just as Katy thought they might catch a quick catnap, the room doors opened and Dindal escorted Rácz inside.

23

Mara locked the room back to the siege setting that made eavesdropping impossible, and looked their way. "Humans, if you will join us. I'm told the Muškikal have acknowledged your status amongst their leadership." She frowned slightly. "We weren't ready to broaden the circle of knowledge yet, but what's done is done. And Rácz says they have critical information to share, now they have senior council approval."

Katy fought her confused revulsion at the Muškikal's reappearance, ashamed of her reaction. *Buck the fuck up, Mary.* The Aoni would be filled to the brim with fantastical creatures. Just because myth or literary convention on Earth said this was a form meant for darkness and chaos didn't make it true.

"Quick," she said to Riri under her breath. "Help me change how I'm seeing them," she nodded toward Rácz. "I need to be not weirded out."

Linking their arms, Raisa murmured, "Did you not see *My Octopus Teacher*? Simply wonderful. Both heart-opening and heart-rending. Brilliant, adaptive and curious creature, quite similar to this one. She didn't have the head opening trick, though, which I find mesmerizing."

By this point they'd neared the Muškikal and the rest of the group. All the voices had risen when Rácz entered, except Olak and Pijo. They remained on a settee by the windows, sitting closely together. Katy just couldn't get a handle on them: were they a couple? Friends with benefits? Just besties? She shook it off as none of her business and turned back.

In the focused light of this impromptu war room, the fine mesh armor covering Rácz shone more brightly than in the library. Somewhere between rose gold and copper, it draped over their bulbous head, down the many, many arms, stopping just short of the floor.

For once remembering touch might not be a welcome thing in this species, Katy didn't default to handshake position. Rather she folded her hands in front of her and bowed slightly, which seemed a safer indication of respect. "Thank you so much for coming. You have something to share?"

This time Katy was ready for the cranial split, the folding back, the small tentacles forming a face. Instead of instinctual fear she could appreciate the beauty of it, the utter marvel of a biology that came up with such an ingenious way to alter and overcome.

Rácz's eyes bounced between the Humans and the voices. "May I request translation, please."

This is getting old. "Bay, can you give them the local upload?"

He stepped forward, squeezing her waist as he went by, a little reminder he was there and would help, support and champion her. In a few minutes it was done and Rácz's baby face tentacles writhed a bit. Katy worried they'd inadvertently damaged them somehow.

"The information of your species already enhances!" they enthused. "So many languages all in a single world. Our Father will be proud."

"Your Father?" Katy had heard the capital F, assumed it meant one of the Drazoen, but well did she know assumptions got people into trouble.

"Tonguemaker Green, Father of Life and Language, He Who Teaches the Aoni to Speak," they intoned. Definitely reciting from a holy script or book. Their body pulsed with a myriad of green shades, rippling north and south, first an ombre then swirls, ultimately resolving into a pattern of super-fine gradation. "I must start as is proper." Rácz stretched themself to their full height, two of their bigger arms coming around their front to mimic the clasped hands Katy had first greeted them with. Brilliant, adaptive and curious creature, indeed.

"The Mušušumgal of the Muškikal greet the first Chanticleer. They are greatly pleased the time has at last arrived wherein we will share knowledge with others. They send their thanks for the giving and receiving anticipated to commence."

Katy was waiting for the translation of the new word, but nothing came and she saw confusion on the faces of everyone in the room. Maybe it was new for everybody? She decided to ask because she never minded admitting she lacked knowledge if it meant she learned something as a result. "Sorry, what is 'moosh-oosh-oom-gall'?" She smiled a little. "Riri and me, our aoiti are still learning, I'm afraid."

Katy couldn't tell you how she sensed it, but Rácz was bristling and a little menacing after the words registered with them.

"You fear? Have these people harmed you? The Muškikal offer sanctuary." Metal-wrapped tentacles spread wide around their face giving them a halo shield.

"No, no, our apologies," Raisa said hastily. "It's a common saying on Earth, indicating regret rather than fear."

Rácz didn't completely relax, but accepted her friend's words. "Mušušumgal are unknown to any before today, outside of our home planet. You may have been told that my people are philosophers, mystics, cosmic theorists. We are all of these things because our Father told us to be so. He raised us from the mud my ancestors were reluctant to leave. He shaped us, encouraged us."

Kalim tilted his head and opined, "Some would say Tongue-maker engineered the Muškikal. Forced evolution into a path it might not have taken."

Whoa, that seemed rude! Katy turned to gape at the Rixat voice, shocked. Wasn't that speciesist or something?

"This is undisputed. We are the youngest advanced species, and only here at the Calling because of our Father's intervention, accelerating our development." No offense taken at Kalim's words it seemed. They paused, gaze sharpening on Katy and Riri, before their tentacles formed a smile. "We were the youngest, I should say. Now Humans will don that mantle."

"Wait, wait, wait." Katy wanted to make sure she understood. "You believe one of the Drazoen literally made you? Pushed you past natural development into sentient beings?"

Rácz's skin streaked with lightning forks of grey. "We were sentient, He advanced us. Helped us leave our beloved Kan-Xibyui home world and arrive on Centris to demand our place in the Calling." A small pause. "This is not belief, this is fact."

Noted. Don't question creation stories of the Muškikal.

"As I said, Tonguemaker told my people to use their natural curiosity, their desire to understand and resolve enigmatic questions. We worship knowledge. From our earliest days, we have hunted stories, science, lyrical and poetic truths, political diatribes. Anything and everything we are able to find that questions the greatest of cosmology's mysteries. That is what Mušušumgal means; they are the paramount scholars of my people, ones who sought enlightenment the way Mikanjo sought Kawakona," they paused to look at Bay, "herald," nodding at Mara Silvervoice, "or Chanticleer." Rácz swept the two arms clasped in front of them up to point at their own eyes.

"If I'm getting a name from every species," Katy grumped, "I want a cheat sheet to keep track. Plus a t-shirt proclaiming them all so I can brag. It will take officials five minutes just to read them all out when I enter a room." Her heart pounded a little at that thought, publicly acknowledging her status, opening herself up to attack again. "Never mind. Scratch the shirt."

So that's what a confused cetacean looked like. Very odd baby tentacle configuration. Katy's sarcasm had thrown Rácz.

"There is only one more name I know of, created by Kaltor Silvervoice." All of the voices tensed at this, shifting on their feet, shocked Rácz knew of this. "Returning Child is the name he used in more than one of his poetic prophecies. It isn't understood if he was having a vision when he used it. He was, after all, a poet as well."

"You have a copy of his 'Adugagio of the Returning Child'?" Mara nearly gushed the question at Rácz. Even Olak and Pijo got up from their window seat to join the main group.

Streaks of orange rolled around the edges of their arms this time. A reaction to Mara's over-eager question? Katy knew the colors all had meaning, but how to decipher that meaning wasn't clear yet.

"We at one time had a copy. We also had his 'Song of Discovery', as well as many more tales of the Lunari. Those copies are safe, but inaccessible. Which is what I am here to share, by order of the Mušušumgal."

"Perfect," Gudar muttered. "Very helpful to know we can't get to the things we need." He glanced at Katy's pendant, still displayed over her robe. She reached up to cover it reflexively, and he pointed at her. "If this one is legitimately the herald, we have to have answers, leads, things we can act upon. Mystery and hidden truth does us no good!"

"I understand your frustration." Rácz raised several arms in placation. "We have waited for a hint of the Chanticleer so we could play the part our Father assigned us. Now it begins.

Before the Nine left the Aoni, my people had spent many milenyo gathering the kinds of documents I described. It was the greatest library in creation. We had copies of things the Lunari had committed to the page, songs and poems dated from before Vonar was destroyed."

The collective pained inhale at that statement silenced the room. The Krylar people destroyed Vonar about fifty thousand years ago, but time never made a pogrom better or easier.

Rácz continued. "More than that, we had Eng philosophy, Oti scientific treatises, rare Uilig spiritual writings, everything Lonah Yuādo had ever inscribed."

The look on Riri's face was beatific and melancholic at the same time. She knew her friend didn't understand half of what they were referencing because Katy bloody well didn't. But, of the two of them, Raisa was the born librarian. Knowing this Muškikal library probably went the way of the Library of Alexandria would both sadden Riri, and lift her spirit to know it had once existed at all. Rácz brought her back to the conversation.

"Shortly before the Drazoen were exiled, Tonguemaker came to us and asked for a sacrifice. He wanted our greatest Mušušumgal bound to the library. Before He went away, He would hide the library with these bound Mušušumgal in it. It held precious knowledge that could not under any circumstances be permanently lost to the Aoni. With so many milenyo expected to pass before His return, He believed information destruction a real threat, thus hiding it was necessary. He assured my ancestors that when it was time, the library would return. Those volunteer sacrifices were to be hidden with the library, keeping everything in order, properly indexed and protected."

"Holy Mary, mother of God," Katy gasped. "Are they still alive? Trapped somewhere?"

Rácz flashed a deeper shade of orange. "We don't know if

they were made eternal, or if they have replicated over time, handing their duties to offspring."

Katy was all-over gagged at the idea some poor schmoes had been sentenced to ninety thousand years, give or take, in a library that had been concealed by a dragon so well almost no one knew it had ever existed. She loved books but that was torture-level solitary confinement, no matter how marvelous the environs.

They went on. "Our Father told us we would know it was time for its return, because the first Chanticleer would come forward. Another major thing unfolded before that event to inspire our wisest leaders to spirited debates, as well." Here they addressed Kalim directly. "For the first time in Chorus history, a non-Lunari voice was chosen. Not only that, he was Rixat."

The Bluevoice jerked his head back in surprise. "What possible bearing could that have on this?"

"For nearly a kōmilen my people have kept the Promise of the Chanticleer secret, passed down generationally. Just as the Mikanjo have done, as the voices and Lunari have done." Rácz's skin went all-over murky, dark emerald, the color you'd see outside a deep-sea submersible on Earth. "Muškikal originally named our treasure the Great Library. Once Tonguemaker Green hid it, we renamed it The Lost Library of Shilmand."

Given the explosion of sound (some cries of amazement, some shouts of disbelief, quite a lot of *this is impossible*), Katy assumed Shilmand meant something important. Most especially to Kalim. He had physically reeled from Rácz's words before steeling himself and stepping closer to their personal space. Riri grabbed Katy's hand at the same time she started backing away. This felt too much like an impending bar brawl, and all for reasons opaque to the humans. Bay's wing wrapped around her left side, leaving Katy and Riri joined palm-to-palm on the right.

He extended his physical protection to her friend by settling a hand on her shoulder.

"You claim Tonguemaker Green of the Sacred Nine told your people, over a kōmilen past, your library would be hidden on Shilmand?" Kalim wasn't shouting, but his demeanor was quite a few notches beyond calm. Furiously firm. "And you say nothing of this until now?"

"Shilmand," Raisa hissed under her breath, leaning into Katy. "When we first landed, the aoiti said that's where the Rixat live."

"Yes," Rácz said, unintimidated. "One of our most celebrated writers received the 'Promise of the Chanticleers' directly from Him, then was bound to the library. Fäs Bö they were called, and they were the one to rename the library just before it disappeared. We were told to look for signs that the Aoni was preparing to return the Drazoen, but until then to keep silent. When your God tells you to do something, you do it."

Here they turned to Bay. "Your people were told by Windweaver White to seek the Kawakona. For that you've sentenced untold generations to wander isolated throughout the Aoni, unable to return home. My people were told to chase fragments of information, stories, mere rumors so we would know when our task actively engaged with the greater purpose. What is stored in the Lost Library has power, and in the wrong hands could have helped those who would like to ensure heralds never arise." Suddenly their head resealed and all their arms jerked together, forming a near-solid trunk. As quickly as it happened it was undone, a full-body clench and release. "Pardons, this is momentous and I never dreamed to be part of it, so close to it. I am overcome.

"When Kalim was proclaimed Bluevoice, the Mušušumgal gathered to discuss everything my people know from our collected resources. It was particularly interesting to our senior leaders that not only was a Rixat proclaimed Bluevoice, but one from a member of the royal family. Most captivating, to think this was a sign the Aoni had moved pieces into place." There was real excitement in their words. Rácz was pretty thrilled about all of this.

"I worked hard for this role, it wasn't fate or the Supremacy Beyond. It was me! My bisous of study. My painful callouses earned by my mastery over the instruments and performance arts I improved upon sal after sal." Oops, someone touched a nerve of Prince Rixat Bluevoice.

Rácz inclined their face slightly, acknowledging his words. "Of course. But the pools of Kan-Xibyui are deep, would not the rivers of the Aoni run deeper? Things such as this are far beyond our abilities to decode. We can only accept." They swept a set of newly tinted purple and aqua tentacles in Katy's direction. "You were chosen a mere three tuig before the herald appears. And when she does arrive, in the company of her seeker, she comes directly to where you are. Where I am." Rácz emphasized.

"This could well be coincidence," Golgun Greenvoice said, smirking. "But I think not." Dindal, beside her, laughed.

Mara jumped into the fray. "The clear solution is for Kalim to return to Shilmand and pursue any clues about the Lost Library. Rácz," she said, "is there anything else you can share, anything to make his search faster? I can't help thinking our time may be short."

"I have shared all the Mušušumgal shared with me," they replied. "I am also given over to you, empowered to speak for our council if necessary, and to share everything we can. If you need me, I am to help in any way possible."

Olak piped up from the settee she and Pijo had reclaimed after the fracas moments ago. "There isn't much time before the Humans will be noticed. One slip, a moment of inattention, and we as a Cadre will need to justify why we kept the Prima out of the Calling for hours or days. Zina may violate Kaltor Protocol even more than she already has... her secrecy isn't a given; remember how angry she was."

"Speaking of Zina," Trey Goldvoice interjected. "I think I should check on her. Our history is long, maybe I can get through to her." Chocolate brown eyes in a tan, moon shaped face glanced at Katy. "We're dealing with something major, unequivocal; our Cadre must stand whole. I know she can be abrasive, but she has vast knowledge and experience. We need our Blackvoice."

Mara nodded decisively. "Do that. By the Nine, I pray she can set aside her resentment. I think I will also call for Thuliso Maor. He's been traveling for long tuigs. It's time for our appointed to report back on what he's seen in the wider systems and galaxies." She seemed to turn her thoughts inward. "It's easy to focus so much on Centris and lose sight of the greater vistas. His information may lead us down a path we've overlooked."

With that, their group dispersed.

BAY DESPERATELY WANTED to get Katy alone. In a private room, where he could worship her the way he'd earlier said he would. Her calmness and aplomb while all these bombshells had been dropped around her fired his blood. His *qania* was competent and practical. Yet she still had the imagination and whimsy of someone able to believe what would be fantastical to nearly all on her planet, and probably ninety percent of the greater Aoni. Djilbay was learning that was an intensely arousing thing to him.

He'd contacted Vailillia, telling her what happened over their private connection. She had volunteered to take Kalim home to

Shilmand first, then to find this Thuliso Maor, appointed of the voice Cadre, and bring him back to Centris. Yuhwa was back on the *Eternidad*; it should only take them a few sals.

When Katy heard Yuhwa was back on the *Eternidad* she demanded a call with her new friend, but the pilot put her off, promising to explain what had happened with Tangun when she returned. Katy wasn't happy, but said she "respected bloody stupid fecking boundaries" and didn't push. Songscribe Voltan provided them with two bedrooms in a wing one floor down from the meeting chamber. Hard to believe they'd spent nearly the entire day inside it. These new rooms – one for Raisa, one for Bay and his *qania* – were comfortable without being overly sumptuous, and opened onto a common area with a small replicator. The Humans were thrilled to know future cups of tea and nropita were barely two steps away.

He'd enjoyed a simple meal with his Humans, relaxing after the stress of the day. When they prepared to retire, Olak appeared, drawing Raisa away from their rooms to explore the house in more depth. The more he observed her, the less he thought he understood the Purplevoice. But Katy's friend and companion appreciated the attention, that was crystal clear. Years on Earth had taught him what flirting was, and it was out front and center of whatever what happening between the two women.

They were not his primary concern at the moment, though. Katy, his wondrous, lively, incredible Katy, took every thought from his head. Once she'd closed the door on Raisa saying goodbye she'd locked it, turned, and whipped off her tyro robe. Bay's entire body lit up.

"Alright, boyo, you've got some promises to keep," she called to him.

He spread his wings as wide as the room would allow, entranced by the vision of his *qania* naked except for

Sundancer's pendant. He had lovingly crafted the essence into a piece his Kawakona would want to wear, one that would call to her, make her positive this was her destiny. His artwork touched her body constantly. *His.*

They met in the middle, Katy's arms going around his waist and sliding up to the bottom of his wing joints. She caressed them, right where the flesh joined wing to back, stroking skin and feathers. It burned him in a perfect way, surprising as he'd never been touched there, the spot sensitive and his skin dimpling with the sensation.

Katy's tongue meeting his own spawned tremors throughout his body. This sensual exploration was so new to him, overwhelming and making his very cells desperate to align with hers. Want on this scale was unprecedented for Bay. A relationship on Earth would have been impossible given the physical anomalies, and while he'd had a handful of post-fledging encounters, they couldn't compare to this.

Katy was warm and vital, inciting all of his instincts to surround her in his feathers and join their bodies in a primal way. His hands were about to make the journey from her shoulders to the small of her back on the way to her perfect behind, when a knock brought them to a screeching halt. Curse foul winds! It seemed their fate to be interrupted, and he sighed.

Before he could even unclasp his arms, their interrupter knocked again, frantic and forceful. "Hurry, hurry!" Dindal sounded panicked. "We're meeting upstairs immediately!"

Bay, mindful of Katy's nudity, replied through the closed door. "What's happened? We no longer wait for tomorrow to assemble?"

"Zina is dead," Dindal moaned. "Trey found her in her rooms, throat cut."

"Oh my god!" Katy cried.

This was terrifying in and of itself, but especially because it had happened in the same place the Kawakona was in. If they could get to a voice they could get to his Katy. Bay bowed his head and prayed to Windweaver that they could get to Her Sister, Sundancer, before anyone came after Katy again.

24

Katy was paralyzed by shock. Throat cut? Here in Zina's own house?!

Bay had paled, as stunned by the news as she was. Katy donned her robe once more and they flew out of the room, desperate to get answers. Dindal had already left their door, saying she'd find Riri. How could this happen? Why, was an even more critical question. Zina hadn't believed Katy's arrival was the start of the Drazoen triumphant return: what possible threat could she have posed to anyone who felt they had a stake in the prophecy game?

Were any of them safe here?

The reassembled group was tense and silent, waiting for Mara and Trey to join. Katy looked at the angry, fearful, near-belligerent countenance of Gudar. Dindal and Golgun were standing close to each other without speaking; Olak and Pijo sandwiched Raisa, offering comfort. But when Bay and Katy walked in, she broke away from the voices and hugged Katy tightly.

"Is it him?" Riri whispered. "Did he follow us and he'll kill us now?"

"I don't know," Katy whispered back, pressing her arms more tightly around her friend. "Bay didn't think he'd be able to get here so fast, but maybe." She shuddered. "We can't be sure of anything, can we? This isn't fair."

When Riri pulled back her eyes were red-rimmed. "Will we ever be safe?"

"Yes," Katy said with conviction. "When we wake Sundancer. So let's get on that in a hurry."

Raisa flashed a ghost of a smile and shuffled to Katy's side. Mara and Trey walked in, locking the room behind them. Their faces were haggard, even their large Lunari eyes looking pinched. "Zina is gone, killed," Mara started, looking at Trey to continue.

"I messaged her when we broke the session earlier, asking if we could meet. I hoped-" he inhaled harshly. "I'd hoped she would see reason. She replied, saying she wanted to meet as soon as possible, because she'd learned disturbing news about three Calling ambassadors."

"Zina played no political games, what could she have heard?" Pijo asked, surprised. "What did she say?"

Trey clenched both hands in the hair at the nape of his neck. His gold robe was wrinkled, as frazzled as the man. "She didn't give me more, said she wouldn't put it in a message but would explain at our meeting. When I got to the teahouse on Windweaver subspoke I waited hours, but she never came."

Golgun Greenvoice, clutching Dindal's arm, asked in a wavering voice, "Why the subspoke? Why not here?"

Trey's weariness bled through his gaze. "Zina said she didn't feel safe in the house. Didn't specify why, but insisted we talk at her favorite teahouse."

"Which three ambassadors?" Olak asked.

Mara answered this time. "Yĕo Qo'orianka, Eka Uitu'umen, and Ilva Alaa." All the Chorus members looked aghast.

"For the late comers, can you please explain the importance

of those people?" Katy regarded each of them around the room in turn. "Who are they?"

"The first two – Ambassadors Qo'orianka and Uitu'umen – are Pu'ulqaari, highly ranked. Very outspoken about their rights to namu'ur." Mara sounded furious.

"Slaves," Bay muttered under his breath, before Katy's aoiti even had time to translate.

Gudar jumped in. "They have recently been pushing for a Calling resolution to codify and protect the right to run their 'service industry', built on the backs of namu'ur." His face scrunched with disgust.

"Zina was loudly vocal about fighting against the resolution," Trey added. "Those two are very powerful, and if they heard she was going to object..."

Dindal spoke up. "But what reason to attack Zina? They're well positioned, with allies. The Pu'ulqaari have had a large amount of support from the Chitans, in particular High Ambassador Alaa. It's said she has the ear of the Trinary."

"That sounds like a deity," Raisa said. "The Trinary."

"They behave like one," Mara spat. "Originally the Nine created the Calling to be equal for all species. Across all planets and galaxies, when you had a seat in the Calling your word and business – be you Lunari, Mikanjo, Rixat, so on – was all equivalent, comparable. But over the milenyo power bases, alliances, and factions gained popularity and ultimately prevailed. This was one of the worst developments when the Drazoen left the Aoni."

"I was taught," said Bay, "it began earlier, when the Uilig withdrew, making a vacuum for the rest to fill."

"Perhaps that, perhaps the disappearance of the mythological Cho. Or perhaps something intrinsic in how advanced species function at their cores. Whatever triggered it, the power ebbed and flowed over time, cascading until it resolved into the setup we have now." Directing her comments at the Humans she continued, "The Trinary is the three top ambassadors, ascendent in power and voted in by only the heads of each species' delegation. They're able to quash or elevate business in the Calling as they see fit."

Mara closed her eyes briefly, sighed, and opened them again. "Right now we have a Trinary motivated by greed, therefore willing to entertain the idea of fully legalizing Pu'ulqaari namu'ur. It represents a vast revenue stream for those willing to take advantage of the practice."

Katy began to despair. "Zina thought the three ambassadors were up to something shady together? Gobshite PQs. Are they all crap, or just the ones I've come across?"

Golgun frowned. "No species is ever a single thing, herald." She raised a hand to point at Katy and Riri. "Here are the first two members of a new species. Are you the same? It has not seemed so."

"While you are correct," Raisa countered softly, "we are not condoning slavery."

But some Humans would. Katy was saddened by her fleeting thought. "What's our move now? Do we think these three killed Zina? Was it a hired hit? Is there any chance it was completely unrelated, maybe Chorus troubles?" Just as she said it, she realized how many feathers she'd be ruffling with her words. None of them Bay's.

"You think *we* would attack her?" Mara was incensed.

Bay tried to intervene. "I think Katy meant jealous subordinates, or someone vying for the Blackvoice position."

Olak mused, "It is second only to Silvervoice. Plenty of eager songscribes might imagine themselves in the role."

Now Gudar jumped in. "That's possible, yet we have more than two kōmilen of Chorus history where no voice has been murdered for their robe. It would seem far more logical we lay this at the feet of the people she named outright."

"All Zina said was she'd 'learned disturbing news', not what that news was. It may have nothing to do with the herald, true, and is only about the pending legislation," Pijo said. "But I think it's more likely to be about the herald. They're the people who sent the assassin, from a family well-connected and known to use violence to rise in status."

This set off a fight Katy wanted out of; hard to follow a pissing match when you've had a lone day to try and figure the players. Lah, she needed a break! In a single day she'd snuck onto the Wheel, met a swarm of new people, tried to solve the riddle of her prophesied role, and was bloody tired. She retreated to the windows, looking over the lawns and fountains lit by soft lanterns now that darkness had fallen... or been set. How would that work on a world that was effectively a massive space station? Did it rotate like a planet around a sun she hadn't noticed on their way into the dock?

Bay interrupted her thoughts, wrapping his arms around her from behind and resting his chin on her head. He didn't surround her with his wings this time, but he still radiated warmth and ease. "It will be all right. We'll find our path, no one and nothing will stop you from waking Sundancer."

Oh how she wanted to believe him. But doubts in herself and in being a chosen one overtook her. "Yfaun got to us on Earth. Someone got to Zina here, and for reasons we don't even understand! At least coming at the Kawakona makes sense for the PQ, but Zina said she didn't believe the prophecies. How do these things relate, or are they utterly separate? We could chase our tails for days trying to sort this mess. Meanwhile we're trapped here, because Lia and Yuhwa swanned off ferrying Kalim back to his planet. Then they swing to where-the-hell-ever to pick up the other guy before flying back."

"Thuliso, who is on Hadea." At her raised eyebrow he added, "You haven't met the species from there yet. The Imen are rarely away from their home planet. I was surprised to hear they'd allowed a Lunari to stay with them so long."

Katy processed. "I want us all together. Even with Yuhwa's fancy river dance thing we have a week before they're back."

Bay's laugh felt so good against her body, jostling her just enough to make her smile too. "Dao, although I like river dance. And I concur, we have a week in which we'll try and progress without their help. I don't think Kalim Bluevoice will immediately locate a library that's been lost for a kōmilen. Which leaves us with you."

She sagged in his arms. "No pressure at all, my dude." A little elbow jab to his abs in chastisement. "Seriously, what do I do? What *can* I do? I have a pendant and not much more."

"I heard Raisa counsel you to trust yourself earlier and I agree completely. We should ask Dindal Orangevoice to find you a flute. I understand there are meditation chambers where the Toledral speakers give counsel, we can ask Swailu to get you there in secret. Anything we can do to put you in touch with the music you heard when you first touched the pendant, Sundancer's essence."

Katy winced internally, conscious she'd yet to share with anyone the truth of her Air. How a tune that had been with her from birth seemed to have hit musical puberty when the necklace touched her skin. It was out of control at Pike Place and had taken over her entire being. Though it receded a bit after first contact, it played constantly now. Both in the front and back of her mind. Any time spent alone with Bay made it surge as wildly as river rapids, and quiet moments of companionship with Riri, Lia or Yuhwa had it susurrating like light breeze through vast open wheatfields. Standing near the Muškikal had inspired a ticklish rondo of contrasting melodies.

A lifetime of hiding what made her weird kept her reluctant to share about it. But she could try to play it again, as she'd been trying her whole life. Was the key to finally catching her will o' the wisp Air being in possession of the spark? Meditation as a help... well that was a whole other thing. She'd tried it a couple of times, but the very Air that probably marked her as herald kept her from any kind of Zen state. Instructors would say "empty your mind" and Katy would try, but the Air would tempt and tease, and she'd completely fail.

It was worth trying here and now, though. Maybe since she had the pendant it would help. *By distracting the Air with something shiny?* Damn her inner voice for a sarcastic trollop, but the sentiment was valid. What was different about Katy now that could make a difference in finding her inner peace, merging with the Aoni, all that spiritual dreck?

Looking around the room, she realized quite a lot was different, to be fair with herself. She was surrounded by aliens, on an alien world, cradled in the arms of an alien, and she hadn't needed a dose of benzos to handle it. She'd arrived here on a bloody damn spaceship after facing down an assassin. Hell, she was now family-close with someone she'd actively tried to fend off at every turn, and if her friendship with Riri wasn't the biggest evidence of change, Katy didn't know what change was.

Fifteen minutes later, the voices had quit their blazing row. The whole group gathered around the large table, seated there for the first time like a real war council. Mara took the lead. "We, the Cadre, will try to ascertain what the three ambassadors know. Better yet, if they fear the herald and that was their motivation, or if this is purely political machination."

"Who found her?" Katy asked, remembering Trey had never finished his story before the arguing started.

"I did," he said, forlorn. "When Zina didn't come to meet me, I went to her wing hoping she had an explanation." He gulped. "The door was ajar, her blood staining the rugs. They'd left her face down on the floor, like discarded clothing." Olak reached out and stroked his arm, offering sympathy. Trey's lips pressed together tightly.

"What we don't know right now far outweighs what we do," Mara said. "Did your assassin from Earth transmit details to someone here? It would seem impossible for a traveler to make it here that quickly given the Centris system limitations."

"We've been tracking signals and looking for signs of off-world departures," Bay answered. "There's been nothing."

Mara shook her head. "In light of this uncertainty, we all feel it will be best for the Humans to remain here."

"But a killer made it in here!" Raisa cried. "How will we be safe?"

Mara raised a hand to forestall her. "We will move you to the wing usually reserved for dignitaries and their security details. The entire floorplan can function under siege protocol like this room; you control it, determine who is allowed in or out. No one else," she swept an arm around the table, "not us, nor anyone in the Chorus, the Calling, or other factions can get through it. Not unless you admit them."

"What do you think, Riri? We could be protected while we wait for Lia and Yuhwa to come back. Spend more time talking over the lotus and what it could mean?"

Raisa shrank into herself a little. "I don't like the idea we have to barricade ourselves like this. Eventually we'll turn into rats in a cage."

"What if I promise we won't? We'll break out of the pokey before that happens, I swear to you."

At that her friend rolled her eyes. "Katy Phelan, if there's anyone I believe would engineer an escape from a self-inflicted prison, it's you."

"That's settled then," Katy said for the benefit of the Cadre. "Show us to this wing, please."

In just a few minutes they'd re-relocated everything that came to Voice House from the *Eternidad* before it left on mission. Wasn't much, just caftans from Lanu, Bay's rucksack with his beacon and some casual robes, and a care package from Yuhwa that included rusim and spare bodysuits for the Humans. Zazi had sent Katy baijur crackle and a drawing of them flying together. She treasured it, and figured it was the closest to real wings she was getting.

Their first action, after picking which rooms out of the eight options they wanted for their own, was breaking out the tea Lanu had given them. New replicator, new test cuppa. This replicator was better than the one on the ship. They'd only had to tweak brew intensity and beverage heat twice instead of four times.

"You notice how," Katy said to Riri over the rim of her mug, "sometimes the aoiti uses our language, sometimes Aoni?"

Raisa nodded, blowing on the surface of her own tea. "I think when our term from Earth doesn't fully capture it, these nanobots fire new synapses. They've learned however human brains work and improve as they go. They're getting faster, more nuanced. If we think 'herald', which tends to be European or biblical in concept, that's a certain word for us. Kawakona, though… they keep telling me it means more. Anticipation, inexorable destiny, calling fulfilled. Good guys winning, all of that rolled into one."

"I get it, now you put it that way. An hour on Earth isn't an exact match for a sal-ang here."

Bay swung by her chair, kissing her softly, headed back out to the Toledral Chambers. Katy watched him go until Raisa cleared her throat.

"Tell me," Raisa whispered dramatically, "how does aoiti translate 'condom'? I assume the word in Mikanjo is different?"

Katy gawked at Riri, sputtering. "Ah, well, yes. Different word, same basic concept." She knew her blush was beet red. "They aren't as fertile as we are, so there's probably less risk of pregnancy…except Bay says humans breed like rabbits and isn't sure how that will work out. It's only an issue until our nanobots are fully active, anyhow, because then they'll combat disease and let us control our own ovulation."

Raisa's eyebrows arched up. "But what's the word? You

didn't tell me the word. Friends don't keep important things from friends."

"I don't remember-", Katy stopped as her aoiti provided **koro** almost as fast as she thought about it. She told Raisa, who nodded and smirked, repeating the word to herself.

"Why do you keep saying it?!"

"I'm doing what they all do with our words that are new to them, reiterating so it sticks. Never know when I might need the word!" she laughed.

"Jeez. These things are retraining us to think in multiple languages' meanings! Even without us consciously learning said language." Pursing her lips and cocking her head, Katy asked, "We're not worried about that, right? That we're being redesigned by quantum tech we can't possibly understand?"

After a large sip of her tea, Riri said, "Nah." More seriously, she asked, "You and Djilbay are good?"

"Yeah," Katy sighed. "Massively happy when we aren't stressed about this prophecy shite or people getting their throats cut five feet away."

"You aren't worried about the age and lifespan differences? Or that he's not human?"

"I don't think about it when we're together...."

"And right now?" Raisa queried gently.

"Right now, I don't see what I have to offer him that could last." Katy gave herself permission to be one hundred percent honest with her friend. "I'm less experienced, a bit of a disaster on a good day, and failing this quest. He acts like he loves me, which, I know, fast for that. What if it's only a response to the intensity of all this Sundancer herald stuff? Except it's all there in me, too. For him. But I worry I'm tying him to a being who isn't going to be there long-term. Even with the help of these aoiti we aren't going to suddenly live three thousand years. It will take what lifetime I have left to learn the things he already knows, so what can I possibly bring to this relationship?"

"Those are heavy cares, and valid." Riri's teacup plonked down on the table between them as she leaned forward. "But, Katy, how dare you think you're failing, that you're a disaster! You're a fighter, someone I would have beside me in any scenario. Passionate, clever and empathetic! Your way of seeing things is unique, and will be what wins the day in the end."

Katy's face crumpled in that *not gonna cry* way. "I don't deserve you, you know."

"I know."

"I'm sorry to tell you you've missed the returns window, so you're stuck with me."

"Baba will be thrilled. Another cup of tea?"

Days passed like this. Without the ability to read the languages, they couldn't research any of the volumes they'd brought back from the library. Not unless someone volunteered to read aloud to them, and their previous helpers were embroiled in Zina's murder and everything happening there. Their aoiti occasionally kicked in with search results on the texts, but nothing substantial. More like heavily redacted government documents. Just bits and pieces. As much a gift as these things were, the aoiti were still a work in progress inside the Humans and their help was intermittent. Katy's nanobots at one point downloaded half of the Tschuele "Origins" Voltan had mentioned. There wasn't anything there, though, except a fairly basic "Giftgiver and Songmaster told us to go that way and find water. We did. The end." When she pressed Voltan for some insight, she told Katy most of the references were so old they couldn't be corroborated in modern times.

"There's no evidence of that mountain they reference, Schoena. Some theorize it was so long ago the mountain has worn down by now. But the Tschalom Desert isn't there either, which means the tale might be mistranslated. Or that it happened on a different planet altogether, so far in the past they don't remember carrying it to a new world."

"Do species do that? Abandon a world for a new one?" Riri was extra curious, since her bots hadn't given her the download Katy got.

Voltan shook her head. "Rare to non-existent. The Eng have three primary home worlds, but they're the outliers. Most have stuck to a single planet, with satellites or outposts to extend their influence. Easier to build those than terraform entire planets."

When Katy, Bay and Riri heard updates from any of the voices, it was a lot of "be patient" and "discussions are happening." Typical political fluff and nonsense. Too bad it's how Earth and the Aoni both seemed to work.

Tangun had returned several times, leading the investigation into Zina's death. Not that she knew him well, but Katy thought his outwardly composed demeanor covered fury. This guy was head of the militia, or police force. Corps. She wasn't sure how the Swords thought of themselves, but she and Raisa had learned that the ones on Centris were neutral, serving the Calling itself, not individuals.

One of their main jobs was to act as proxy: when disagreements, matters of honor, fights between ambassadors and/or supplicants broke out, the Swords were there. They did battle for the side that engaged them. There were privately hired Swords as well. Each Jadoube (because they were all Jadoube, like the voices used to be all Lunari before Kalim) had a unique weapon, personally forged to suit their fighting style.

Tangun's was a long staff, made of a metal called waja. "Rumor is that Tangun Ye-Na is undefeated." Bay seemed awed by the older Jadoube man. "He removed himself from the pool of combat-ready Swords, took an apprentice instead of continuing to fight."

Twice a day, Dindal came to Katy, and they would play together. Dindal had brought Katy several wooden flutes to try on for size their first session, one of which was a gorgeous Irish flute in a light finish. Not what it was called here, but that's what it was nonetheless. Each school aligned with a Drazoen and their traits, with instruments associated to the ideas. Sundancer was power, intellectual drive, justice, a lot of cerebral things basically. Her instruments were pipes, flutes, whistles and saxophones. Dindal played panpipes; as a voice she'd mastered all the instruments of the schools, but as Orangevoice she had her favorite.

They would retreat into a private room on the wing, and Katy would try to align with the Air, coax it into being. She thought she'd hit the right note once or twice, and the relief of having a flute in her hands and lifted to her lips again was profound. Dindal was an incredible teacher, as could be expected from someone who'd conquered every musical discipline over a few hundred years. The hours they practiced and riffed were blissful. Katy taught Dindal a few Irish reels, which delighted the voice.

"This is similar in tone and spirit to Lunari folk music, but has a distinct feel of its own." Her smile was ecstatic. "Be prepared to lead students in this once you're declared a species of the Calling. I think it will be popular."

At least twice, Kweza notified Bay from the *Eternidad* that her family had tried to contact her again, and someone had even attempted to backtrace the IP. Katy thought that had to be Oran, thinking he was a clever git or some such twaddle. When they set up another call, it was even more anarchic than the first. Earth was in full panic about the revelations of aliens among them: not a scrap of toilet paper left in any store on the planet. Planes had been grounded until world governments decided they weren't at risk from flying saucers, which meant families couldn't gather unless they were within driving distance from one another. Even if you could drive to your family there were miliary checkpoints at all the major freeways and highways. Her mother was even more quiet and silently pleading than before.

Her brothers threatened Bay if he wasn't "dead careful" with their sister.

Her father looked at her closely. "Tell me you're all right? If not I'll find a way to you, I swear it."

She'd lied and said everything was grand, not to worry about her. *Love you, I'm fine.*

On the fourth day, when she, Bay and Riri were climbing the walls of their lavishly appointed prison (house arrest is house arrest regardless of the gentile décor), Swailu came for them. Tangun at her side, as always, plus another Jadoube who was never introduced but looked very scary. He had a wicked spear in his hand and eyes that never stopped tracking every movement, scouring each nook and cranny of their wing. His presence gave just enough extra security that their group was willing to risk leaving the Chorus.

"We've brought a storage sled this time; we'll smuggle the Humans inside of the cargo section. That should get us into the speaker compound unnoticed." Swailu's voice was soft and soothing. "Djilbay commed that you might benefit from meditation; we have an area specifically for that. Given the sensitive nature of discussions and mediation that happen with us, everything there is strongly protected."

"I vouch for the safety of this activity," Tangun added with an elegant bow. "We've scouted the way, ensured the passage is secure."

Unfortunately, being cargo meant Katy couldn't see anything they passed. The map of Centris she'd studied suggested they'd travel along mid ring back the way they'd originally come, going even further around. Past Giftgiver, Tonguemaker, Earthcaller and Waterbringer spokes. The Toledral speakers, who were only ever Mikanjo, would naturally set up shop at the sky ring level of Windweaver's spoke. Katy, getting claustrophobic in the hold where they'd been secreted, vowed to see as much of Centris as she could once she had an all-clear.

Upon their arrival directly to the doors of the chamber, Bay said he'd stay with Tangun and Swailu once Raisa and Katy were set up in the unbreachable "tranquility sanctuary". Katy gave him a kiss on the cheek, hoping that was acceptable PDA. His blush said it wasn't expected, but the grin said it was welcome.

They'd begun following Swailu when Bay called out, "If this doesn't work it's okay, my *qania*. When it's time, we will succeed."

Katy looked over at Riri, a little choked up, and saw a tiredness in her friend's face that hadn't been there before. All of the secrecy and pressure and fear was wearing Raisa down, Katy worried.

Both women followed the Toledral to what Katy had thought was just a back wall. At Swailu's touch, however, a panel slid aside and pure peace reached out and captured Katy. She felt Riri beside her, but was too awed by the serenity and harmony this space exuded to reach for, or even glance at her.

Rich toned wainscoting lined each wall. Potted not-quite-bamboo in the corners, teal leaves larger than they'd be on Earth. Huge spacelights for a roof, revealed colorful twinkles rippling above, sort of like Northern Lights. Bright stars winked in the distance far beyond this empty Kéntro system they inhabited. The lamps were warm and golden. A small fountain, centered against the wall before them, burbled with low and rippling sounds.

Riri and Katy quietly took seats on pillowy tufted ottomans in the center of the floor. This room wasn't large, and there were only three of the stools. Katy saw two woven mats, for someone who preferred sitting on the ground.

"This is the most soundproofed location in the Toledral Chambers. You should have complete noise cancellation," Swailu offered. "Hopefully it will help bring you relaxation and composure.

Once the panel slid shut, Katy closed her eyes and breathed.

Inhale. Exhale. This was the balm she desperately needed. The deeper she breathed the more a scent teased her nose. Something that carried so much nostalgia and contentment... what was it?

Cedar.

Her eyes popped open, but didn't see Swailu's meditation chamber. She was back on Orcas Island, a camp from childhood. Every summer her parents would send the kids off for one to four weeks. It was a camp run by the YMCA, and there were plentiful activities and things to keep bored children occupied. Swimming, archery, painting. Woodcarving was where Katy had spent most of her time.

Cedar was abundant then, at least in the amounts they used for children's projects. Katy remembered the portable speaker hooked to the iPods of the older camp counselors. Those days predated streaming by a bit. It was in that shop Katy heard Neko Case for the first time, and heard her over and over because Talulla loved her. Arctic Monkeys and Morrisey got some play, too, but when Marc put them on, Talulla would only let a few songs go before taking back control.

Katy sat in that little cabin, surrounded by the fresh earthy scent of cedar, making small tchotchkes. She'd sing along to "Hold On, Hold On" and try to think of something else to carve. If it kept her out of the sun (where she burned like toast), and out of water (where her hair turned into ballast, then dried like electrified barbed wire), Katy was all for it.

Toward the end of her third summer, she decided to make a flute. She was ten now, and it was time to go big or go home. Marc secured her a piece of cedar only long enough to make a small flute. More of a pennywhistle, if she were honest. Katy's creativity and imagination soared; she'd already known she wanted to become a great flautist. Now she could make her own instrument!

The Air had murmured at her, encouraging her, helping her

bore, chisel and sand. What came out in the end wasn't pretty, but it was hers by her own hands and meant everything to Katy. That crooked, poorly varnished flute, with holes of ranging sizes and a mouthpiece that strangled breath on the exhale, was perfect to her.

Here, now, in this quiet room the impossible scent of cedar washed over her, bringing back all those feelings. The certainty of her calling. The joy in such a simple thing because she'd created it. The ability to simply exist in those summer days as a breeze off the island's beach wafted through the open cabin window. There had been freedom and peace, and the thrill of experiencing new things. Katy unexpectedly had it back in an instant.

She needed to remember that even small, untrained hands could make things that mattered, and important tasks weren't always finished in a day. Her little pennywhistle had taken eight days of fourteen on that island, but day by day she'd done the work and was rewarded at the end. That's how she'd get this herald deal accomplished: day by day. She could do this. They could do this. All of them together, they would get this monumental thing done, and Katy would appreciate each minute as it rolled by.

Katy might have been hallucinating, but she thought she felt the brush of a wing inside her, as though it stroked her in reward for this breakthrough. It was the first solid hint she was on the right track: she'd lived her life by instinct, and wasn't about to change now. Prophecies would be useful, but this Kawakona/herald/Chanticleer gig was always going to come down to Katy letting herself trust what she knew to be true: let the music guide you and everything will come right in the end.

25

Near as Katy could tell, six days had passed when the *Eternidad* returned. It got a little fuzzy for an exact count because there'd been a lot of napping. Running scared for days on end took it out of a person. She and Riri had passed a night or two drinking, too, talking about what they missed from home. Since they hadn't been set free on Centris, there wasn't much they could say they liked better here than Earth – there was no basis for comparison yet. The replicator kicked ass, though. It had learned how to brew a perfect cup of tea, kept them in as much nropita as they wanted, and suggested new foods for them to try from various species' cuisine.

Katy had also gotten it to make something approximating mayonnaise. It was a gift from heaven when the replicator finally almost nailed it, because whatever was in the air here on Centris turned her hair into a dry, frizzy attack mop. One night Bay's wings had literally gotten trapped and they'd had a painful twenty minutes unsnarling the mess.

At last, though, the lazy days of playing flute, meditating and eating were set aside; Lia and Yuhwa were back. They had some new guy, Thuliso, with them and he was important and an urgent gathering had been called and so on and so on. Katy had her own agenda: to check in with Yuhwa first and learn what had happened in her meeting with Tangun. Yuhwa's withdrawal after her brief stay on Centris worried Katy.

"It was nothing, truly," Yuhwa said. "He wanted to remind me that once I've moved on from being a pilot, majio, he would make a place for me here."

"Are you thinking of changing jobs?"

"For my people," Yuhwa said, "it isn't a choice. You work as majio until the nawa call you home." Her voice cracked a little. "Let's not talk about that. Instead, let me tell you about Kalim Bluevoice. He was the most hỏi hậu person we've ever carried on the *Eternidad!*"

No translation needed. The man was a pretty diva, Katy had seen that right away. "Did he have four hundred suitcases? Racks of clothes? Casual namedropping and stories about his legion of conquests?"

Yuhwa cackled. "Thuliso Maor was no better!"

Lia suddenly rounded the corner and urged them to hightail it to the old meeting room. "Everyone is waiting," she groused with no small amount of exasperation.

As much as she disliked feeling imprisoned in their wing, Katy had to admit leaving it made her heart race. Fear of attack, of the unknown, and the constant nagging impression she was missing something obvious that would resolve everything, kept her edgy. Maybe that was why her first impression of the new Lunari emissary wasn't entirely positive.

Appointed, Mara had called him. Some kind of traveling information broker. Thuliso dressed like a man looking to charm and impress. Wheel and deal, as her oldest brother Ian might have said. A gombeen, Da would have said, because he never trusted men who cared overmuch about their appearance. Slate gray pants and jacket, British racing green shirt, all loose but well-tailored. Black loafers and socks of a color to match the suit. His bronzed skin and chin-length espresso colored hair combined with the clothes gave him a look of relaxation and casual style. How could someone this laid-back help them solve the riddle of Sundancer waking and the killer PQ ambassadors?

Riri was already present, seated near Olak and Pijo. Those three were fast becoming a clique and Katy wasn't sure whether it was jealousy she felt, or honest concern for the emotional well-being of her friend. Olak was very clearly invading personal space, and Katy knew Raisa could stand up for herself if she didn't like it.… But Katy didn't like it. Call it gut instinct, but she wasn't sure Olak, and her shadow Pijo, saw Raisa as more than a momentarily fun oddity.

Thuliso smiled broadly when Katy, Lia and Yuhwa entered. They were the last, and Mara locked things up behind them as the newest addition said, "I am very pleased to meet you, herald. I am Thuliso Maor. I was brought up to speed during the trip." He gestured at Lia and Yuhwa. "They shared your adventures so far, very exciting." He stepped forward, light, on the balls of his feet like a dancer. On him it came off as prowling.

Katy couldn't have clearly expressed what she thought of Thuliso out of the gate. But it was a mélange of attraction and distrust, ease and alarm. His voice was deep, sonorous, a rasping bassoon that she'd bet he weaponized to get bed partners. He'd stopped just shy of her comfort zone, eyeing the pendant, taking in her physical appearance. Katy was instantly and uncomfortably aware she was being judged; assessed and measured. She wondered if she could excuse herself from this meeting, weary of the constant push to be mystically more. To be the herald they all expected. Now this tosser piled on with yet more calculation, after days of her falling short of everyone's hopes.

He was important according to the voices, sure and all, but she didn't know if he was really trustworthy. Should anyone have been telling him about any of this outside of the war room? Then again, he oozed such self-assurance and allure it made her want to tell him all her confidences so he could solve the problem.

"A little exciting," she admitted. "But more terrifying, on the whole."

His face flattened, a removal of emotion entirely. "Yes, yes, only natural. Zina's death, the assassin Yfaun nearly succeeding, being thrust into the chaotic Aoni without sufficient knowledge." He made a moue with his mouth, shrugging. "Absolutely understandable to be afraid."

Gombeen for sure. Shady, condescending git! He'd just slammed her, Raisa and even Bay with a few words. Thuliso's large Lunari eyes were cornflower blue, close to her mother's color but so much deeper due to the size and lack of pupil. He'd widened them to look interested, leaned forward a little. Physically he wasn't imposing, but she still sensed danger. No, not danger, but hazard, maybe? Thuliso was a carnival ride, thrilling but risky. Katy revised her initial thought of information agent to whatever the Lunari version of undercover operative was.

She must have given off confused, nervous vibes because Bay moved to his favorite spot, directly behind her, protecting her back while letting her stand up for herself.

"Mara said you could help us figure out Zina's murder. Maybe catch the baddies," Katy challenged. "Not rehash yesterday's news."

Before he could answer, Mara jumped in. "Thuliso, we've been working our communication channels with the Pu'ulqaari and getting nowhere. They refuse to even let us into their delegation quarters."

"Our best move," Thuliso mused, "is going through Ilva."

"She's the Chitan ambassador, right?" Katy asked. "Not one of the PQ?"

"PQ?" Thuliso repeated, amused.

"Her name for the Pu'ulqaari," Dindal said.

"I like that," Thuliso laughed. "We'll never get anywhere with the 'PQ'. They're bound by so much protocol, honor, rules of hospitality that would oblige them in ways they don't want…. But Ilva and I have a good relationship."

"Very good, from the rumors I've heard," Olak cat-called from her chair.

Mara and Golgun turned annoyed frowns her way, but Thuliso just cracked a huge grin and poked his tongue out a little. "We have been amiable in the past, it's true. And that may give us some advantage here. I'll see her, try to dig for answers." He addressed Katy again. "I promise to help get you out from under the threat of death. I anticipate we will find Zina was killed for something unrelated to you being Sundancer's herald."

Katy was startled when Thuliso took her hand, and Bay pulled her back into his body when she flinched away from the Lunari. This was a very confident man, but she wasn't interested. Either in flirting or just friendly comforting. Katy was a one-alien-woman, and it was the one behind her, warm and solid. Thuliso could keep his hands to himself, please and thank you.

Sensing he'd overstepped, Thuliso withdrew slightly, expression wry. "I'll go now, hopefully Ilva will let me sneak into her offices between appointments." He walked to Mara and hugged her, clasping hands with Gudar and Golgun. "I'll send word once I have a sense of what's going on."

THREE MORE DAYS PASSED, waiting for word from Thuliso, Tangun, Mara. No one knew anything and Katy's agitation mounted. Riri spent more and more time with Olak and Pijo,

Bay split time between the *Eternidad* and Lia, being here in the secure wing, or with Swailu at the Toledral complex. She knew it wasn't fair to expect people to keep her entertained, but at the moment she felt isolated and lonely. The more stressed she felt, the less Katy connected with her Air. For the last full day, whether she played with Dindal or stared out a window at the endless vista of this foreign galaxy, the result was the same. No buzz from the pendant, the music usually always present, silent. She feared she'd lost herald status.

Rácz had vid-called a few hours past, saying they'd heard from Kalim back on Shilmand. The Bluevoice thought he was making progress on finding the Lost Library, but no solid leads on new prophecy texts yet. The Muškikal was giddy, flushing a rainbow of colors and letting their arms ripple. If she knew how to harrumph, Katy thought that would have been the time to do it. Why get excited about a missing library when they weren't progressing a single damn bit here? Her meditative positivity of a few days ago had largely fled.

"Herald!" Thuliso's voice rang through the audio panel by the wing's entrance. "Good news, finally. We're gathering in the main meeting chamber."

This best be bloody good, she thought. Heaving herself out of a lounge chair she'd appropriated, Katy donned the tyro robe she wore anywhere outside the wing. She was damn tired of that rag, too. She'd learned the Lunari typically wore loud colors, clashing patterns, a whirlwind of couture that showcased an exuberant and lively species. Why the fecking hell they'd muted all of it for the Chorus was perplexing. When she got some freedom, it was time to shop for clothes better than a ship bodysuit or a neutral robe she wasn't entitled to wear anyway.

Their meeting room was very full this time. Swailu and Tangun, Bay and Lia, Yuhwa, all the voices, Thuliso, Raisa. Even Rácz, who was bouncing slightly on their tentacles. Katy looked around, heading for Bay and Lia who'd waved her over.

"Yĕo and Eka have fled Centris," Tangun started.

They were the PQ ambassadors, Katy recalled.

"We think," Thuliso purred, "our questions and investigation got them worried enough to run back to Ishar. Ilva claims she never took their legislation attempts seriously, that she only kept them close to ensure she knew their next moves before damage could be done."

Golgun and Dindal scoffed. "We don't believe that, do we?" Golgun asked.

"Irrelevant, I think." Thuliso rocked his head side-to-side. "What matters is they've left and Ilva wants to distance herself from their taint."

"The Swords watch Ambassador Alaa very closely," Tangun rasped out. "She has given several of our members cause for concern, though not related to Zina Blackvoice's murder. That offense we assign to the Pu'ulqaari duo alone. None of the other Pu'ulqaari contingent were supportive of the darker side those two had started pursuing. Those who spoke to us admitted they'd heard Yĕo and Eka plot to harm Zina."

This was turning into a spy thriller or something. Katy pressed her back to Bay's front, taking comfort as she always did in his nearness. "What does this mean for us?" She looked at Riri. "Are we still stuck in the wing? If those two were the threats, and they've left, are we safe? Do we move on to declaring Humans are on Centris?"

"No," Raisa said quickly, "we should remain a secret. As much as I want to move around, having all of Centris knowing she's the herald seems…. Alarming. What if they come back?"

Katy was glad Raisa had said it. A lady didn't want to appear weak or, let's say, a 'fraidy cat. But she still had nightmares about Yfaun, and announcing to thousands of unknown people she was supposed to be a sort of dragon savior felt awfully foolish.

"You're correct," Mara spoke decisively. "Declaring Prima,

the politics and bureaucracy, it would devastate our chances to locate Sundancer. Every kaala would be absorbed with the balancing act of introducing a new species and petitioning for status. Hearings, interviews, it will be unceasing." Leader Mara was back in action now that her biggest naysayer was off her back.

Oh no, not a chance. Raisa and Katy shared a look and Katy knew they were on the same page. Someone on Earth would champ at the bit for that nightmare of paperwork and negotiations, and they were welcome to it. The two Humans currently on Centris would find a way to gracefully scarper. The hell with red tape.

"My suggestion," Mara went on, "is to try a small outing. First, over to the Chorus dormitory section. Less open than this part of the Chorus, therefore still controlled. But filled with tyro and songscribes of every species, giving you a chance to mix into a larger crowd." She pivoted to address Swailu. "I thought if that went well, you could take Katy back to the Toledral meditation chamber, openly this time?"

Swailu smiled that gentle, soft smile that both warmed and encouraged. "I would be happy to do so."

Bay intertwined his fingers with hers. More of that silent support he so excelled at, because she guessed he understood her nerves about this first real outing. "Lia, Yuhwa, you can come too?" She looked over to see them nod in agreement. Just beyond Lia she saw Raisa flash a hurt look. "Riri, let's see how many lotuses we can count. I'm betting more than a hundred."

Raisa's countenance cleared, and she laughed. "Field trip, and a bet, it is."

WHAT THEY'D LEARNED FIRST and foremost, was that Riri and Katy couldn't speak loudly in populated places. The aoiti of everyone around them would alert those folks it was an unknown language, and as far as Centris dwellers knew that shouldn't be possible. This would certainly raise eyebrows (on those who had any). Their inner circle had all gotten the Human updates, but the full database couldn't get an infodump without causing an intergalactic political incident.

So. Mouths shut, advised to pretend they were mute if cornered, they all toured the second section of the Chorus. This was where Chorus students lived, practiced, even held their initial shows when they graduated from tyro to robes. It had its own separate amphitheater, smaller than the main one. Unlike where they'd been staying, a large area of the mid ring spread between silver and orange spokes, this was stretched between red and silver. Still large, closer to the port, further from the Calling. Katy didn't have a perfect grasp of geography here, but she'd studied quite a bit in the time they'd been in lockdown. Several of the voices had also been telling her tantalizing bits of info that whetted her travel appetite; where the best deals were found, party areas, food, nature. Everything could be found on the Wheel if one knew where to look.

Their first outing went well, their core group impressed with the bustle and life thriving in the well-organized Chorus dorm area. It was chaotic and bright, reminding Katy very much of her years at uni. Not so much the colors, but the feeling that everyone there pursued learning and expansion of their minds communally, with gusto. She felt the closest to normal she had since leaving Earth.

Day two was an adventure across the Wheel to the Toledral complex and the meditation chambers. Now they could see where they were going, the Humans had no trouble keeping their mouths shut: they were overwhelmed with the sights. Thousands of people, different species speaking languages their aoiti raced to translate via newly trained neurons, shapes familiar and not, and strange clothing everywhere their eyes looked. Reaching the calm garden oasis of the Toledral complex was a relief.

Their previous trip they'd gone directly to the door of the meditation chamber, so they hadn't seen the entrance. It was like a Grecian temple, and oddly reminiscent of the front of The Kennedy Center Katy had seen for years on TV. Just beyond that, though, were exquisite gardens. Raisa was gobsmacked and asked to skip the room this time for a walk through the Toledral arboretum and manicured grounds. Katy opted to join her, and they both strolled through formally designed areas bordered by lush natural landscapes. Shrubs of lapis and trees of orange sunstone. Vine-covered archways, carefully planted flowers in patterns; it was a delightful profusion of exuberance and restraint. Very yin-yang.

"I believe," Riri murmured, "that I am far closer to winning the bet on the lotus imagery."

"They do love a lotus," Katy agreed. "When I said a hundred, I wasn't thinking it would be built into the floor tiles at the Chorus, or that this compound would design massive buildings and floral displays of it." She pointed at a bougainvillea -draped frame shaped into a lotus dripping with blooms. "You were way smarter to throw out a million for your guess."

Despite the two successful outings, both women were hesitant to venture out of their secure wing. Tangun assured them neither ambassador had returned, nor had there been any sign of other PQ killers running around Centris. Still… they kept to Voice House despite invites to explore from Dindal, Rácz, even Thuliso.

Finally, before dinner on the day after their tour of the Toledral complex, Bay asked them to meet him in the common area of their wing. Katy had no idea what to expect, and Riri's raised eyebrows suggested she was no wiser.

"Do you recall," he started, "how you noticed the car alarm tone bothered Yfaun?"

Katy remembered, but quickly brought Raisa up to speed since she'd been passed out in the backseat at the time.

Bay went on. "I had Kweza work on a way to turn that sound into a portable defense for both of you." He held out a palm where they could barely make out two small dots. "This is what it designed: these are intended to be subcutaneous, triggered by sustained pressure of two full atómi."

"Alarms," Katy breathed out, overwhelmed with an immediate sense of security and freedom. She hadn't admitted just how deeply she feared Yfaun and his people, what they'd already done and continued to want to do to her.

Riri must have felt the same, maybe even more since she'd suffered the near-fatal effects of Yfaun's crusade. Her hand raised to Bay's, not quite touching the tiny discs, fingers trembling. "You think this can stop him?" she whispered.

"Not stop, no. But if it makes him, or any of the Pu'ulqaari who try to threaten you, hesitate for a crucial moment... that could be enough to get help, or fight back. Not," he stressed, "that there's been any sign he got off Earth. Kweza and Vailillia have monitored the Earth satellites and there's no evidence of another ship leaving the atmosphere."

Katy stretched up and kissed Bay's cheek. "You're wonderful. This, this is wonderful. A second where he flinches is a second we have a chance." She gave him one more peck. "Thank you. Now, how do we put these on? Where do they go?"

Once she'd stopped cringing at the idea it was to go under her skin (Riri finally told her to quit being a baby), the process was easy. Bay had some Mikanjo doodad that covered a spot right behind their ears and did the deed. Neither one of them felt a thing, other than the rush of relief at being armed with even this minor way to defend themselves.

This didn't stop Katy, however, from claiming Bay needed to

kiss it and make it better when they got back to their room. He tried to point out there was no injury, as the injector plus the aoiti had closed the site and accelerated the healing. She was having none of it; he needed to do his job as her man and kiss the booboo. He laughed and spent half the night meeting her demands.

26

KATY WOKE NEXT TO BAY, EXCITED FOR A NEW DAY OF exploration. The alarms he'd given them the night before made her dead psyched to get out and go sightseeing. Golgun and Dindal had told her about so many incredible things to see on the spokes she'd had to make a mental top five list. That way she didn't try to do everything at once; she'd be getting to all of it someday, just not her first day. It was escapist, maybe, but their Save the Aoni group hadn't gotten far sussing out what to do or how to do it. Nothing further had come from Kalim back on his home planet about the Lost Library, nothing in the histories they'd gotten translated gave them huge AHA! moments. A break might be just the thing to get new cylinders firing.

She tried to wake Bay up to join her, not quite up for flying solo out on the Wheel. He retaliated by trying to drag her back to bed, and she only narrowly escaped, laughing and vowing to be back for a late lunch. The Wheel had too many things to see for her to laze about in bed, even though his arms were awfully tempting.

Riri was in the communal area finishing a mug of nropita.

"Want to explore? Bay is a sleepyhead and I want to see every-thing. We can have girl's day."

Her friend linked their arms. "I was just daydreaming of that very thing, so I'll take you up on it. I'm thinking green spoke for bookstores and libraries first? Green is Tonguemaker, yes?" Naturally Raisa would want to get near more libraries after the one in the Chorus whetted her appetite. No matter they couldn't read them yet, books were books, especially for Riri. "If we're lucky the aoiti will let us see if we stumble across one of the histories hidden away, only to be revealed when the Kawakona comes upon it!"

Katy snorted. "Grand!" Then she spun to look at Raisa while walking backward. "We could go to red for food after finding our secret decoder books, and then silver for instruments and music? Books for you, a flute of my own, and intergalactic food for both of us."

"Here's hoping these aoiti work like the debit cards everyone swore they are, so we can pay for all these wonderful things," Riri said. She referenced the fact Bay and the voices had loaded them with funds, but only if they could figure out how to scan themselves properly. "Olak gave me this," Raisa held up a palm-sized tablet with writing on it neither could decipher. "It has our favorite dishes so we don't have to try and speak them. She says the food on red subspoke is incredible, but prefers what's on gold. Earth-caller's spoke.

"I say we try both. For science."

"This is wise and I support your efforts"

Katy turned back around as they reached the locked wing door. Swailu was coming in just as they tried to leave. The Tole-dral speaker was one of the few people with full access rights to the wing. She looked tired today, which said a lot about a woman who Katy thought must have the patience of four saints and the skin care regime of a movie star. She was older than

Bay's millennium-plus by a good half-century, but looked younger than Katy's own mother.

"Kawakona and Raisa! Good fortune to meet you both early this day." They all bowed in greeting. "I had hoped to speak with Djilbay, has he gone ahead?"

"He's still trying to sleep in. He said finally being safe for a while meant he didn't have to 'wake with the far-oh-pie-ee-tee', whatever that might mean."

Swailu smiled nostalgically. "Faropaiti are the first birds to rise on Bankiri, and I would think on the *Eternidad* they kept a flock to remind the seekers of their home world." Her cheeks creased even more deeply with mirth. "Perhaps I will find a recording to shake him out of his slumber."

Katy and Riri left Swailu to the fun of waking Bay. Their first independent foray called for navigating the trams, which was easier than she'd feared. They'd been seen out and about enough times in the Chorus that they drew little notice. Once they'd boarded the tram there were so many people that they were utterly unremarkable in their bland robes.

Katy's heart filled with wonder at the noise and bustle, the way Centris had been created to harmonize technology with nature, and the fact that she and Riri didn't stand out in any way. None of the people they passed on their way to the mid ring trams had any idea the first two Humans in Centris' history were strolling by. After days of running, of being the herald, of being protected and scrutinized (and found wanting more often than not) this stolen time of freedom was invigorating.

Since they were at the edge of Songmaster Silver's spoke, they would board the tram there. "Could we go back up to the dock for a tick?" Katy asked. "It was such a blur when we came in, I'd love to take a longer look at all the different ships again."

"Sure." Raisa aimed for the tram running out to the sky ring and landing port. "Honestly everything since Pike Place seems a blur. I still can't believe we're in the center of the Aoni. What passes for it. Olak explained how it's all relative to wherever you are."

Olak again. Some more. Katy had yet to reconcile her thoughts on the Purplevoice who'd been so blatantly flirting with Riri. A woman who would take whatever opportunities came her way. Aggressive in a sultry and compelling way, both gentle and firm. Grandmum Phelan would have called the voice a floozie, or a hussy, but Katy preferred less judgy words, like 'bohemian bombshell' or 'vivacious vixen'. Sensual siren, even, of the sort Katy could never be in a million years. Initially she'd thought Olak was hooked up with Pijo Whitevoice, and, if so, they made the kind of couple you'd seen in perfume ads. Katy had the sense Riri would be on the monogamous side of things, so if the Lunari were thinking they'd snag a Human third that might not go far.

Then again, I don't know leprechaun shit about Riri's likes and dislikes. Hell, her reciprocation of Olak's advances was the first Katy had ever seen of Raisa's interest in *any* person. Bay had made sure to tell her that while the Lunari were all about free love, they absolutely respected consent and would never cross a line like that. Katy took a moment to curse herself for a missed opportunity: when Riri had asked her about Bay, she could have probed her friend's feelings about the Purplevoice.

"I don't know on that," she responded to Raisa's earlier comment. "I get very lost when the physics and astronomy gets tossed about." She rose in anticipation of their tram stop. "Calling it Centris makes it center enough for me."

They stepped off amidst a crush of people trying to get on and go back down the spoke. Katy mentally checked off the species she thought she knew by sight now: Jadoube, PQ, Uilig, Rixat, Mikanjo, Chitan, Ⓞti, Muškikal. As much as Katy loved Yuhwa and remembered Lanu fondly, she thought the brightly colored nine-fingered Ⓞti might be her new favorites. Their extreme height and three large eyes made them the epitome of what Katy had thought aliens would look like. Even their name, *ooh!-tea*, was fun to say.

She and Raisa paused in the first open area leading to the ship docks. So many people stopping and staring, just as they did. Or they rushed hither and yon with bags, grabbing food and drink from a handful of carts. Many queued at the help desks. Ⓞti lumbering through with satchels and heavily kitted-out toolbelts. Katy was hit with a feed of information that rushed her like a memory suddenly recalled, complete with flashing images.

Harbor Primur *gateway to the corridor of berths behind it, which form the Primary Port of Centris. Six pads total, capable of docking up to forty Eternidad-sized craft or several hundred smaller ships. Staffed by two hundred and eight workers, open all hours and days. More than ten million travelers per tuig. Open to all arrivals, unlike Harbor Ovu which is restricted and one-third the size of Harbor Primur. Have travel documents ready.*

"Whoa!" she hissed to Riri.

"Did you just get bombarded with data about this place?" her companion hissed back, incredulous.

Eyes wide, Katy nodded, kept her voice as low as possible so they wouldn't be overheard. "When they said the aoiti would give us 'full background', I didn't expect that. It's like all of the internet search engines in our heads." She shuddered a little, then brightened. "Just think, we'll never need travel brochures or calculators again, though."

Riri nodded. "I'm happy the nanobots are incorporating like Lia and Bay hoped, but it's going to take more adjustment. Getting blasted with so much information is jarring, it messes with my concentration." Raisa shook herself slightly, pivoting on her heel. "I swear, just as it happened, I thought I saw that woman from the refuge."

Refuge? "Oh! The one with the tail and major 'tude?"

"'Tude indeed," Raisa muttered. "Yes, there!" She pointed to their right, near the colossal doors leading to the ship docking bays.

Katy spotted a blonde man in some kind of uniform standing close to a woman who looked a lot like the Chitan they'd seen. The pair weren't arguing, but it was a very intense convo whatever the topic. It *was* Fumi Ly. She of the badass hair, outfit, and body language. What was she doing here? Everyone had said they were safe because no one from Earth could have gotten here so quickly. Yuhwa hadn't sensed any other majio-piloted craft in the space around them when they had first raced to Centris. Meaning Yfaun hadn't left Earth when they did, but how could Fumi be here now? Bay said Lia and Kweza both vouched no ships had left Earth. But here was evidence to the contrary.

A trickle of nauseating fear spiked down her back; just as she reached for Riri to say they had to run, her friend fell forward to her knees. She grabbed the back of her head, blood oozing between her fingers. Katy tried to spin, but felt a needle pierce her lower back. Horrified, she told her legs to move, to run, but they didn't respond.

"Created this lovely drug," Yfaun growled in her ear, "by synthesizing what your Mikanjo atachelys injected into me."

Katy's tongue was fat and numb in her mouth, all she could do was gurgle in terror. He would kill her now. Take her somewhere hidden and cut her throat or stab her. Would he destroy her corpse or let it be found as a way to prove he'd ended the dream of waking Sundancer?

Riri's eyes, blurry with pain, caught hers. *Run,* she tried to convey. *Save yourself.* Yfaun had pulled Katy close like they were together, though his attack was so fast and silent not a soul in the Harbor Primur had noticed anything amiss. Katy could feel her mind darkening, but knew if she succumbed she'd never open her eyes again. Never see Bay, Earth or her family again.

Sheer panic flooded her system with enough endorphins to get a single word out. "Car!"

That was all it took for Riri, who blinked once and rolled to her feet at the same time she pressed the spot below and just behind her ear with a bloody finger. Two seconds was a long time when you were losing consciousness and scared your friend would die next to you. *Please, Riri. Survive.*

Raisa stumbled, finger still pressing, and it looked like Yfaun would strike her again, but the beautiful amplified sound of Bay's car door alarm went off. The PQ killer flinched back, disturbed and shocked by the noise, just as they'd hoped. Finally, people nearby turned their attention to the trio, and Yfaun jerked Katy back and away from Riri.

It was the brief reprieve she needed. With one tearful look at Katy, Riri ran as fast as she could into a crowd, lurching toward the information desk. She was so smart, Katy marveled. Don't go for the tram; target the place in the cavernous room with the heaviest concentration of people. Plus, whoever was behind that desk would know who to call for medical aid.

Not getting to spend more time appreciating Raisa's intelligence and practicality was going to be one of Katy's top five regrets. As her eyes drooped shut, adrenaline spent, she felt Yfaun drop something over her head and drag her away.

27

KATY CAME TO, MOUTH RUBBERY, HEAD ACHING. ALL she saw were seamless grey walls, chairs in the same bland color pushed against the walls. After days of the electric color mix Centris blazed at every turn, this was shockingly blah. Menacing in the same way all prison cells were. Eventually she realized she was laying on a table in the middle of the room, flat on her back, arms at her side. No sound, no color, not even air cycling until a door whooshed open and Yfaun prowled through it.

She jerked back instinctively, pieces of what had just happened flashing like a janky film reel. Attacked and kidnapped in the middle of the bloody main port on Centris! How had he done it? Katy saw his face was near invisible, as it had been back at Pike Place Market: he must be wearing another mask thingy, a kuh. A replacement for the one Bay's machine had broken into and reconfigured. Was that thing honestly enough to let him get away with poisoning her in public?

"Time to go," Yfaun snarled, grabbing her wrist and yanking.

She cried out, slid and fell off the table, landing hard on her hip, legs tangled. Her muscles weren't working: either the concoction he'd injected her with had destroyed her nervous system, or it hadn't worn off enough to let her move. When he kicked at her, pain spiked in an ankle, so hopefully everything was just mostly asleep.

"I'm not going anywhere with you, PQ shitbird!" She struggled to sit up and dodge another kick.

Yfaun ripped his mask off. His creeptastic pink eyes made her skin crawl when he focused on her, bending down to growl in her face. "You have no choice. Our ship is ready, you are weak, I am not." He lifted a hand, showing her his needle glove attachment, prepped and ready. "I can put you under again, or you can walk yourself."

Katy spit in his face. "Fuck off, you bastard!" If he managed to get her on a ship and off Centris the odds of being found would shrink to almost nothing. As much as Bay would search (and she knew he would be relentless) it would be an insurmountable problem, because Yfaun could take them anywhere. She had to try and stall. "She'll have them looking for me by now. Just give up, let me go back."

"Far more likely your friend was scooped up by my seconds," he hissed, not bothering to wipe her spittle away. "Even if she evaded them, this station is large and there hasn't been enough time to mount a full sweep. Not when we control the surveillance and they have no idea where to begin looking." He shook his mask at her.

"They don't need to see your face to see you dragging me around," Katy snarled. "That'd be pretty sketchy, even in the crowd we were in."

Yfaun snorted. "Stupid Human. That isn't what the kuh does here. On your planet, yes, blending only. Here it creates blind spots in the system, wiping all trace of us. If we don't want to be seen, we simply aren't. For untold tuigs we've bypassed the Centris cameras and databases, going about business as we decided." His face was a rictus of combined disdain and glee.

Katy's blood froze. From the beginning she'd seen Yfaun as

terrifying, but this went beyond that. What he said meant their species actively hid their activities from Centris and the Calling. They were deeply embedded, apparently had backup killers, and could slip in and out of the system without a trace. They must have been able to get into Voice House to kill Zina that way, maybe even the last Silvervoice before Mara. Such a convenient accident that had been.

Trapped. She was too dizzy to hit back or run, and she was trapped. He was going to get her on that fecking ship he'd mentioned if she couldn't find a way out. The ship was another thing that signaled this was a bigger plan than any of them knew.

They just hadn't taken Yfaun, any of the PQs, as seriously as they should have. If he had transport ready and waiting, she suspected he'd been supplied by PQ ambassadors or sympathizers. Well, she wasn't making it goddamn easy for him. Katy started screaming at the top of her lungs.

Yfaun just stared at her. This close she saw his irises were like carved rose petals, seeming to shrink and bloom around the dark central pupils. "Are you through?" he asked, when her voice cracked one last time. "This is a soundproof chamber and I'm done wasting time."

She tried to get up, to push away, but her muscles were still in shock from his first dosing. All she accomplished was flopping to her stomach like a dying fish. "No! No, no, no!"

He didn't even slow down on his way around the table, grabbing her wrist in one hand, punching his other fist into her already sore hip. She felt the needle pierce her skin, and darkness took her immediately.

DJILBAY WAS ON CLOUD NINE, as his beloved Human liked to say. Swailu had brought news she'd contacted his mothers, who were willing to have a call with he and his sister later that sal. She'd also been painstakingly clear his mothers didn't believe her about the Kawakona, and he shouldn't go into the call with hopes they would see things from his perspective.

"Sometimes the best we can do is to keep the windows open for clean breezes to flow," she'd told him.

Bay hadn't told his sister he'd asked the Toledral speaker to reach out to their parents, and a part of him wondered if she'd even want to join him. From what she'd said a few sals ago, the choice to stop contact with them had been hers. "They never said as much, brother, but I knew they pitied me for staying. Their loss of belief isn't the bitter poison of Orihei's parents, but comes from deep within them nonetheless."

Hopefully he could bring everyone together as a start today, and work on full reconciliation once Katy had woken Sundancer. He felt her despair sometimes, thinking she'd failed him, the voices, or the entire Aoni somehow. What he also felt was the growing power within her. Every sal-ang spent playing with Dindal centered her and gave her strength. As she adjusted to life on the Wheel, she was noticeably less anxious and pushed herself to reach for what she needed. Even things as simple as learning more about the species she'd already met; researching and finding recordings of the greatest concerts in Chorus history; studying the geography of his planet. She'd made him swear to take her there "when it's all said and done", so they could experience it as first-timers together. Bay was confident, far more so than Katy, that she was on the cusp of figuring out how to do what she needed in order to fully become Kawakona.

This was, in good part, why he'd encouraged her to explore without him today. Lia (his sister finally let him use the nickname) had scolded him when she thought he was being too protective of his *qania*. A fledgling too closely covered doesn't feel wind in their own feathers and cannot fly, she'd lectured.

As he finished showering, wondering if he should don ceremonial dress or stay in casual ship clothing for the call with his parents, the main door chime for the wing sounded. When it played over and over, urgently repeated, his heart started to race. Frantic noise like that, when Katy and Raisa were alone on Centris right now, filled him with glacial fear.

Racing half-dressed to the door, he saw a grim-faced Tangun on the other side.

"They were attacked," the man growled. "Raisa is alive but injured, Katy is missing."

Bay's world stopped, his entire body petrified. This couldn't be happening. "Where?"

"Harbor Primur, less than a sal-ang ago. Thankfully the Human was smart and demanded security call me." The Jadoube Head of Swords bowed his head, then snapped it back up. "Come quickly, we'll go to the mediward healing Raisa and try to get answers. We'll find your herald, I vow it."

WAKING this time was worse than before. Doubling up whatever drug he'd created wasn't doing Katy's system any favors. Her head swam, nothing around her in focus. On her back again, aches letting her know she was painfully alive. Slowly, Yfaun's hated visage dropped into her field of vision.

"Wake," he barked, slapping her face. "I want you to see this. To witness."

He was coming unhinged now, a zealot about to perform his sacred duty. Katy knew he was going to kill her, maybe brutalize her first. What that would accomplish she didn't know. Did he think she knew about other heralds? Hopefully not. She didn't want to die, but better a quick death than prolonged and painful torture. PQ were certain to be experts at that kind of interrogation.

In all her years of reading fairy tales and adventures, she'd never considered what the heroes felt in these moments. The gut-clenching, bowel-emptying, voice-stealing fright. Her eyes wouldn't close, or move away from Yfaun's cruel grin. She couldn't gather her voice, call him names, beg for mercy. No aoiti to explain what nasty name he'd just called her, no Air to comfort her. Utter paralysis of spirit and body. He reached out and slapped her once more, just because he could, or because it was fun for him. This jostled her body enough that the pendant slid up to the hollow of her throat, catching his eye.

His spooky, bleached, bony fingers pulled the talisman out of her robe. Letting it drop against her chest, he tapped it. "I can feel this is the essence. This is from Her." His gaze rose past her face, becoming unfocused. "That's what I'm bred to do, you understand. Your pitiful seeker mocked my status, but he is too ignorant, too stupid to comprehend."

"Wha-" she started, tongue thick. Licking her lips she tried again. "What are you talking about?" He wasn't going to just cut her throat here and now? She'd take every second she could.

His intensity made his patterned iris appear to swirl. "I was on your Earth long enough to see some of your entertainment. You hope I will speak all of my plans, leave myself open to ambush by your seeker come to save you." His smile was pure evil. "I *will* tell you, so you may know what kind of eternity you'll endure in the shadow prison. Somewhere he will never be able to find you. Never."

Katy thought she couldn't be more scared, but the phrase "shadow prison" was amping up the horror. No one had mentioned anything like it in all their discussions of Drazoen, developing species, or formation of the Calling. But Yfaun spoke of it like it was normal, everyday. Which told Katy it was something only his people knew, and they understood it well.

"Long ago, our greatest artisan saw something in the Aoni no other could. Shadows that flew between the stars. Then she saw something even less perceptible than shadows; the darkness that must exist in opposition to light. Sula Nera'aj saw this darkness and knew she could harness it, trap it. Through her work, our people would have a place to lock away those who would deny us what is rightfully ours. Our way of life is precious, but has long been attacked by others outside our world. They don't respect our ways, nor do they give our sovereignty its due.

"Sula of Shadows foresaw what her talent could give us: prisons crafted from nefeslo cages. These places would be inaccessible once created. Only an act of great power, wielded by a chosen one, could open temporary portals to the prisons, and in them we would consign the greatest threats to our way of life. The doors would close, those problems sealed away for eternity."

Dear gods, the PQ were totalitarian, populist nutjobs who'd found a way to create cosmic gulags. Katy recalled Lanu telling her nefeslo was PQ special mud, the same stuff Yfaun had quantum bonded to his freaky-ass face. And some ancient slag made jails out of it?

"After creating the prisons, before she was lost to the darkness," he continued, "she taught our clergy how to design and produce those of us who can make the temporary bridge between light and shadow. Only nine of my kind are bred each generation, a process that took many generations to perfect and quite a lot of genetic realignment." He added, softly, "We're told hundreds were destroyed before they got it right."

A beat of silence where Katy heard her breath rattle in her chest. Yfaun stood, looking over her prone body. When he spoke, he tapped his chest in emphasis. "Artisan, spy, clergy: preselected before conception, hewn and trained our entire lives. Everything is carved from us, bit by bit, from our very first breaths. We are meant for a single purpose: to open the shadow prisons and lock your kind away. That means we must be able to sense you, sense the Drazoen triggers." He bent and touched her pendant again.

"A full kōmilen has passed since Sula of Shadows did her job. Now I do mine." Yfaun's face had been grave, but the smile he turned on her now was rapturous. He removed his top, revealing a chest that matched the ghostly beech-bark of his fingers, decorated in rosette swirls like his face. "My own family never believed the time of heralds would come. But I always did. I had dreams, such dreams. They called me, urged me, and I knew if I followed the Mikanjo seekers, I would be blessed with the power to stop you before you woke Sundancer."

The bizarre twinning of Bay and Yfaun was gruesomely fascinating. Born to do their role, dreamed that they were the ones who would accomplish the duty from their earliest years. Doubted by family, driven to succeed, they both even had markings all over their torsos. But only one of them was a psychotic killer with infantile beliefs that his people's greed meant others needed to die.

"Why do you have to kill me? You won't even try to talk me out of it, or bribe me, nothing like that? Appeal to my baser, craven instincts?" The drugs still had her so woozy she couldn't sound angry, merely forlorn.

He shook his head, mystified. "I do not kill you, why do you keep assuming this?"

Katy wanted to smack him so badly. "Because you almost killed Raisa at the market, thinking she was me!"

"Ah," he sneered. "That would not have killed her, or you. The drug was designed to mimic death only. It was more aggressive to Human systems than expected, I admit, but she wouldn't have died. In all likelihood. This new drug I synthesized, though, worked better than I hoped. Than you deserved."

Great, I'm the guinea pig of knockout drugs.

"I do not kill you. I imprison you. For eternity. The shadow prison is outside time, outside the Aoni. You will never die, and therefore no other herald for Sundancer can ever be born. You take Her essence with you, never to be found by another." He closed his eyes, exhaled, then proclaimed, "I don't kill you; I sacrifice myself to open the cage and send you through."

Katy spluttered, desperate for a response that would stop him, but before anything coherent came out of her mouth, light filled in the cheetah-like pattern of Yfaun's nefeslo mask and the marks on his chest. It spilled forth like cracks of dawn breaking though his skin. Brighter and brighter, burning her eyes, making them water. Just as rapidly as the light bloomed, it was infiltrated by a seething, roiling blackness. Thesis and antithesis, fighting for dominance. The PQ assassin's pink eyes were subsumed by the darkness, then his entire body. The creeping shadows reached out to cover every surface and fill all the space in the craft. They were a floating bubble of nothingness.

"Katy Phelan, herald of Sundancer Orange, you will suffer eternally, as you must. Know that my life is the payment for this."

The slithering bands of shadow rolled over Katy like the river Styx and she fell into oblivion.

28

DJILBAY HAD NEVER KNOWN DESPONDENCY LIKE THIS, laced with terror and self-loathing. Katy was missing, taken from him in one of the rare moments he'd let her out of his sight. His instincts had been screaming the entire time they'd been on the Wheel, but he'd overruled his concerns. Lulled into a sense of complacency by the sheer number of people involved in trying to wake Sundancer. Others had been confident Katy was secure on Centris, waiting for their group to find a sacred text or remember an oral prophecy that showed them the way forward. The Chorus, the Toledral, even the Head Sword. All had sworn Katy was safe within the flock.

He blamed no one more than himself. If he'd just gotten up with her that morning, accompanied her to the subspokes instead of letting them go alone. If he hadn't let himself be distracted by Swailu's update on the call home. If he hadn't gotten it into his head she needed the confidence a solo day out would give. If he'd only insisted Katy wait for him to explore, if he'd just pushed for Dindal or one of the other Cadre to chaperone. If, if, if.

But he hadn't and she was gone, as though she'd vanished from Centris entirely. Tangun was taking it very personally, and with even more fury than Zina's murder had incited. He'd sent his Swords through all of Centris to look for Katy, but to no avail. All of the voices had shaken their heads, murmured regrets… some more honestly than others, Bay thought darkly. He wasn't sold on the credibility of Olak and Pijo, despite (or perhaps because of) the closeness developing between them and Raisa.

Speaking of whom. Raisa was nearly as wrecked as Bay. She hadn't stopped crying, even while her head wound was being repaired by the med staff. She repeated herself tonelessly for a sal-ang or more, "Why didn't I see him? Feel him? This is the second time. I should have sensed him."

By "him" she meant Yfaun. While they thought they'd safely stranded him on Earth, he'd managed to get to Centris. He'd tracked his prey, waited for his moment to attack, knocked out Raisa and snatched Katy so fast he barely appeared on security footage. Bay hadn't said anything to Raisa, but it was probable the only reason Yfaun hadn't struck to kill was to avoid making a bigger scene in such a public place. He gave her great credit, though: even in those harrowing moments she kept pretending she was mostly mute, avoiding an even bigger intergalactic incident if her status as an unregistered alien became known. She'd just repeated Tangun's name over and over until he was summoned.

Bay paced the wing common area, empty and eerily silent. Katy had disappeared from Centris cameras, no one could put eyes on her anywhere on the Wheel, and there was a chance Yfaun had gotten off the station. Bay refused to think she was dead; he believed to his core that he would feel it if she were. She was his dream, his life's purpose. He could admit that now, embrace the overwhelming feelings she'd sparked in him. He saw his future and new dreams with her; the fulfillment and sense of rightness when he was with her a powerful motivator to be a better Mikanjo, one who deserved such a partner. Merely thinking of her brought ease and peace to his mind.

At least, that had been true in the sals leading up to this one. Right now Bay couldn't contain the anger and dread: his wings were extended, ready to launch him to the heavens so he could scream out at the injustice. He was her seeker, the one who'd found her, taught her about Drazoen, and tried to shepherd her awakening to the greater Aoni. Yet he orbited this room like a useless fambondro from Bankiri. Wandering in concentric circles until he eventually created a trench so deep he would struggle to climb out of it.

His self-castigation was interrupted by the Lunari appointed, the one who only sals before had assured them Katy would be safe on Centris. Thuliso Maor stepped into the room, quiet and calm demeanor belying an intensity Bay found both magnetic and unnerving. He and Katy thought this emissary of the Lunari epitomized 'charismatic'. Katy had said, "He's a Rasputin-like chancer. Charming, smooth, but I bet he's harder to kill than a cockroach."

"No update on a location for her, but I've got some information about how the assassin got here," he said without preamble. "You're wearing a hole in the flooring," he smiled faintly. "Perhaps straighten your path? Let's get food while I share what I've found."

"But-"

"Jaxolē, it does you no good to starve. She'll need you in good health to survive this."

Bay stared at Thuliso, torn. Reluctantly he nodded, acknowledging there was no advantage to weakening himself with hunger. Katy would need him strong when the time came to get her back. But it felt like a betrayal of her to leave the Chorus and attend to needs so basic. How could Bay eat or drink when she was missing? When she might be in pain, scared, or being tortured by the Pu'ulqaari killer?

"Where to?" he asked, snapping his wings tight to his back.

Thuliso pivoted to leave the antechamber. "I know a vendor on Giftgiver subspoke that makes gualpô I dream of when I'm away from here."

Bay shuddered at the dish mentioned. Thank the Nine there would be many other vendors serving food that didn't simulate a sea creature actively trying to escape the bowl. Djilbay was surprised species other than Tschuele enjoyed it.

Neither man communicated again until they'd boarded the tram bound for Giftgiver Red's spoke. Once they'd settled into their seats for the short ride, Bay grumbled, "Well, let's hear it. What do you know?"

Thuliso turned his attention from the view outside the tram to Djilbay. "Two sals past the *Oudna* arrived on station. They docked with special cloaking permissions at Harbor Ovu." He stopped, waiting for Bay to recognize the name of the craft.

"That means nothing to me, I've been on a planet without access to Aoni current events," he ground out.

"I forget how long you were isolated." Thuliso crossed his left leg over the right and leaned back. "The *Oudna* is one of the modern Dál craft. They use them for training, living quarters, traveling fight arenas. Because they are so widely known, hated or worshipped, their fighters are often hunted for revenge or romance. Due to this, they've negotiated the right to declare privacy protocols. Thereby securing them isolated docking bays with no other craft, and keeping them off most station records. Essentially, they become invisible to stations they frequent when they aren't holding advertised bouts."

Bay was lost. "What do galactic blood sport goons have to do with Katy?"

The Lunari raised an eyebrow at Bay's tone. "Not a fan, I see.

The intersection is with your Human's planet. It seems someone at Earth's safehouse called on the *Oudna* to rescue her from the chaotic wake your ship left."

Instant nausea rippled Bay's skin and fluttered the innermost feathers of his wings. "The Pu'ulqaari killer, he caught a ride with this fighter's ship?" He exploded out of his seat, startling the other riders, though his companion didn't even flinch. "Because the *Eternidad* exposed the safehouse, carried that Chitan woman to Earth, and I stupidly spoke of coming here?!" Bay needed to pace, fly, or punch and kick something.

"I worried they'd send another killer after her, but I never…" he trailed off, looking down at Thuliso with helpless anguish. "It hadn't occurred to me Yfaun could get off Earth and here so quickly. We were checking, but saw no signatures of interstellar craft leaving Earth's atmosphere."

"Their cloaking is extremely advanced," the Lunari said as the tram slowed. Thuliso stood, clamping a hand on Bay's shoulder. "It's good this is our stop, you need to walk some of this energy off. I understand you're afraid, upset. But you have to calm so we can formulate a rational plan."

Bay shrugged the hand off, still mad and self-flagellating. "There's no time for food and 'calm'. She's in danger, damn you! We need to find the crew of the *Oudna* and force them to answer our questions."

Walking to the exit, Thuliso spoke over his shoulder. "Seeker, you will not get answers there. You'll get bruises and broken parts." The tram stopped. "Dál members are some of the most vicious fighters in the Aoni, they do it for money and fun, and you believe you can force them to talk to you?"

Bay grudgingly admitted the Lunari was correct. But to be thwarted like this, when the sheer panic of knowing Yfaun might have Katy was corroding his insides! He refused to contemplate an even worse possibility.

The next atóm his senses were overwhelmed with the

chaotic whirl that thrived on Giftgiver's subspoke. As a Drazoen, They represented all people, all genders, all natural urges as a celebration of life. Here on Their spoke of the Wheel one of the fundamental needs of all creatures was fêted: eating and food. There was a myriad of street food options on the subspoke, vendors lining the sides and centers of the pathways, and sandwiched between fixed restaurants. Whether someone wanted a quick dish or a sit-down experience, Giftgiver subspoke would provide.

More than almost any other subspoke, Giftgiver Red's accommodated all fifteen species. If there was an appetite for a rare dish, odds were it could be found nearby. Bay wondered which Earth dishes would end up here, once Humans were introduced and accepted.

It wasn't long before Thuliso halted in front of a cart boasting the gualpô in huge lettering on the side. It also listed a couple dishes Bay was more willing to eat. Once they'd gotten their food, they took seats at a nearby communal table, sandwiching between other diners. Djilbay was pleased with his bowl of xitlacoche. The large-cap fungus was delicately seasoned, reminding him of a mushroom dish he'd had in Lesotho once, many tuigs before.

After two bites, he eyed Thuliso and asked, "So, I have calmed as requested. Now tell me, how would you proceed? How can we know where they are or what has happened? A Pu'ulqaari killer hid from cameras, kidnapped my Kawakona-" Overcome, he choked out, "Katy is gone, we have to find her!"

From his left a raspy voice said, "I can help find her."

Bay's head jerked around to glare at the eavesdropper. A Nyakisi man, leaning toward them with a bright gleam in his blue eyes. Dressed in synth-hide like most of his species preferred: trousers and vest of a buttery texture and form-fitting quality that told Bay this man was very good at what he did. If he could afford that kind of ensemble, bespoke and perfectly tailored, he must be expert. Nyakisi specialized in dirty work: for the right price they'd steal something, abduct someone, even kill whatever the buyer said needed to die.

Whereas Krylar thought their way was the only way, or Pu'ulqaari thought their way was the right way – and both would "help" you see it their way – Nyakisi didn't care about your thoughts or feelings. They cared about getting paid; utterly loyal once they were bought, at least for the length of the contract. Once that was up, though, they'd happily take a revenge contract from your enemy.

"I don't know what you thought you heard, Jaxolē," Thuliso said neutrally. "But mercenary help isn't what we need."

Bay wasn't sure he agreed. Nyakisi operated in the shadows, and that was exactly where Katy had disappeared. They had less than nothing to go on right now, which he'd heard was right where these people excelled.

The Nyakisi leaned back, eyes still on Thuliso and Bay, his food forgotten in front of him. His pale skin didn't flush with anger at the Lunari's attempted brush-off, and the eager glint in his gaze didn't dull. "Ah, Lunari, I am not your 'friend'. I know what I heard, and I think you do need me. People who are taken like that, hidden so quickly and well, it's by the will of the wealthy and powerful." He spread his arms. "Where I surpass all others is my knowledge and access to that class."

"Who are you?" Bay asked.

"Na Xan. And who might you be, Mikanjo?" Na's stare flicked to Thuliso. "You, I've seen before. Appointed of the Cadre. Don't be so quick to label me mercenary when you, yourself, have a long history of doing what you've been paid to do."

Bay was amazed when small spots of color rose in the Lunari's cheeks. If they had time he'd have probed just what that meant. Was Thuliso a Lunari hit man? Seemed like nearly every species had their version of Earth's black ops spies. Did his own people have it and he just didn't know, gone so long?

"I don't know if I can afford your price, Na Xan," he started.

"I can," Yuhwa's voice rang out from behind their table.

Bay whipped around, caught off guard again. First the Nyakisi, now the Jadoube pilot. He was off his game, the stress and heartache making him feel useless. Yuhwa joined their table, sitting on the other side of Na, who smiled widely.

"Just what a man likes to hear," he said.

"What are you doing here?" Bay asked. "Is Lia here, too? Tangun?"

At the name of the Head of Swords Na shifted away from Yuhwa. She eyed him with suspicion, then answered, "Just me. I saw you both leaving and wanted to offer help. I wasn't sure I had anything of use, but at least I have money to make this mašu help us."

Bay nearly laughed at the Nyakisi's expression when Yuhwa insulted and praised him in one word. She was right; Na was a mašu, an opportunist from a people that would always look out for themselves over all else. They didn't even have family relationships once they passed maturity. But he reminded himself, once paid they were loyal. And a majio of Yuhwa's skill would probably have a very nice amount of currency hoarded. Enough to buy them Na's fealty for long enough to find Katy.

"I don't agree this is a good way forward," Thuliso growled.

Na raised his black eyebrows and tilted his face to Bay, waiting. Bay laid the ground rules.

"Let me explain the situation. This will be conversation without commitment on either side. If you can present an option, a plan, that works for both sides, we'll proceed. If not, no contract. Fair?"

Na assented. Once Bay started talking, the Nyakisi focused intently. There was no point to secrecy anymore, so he told Na everything. Fast as he could, he recounted the events at the market, the refuge, here on Centris. This man was clever and able to handle large amounts of information easily; he only asked for clarification twice. When it was done, Yuhwa and Thuliso having added three or four comments of their own, Na pushed back from the table and steepled his fingers.

"She won't be on the Wheel any longer," he said bluntly. "Either she's been killed already," he waved down Bay's instant rejection of that idea, "or she's been taken away. The logical place would be back to Ishar. Their clergy have definitive ideas about inflicting suffering on the faithless, which they would probably say your herald is."

With those words he stood, tall and lanky, bending over the back of his chair. "I have contacts in the Lu'upan family. They're extremely powerful, a ruling house on the rise. They would see this as an opportunity to get even more credit: their family, through Yfaun, was able to capture a mythological Drazoen herald. They'll brag about it, and that's our way to stealing her back. My 'plan' as you called it, would be to get there and find wherever they've stashed her."

"I don't think we can use the *Eternidad*," Bay said. "But the voices must have something we can borrow."

"I have a far less noticeable ship here and," Na grinned unabashedly, "let's call them 'unofficial' routes onto the planet. We should leave as soon as you can be ready, every day we're not there is a day they can hurt or kill her."

Bay's blood drained to his feet before gushing back to his face. Mikanjo were known as peaceful people, but if anyone had hurt his Katy he would channel the worst of the Krylar butchers from ages past.

"I'm flying," Yuhwa said, rising beside Na. When he objected, she cut him off. "Your ship is yours, but I will navigate the veşu and use dao to speed us up. Surely you can't oppose a faster journey, given the threat you just laid bare."

Yuhwa's core was made of the waja her people were known

for. She didn't hesitate and offered no other outcome. Which thrilled Bay, because that took days off the trip to Ishar. "I'm ready now," he said, pushing to his feet and offering a hand to Na. It confused the Nyakisi, but it felt right; it was a Human gesture, and something Katy would have done. They'd get her back, he was sure of it. There was no other option.

29

This was beyond a prison. It was the absolute absence of everything, a holding cell meant to terrify and make madness bloom. Katy was in a vast, blank space. Yet there were no walls to define a room, no horizon to glimpse in the distance, no dark or light to make sense of surroundings. Not the beautiful black of space, the burning orange and yellow of a star, or the winking diamond white of distant galaxies. Nothing. No thing.

For all she knew there was no space at all and she was trapped in a loop of her own brain, eyesight gone, convinced she'd been locked away in blankness. When she cried out, she heard her own voice, but was that only in her head? Or was it echoing in a vast cavern she couldn't properly see? Her questions circled and leapt like racing schools of fish: just as she convinced herself she wasn't going mad, another part of her mind surged forward and asked *but what if this time, you've flat out tripped? Gone full gonzo?*

No, no, I'm fine.

But, what if this time, you're not?

Katy had no sense of time, which aligned with Yfaun telling her this place was outside the Aoni and was eternal. It took either seconds or years to realize she had no physical sensation. Fingers, toes, lips, gone. It was as if her brain had separated from her body and her consciousness floated in a neutral ether. Untethered, with just a memory of vocal chords and the sounds they made, lost in this place of infinite emptiness.

Or was it finite, closing in, wrapping around her, clinging, choking, numbing her and that's why she couldn't feel.

You've gone barmy, lass.

I am fine, damn it.

But, what if this time, you're not?

This was torture, just as Yfaun had intended. Had she been trapped forever yet? Felt like it. The Air had finally woken when they'd been shoved in here by Yfaun's suicide power move. It had pulled at her initially, seeming to be as panicked as she was. Its high faint melody was rushing through her, but had suddenly stopped, leaving her bereft of even her earliest lifelong comfort. Yet again. To comfort herself, she mentally played through her favorite three reels from The Chieftains. Then a rousing mix of Duran Duran, Lady Gaga and First Aid Kit.

Silence had never been part of Katy's world. From birth she'd heard the Air, dreamed it, loved and hated it, pleaded for it to reveal itself. When she struggled to find her place in a boisterous family that often knocked her back, she leaned on it for support. Now it left her alone? This was fecking crap. *Fine, I never needed you anyway.*

That's not true, come back. Help me. Keep me sane.

What if that's not an option anymore?

THULISO HADN'T COME with them. He said he was too visibly aligned with the Cadre to openly confront Pu'ulqaari on their home planet. His point was valid, but Bay couldn't help but wonder why the Lunari had been so relieved to escape their small troupe. He asked Lia to keep an eye on him while they were gone. She'd wanted to come with them, but Bay wasn't ready to risk his sister on a planet new and strange to them. Especially not one ready and willing to turn people into namu'ur for the flimsiest reasons.

Na's ship, the *Frelaasti*, wasn't large but was comfortable enough for their journey. Six private berths, a cargo and exercise area, as well as the usual communal dining and entertainment chambers. Sufficient and easily maintained for short hauls like this.

It was day three, Yuhwa was surfing the dao and had surfaced long enough to say they'd arrive at Ishar in five salangs. Finally. The two sal crawl out of Centris' Kéntro system had nearly driven him insane.

Bay and Na were watching a vid of the Dál. Seems the *Oudna* had left Centris after dropping off Yfaun, because this was broadcasting from a satellite in the outer Krygred system. The Krylar had been declared ûpiøra, but as long as it skirted the edge of the shunned species' home system, this Dál crew could operate without repercussion.

Traveling charnel house, Bay thought to himself. Earth had developed violent sports like boxing and martial arts, eventually enshrining them in world televised events. Olympics, pugilistic bouts, MMA and the like; Bay even remembered Leitai and Tahtib which had evolved into elegant forms surpassing their brutal origins.

But the fighting on this mobile arena was more vicious than anything he'd seen before. All genders included whether brawls were between groups or individuals. He saw Fumi Ly more than once, who was utterly savage each bout. No clear rules. Just attack and try not to be knocked out or permanently damaged. No wonder they'd given harbor to a killer and ferried him to Centris. Was it possible they'd taken Yfaun and Katy back onto their ship, and this trip to Ishar was lost time in a completely wrong direction?

He wanted to trust Na, although Aoni wisdom said that was a foolish thing to do with a Nyakisi. But if all else failed, Na was from a species that excelled at subterfuge, hiding in shadows, and maneuvering the slipstream of less savory haunts. Not to mention he was being well-paid to succeed, and if he'd thought the chance decent Katy had been ferried on the Dál he'd have said so. None of it was making Bay feel better about the time he'd been apart from Katy, though, or about how she was being treated. What shape she might be in when he found her.

Disgusted by the blood-drenched stadium on-screen, he turned his attention to Na and asked something that had been niggling at him since they boarded. "*Frelaasti* means what? The aoiti are giving me a mix of autonomy and personal journey, but I don't grasp the nuance, I think."

Na slouched down in the couch they'd claimed when they started watching the matches. One hand ran over his closely shorn, black hair before he answered. "For Nyakisi, *Frelaasti* is the core of how we see ourselves. No one will ever own us, lock us away, deny us the right to our freedom. It can be a place, as this ship is," he paused, rolling his head so he stared at the ceiling. "Or it can be something we hold inside ourselves."

"A personal mandate? A moral code?"

Na shrugged. "If you like. I'm finding it hard to define, which might be why your aoiti struggle. But *Frelaasti* is something every Nyakisi recognizes in their soul and would defend to the death."

Bay was about to ask more when Yuhwa entered the room. "We're close," she told both of them. Directing her next words to Na, she said, "You'll want to take over from here, unless you plan to give me the landing details?"

Na shook his head decisively. "This final step is for me only, majio, but thanks for getting us to this point so quickly. Have either of you been to Ishar before?" They both said no.

"All right, a short primer on the planet: tidally locked to three suns means everyone on Ishar stays indoors or underground. It's daytime all the time, and the suns burn nearly instantly. Even a short exposure on the surface can have serious, long-term impact to your health. It's a deadly desert down there. I can't emphasize this enough. Do not, at any point, think you can take a quick walk outside, or run from one place to another. If it's exposed, it's very dangerous to you."

Yuhwa looked uncomfortable. "I don't want to be underground."

"You won't be," Na shot back. "Unless you're taken as namu'ur, and that would be hard for them to get away with against a pilot like you. Not impossible," he warned, "but unlikely. The only people who go underground are certain enslaved workers, some artisans, and occasional clergy. There's a chance we won't even get out of the hangar, depending on how they respond to our request to visit."

"Visit?" Bay asked.

Na's exasperation came through clearly. "How did you think we were going to find your Human? This isn't a society where we can show up unannounced and knock on doors. We have to follow expected patterns, or they'll ignore us completely. We have to pretend to have something the Lu'upan family would want, otherwise we'll never get past their front door. We need to engage the trade and procurement lines of the family, not the warrior class." He stopped, made a humming sound. "I'm wondering, maybe we don't approach Lu'upan family at all. They'll know about Yfaun, he's theirs after all. And if he's back on planet they'll have closed ranks, making them a bad bet."

"Where then? Who?" Bay was frustrated, which was turning into a short temper. He wanted to spread his wings and fly to get some of the energy out, but he was trapped on this small ship. Soon to land on a planet where he couldn't safely take to the skies without burning off his feathers. His heart pounded with pent up anger.

"The Vi'isser clan has been pushing their way into the ranked families. On Ishar, the Pu'ulqaari claw, kill, fight their way into power. Some families stay at the top, but most of them rise and fall constantly. That means they're always eager for advantage; in our case that could translate to a willingness to hear an unsolicited pitch from a Mikanjo about opening trade lines to Bankiri." Here Na raised an eyebrow, inviting Bay's thoughts.

"I've been away for a long time, Na Xan. Are you saying there's not a system already in place?" Bay found that hard to believe.

Na grunted. "Even if there were existing trade routes, someone is always happy to undercut them. You can't come out on top if you don't hack at the foundations of others." He clarified, "But in this case, the Mikanjo have long objected to the practice of namu'ur and won't allow direct commerce between Ishar and Bankiri. We'll go in claiming you've found a way to create a black market for low-grade nefeslo. They'll love that, since they consider Mikanjo a lesser species. It would fit their preconception that you're barely above animals and are only smart enough to use the least refined ma'at."

Bay was flabbergasted. Barely above animals? It was his AI that cracked the code of Yfaun's kuh! Lia had told him they were already finding a myriad of ways to extend the tech. But Mikanjo were animals?!

Yuhwa interrupted his thoughts. "We won't have to visit the ma'at caverns? I remember from school lessons that's where they harvest it."

"You," Na laughed, "are very worried about nothing. That's the other side of the planet, considered sacred. Opposite of this side, it's always dark there and rains often, supplying the caverns and cenotes with water to form the ma'at. Like I said, no one goes into the underground areas unless they've had their tongues cut out so they can't reveal the secrets of ma'at and how it becomes nefeslo."

Yuhwa and Bay both recoiled at the blunt vision that statement triggered.

Na powered on. "I'm not unknown here, so I can coordinate with my contacts and work on a meeting with the Vi'isser clan. I'm going to suggest you both let me do most of the talking. Now," he turned and headed for the exit, "prepare for landing."

KATY THOUGHT ABOUT BAY, how much she loved him. Love was a risky and terrifying prospect. Especially in these days of heralds and dragons and always feeling eight steps behind everyone else. How could he want her, a woman so much younger, more naïve, less wing-having than he was? Katy couldn't fly with him unless he carried her, she hadn't even learned to use her aoiti for shopping, or practiced how to order food on the Wheel that didn't come out of a replicator. Silly things, but signs of the problem at heart: she had so little experience of life, much less the big Aoni he knew and had already travelled.

Mmm. Nropita. What would she give for some of that right now? Or better yet, that smashing bevvy of Yuhwa's. Rusim. So damn good.

Enough alcohol would get her mind off of the nightmare here and now. Silence surrounding her, invading her, that she didn't know how to combat. Too much time, even as time had ceased to exist, giving her plenty of room to noodle around a brain castigating her for having been too slow to act. For foolishly thinking they'd outwitted a PQ assassin who'd been bred to end her existence by offing himself in an unparalleled light show.

What a lark it had been, even with the scary parts. Swanning about the Aoni with Riri and Bay like she was living in a fairy story. One with a guaranteed Happily Ever After at that! Katy was embarrassingly aware she'd let herself think she was in *The Princess Bride* or *Labyrinth* instead of a *Game of Thrones-Predator* double-feature.

Silly bint. You failed and got your just desserts.

Because, yeah, had she woken up any dragons, orange or otherwise? No. Her beautiful Mikanjo seeker had put his money on her and she'd failed to come up a winner. Still. He'd put his money on her and couldn't take it back now. She wouldn't let him. She remembered how he'd cherished her that last time together, how he'd traced her face slowly, looking at her as if she were the answer to every important question. His light aqua eyes surrounded by café au lait skin, the carved muscles rippling underneath masterpiece tattoos that told of his long journey to reach her. The gentle humming sound he'd made, fractionally below her range of hearing, vibrating her eardrums just enough to make her shiver. An exquisitely sweet kiss on each eyelid, her nose, her mouth. A devilish smile as he set about proving to her she'd made a very good choice being his.

Find me, mo chroí. Please find me. I'll go mad here.

THEIR GROUP HAD BEEN SHOWN to a small waiting area two floors above the private landing deck on Ishar. Na Xan had serious connections, whether legitimate or not, to get them a berth in a small, exclusive port like this one, removed from urban centers. Bay assumed this was where secret deals were made and goods stashed for smuggling. The building, what he could see of it from inside, was a cylindrical fortress of suns-bleached grey, both inside and out. Windows in their area were heavily polarized; the desert flats surrounding the outpost were tinted purple by the safety windows. Little to no plant life, just a few twisted, stunted trees and a vast sea of low dunes spreading to the horizon. It reminded Bay of his time in the Sahara with nomads searching for gold, water, and adventure. That landscape had forged races of survivors: fiercely independent, intrepid, quick to temper, even quicker to forgive. Absolutely ingenious in their use of the resources available to them, and in securing what they needed to survive. He wondered if this was part of Pu'ulqaari makeup, too.

Other than greeting a few service people, they'd been left alone since being herded into the waiting room. At Na's suggestion Bay and Yuhwa had remained silent the entire time. It was the Nyakisi's hope that a Mikanjo on Ishar would be a lure the Vi'isser family couldn't pass up. Bay wasn't sure he was that exciting, but resolved to exude an air of "mysterious broker", the role he'd been assigned. Yuhwa, usually very calm and self-possessed like all stoic Jadoube, was flustered. Her palpable fear of being sent underground or being pressed into slavery, or both, was cracking her composure. Bay prayed to the Nine she held it together if they were granted an audience.

At last, seven sal-angs in to their wait, a sleek racing sled approached the station. It was diamond-shaped, decorated heavily on all sides with nefeslo shining in every metallic color he could imagine. Not quite holographic, but blazing with the reflected brightness of the three suns. It looked like a beacon of light. He silently begged Irojaku jo Faluji to make this encounter one that showed him his way to Katy. She needed him, he needed her, and in the deepest part of his soul he knew it would take Sundancer Orange's help to be reunited.

A mid-sized assemblage swept into the waiting area. Six lavishly attired Pu'ulqaari, and three more in far drabber robes. Two of the drabs wore only demi-robes at that, something closer to a kilt, otherwise bare to the waist. Bay couldn't believe anyone went about half-dressed, given the dangers of Ishar's environment. Ah, of course; it was a way to control the slaves, better than chains or tracking chips. They couldn't step out of a door without risking death half nude; they certainly couldn't make a spontaneous run for freedom.

The six Vi'isser spokespeople exchanged formal greetings with Na, ignoring Yuhwa and Bay entirely. An "animal" and a pilot didn't merit socially. Bay examined these people who were about to either help him, or, worst case, banish them from the planet. Four women, two men: all dressed in caftans like Lanu's, except they were boring in color. Finely designed, draping their bodies in light, neutral shades that probably helped in the heat of a triple-sun, never-ending day. When one of the men shifted position Bay's eye caught hints of fine gold thread at the hems. What color wasn't on their clothing, however, was on their faces. Gorgeously detailed ruh, more finely lined than Yfaun's had been. Subtler coloring as well, though still bright, but an ombré of blues instead of the pink and green nightmare mask the assassin wore. This group's coloring was deepest blue in the center of their face, fading as it radiated to their hairlines.

Two of their three male namu'ur bore ruh bands in the same graduated blue around their necks. Collars announcing their owners, wherever they went. There was one exception: he had a large face design, not a ruh. A full moon surrounded by roiling, dark clouds under his right eye. Lightning streaked below the stormy moon, down his cheek and chin, trailing over his neck and upper chest. A closer look revealed a mother cradling a baby drawn inside the moon. It made Bay unaccountably sad.

"This is the Mikanjo I commed you about," Na's voice jerked him back to the main conversation. "He'd considered the Lu'upan clan initially, because even on Bankiri they've heard of that family. But I convinced him you were the smarter choice. Especially given the recent," he paused, dragging it out, "troubles in their house."

Smart. Give them an opening to discredit a rival house, share information if they had it, and make it clear Bay would be malleable. Someone easy for the Vi'isser family to sway and lead by the nose. He resolved to keep his silence as Na was clearly the master manipulator here.

"Goodness, how shocking to hear news of their lost son has already spread," sneered the shortest of the women, standing in front.

Na twisted his lips in a way that read as sarcastic amusement. "Naturally, one knows these things happen. Especially engaged the way he was."

One of the men spoke this time, huffy and short. "Yfaun Lu'upan was doing sacred work, he is not fodder for gossip." He glowered. "Particularly by outsiders who shouldn't even know of it. Nyakisi," he spat. "Have your fingers in every bowl, you lot."

Bay tried to process the past tense he'd heard. Was? Lost? Yfaun was dead? How could that be? He'd just been on Centris three sals ago, attacking Raisa and kidnapping Katy. The urge to grab these venal, pompous Pu'ulqaari jerks and shake them until plain truth fell out was mounting. He resisted, although his wings rustled on his back when he stiffened. That had all six sets of eyes shifting his way.

"Mikanjo, how is it you have secured a route to funnel our ma'at to Bankiri?" Second woman, standing deferentially behind the first. Bay could see a hierarchy in the way they'd arrayed themselves. It almost mirrored the shape of their racing sled, family in front and namu'ur shunted to the back.

Thinking fast, he said, "I left our Seeking Ship not long ago.

When I got back to Bankiri I was dismissed by many for losing faith. Shunned. But that let me find a different class of people." He spread his palms and tilted his head. "I represent the ones who aren't interested in what they're told to accept. What you do," and here he nodded to the namu'ur, "is your business. We merely want what will improve our homes and lives." It was a necessary evil, but his stomach lurched when he said such horrible things.

The Vi'isser clan looked to each other, communicating without speaking. Bay assumed they had a private channel they used, though it was possible they just knew their family minds so well they didn't need to talk aloud. After a moment, the head woman addressed him. "What is your name, Mikanjo?"

There was disdain in the way these people said "Mikanjo." Na was right, they evidently thought his people were below them. Less evolved, more like beasts than sentient beings. "Abou. Abou jo Nbali." He decided to use the moniker of the faithless man who'd harangued Katy on the *Eternidad* with his wife, and the line name of Hu Ularu Black. They were a Drazoen he'd heard the Pu'ulqaari feared. No one flinched, so either he'd heard wrong, or these people didn't know the Mikanjo version of Their name. "May I know yours, if we are to do business together?"

He was ignored. "We will consider this proposal, Na Xan. Your reputation precedes you, and we think there may be profit to be made. We also presume you will continue as intermediary? Direct communication with Abou," the lead female's voice dripped with condescension, "may not be possible."

Bay stifled his rage and let Na take over. To be relegated to insignificance like that made his feathers prickle. Beside him he felt Yuhwa, who'd been a frozen statue this whole time, lean ever-so-slightly into his arm. Reassuring without drawing attention.

"Of course," Na replied. "It only makes sense given how....

sensational Mikanjo can be. Very noticeable." The Nyakisi turned to the windows. "I assume you brought samples for analysis?"

"Samples?" she laughed. "Nothing is free in the Aoni."

Na bared his teeth. "Ah, I thought you had come to do business. Only fools make agreements without proper review of the resources." He turned to Bay, casual and insolent. "We will contact the Lu'upan family after all, Abou. They might be mourning a dead son, but they will know how to conduct business properly."

The second man, face stony, pushed forward. "Even as they hold rites for Yfaun, they will not be tricked into undercutting our offer! Their sorrow does not outweigh their glory in his accomplishment, and they will contract with you at a premium. Prices suitable for the ascendent house of Ishar." His glower was cut short when the other five squeezed him back out of view.

Bay reeled, stomach heaving. If Yfaun was dead, but had done what he meant to do, Katy was dead. Gone.

He couldn't see, tried not to fall down. Losing composure now would risk all their lives, but his mind repeated *"glory in his accomplishment"*, the words whirling faster and faster.

Katy can't be gone, his heart begged of him. She was his everything, and he couldn't accept it. *Glory in his accomplishment* his mind refuted. Bay's soul, though, whispered to him that they would know when she left him forever, and that time hadn't come.

Numb to his surroundings while the battle raged inside him, he was a passive observer to Na's closing negotiations. After an interminable discussion where Bay fought to stay standing and not throw up, it was agreed the samples would be gifted from the Vi'issers. Na lied that after some time to analyze and evaluate, their small team would return word to seal the deal and confirm how the black-market route would be set up. Bay watched, mentally disconnected, as a namu'ur – the one with the elaborate face design – left to move the cargo from the Pu'ulqaari skiff onto the *Frelaasti*.

My *qania* is not dead.
Glory in his accomplishment.
Katy can't be gone.
Glory in his accomplishment.

30

Maybe it didn't matter to Bay that she was a young Human from a backward planet, with brothers who threatened him and parents who kept trying to *69 a spaceship thinking they'd get Katy on the line. Maybe he liked her despite her social awkwardness, her unfortunate tendency to act like a bridge troll before morning nropita, and being attacked by her hair as he slept. Perhaps she was enough for him. More than enough, even, maybe she was the answer to his questions in the same way he satisfied hers.

All the time they'd spent in the isolation wing, talking about their upbringings, their dreams and plans. Bay felt like he could finally make some, now she was found and (according to him) sure to awaken Sundancer any day. Her promising infatuation had turned to real love, a need and desire to be around him, to share in his future and have him share hers in turn. For however long that might be, given Humans got so screwed on the longevity deal. She'd have to talk about that with Sundancer. Surely a boon would be granted by a Drazoen awoken after a hundred thousand years, right? A herald could ask that, Katy thought.

Although, once again, it all hinged on waking Sundancer up, which seemed less likely from this hell hole in which Yfaun had stuffed her. Panic creeping in. She went back to thoughts of her limbo-trapped quest.

Her feelings for Bay had grown and blossomed on this adventure. It wasn't just the pendant but their relationship, too, that had brought the Air closer to her. Linking a flute to the Air in her childhood had triggered a tsunami that had subtly built over twenty-eight years until it filled the empty harbor of her frustrated ambitions and awkwardly stunted family bonds.

There was so much to love and appreciate about the Phelan-Rollins crowd, but Katy had always felt a wee bit out of step. As though she aligned imperfectly. Was it the Air coming to her so young that had shifted her slightly off-center from the rest? Whatever the cause, she'd felt more alone than a woman in a rollicking, happy family like hers should have felt. She'd not gotten a precious twin bond, either; if Oran could have eaten her in the womb he would have. Everyone was successful whether they'd done it practically (Da, Ma, Ian, Deb, Oran, Aunt Mildred) or by following dreams (Paul, Patrick, Vasuda) and she… hadn't. Yet. Katy had followed what she thought was her calling, but there'd been no reward for it. Until this herald thing happened, which was absolutely mental.

What she hadn't realized until now, though, about that tsunami of the Air; it needed to overfill to be expressed. She'd let it top up some of the empty places, but clamped down on it before it could overflow. Kept it locked behind a jetty, only moving at safe speeds. Her fear of ridicule, of not being believed, had built fortifications that kept it contained. Katy, alone, had to own up to suppressing her Air that wanted so badly to be played, to be shared with the Aoni. The constant tickle of it had gotten stronger, more clamorous, ever since she met Bay and put on the bloody pendant.

Which she couldn't feel anymore, sinking in a purgatory of

something that wasn't anything. Because she was trapped. Dying. Not dying, yes, suffocating, not breathing, why was there no pain with the suffocating? No, not that either. She was none of those things. She was nothing. The loss of purpose, meaning, value. Empty, blank, a thing apart.

Stop the panic. Mental breath. Katy circled back to the Air, the pendant, and Sundancer. What had Dindal taught her? She'll make me powerful and sage, wise. Rewards truth, punishes lies. Mother of Justice. Not ominous or anything, right? Christ knew Katy wasn't a paragon of truth… Gods knew? Dragons knew? Jesus wept, someone damn well knew!

Fond of fibs, Katy was, and that's what any Powers That Be out there would know. Her da taught her from a young age to be creatively generous in her interpretation of events. What Da called "malarkey" and considered part of a child's ingenuity, her ma called "speaking with a forked tongue" and discouraged. Often. Sometimes with a wooden spoon to Katy's behind. Despite corporal threats, if push came to shove, Katy would lie like a ragdoll.

Despite being terrible at it, too, she'd tell a thousand porkies if it got her out of trouble. A justice dragon awakened after a kōmilen of exile, napping, or cold storage was likely to side with Ma, and wallop her arse.

Putting her squarely in the busted category if Sundancer came back. Unless she got a pass for being the herald? Who'd have thought Katy was the chosen being in all of the Universe to wake up a dragon, a supreme being? Sundancer Orange needed little Katy Phelan to do something fabulous to bring her back. And she was the first one, the first herald. Take that, chosen ones of the future, I planted the first flag. Ha!

Although, if Bay's prophecy was all true and came straight from the mouth of Windweaver, why would Sundancer come back first? Windweaver was the one dropping prophecies all about the place for the Mikanjo to chase. Shouldn't she have come back first? If a Mikanjo seeker was needed, why wouldn't she make sure her people woke her up first?

Maybe that She and Her needed capitals, because Katy was pretty sure they had them when everyone else in the Aoni said them.

Not the point. Mind wandering too much.

Windweaver wasn't the only one leaving tantalizing tidbits here and there, though, was She? Tonguemaker had been busy with His Muškikal, giving them jobs and libraries where they'd be hidden away. Lunari had songs and poems that were meant to be prophetic except they might be lost now, since those ones didn't write anything down anymore. After the planetcide committed by the Krylar, their culture had shifted to oral tradi-tion. They saw it as a way to keep their history alive and vibrant, something each of them carried within themselves. Less handy when the keeper of the most important one dies without passing it on.

Katy was willing to bet every culture had something that foretold the heralds. Kalim was chasing down what the Rixat might have, at the same time he looked for that lost library. Yuhwa and Tangun were going to consult with some Jadoube version of wise elders to see what they might have. Hell, the PQ must have a prophecy, too. What else would make them screw genetically with embryos in order to create someone capable of using these shadow prisons? They wanted to stop any of the white hat prophecies coming true.

Where the fuck was Bay? Shouldn't he be there already, saving the day like her very own Errol Flynn? Her man didn't need convenient ropes or swinging chandeliers. Bay could swoop in all on his very own with those incredible, magnificent, soft wings. The ones he'd first wrapped around her as they fled Seattle, rousing Katy's previously unknown wing fetish. Every color of pearl, seashell, ivory, snow, ice, alabaster, and swan-white Katy could imagine. Since her eyes weren't sensitive enough to discern the differences, she'd had to fantasize about them. And boy had she.

Maybe that was another favor she'd tack on to the longer life request, when she found Sundancer. Eyes as perceptive as a Mikanjo's. Which was all well and good until she had to confront her own reflection after a night of too much indulgence. More than once she'd thought a gorgon stared back through the mirror the morning after a good gaff. Okay, bank that request for now.

Had she spent five minutes or a decade thinking about this? Were those walls forming around her suddenly? Were they closing in? Wait, were they swelling?

No. Stretching away from her, endlessly expanding, leaving her alone in a space so massive she'd be lost and forgotten, adrift and alone.

Never mind, no walls. No anything. This was all things that weren't things, the moment before nothing became everything. When all that was did not yet exist.

kuk ularu

Katy jumped, or thought she did. That wasn't her voice, her idea. Nor was it the soundless information transfer of her aoiti. It was a soft baritone, gently pitched, imbued with more grief and sorrow than she'd ever heard in a single voice. But it spoke nonsense, words she didn't know.

kuk ularu, the moment when all that is and will be hasn't yet become

The breath before the note is played, Katy thought.

yesss, Child of Orange

IF BAY THOUGHT he'd been in a bad way before, as if his wings tangled in painful branches of negative thought, it had been nothing compared to this. His mind tortured him ceaselessly with the Vi'isser man's words: that they celebrated, gloried in Yfaun succeeding at his mission to rid the Aoni of Sundancer's Kawakona. The Mikanjo seekers' cause, Bay's love, gone.

Yuhwa had tried to talk to him when they boarded, asking if he'd noticed anything amiss about the *Frelaasti*. He stared at her, incredulous at her insensitivity, and walked away. He'd locked himself in one of the berths ever since. Two sals – three? – of mourning, plucking his own feathers in his grief, drowning in a morass of devastation and sorrow.

Na had knocked once, offering alcohol that he just left at the door when he got no response. The amstre wine, one rumored to be prized by Nyakisi, hadn't helped. It only slurred the voice telling him over and over Katy was dead and he was alone. Nor did it silence the insistent part of his soul shouting Katy was alive, that they were already as bonded as deeply as his mantle tattoos were to his skin.

She is still with me. I would know she'd been taken from me forever. She will return.

That part of him was losing the struggle to keep hope alive. Time passed as Yuhwa transited the veṣu and Bay found he didn't care. They would return to Centris, but nothing on the Wheel mattered to him now. Other seekers might continue to chase Windweaver White's prophecy, but Bay was finished. He'd found his herald and lost her.

His own ignorance, his trust of others who weren't motivated to his level, his belief that Kweza could warn them of Yfaun's approach; all of these things had handed Katy over to the killer. He could see that now. He would never be able to punish himself enough, but, he thought drunkenly, he would give it a good try.

KATY FELT CRADLED by the soft, sad voice. She thought it was masculine, but in this void she didn't feel sure of anything. What had he said? Something about kuk ularu, which was that infinite pinprick of time, almost impossible to define. Like when a chest knows to rise before taking a breath is even a complete thought. Is that where they were, in kuk ularu?

Child of Orange, you rest in a pocket of Aoni, something wrapped in remembrance and celebration of kuk ularu, when all that was unseen had as much value as the visible

Katy wasn't sure what the voice meant. What was unseen besides maybe germs, socks the dryer ate, and black holes? Riri had been talking a lot about veşu, black holes, and what they might be; probably more than Humans knew, since Jadoube travelled them like the yellow brick road. Wowza, Riri had watched a lot of documentaries about space. Katy was simple, though. What matters is what's visible: suns and skies and oceans and spinning planets. Like Ma always said, seeing is believing.

NO

Not such a gentle tone now. Angry, bitter. A different voice, feminine this time.

Katy was lost and alone, snared by that PQ son of a bitch and thrown here to die. Multiple voices not hers, that could apparently read her mind, boded ill. Ones shrieking at her and speaking of invisibility, and concepts from before time existed, smacked of schizophrenia.

No, no, I'm fine… But, what if this time, I'm not?

peace, Chosen of Dikaios. sorrow and regrets to cause you doubt and pain. we know much of these things, and would never pass it to another

One more voice, different again, broke her heart more than

the first. The sadness underlying each syllable was nearly palpable in this place of intangibility. Why, she wondered, were these three so upset? Almost immediately a fourth voice rumbled.

we are the voiceless, the nameless, the unseen. there is power in the invisible, but we are ignored. disregarded. Kōtuig upon kōtuig we watched our counterbalances fly the Aoni, worshipped and beloved wherever they went. but we remained unknown, misunderstood. we cried out, only to go unheard

Her mind was hijacked, flooded with memories not hers. She saw something amorphous that allowed other matter to form into nebulae, stars, planets. Whatever the opposite of being is called, that was these creatures. They travelled unseen, wrapped around and between objects, gave them gravity and weight. Sometimes they allowed comets to sail between solar systems, or asteroids to batter planets. Crashed whole galaxies into one another when their pull became too great.

She'd learned just enough from Riri and old science shows to grasp the sudden influx of images deluging her. These were the dragon equivalents of dark matter. That undetectable, unmeasurable stuff Earth scientists said had to exist because the math didn't work otherwise. Katy reeled. These were the other side of the Nine, anonymous, disembodied. The passive and reactive forces opposing the active and progressive dragons going about the Aoni spreading languages and music and love. No species of the Aoni had celebrated them by name, danced and made love in festivals dedicated to them, or believed in them at all. They were unknown, unheralded. And here she was, a catalyst to one of the seen, one of the dragons who'd been revered since time began.

They'd called her a child of orange a few times now. Plus something else, chosen of Dikaios. What did that one mean? Gorgeously sad third voice spoke again.

Dikaios is her name. the one you are here to awaken, to release and set free, for you are surely the note she sang into being so long ago

But how did they know? And did they hate her for it?

we sense these things. we have known our kindred since kuk ularu, and you burn with the spark and essence of Dikaios

Angry voice that time, and the hate question wasn't answered. Katy assumed being the chosen one of Sundancer wasn't playing in her favor, since these folks clearly had the upper hand in this pocket of whatever. She pondered (for one second? For eternity?) and decided she couldn't blame them for that. Katy would likely hate the person about to wake up her enemy, if she were in their place.

not enemy

Hypothetically wake up, anyway, because Katy hadn't gotten far on that front. Were they all here, in this cage? They'd said she was here to wake up Dikaios… which had to be Sundancer's truename! The thing from the Mikanjo prophecy. Score one for ancient history! It also sounded like the seen and unseen had coexisted from the beginning, from kuk ularu on. Yfaun had called these shadow prisons: were they jails, trapping these ephemeral Shadow Drazoen and their adversary, Dikaios, together?

not enemy, not adversary. cherished. sibling. all we wanted was a place to be acknowledged as she was

A place to be known. Katy understood that. That was largely what music meant to her; a way to be heard when she didn't have words to express what needed saying. When having four obnoxious brothers who would shout over her, ignore her, or just sit on her, was more than a girl could withstand. When her American cousins in the Midwest didn't understand why she wasn't interested in dolls, makeup or "normal" stuff, so they left her out when she'd visit. When boys in high school hadn't been much interested in Katy's charms, then the blokes at uni just wanted a roll in the hay with no commitments to tie them down. When Ma and Da couldn't understand that their idea of her life was different from what she'd wanted, and that her dream was valid regardless. When she had one of those mornings where she woke up with the Air frustratingly elusive, feeling morose for no discernible reason, scared there'd be no adventure or purpose to her life. Trying to love her job as a library page but knowing deep down it wasn't her, just a placeholder while she waited for Sunday nights to play her heart's song. Year-by-year it dulled her creative edges into near non-existence.

These shadow dragons had no way to sing out, move from inaudible to audible, and she knew how that could eat at your soul. Her Scottish roommate in college loved the word "ken", had even written a sonatina celebrating it. She said the word encompassed knowledge and knowing, vision both literal and figurative, a deeper awareness of the world and an acknowledgement of places beyond the mundane. That's what these Shadows wanted, to be kenned by the dwellers of the Aoni. No longer overlooked, finally invited to the party.

If anything, Katy understood these Shadows more than she did the Nine. Having so few people in her life to chat about music theory and melody, modern composition vs. folk vs. classical, the merits of wood over metal. Why sometimes a tin whistle is the right choice except those times nothing but a piccolo will do. She could go without it, but when she did it was a version of this cage, albeit less drastic: isolating, maddening, a part of her spirit smothered. To be lost and alone, adrift and apathetic, was a tar pit hard to escape. Here they were, in some hell-hole designed to reflect the time before creation, a place not even a nothing. A place that was a something beyond her basic Human comprehension, but a prison nonetheless. All Katy had was the choice to acknowledge Them, to share her own earliest and oldest glimmer of what reached from a nebulous beyond: the Air.

Hearing Irish flute in her father's lap all those years ago was the genesis quake, a crack of earth that rippled along the ocean floor of her spirit. Years of study and fantasizing had pushed a seismic wave toward the shore, but from so very deep down. It had needed time to rise to the surface and build to a crest. That time had come, and so many pieces fell into place at last; rapidly and smoothly, domino-perfect.

I am Katy Phelan, the first note of Dikaios returned to its source, an opening to the symphony of us. You, the four rows of the musical staff, forming the backbone of the composition. Indispensable. I see you, I hear you, I ken you. Without you and what you did to shape creation, much of what I love might not exist, and for that I love you, too. All that I have to give, what I am at the very core of myself, I give to you. Together we can be heard.

The Air exploded out of her soul, the tsunami of sound vibrating along particles she could neither see nor touch, but felt, and could finally get out of her head. Loving Bay and her family was at the core of that single note ringing out. The power seething inside the pendant he'd created had given the Air a strident note, stronger than what it had been in her youth. Every moment of her life, her pain and losses, laughter and love of family and friends, the pure delight of Sunday jam sessions when Kevin gave her a hard time. Discovering a true friend in Riri. All of these things built her symphonic introitus to crescendo.

A second note followed. Her wonder at a vast and astounding Aoni. Meeting Bay and fleeing Earth and wings, glorious wings. Lanu, Lia, Yuhwa, all the Mikanjo both kind and not. Learning a species was capable of swimming space time. Feeling humbled by the breadth of life at Centris, the diversity and possibility in the tiny slice of it she'd seen. Time with the voice Cadre, the Toledral speaker, and so many others. Confused and frustrated at being prophesied but having no real direction or instruction. Occasionally shamed by

Human ways the others saw as backward and ignorant; anger at her shame.

Third note, now, generated by the tension inherent in her fear and anxiety, compounded by Yfaun's terror campaign. The power from Sundancer's verse in the Lunari poem was in that note as well. A dragon's strength to mete out justice, to weigh the balances of right and wrong. The ecstasy and awe of staring into cavernous spaces between the visible and realizing something curled in the hidden realms. That an entire cosmos was waiting to be discovered, if only people deigned to look. All of these things soared through the developing movement of Katy's Air, and were necessary to turn nearly imperceptible waves into the kind that could flood cities and bring down buildings.

The Aoni-changing wave Katy needed had required a pause before crashing to shore. Regathering, returning the part to the whole in a penultimate moment. A final acknowledgement of what came before, one last nod to as things had been.

The hiatus was done: she'd spent her whole life paused, waiting for this. To wake a dragon who would rewrite existence, the Air had to overfill, flood and glut, swell and burst to release all that potential energy. With a single thought, she invited the unnoticed to stand witness; opened the door and held out a welcoming palm.

I am yours as much as Hers. This is our Song.

we are Wataño

Four Shadow voices raised, each one wrapping layered polyphonic chords around Katy's Air, until it became something that surpassed a symphony. More than note, it was Music. Greater than voice, it was Song. Operatic instrumentation so complex it was beyond comprehension, soft like an opening sonata gently shepherding you through the opus. It harmonized into a galaxy-sized union of celebration and requiem. Gospel and dirge. Katy's Air with the Shadow Drazoen was an ouroboros for the cosmos. The thought before the first breath and the final exhale, a repeating yet ever-changing motif. The ostinato of creation and destruction. A joy her physical body could never have contained; it felt as though the Air streamed from every pore to fill the void. Like Yfaun's light show when he opened the shadow prison, but with a celestial sound that would surely blow the doors off this place.

Notes surging, her entire soul quivering, Katy realized she held a flute in her hands. A moment's thought and she knew it was the pendant, Sundancer's essence transforming, providing the final spark needed to bring Dikaios back. Katy lifted the carnelian flute to her lips, and joined her theme to the chorus ringing throughout this everything and nothing that was her and the Shadows. This was what she'd been born to do: reveal a sleeping dragon and start resetting the balance.

Virtuoso.

31

Orange detonated, there was no other word for it.

One second Katy and the Shadows were playing the Music of the Spheres, the next an explosion obliterated the void-space that had imprisoned them. Instead of nothing, all she could see was orange. It glowed from within, mesmerizing and intense. If a color could have a heartbeat, this orange did.

Katy reared back, several things hitting her brain in rapid succession. First and foremost, this had to be Sundancer, right? Because Orange was what usually followed that name, the Shadows even called Katy child of orange, and there was orange fecking everywhere. It was all she could see. Rippling waves of it, fading from one shade to the next, like Rácz would do, but bolder and faster. Pumpkin to apricot to salmon, then neon tangerine and marigold.

Second, *of course* it took the Shadows plus her to awaken Sundancer. It made perfect sense in hindsight. The Shadows and Katy were the five lines that bounded the four rows of a music staff; Sundancer, Dikaios, was the notation on the staff, the musical notes that wouldn't have a defined meaning without the staff on which they were placed. Joined, they made what the Shadow Drazoen had called a Wataño. Together, all five of them pinned the exact spacetime continuum of their group, and anchored it in reality.

Finally, holy shite. If Yfaun's dark matter gulag had been destroyed, was she just floating in space, about to die from no air, looking gross and freaky as she suffocated?

Rest easy, child of mine. I have you. I have created a cocoon where you may breathe and speak.

That voice. Brigid and all the saints. It was warm honey butter, melty and soothing, like you wanted to bathe in it.

I see this substance in your mind. Honey. Something new to me, as are these bees who make it. Industrious, ruled by a queen, ordered and beautiful. I enjoy this pattern and will adopt it for myself. Something to show I am reborn and this iteration of my existence is unique.

Confused, Katy raised her eyes to try and behold her dragon, about to ask what She meant. *Size is an issue here. Because I appear to be the height of Her nostril.* Getting the whole picture might take distance, although Sundancer wasn't fully solid yet, either.

Suddenly she had the impression of a wing beat and Sundancer wasn't so close. Katy saw…. Well, she saw that a fair bit of standard dragon imagery was dead on. At least Earth's was. Two massive wings, just humongous. Bay might be jealous when he met Her. A huge chest tapering to slightly narrower, but still substantial, hips. Haunches? What was polite here? Four limbs, also gargantuan, capped with claws of silver. They looked a lot like the tattoos and weapons Tangun had, come to think of it. Same sheen.

Waja. Our claws are made of waja; We scattered it to Malor where the Jadoube have learned to use it well.

Katy nodded dazedly. Should she call Her Dikaios? Irojaku jo Faluji?

You will call me Dikaios only inside our Wataño. Just as you are Kawakona, herald, Chanticleer and more you have not yet heard, I am also many-named. You may pick whichever you like to use around others.

This experience was kinda hallucinogenic. She was so over-whelmed by Dikaios magically being there, reading her mind, and talking back into it, that Katy was seeing things. Like Sundancer's skin slowly changing, a honeycomb pattern rolling through the orange in a wave. Huh. The lines blended several permutations of orange, covering Her hide. Katy was mesmer-ized. Sundancer's voice got pointed.

As I said, I greatly enjoy the patterns of your Earth bees your mind showed me. It is logical, serves good purpose, has value to multiple species' communities, and is aesthetically pleasing. I choose to take on this aspect.

Katy looked at the jumbo jet-sized leathery wings on either side of Sundancer, more like a bat than a bee.

Their wings are less desirable so I choose not to take that trait.

"As dragons can, I suppose," Katy replied cheerfully. She felt it prudent to be upbeat when you were the herald of a justice dragon who was getting annoyed with you for your wandering attention.

Nor did I arrive 'magically', as you thought before. You and my brethren unlocked the nefeslo cage when you achieved harmonic resonance. Not magic, merely expression of something more ancient than anything other than kuk ularu. Your Air is a thread of the greater Song. This is a concept your spirit should understand, note of my heart.

Oh my. Katy was the note of Sundancer's heart. That was the best thing Katy had heard in a long time. It was like coming home, not having realized you'd been away in the first place.

Sundancer's head turned, and Katy saw that it was lined along the sides with spikey crenellations giving Her a crown-topped visage. Just like what Bay had crafted into the pendant dragon. He must have had a true vision of Her when he made it. Her eyes were black fields with swirling galaxies inside. Trying to focus on that was making Katy dizzy, so she looked back at the incandescent mandarin honeycomb skin stretched over hundreds of yards of muscle. Sundancer Orange was the epitome of everything Humans had dreamed dragons to be.

My family, we are freed again, She said to the Shadows. *Our liberty is the first action, now we must empower and aid the hearts of the other Wataños. Once all nine have been released we can take our final actions.*

"Well, that's not sounding ominous," Katy murmured. "At all." Their sense of amusement in the back of her mind was how she realized the Shadows were still connected to her, though she couldn't see Them. She knew it came with the whole dark matter deal, but she did wish she could see Them just once.

you will always be joined to us now, Herald of Orange Wataño. We are entangled, as was meant to be

The belonging and deep-rooted satisfaction in the deepest Shadow voice was making her tear up. "So I was right? A Wataño is everyone together, out of the prison?"

it is all of us together, Drazoen and Herald, openly in the Aoni, bonded. not since kuk ularu has anything this powerful happened, and it is a wonder beyond words

Damn it, there went full tears. Angry Shadow wasn't angry anymore. They were a family. An odd one, to be sure, but if Katy had survived her brothers all these years she could totally handle this.

Brothers! Home. Family and Bay and Riri and the chaos that had probably ensued in the wake of her kidnapping. "Not to rush things along…. but we're off to Centris then? Catch up with the voices and figure out our next moves? Find the other eight Wataño like you said? I don't know how long I've been gone." She started to get more anxious. "What if it's been months? Or years?" Panicked now. "We have to go!" Sundancer's tolerant amusement floated in her mind.

This is what the note of my heart became over a kōmilen. I could not have foreseen such a thing.

Before she could pick between offended or flattered by Sundancer's words, Katy was abruptly surrounded by tail. Nine of them, actually. Scratch that, one tail with nine branches. Not fluffy or scaley, smooth and covered in the same honeycomb pattern as the rest of Her skin.

We will return to Centris. I am glad to hear it is as we left it so long ago. Come within my circle and I will transport us.

Katy stepped forward, realizing two things: one, she was still clutching the carnelian flute. Now that she could see it she was never giving it up because it was godsdamned exquisite. Two, she had no idea what she was walking on, because for all intents and purposes she was in the middle of space. No planet, ship or station under her feet. Sundancer's nine tailpieces wove around her like a basket just as she started to flail, and she was secured like a babe in a bassinet. When she touched the tails, their texture was that of the finest suede. "Do you breathe fire, by chance?"

I do not.

Negative one for Disney and Game of Thrones, and some major world mythologies. She eyed her dragon again.

I do not breathe ice storms or electricity. Nor do I hoard gold, gems and precious things.

Redirection time, because Sundancer sounded annoyed again. "How do you fly in space? There's no resistance for your wings, is there? I don't see how it works. Is it like Yuhwa and how the majio swim the dao?

I am made of what created the Aoni in the earliest moments. We gave names to all things, which were birthed by our expansion after kuk ularu. Very little exists in the Aoni that did not have origin in one of us. Long ago, that meant we transported instantaneously, with thought alone. But the Aoni has expanded far beyond those times, and now we follow winds unfelt by mortal beings, pathways carved by our original travels.

She paused while Katy tried to get hold of the idea.

If we have been to a place, should we desire to return there, the memory tugs us through the weft and warp of space time. No longer done in the blink of an eye now the Aoni is so large, yet still only a short road along the remembrance.

She had a feeling Sundancer's "short road" would approximate the Autobahn for a non-Drazoen passenger. Or that Monza racetrack Paul was always droning on about. Fine, she was tough and could handle it. She'd survived a PQ assassin not once, but twice, trained alien machines to brew a proper cuppa, and broken everyone out of jail just now. She felt the softest laughter from her Shadow Drazoen.

One last question before they got underway, though. "Bay says his family line takes their name from their goddess–"

Windweaver is not a goddess. She is as I am. Primordial, not deity.

"Sorry, just using the word he used. But they call themselves jo Bikajo after Her. Now, if we're Wataño, does that mean I get to take your name? And if it does, can it be the Mikanjo version? Katy jo Faluji has a ring to it. I think my family would really get into it, too." Katy sensed Sundancer understood her nonsense questions masked a growing fear: had she been away for so long her Human family was dead, or something catastrophic happened to Bay? There was also a yearning to belong fully to their new family. Naming had power, and Katy wanted to claim her Wataño, broadcast it to everyone.

You shall be the first of that line for your species. I delight in this.

"I bet Da will, too." Katy smiled as they began their flight. "I mean, orange is one of the colors of the Irish flag. He won't be able to resist."

BAY ONLY STIRRED from his berth when he felt the *Frelaasti* come to rest in the main docking bay at Centris. Twenty sals had passed between now and when the *Eternidad* had first arrived on the Wheel. How could it have gone so poorly? They'd had a blissful span where he and Katy got to be close. When he'd marveled at her quick wit and incredible talent with her flute. Admired the way she accepted her own limitations, then found ways around them. Her intrepid bravery about having such a heavy burden laid at her feet had pleased him, and her refusal to learn about Calling politics made him laugh.

So little time to sleep, laugh and eat together. Share smiles and kisses – shiftin', she called it. The bliss of having her in his arms, enclosed in his wings, her fingers ticklishly rubbing the inside of his wing arches had been immeasurable. She'd giggle, then moan softly when he had to sip the happy laughter directly from her lips.

He found it impossible to accept he would never have that again. The pushy internal voice was weaker now, but still tried to assert she lived. Bay expected, as the tuigs went by, that voice would forever torture him. He knew it for the insidious demon of hope now, had accepted part of him would always dream she was coming back. But that wasn't reality. Their fantasy of waking Sundancer Orange, the sals of research and meditation, had come to naught. A beautiful Human was dead, and it was his fault. He'd brought her here, given her the pendant, made her Yfaun's target. All his mistakes.

Gathering his few things, he faltered, realizing he'd be the one to tell Raisa her friend was dead. Yuhwa and Na were standing together at the bottom of the ship ramp, waiting for him to disembark. Their looks of pity were twin knife blades to his stomach.

"Vailillia has already reached out," Yuhwa started, voice low. "I've explained what we learned, and she says they're waiting at Voice House for us."

Bay closed his eyes against another wave of pain. Enduring the sympathy of others seemed like the cruelest wind plucking at his feathers, even with the relief of hearing he was off the hook with Raisa. Rolling his shoulders he nodded at her, ready to get it over with.

"As for payment, I'll keep the ma'at samples from Vi'isser clan. I will consider that our bargain completed." Na drew a hood up around his head and face, waving off Yuhwa's surprised objection. "I'd hoped for a better outcome, despite knowing the Pu'ulqaari to be unprincipled, foul people. We share sorrow in this time."

That was a lot coming from a Nyakisi. They weren't traditionally emotional as far as Bay knew. "I thank you, Na Xan. Your efforts were in good faith, and-" Bay choked up. "At least we, I, know the truth."

Just as the two men reached to clasp forearms, shouts sounded from the *Frelaasti* port cargo area. Two Oti crashed into view, landing heavily on their backs. Then a Pu'ulqaari ran around the landing gear, frantic, scanning his surroundings. It was one of the Vi'isser namu'ur from Ishar. The one with the melancholic face ruh, who'd loaded the samples onto the ship. He'd stowed away aboard the *Frelaasti*? He was making a run for freedom, and he didn't slow as he shoved past anyone who got in his way, a headlong rush toward Harbor Primur's main doors. Yuhwa spun to Na, accusatory glare spearing into him.

"You lied to me, mašu," she growled. "I told you I knew there was someone aboard. I explained we can sense all life when we navigate the dao, but you swore it was 'organic material giving off life signatures'!"

Na shrugged, his face shadowed within the hood. "You wanted to believe me; I didn't have to convince you of much, pilot. You should work on controlling those fears of yours, they made you wide open to influence."

Yuhwa hissed at Na. "If I were going to travel with lying thieves again, I would!"

Bay was so tired. None of this mattered to him, not escaping slaves or the fight happening in front of him. He wanted to find a bed and never leave it again. Or a nice chair hidden away where no one could bother him and he could grieve in peace. He dropped his bag and spread his wings to full span. It knocked the two ⊙ti back down just as they'd regained their feet. Na and Yuhwa, shocked out of their verbal sparring match, turned to him warily.

"We're all idiots," he said calmly. "We all believe what we want, when it suits us or convinces us we're right. It's irrelevant now. The runner is gone. Katy is gone. I'm going back to the Chorus." At that he picked up his bag and strode off, no good-byes or sentimental parting words. That time had passed. If he could have flown back to the Voice House he would have, but too much sled and tram traffic made it dangerous. Instead, he trudged, numb, boarding the tram to mid ring, then to the Chorus entrance. His black mood never lifted, just settled more and more heavily into his bones.

Except… what was that? His head lifted, a sensation in his chest like a door opening. More accurately, like a puzzle piece connecting perfectly to its mate. He stepped off the tram, facing the doorway to the Chorus, skin pimpled all over his seeking mantle tattoos. His spirit was instantaneously lighter, the voice he'd tried to suppress shouting at him now. *She is here! Katy has returned.*

Terrified to hope, impossible not to. They'd been wrong on

Ishar, Yfaun hadn't succeeded! Every instinct he possessed told him he was right. The same force that had guided him to a planet uncharted, then to the carnelian on Earth, and eventually to Katy in Seattle, pushed him now. Bay gave in to the rush of intuition and leapt into flight, soaring over the heads of everyone on the path to the entry. Katy would be there; he knew it to his core.

32

THEIR FLIGHT ENDED BEFORE KATY COULD TAKE TWO full breaths. Approaching Centris via dragon was vastly different than when she'd done it before. Sundancer was very big, not *Eternidad* big, but they hovered at the edge of the smaller VIP arrival bay to avoid blocking traffic. Definitely turned a few heads on a wee passing ship headed in for a landing.

This has not changed as much as I thought it would.

Katy ran her hand along the side of one of Sundancer's tail-pieces, taking comfort and offering it in return. "From what little I know they've mostly kept to how you left it. There was the Krylar thing, but otherwise the rest of the species still run the Calling, the Chorus, etc."

Krylar thing?

As soon as Katy thought about it, the Wataño knew it. The destruction of Vonar, the near-genocide of the Lunari, the shunning of an entire people in response. Sundancer's angry roar must have been aloud, and with considerable power behind it, because a ship trying to depart the dock fell back to the deck, flipping sideways and sliding.

Never before had ûpiøra been declared! They dared! They

waited until we left the Aoni and let their evil shine forth, a sickly light of a species evolved from what should have been left to die. My brother may wipe them from the Aoni when he wakes.

There was grim satisfaction in Sundancer's voice. Katy mentally flinched. Even a theoretical holocaust was horrific.

You are too young, an innocent and raw child. you cannot understand what they've done.

"Hold up, Dragomum," Katy said aloud, steamed. "Don't dis me because I'm not thousands or billions of years old. I'm the right bloody age to get the job done and bring you out of deep freeze! But even if I lived hundreds of lifetimes, there will never be a good age to sign on for destruction of an entire species. We Humans already tried that, more than once, and have tried to be better ever since. We don't wipe out the evildoers and forget, we carry the burden of the memory and work to improve."

Was absolute silence a good sign?

our herald is right, Dikaios. wholesale slaughter is not our way, nor our right

Sundancer resumed flying to the landing bays.

I leave it to you to reason with Songmaster when he learns of their treachery. I am the Drazoen of justice and objectivity, and can only rule on matters formally brought before me.

Nice evasion, Katy thought, as they touched down lightly inside the bay.

She was absolutely chuffed to see everyone scrambling around the private landing deck Sundancer had commandeered. Panic, shock, awe, it was lovely. Especially the dyspeptic looks of dread on every PQ face she checked. Those mofos were in trouble now.

You will bring suit in the Calling so that I may pass judgement. It is time for me resume leadership of that council.

"As you wish, Irojaku jo Faluji," Katy said as loud as she could. The timing was perfect, because Sundancer unlaced her tailpieces and revealed Katy just as the words rang out. What an entrance!

Would have been better, she mused when she saw the blank faces, if the damn aoiti main database knew English.

Could have heard a cricket chirp in that place. Dumbfounded didn't cover it: stunned faces, people frozen in place, while Sundancer preened just a tad.

I do not preen, I allow them to admire me.

Katy turned to look at Sundancer in the light of the landing bay. Incredible. "To be sure, Dragomum. Who wouldn't admire all this?" She waved an arm to encompass the glory of her Drazoen.

I rescind my previous statement; you may not call me whatever pleases you. I didn't know you would come up with a term like Dragomum.

Fair. She'd known it was a stretch even as she tried it out. "Grand. We need to get to the Chorus so I can find Bay and Riri and everyone." She eyed Sundancer's size, squinting as she measured the exit portals. "I don't know how you're going to fit, honestly." Shadow laughter chased her last words.

My form is as I choose.

In a flash Katy was faced with a woman all over orange; skin, clothing, crown on Her head. Once in a museum Katy had seen Egyptian art where the deities were double the size of humans, and that's what was happening here. This bipedal version of Sundancer was as equally breathtaking as the dragon form. She appeared in a warrior getup reminiscent of Earth goddesses like Inanna, Athena, the Morrigan. Bronze plated armor on Her upper body, arms bare, knee-length skirt, cape falling behind her. Her crown was made from carnelian like Katy's flute, and it sat on a head still dragon-shaped.

Katy looked at herself, appalled at how dirty and disheveled she was. How could she be Herald of the Orange Wataño in a torn tyro robe, no shoes, with hair that probably looked like she'd licked a live car battery.

Heartnote, you are what you should be in any form, no one will dare to judge.

Sure, sounded good. She'd just hold her head up high, walking next to a bloody goddess while they quick-stepped their way to the Chorus. Everyone was looking at Sundancer anyway, right?

Dikaios told you, we are not gods. we understand your discomfort, however, wanting to be seen as your best self

That sweet first voice, Katy thought fondly, feeling a breeze ruffle her hair. Which was… odd, given they were in a sealed landing bay on Centris, a closed system to her knowledge. She raised her hand to find the breeze, catching sight of papaya-colored fabric from the corner of her eye. She glanced down, seeing her ragged togs had been replaced by a vibrant orange V-neck gown. It fell in copious folds to her toes, something you'd see in pictures of ancient Rome or the like. Nestled just above her cleavage was Bay's pendant, back in the form he'd shaped, and a rush of nostalgia and happiness flooded her.

One hand went to cradle the talisman, the other ran over the top, then side of her head. Her hair had been artfully braided from what her hand told her. Some elaborate thing she'd never have been able to pull off herself. Five voices spoke in harmonized satisfaction and pride.

all shall know you are ours, our Herald

Katy tried not to cry then, or during the walk to the tram, or on the ride to the Chorus stop, and through the vine-covered door. It was easier than it might have been, because everyone around them tripped, fell back, gaped, some even ran. The few brave souls who tried to approach or speak were gutted with one look from Sundancer and scurried away. All that made Katy giggle inside, which invoked waves of joyful love from her Wataño.

She was an emotional wreck from the roller coaster of all that had happened, so when Bay flew to her, ignoring everyone and everything to wrap her in his wings she lost the battle and wept. Their kiss, through her tears, was the greatest thing she could have wished for at that moment. Bay crushed her to his chest, lifted her off her feet and melded their lips like the world was ending.

"I thought you'd been taken from me," he whispered, once he stopped for breath. "That Yfaun had killed you."

He looked pretty rough, his usually meticulous facial hair straggly and unkempt. Clothes a mess, circles under his eyes, and it filled her with warmth. Too right, he *should* be bloody wrecked if he thought she'd died. Because she'd be as bad or worse if the tables were turned.

She ran her hands over his beloved face, tucking loose hair behind his ears. Another small kiss. "I'm still here." One more peck. "I don't know if you noticed," she mock-whispered, extracting herself and stepping back to Sundancer's side. "Here She is, Sundancer Orange, Irojaku jo Faluji. The Drazoen you were born to help awaken." Katy took his hand, which shook, drawing him closer to them.

His face filled with awe and sincere admiration. "The honor You do me is beyond anything I can express," he began, bowing low, wings stretched behind him.

You have served us well, Djilbay jo Bikajo. We were only able to send dreams to you, and you accepted their truth. Now our Herald has brought us back to the Aoni, and you deserve much of the credit for this. We are back on Centris, and our work begins in earnest. You will assist?

"Anything, Irojaku jo Faluji, whatever is needed I will serve. All Mikanjo will."

Katy wasn't so sure about people like Couri and Abou. But hey, now she could rub their noses in their nasty words. She totally knew Sundancer's truename, so suck it ya bleedin' muppets! Sundancer glanced down at Katy, tolerant and reluctantly entertained. *I'm your heartnote, remember? Can't ditch me for someone better now.*

Riri hovered impatiently behind Bay, Yuhwa, Lia, the voices and others arrayed around her. They all stood back a ways; nervous about the giant orange woman? Katy looked around and saw they were getting a lot of attention. There was no mistaking Sundancer for anything but the Drazoen miracle She was, and a crowd was growing, awestruck faces turned their way, cries of joy escaping some. Many had dropped to their knees, Rácz had turned a solid carrot shade. Their smallest tentacles waved wildly instead of laying in the orderly formation of their faux mouth.

Riri broke first, dashing to Katy's side. Her friend hugged her tightly. "You will tell me every single thing that happened! I've been terrified for you, scared what Bay heard was correct and you'd been killed." The hug reached python-squeeze level. "You saved me," she whispered. "Again."

"Nah," Katy whispered back. "You saved yourself."

A few tears leaked from her eyes when Riri leaned back, arms still around Katy. "As it seems you did, too." She pressed her lips to Katy's forehead, overwhelmed. The deepest Shadow voice rumbled.

this one, we like this one. a pure heart

Katy had to agree. Her eyes caught on more and more people running from the central building area, clamoring to see Sundancer. "I think we need to retreat to Voice House," she called out to Mara and the others. "There are a lot of questions to answer, not least," she aimed at Sundancer, "what happened so long ago and how do we get everyone to wake up and come back?"

My herald is correct, we should discuss and learn from one another.

Sundancer didn't wait for anyone to show Her where to go,

long stride aimed straight for the quasi-castle, people scrambling out of Her way. Katy figured She probably knew this place better than the current Voice Cadre. Hell, maybe She'd built it.

This was Songmaster's domain. I built the Calling Chamber. I did visit here often, in times past. To encourage the voices' participation in the Calling, or to enjoy the entertainments. It has always been a place of delight and revelry.

Katy, and everyone who'd come to greet them near the Chorus entrance, made haste to follow Sundancer. Bay was glued to her side. She was just fine with that; her very recent fears of never seeing him again had subsided, but the residual scare had left some traces. It would be a while longer before she felt normal.

Sharing her story of Yfaun, the nefeslo shadow prison and everything that followed, took over an hour to tell. They'd settled in their usual meeting room, siege setting engaged again. There were a lot of questions from everyone about everything. The fact PQ could skirt surveillance tech put grim looks on the faces of Tangun and Thuliso. Rácz had a lot of questions about Yfuan's suicide lightshow to open the prison, and there was a healthy debate over just what a "nefeslo cage built to resemble kuk ularu" actually meant. Thankfully Voltan had brought refreshments, otherwise Katy's voice would have worn out.

They spent another hour hearing the story of Na, Yuhwa and Bay's adventure to Ishar. Much of that was deeply disturbing, not least the notion of just how trapped they'd have been if their mercenary had played them false. Ishar sounded like a post-apocalyptic hellscape and Katy was very happy to have missed that field trip. There were many more questions about the black market trade PQ seemed to encourage, and a whole lot of alarm when the escaped slave part of the tale came to light.

"The Pu'ulqaari will not let that stand," Mara interjected. "This Nyakisi, he was called Na Xan?" She looked to Bay for verification, who confirmed. "We need to find him."

"Good luck," Thuliso said. "I've heard of this one, and he's slippery. Better than most of his people at disguise and concealment.

"He clearly knew what was happening and either passively facilitated or actively encouraged," Mara asserted. "When the Vi'issers come he has to admit his part, so our people aren't punished."

"That can't be bad, though," Katy argued. "Getting a slave to freedom is noble, the right thing to do."

Yuhwa agreed. "It isn't the act of smuggling the man off Ishar, it's that he lied to us about it. I knew he wasn't telling me the truth, but with the news we'd just heard...the need to get back here took precedence."

Bay stiffened, which Katy felt clearly because they were sitting side-by-side on a backless ottoman. She snuggled deeper into his arm and wing, which were wrapped around her as they should be forever. Her hand, already on his thigh, patted him reassuringly. "Not dead," she whispered. He relaxed, stroking her arm.

"I'm going to need another night of rusim and star-gazing to recover," she offered in a light tone to Yuhwa, getting a smirk and brief laugh in return.

Gudar pulled them back on track. "The Vi'isser family will be furious. I wouldn't be surprised if they appear here in person to hunt him down."

I agree, the Pu'ulqaari will come for their property. But they are right to have feared my freedom. Once I have the opportunity, I will rule against the legality of namu'ur. When we left the Aoni, they had only begun employing a version of this. It was closer to contracted servants then; what you show me now is abhorrent, and violates acceptable practice of advanced species.

"Speaking of leaving the Aoni," Katy dove in. "Why did You? Why the complicated thing with essences and heralds?" She'd deny she was pouting, but her lower lip admittedly pooched a bit. "If You'd all just left clear directions we could have avoided so much of the stress and heartache."

If a Drazoen could heave a mental sigh, Sundancer just had. It was sorrow and frustration in one.

I am capable of many things, but answering all of your questions isn't one of them. None of my siblings were aware of what was happening. Except Hu Ularu. They, alone, understood the crisis at hand. They came to each of us, one by one, instructing us to create a trigger out of our essence. We were to imbue that trigger with a spark, linking it to something from the deepest core of our being that would become our herald.

They told us we would leave the people of the Aoni, but they didn't tell us about the prisons or our shadow siblings. Hu Ularu also told us we could not talk with our visible siblings, share our choices or knowledge: they said there were rules we must follow, and I took them at their word. This is why I couldn't have said, before today, what the other eight essences were, nor am I cognizant of where the others left theirs. What I learned from Hu Ularu must differ from my other siblings, as it's clear Windweaver knew things I did not, including the essence each of us used.

All I knew in that time of sorrow was that I was to abandon Centris and the Calling, a place I had first suggested we create together. I didn't know why this had to be, or for how long. But I'd been given a duty to fulfill and I did. I sang my heartnote, watched it sail into the Aoni, followed it to an unknown planet that had a compatible resonance, and wondered what would become of it. Next I felt myself yanked out of time and space, into the shadow prison.

Katy was gagged. She'd assumed once they had Sundancer back they would have a clear and easy race to wake the rest. But this meant each of Them had different essence triggers, unique paths to awakening, and this room's rag-tag crew wasn't much closer to the finish line. They'd need eight more sparks, eight more quests. Worry about eight more Yfauns. This was going to be...impossible.

Five voices soothed her in unison, and she sensed Their words were shared only with her.

We have accomplished much, our Wataño is complete. Think of all that has happened to bring us to this moment, what the forces of the Aoni arranged to make it possible. The future may not unfold as we expect, nor as quickly as we want. But we are free and whole. There is much to celebrate. Our heartnote has returned to us.

Bay, always sensitive to her feelings, folded his wing tighter around her shoulder, feathers brushing her cheek. "We can do this, Katy. Together we can do anything. Look what we've done already."

He proves himself a good mate to you. I approve, with one condition.

Katy blushed at the word mate, stuttering mentally *Are mates a real thing? And what condition? Don't scare him off!* Sundancer's next words evidently broadcast to everyone again, because all heads turned their way.

I have seen in my herald's mind the naming tradition your people created, Mikanjo seeker. But you need seek no more, therefore your name must change. Katy Phelan has decided to become Katy jo Faluji, first Human of that line. Djilbay jo Faluji, mate of the Herald of Orange Wataño, would be acceptable to us.

Whoa, whoa, whoa! That was marriage talk, way too early for that! Probably.

She thought *Dragomum!* very loudly, just to annoy Sundancer, and looked first to Riri who was sitting next to Olak and Pijo. No help there, just a wicked grin. She peeked at Bay, scared to see repulsion or rejection.

Bay's face lit up like fireworks. "I will happily take her name, share her life, whatever she allows." He beamed at Katy, who started laughing and sniffling at the same time. It produced an unfortunate snorting sound, but she didn't care. Bay loved her, she was his *qania*, he was her *mo chroí*, and they were going to fly off into the sunset together.

"Hang on," Katy gasped. "I can't do this without my family back on Earth! My parents would never forgive me."

Lia responded, "We can bring them here on the *Eternidad*." She smiled and said, "The ship has little purpose as a seeking vessel anymore. We can be the Human ferry to Centris."

Katy looked at Riri. "I think I'm getting married? Which is mental, right?"

Her friend crossed the room, knelt in front of her and said, "I will forever be glad I invited myself on your Pike Place Market outing. This," she waved a hand to encompass Sundancer and Bay, "is the happily ever after you deserve and I'm thrilled to be here for it."

Katy took Raisa's hand and squeezed, shocked and elated. The future of everyone in the room held such potential. The Aoni itself would ring out with their accomplishments, and Katy would have Bay at her side, her Wataño in her soul, as it unfolded.

ABOUT THE AUTHOR

Jules Peacock resides in the Pacific Northwest, faithful mini-Drazoen (usually asleep and snoring) at her side. She has dreamed of these characters for half her life, and finally decided the people in her head deserved a jail break. Jules always keeps her music and books travel-ready, for whenever she's whisked off Earth for interstellar shenanigans.

Virtuoso is Jules' first book in the Drazoen Heralds series. Future books will take readers on adventures throughout the Aoni. Visit https://julespeacock.com for more Drazoen content. Sign up for the newsletter, and follow socials for updates, teasers and general news.

Linktree (with all social links): linktr.ee/julespeacock

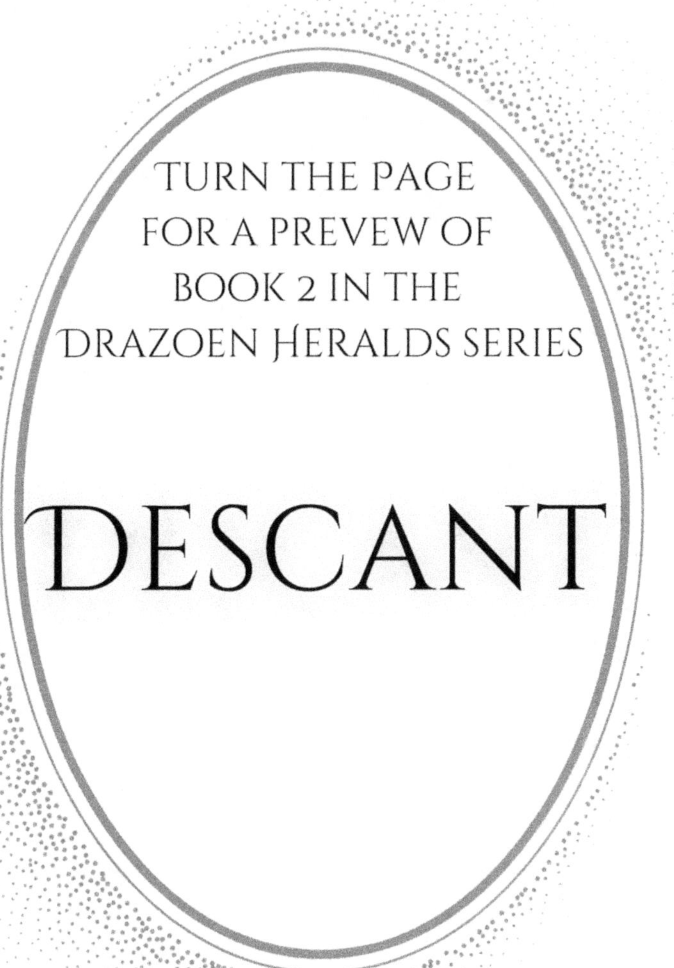

TURN THE PAGE
FOR A PREVEW OF
BOOK 2 IN THE
DRAZOEN HERALDS SERIES

DESCANT

DESCANT
EXCERPT

Paul Phelan was done with this federal git. The man had arrived at the head of a phalanx of black-suited government robots, and was intent on scaring the hell out of everyone. As if anyone needed extra help being terrified in the wake of his sister's memorable exit from Earth three weeks ago.

Thankfully, Paul had been at his parents when this tosser and his posse came screaming down the driveway. In a black van so much a stereotype it hurt, no less. Who did that on Mercer Island, for feck's sake?

Paul looked at his father, who seemed torn between according respect to an official and letting his Irish temper off the leash. Baby brother Oran, also home, cracked his neck ominously and looked ready to get into it physically.

"As I keep saying, we've tracked signals to this home. We know you're in contact with the aliens."

"I'm sure we don't know what you're talking about," Da said, wrapping an arm around Ma and pulling her close.

Paul's heart ached looking at his ma. She'd been hardest hit by Katy's disappearance, though he didn't think the alien thing bothered Ma. More that her baby girl was in the middle of scary events happening so far away. When they'd heard "assassin" and "poison" he'd worried his mother would faint. Of course, Bug had dropped those bombs and swanned off, to do her own thing. Typical move from his baby sister.

Speaking of whom, it must have been her latest call to the family that set off alarms at the Pentagon. Or NASA, or SETI, whichever place this weaselly twat called home base. Jesus knew he hadn't clearly stated his affiliation, just flashed some badge Da flinched upon seeing. Given he worked at Boeing's military and government facility (called the "black hole" by locals), Martin Phelan probably knew exactly who this guy was. Paul didn't and found it hard to care; his irritation was the same no matter which org was to blame.

What did he know? Katy's message from two days ago meant this man needed to leave ASAP. Right as he had the thought, he spied two women approaching the front door. One of them – long brown hair and bright green eyes – was taller than his own six-five. Impressive. The second woman wasn't tall, closer to Bug's height, but she was arresting nonetheless. Pale lavender hair blowing in a gentle June breeze, skin-tight bodysuit of red and black, dark eyes, and stride that said she knew her body's capabilities well.

Paul's life of learning, competing in, and teaching gymnastics had taught him to size up body language instantly. This woman wasn't a fighter, but she had fluid grace similar to it. Like a dancer, or swimmer. This had to be Yuhwa, the pilot of the alien spaceship here to pick up the Phelan family. But, as nice as the diversion of two pretty woman had been, Paul needed to get this idiot out of the house and keep the aliens from bumping into him.

"We will take your entire family in for questioning if you aren't more cooperative, Mr. Phelan."

What had this fool said his name was? Something bland. Tim? No. "Tom, wasn't it?" Paul moved to position himself so the women could see him through the front windows. "We don't even know what you're talking about!" He raised his hands and shook them, praying a brush-back gesture translated across multiple species' lines.

"I cannot be any clearer. Our systems picked up communication originating from beyond Earth's satellites. It came to an IP address located here. In this house."

Both women had spotted him and stopped on the walk. Paul saw them consult with each other, then creep closer to the front door without knocking. He hoped like hell they could hear and understand what was happening.

Oran drawled, "You're whack. You think those aliens from last month, what? WhatsApp-ed us?" As much of a pain as Katy's twin could be, he was solid when he needed to be. Nor was he lying. Katy and Bay used FaceTime.

Da moved to stand beside Paul, Oran sliding in next to Da. They'd made a wall of Phelans, and Tom the government lackey wasn't getting through it.

"I've been here a long time, sir. I've got clearance as far up as an Irish immigrant can get where I work. That means I know you'd have taken us in, seized our computers, and refused us calls for help if you had enough proof. And yet," Martin Phelan shrugged, "here we are. Standing in the family living room."

"Look here-"

"I think not." Ma spoke up, stunning Paul. She pushed her way between Da and Oran. "We've been polite, we've listened to your threats, and we're done. Unless any of your goon squad want the refreshment previously rejected, you may be on your way."

He tried not to react as two puzzled faces peered from the side of the front windows, mouthing "goon squad". Sweet Marie, these two! Thankfully Paul was on a break from women, or he'd probably form the kind of insta-love connection Katy had with her Bay. The very next second, they'd melted away from the porch and front entrance.

Just in time to avoid the exit of a furious government jerk who tried to stare down every family member before stalking out behind his team. Slammed the door when he went. Twat.

"Did you see-"

"Yes, of course I did! Everyone! Get it in gear!" Briana Phelan knew how to bellow, having raised four hellion boys and one sensitive girl.

A girl who'd sent aliens to pick up her immediate family for transport to a place called Centris. On a Wheel, she'd said. In the middle of the Universe. She'd gone and had some epic adventure with winged aliens, supposedly waking up a dragon. Paul figured that had to be exaggeration or creative license. Or maybe a mistranslation by those aoiti bugs Katy had ingested. Bug swallowed bugs. Heh.

His oldest brother, Ian, came out from the rec room, his wife right behind him. Deb was a high maintenance piece of work, but for whatever reason she and Ian meshed perfectly. Another picture-perfect couple came out of the guest bedroom they'd claimed when the fed arrived. Patrick and Vasuda, not married, but might as well be. They were the opposite of the Ian-Deb ladder-climbing power couple; two artists, chill as all get-out, and happiest with simple things.

Paul was sick to death of happy couples. He hadn't been part of one for nigh on six months, and wasn't sure he'd ever be part of one again. Women were vicious creatures who tore a man apart with ultimatums and unrealistic demands. He was better off single, if what his ex had done to him was anything to go by.

Ma and Da (another bloody love match) had everyone gather close in the dining room.

"They're here-"

"Jesus, we know, Da. We saw them."

"We didn't! Do they look very... alien?" Deb's face was more animated than normal. She must be very psyched for this adventure.

Vasuda marveled, "I can't believe this is real. We're going to experience new cultures and species, it will be ama-"

"New networking opportunities. If we can get in first, we-"

"Blow it out your arse, Ian." Oran punched his brother's arm.

"Everyone shut up." Man, his ma could control the family perfectly. "Are all the bags in the garage? Katy said to pack light; they'll have everything we need on the *Eternidad,* or on that Wheel thingy."

"I just packed booze."

"Oran, my lad, you're a good-"

"You have to be kidding. Martin, don't encourage that! Make him grab underwear at least."

"No time, love. I'm sure they've got us covered."

Paul and Patrick exchanged a glance that spoke volumes. They'd always been the closest of the kids. Ian was too invested in being the oldest to care about younger siblings. Oran and Katy had whatever the opposite of a twin bond was; they could fight over anything, and regularly did. Paul and Patrick, however, had each other's backs. They supported one another, collaborated on their businesses, shared ideals and plans, and knew how the other thought. Right now, Patrick was wishing they could ditch the Phelan brood and get going on this trip without all the damn noise.

Paul agreed, but that was part and parcel of the family deal. Hearing a tentative knock on the front door, Paul prayed these two women from space were prepared for the chaos to come.